THE ACCIDENTAL PRESIDENT

Volume Two of The Accidental President Trilogy
A Political Fable for Our Time

by

Dixie Swanson

Cover Design by Joe Thomas at Left Brain Digital

ISBN: 0983329311
ISBN-13: 9780983329312

Library of Congress Control Number: 2011910891
Prose Publishing, Houston, TX

This is a work of fiction. Names, characters, places, and incidents either are the product of the author's imagination or are used fictitiously. Any resemblance to actual persons, living or dead, business establishments, events, or locales is entirely coincidental.

For A.D. and D.H.
The Muse and the Midwife

CHAPTER ONE

REALITY

Thanksgiving morning, 3 a.m.
The Oval Office study, Washington D.C.

The phone jangled. Once. Abigail put the phone to her ear without lifting her head, just as she had done countless times in hospital on-call rooms.

"Thisdoctoradams," she said, sound asleep. She would awaken only if required.

"President Adams. Cristo Salazar in the Situation Room. Sorry to disturb."

Abigail was suddenly awake. She sat up and flipped on the light in the little study off the Oval Office. *Please, oh please, let this be something I can handle.*

"Yes, Cristo, what is it?" Abigail could not hide the anxiety in her voice.

"The President's body has just been recovered."

Abigail felt the world falling out from under her.

Just a year ago, Abby put aside her career as a Pediatric Emergency Physician to care for her dying sister, Texas Senator Priscilla Adams Logan. Without even asking Abby, Pris extracted a deathbed promise from the Governor, Lawson Gray, to appoint Abby to serve the few months left in Pris's term.

After Priscilla's funeral, a very ambivalent Abby entered the Senate. First, though, she had a crash course in media skills, she memorized the Constitution, and professionals taught her how to dress and groom herself as befits a woman of authority. Once on the job, she had demonstrated exceptional independence and backbone in the stodgy Senate.

Abigail "was" her sister in the Senate: same committee appointments, even the same Senate seniority, though she was just thirty-seven. Yesterday, she was taking her turn as President Pro Tem of the Senate. The Senate Rules Committee decided to rotate the position of President Pro Tem after 9/11, lest some senile, orange-haired Senator become President. Abby did the occasional ceremonial chore, but she stood fourth in line of succession for the Presidency. Thankfully, the three people ahead of her were perking along as usual.

Yesterday had started so normally. Abby took her "family," Regina and Duke Temple on a tour of the Senate. Regina, an African-American woman of advancing years, was the only mother she'd ever known and Duke was her nephew.

Abby and Pris's dad had been a wildcat oilman, rich one day, busted the next. He paid cash for everything, including the house they lived in. Their mom made rice and beans some nights, steak on others. One day, her dad did not even have money to pay Regina, the family housekeeper. Regina bartered herself a share of the well in progress. The well hit big, and Regina's dreams of college could come true. He plowed his money back into another well and hit a dry hole.

Then he and his wife were out one night and died in a car accident, orphaning the girls. No distant relatives wanted penniless girls. Regina wanted to go to teacher's college, but she would not allow these girls to go into foster care; she loved them.

She hired a lawyer and became their guardian. She gave up her dream so two girls could have dreams of their own. She figured that was a fair bargain, especially since their dad had made her rich, unless of course the well ran dry. So far, it was still pumping.

The issue of race raised a few eyebrows in their upscale Houston neighborhood, but soon the community saw Regina as the regal woman she was. When Abby was twelve, Regina's youngest sister died in childbirth and the three took in baby Duke. He was now a third-year law student at Georgetown. He was the apple of Abigail's eye: part nephew, part little brother, and at six-five, part very big brother.

Yesterday, during the tour someone rushed past them saying President Harrington, an expert skier, had been in an avalanche while on an early ski trip in the Rockies.

They joined the rest of the nation glued to television sets.

Then the chain-smoking, overweight Vice President collapsed and died upon hearing the news. Was this the second plane hitting the World Trade Center?

As an emergency doctor, Abigail knew to plan ahead, stay calm, and melt down only in private. She went immediately from the Senate to the Supreme Court. Why? If evil was afoot, no one would think to look for her there.

However, there was no evil, apparently, just bizarre chance.

The Speaker of the House, well known for his atrocious table manners, choked on a piece of meat upon hearing the job would fall to him.

That left Abigail.

The Chief Justice swore her in and drove her to the West Wing, where she had been ever since. She had been in office only minutes when her Senate nemesis, Secretary of Defense, P.J. O'Neal, insulted and challenged her in the Situation Room.

"Abby, I'm sure you were a good little baby doctor," he said, "but you're in way over your head here."

Abigail was incensed, but her voice held ice shards.

"That may be, but under the Presidential Succession Act of 1947, if I resign, that leaves the Secretary of State. She cannot serve, as she is foreign born. The Secretary of the Treasury is too young. That would leave you, Mr. Secretary.

"You serve in the Cabinet at the pleasure of the President, and your outburst displeases me.

"The country thanks you for your service, but you are hereby relieved of all your duties. Marine Sentries? Please take the former secretary to the Pentagon and have him locked out from all access."

When she finally went to the Oval Office, George Washington stared her in the eye from his portrait on the wall. His monument was just outside the window. As if that wasn't spooky enough, she heard her late sister's voice as clear as a winter Texas morning.

"Relax. You are standing on the shoulders of giants."

Abigail spoke to the nation that evening and set up camp in the President's study just off the Oval Office. She felt it would be rude to sleep in the White House, the Harrington family's residence.

Regina sent over clothes for today, but forgot pajamas. Mortified, Abby asked a Marine Sentry to give her a tee-shirt to sleep in and, in the privacy of the little study, she cried herself to sleep. She had never wanted to be President. She hated politics, but she was damned if she'd let that arrogant gasbag P.J. O'Neal have the job. The thought of wearing panty hose for two more years prompted more sobs. Nevertheless, she had taken the Oath of Office. She had assumed a Constitutional duty. *Duty. Honor. Country.* She remembered the West Point motto from Pris's funeral. She fell asleep hoping Harrington was alive.

Now that hope was gone. She was President of the United States for the next twenty-six months. Accidentally.

"Does Mrs. Harrington know?" She reached for a pad and paper.

"No, ma'am."

"Have the Special Agent in Charge inform her in person. How about the rest of the party?"

"All recovered." *Two Secret Service agents and two local guides were gone; four families would be devastated.*

"Notify all next of kin in person. After that, I'll release a statement. Make sure you get correct spellings of their names," Abigail ordered.

"Yes, ma'am. As you ordered, I've also confirmed Harrington's nuclear football is safely aboard Air Force One," Salazar said. *Thank God, I've known and trusted him since my Senate days.*

"Are his launch codes and the VP's deleted?" Abigail asked.

"Done."

"Where exactly is Air Force One?"

"In Aurora. At Buckley AFB."

"Thanks," Abigail said, hanging up.

Abigail dialed Mabel, the head operator on the night shift.

"Mabel, I'm sad to say they are all gone," Abigail said gently. She heard Mabel muffle a sob.

"I need to speak to the medical examiner for Beaver Creek, Colorado, please," Abigail said.

Abby got up and went to the bathroom. Her phone rang moments later.

"This is Dr. Sandijay. With whom am I speaking?" The sleepy man had a pronounced Indian accent.

"This is Dr. Abigail Adams. I am the President of the United States. Are you the medical examiner for Beaver Creek?"

"Yes, for all of Eagle County, madam."

"The President's body, as well as those of two Secret Service agents and two local guides, has been recovered."

"Madam, they are medical examiner cases," His tone was cautionary. He had the legal right to autopsy anyone in his county who died accidentally.

"Can you do five autopsies before close of business today?" Abby asked.

"No, no, of course not. It would take at least two days. I am very short staffed."

"I understand. What would you think of doing the autopsies at AFIP?" Abigail asked.

The Armed Forces Institute of Pathology in D.C. is to medical examiners what Harvard is to high school seniors.

"I am not sure, madam," he said, wavering.

"You'll get to ride on Air Force One."

"In that case, I'd be happy to assist."

CHAPTER TWO

THANKSGIVING MORNING

November 23, Thanksgiving Day
5 a.m.

Cristo woke Abby at five with another call from the Situation Room.

She might as well get up and get dressed. She put him on the speaker.

"All bodies aboard, all families informed. Air Force One will take off as soon as Mrs. Harrington is aboard. Some Indian doctor showed up at the scene. Did you really tell him he could ride to D.C.?" Cristo asked.

"Yes, he's Dr. Sandijay, medical examiner. Avoids turf wars. Bring him along and then send him—and the bodies of the local guides—right back to Colorado after the autopsies."

"Yes, ma'am."

Abby put in her contacts, her eyeballs screaming at their lack of sleep.

"If either of the guides' families are financially strapped, let me know. I'll pay and say Uncle Sam did it. That's cheaper than a media circus," Abby said. Pris's horrid marriage produced a gigantic divorce settlement that the frugal Abigail inherited.

"Yes, ma'am."

She was quick with her makeup. She'd likely redo it twice that day, anyway. She wriggled into sheer black panty hose, put on the charcoal suit and slipped her feet into black pumps.

"Order the head of AFIP to get all autopsies finished by 5 p.m. You and you only, are to take all the autopsy photographs and bring the camera here to me. I want all five D.C. bodies—President, VP, Speaker, and two Secret Service agents—in matching, flag-draped coffins and at the Capitol Rotunda by 7 p.m."

Abby swept up her strawberry blonde curly hair, pinned it, and put on enough hair spray to trigger an EPA air quality alert. *Thank goodness, Andre Callas taught me hair and professional makeup. Ditto for Laura Rowe and Kim Tran dressing me for the Senate. A year ago, I had wild, frizzy hair and worked in scrubs. Lip balm was the closest I came to makeup. I may not feel presidential, but at least I look it.*

"Mabel, could you find Bob Wicker and send him into the Oval Office, please?"

"Yes, ma'am."

Within moments, her media coach appeared. A former broadcaster, he was a successful media consultant in Washington. More importantly, she trusted him. He'd been with her last night when she spoke to the nation. He'd probably slept on a couch somewhere in the West Wing, though you'd never know it. A consummate television pro, he probably had an electric razor, toothbrush and fresh shirt in his briefcase when Abby sent for him yesterday. He looked camera ready.

"Sorry to say, but they are all gone, all five of them. Get with Cristo in the Situation Room and draft a release. Don't send it until I see it."

"Yes, ma'am." He headed to the Situation Room below ground.

"I want to talk with Mrs. Harrington. I assume she's awake," Abigail said to Mabel.

"I'll get her on the line."

In a moment, the phone rang. The First Lady was on the line. It was 2 a.m. in her time zone.

"Good morning, Madam President," Evangeline Harrington said. Abby barely knew the Harringtons, but she liked them. Both had made time to visit Pris the day she died.

"Ma'am, you sound remarkably composed." Abby said over the speakerphone. She added her accessories: pearl stud earrings, a pearl choker, gold watch and pinky ring. She stuffed the launch codes and thumb drive into her bra, and was ready for the day.

"Composure is in the job description. I'll get through this, Abigail, and then have a meltdown. I'm so sorry this has fallen to you, but I have faith in you."

"Thank you. I was wondering if you had a message for the nation."

"Yes, please thank them for their prayers and tell them to go on with their Thanksgiving plans."

"I hope I'm not overstepping here. What would you think of a joint funeral for the President, Vice President, Speaker, and the two Secret Service agents on Sunday, followed by separate burials?"

"My thoughts exactly," Evangeline said. "Besides, Sam and Toddy were Walter's favorites," she said, her voice quavering with emotion. "O.T., the White House curator, can do everything. His taste is impeccable."

"It will comfort the country to have you home," Abby said.

Abby said good-bye, willing herself not to cry. Wicker reappeared with a draft statement on his laptop.

Abigail proofed the copy and added the First Lady's remarks. When both were satisfied, he hit the Send button. Without a sound, the world would know in moments that Walter Harrington was dead and Abigail Adams was now President of the United States.

Abigail ordered breakfast for the two of them. She was in dire need of caffeine and predicted Wicker was as well.

It was still dark outside. Just yesterday, Abigail thought she'd awaken to the smells of Regina fixing Thanksgiving dinner. She looked out the door of the Oval Office. The Marine Sentries stood, fully alert.

Hitchcock's night replacement jumped to his feet, the nuclear football briefcase was at his side.

"Capt. Shad Dabaghi, ma'am," he said, offering his hand. One does not salute his Commander-in-Chief indoors and in plain clothes.

"Do you telecommute to the Pentagon the way Capt. Hitchcock does?" Abigail asked.

"Yes, ma'am."

Abby introduced the two men. Then she and Bob Wicker went in to breakfast.

"Bob, I need you to stay as Press Secretary. Can you wangle that?" Abby asked, the reassuring scents of breakfast and coffee buoyed her.

Wicker Washington could run without him. He tutored Abby in the basics of broadcasting and found her, oddly enough, a natural in front of the camera. Doing two years as her Press Secretary would only burnish his company's reputation.

"I'd be honored," he said.

Black bordered pictures of President Harrington and his two Secret Service agents were on television around the world within minutes.

The two ate quickly, and Wicker headed out to deal with a ravenous press. At least he did it well fed and well caffeinated.

Abigail could find her bathroom and study, the Oval Office, and a few other places in the West Wing. She knew the Constitution by heart. She learned as much government and history as possible in the Senate. She could keep herself well enough groomed and dressed to be photographed all day. As a presidential skill set, it was pitiful indeed.

While she waited for the Presidential Daily Briefing, whatever that was, she did the Presidential equivalent of checking the crash cart in an emergency room. She read the manual on how to start a nuclear war. *If you're ready for a complication, it doesn't happen.*

Abigail was cold from sleep deprivation and fear. She asked for a fire in the fireplace. As people filed in for the Presidential Daily Briefing, she noticed they gathered on the sofas. She took the armchair to the right of the fireplace. Capt. Tom Hitchcock came in with the nuclear football. Dabaghi, apparently, was gone for the day.

"How's your wife?" Abigail asked of the soon-to-be father.

"T minus five weeks and counting. Grouchy as hell. I would be too," Hitch offered.

A weak November dawn seeped down the Mall starting at the Capitol and ending at the Lincoln Memorial. *Everything gets better in the morning, I hope.*

"I imagine this is a huge loss for each of you personally. Before we begin, let's have a moment of silence, shall we?" Abigail addressed the room.

All bowed their heads.

The Presidential Daily Briefing details for the President what has gone bump in the night.

The process is a winnowing of whatever data miners, satellites, spies, and snitches all over the globe murmur to the Lord High Muckety-Mucks. The Muckety-Mucks massage it and pass it on to the Grand Pooh Bahs of Intelligence, and they, in turn, try to scare the pants off the President.

This particular morning, they were rather successful.

As expected, Muslim extremists were gloating about Harrington's death. "The beginning of the Collapse of the Infidels," Paul Scoggins, director of the National Security Agency, the electronic spymaster, said.

"And you won't like it that you are now called the 'The Whore of the West.'"

"Ouch. Already?" *I've given it away, but I've never sold it.*

"Yes, ma'am," Scoggins said. "I don't think you should take it personally."

Abby gave him the cocked left eyebrow she'd learned from Regina. In the family, it was known as The Look. Everyone in the family believed it could stop a charging rhino in its tracks.

"Al-Qaeda in Iraq says only a weakling woman is left," Michael "Spooky" Petersen, head of the Central Intelligence Agency, said.

"Do we need a show force option?" Abigail said.

No one spoke. Her spectacular firing of the Secretary of Defense just minutes into office showed she had balls, even if she did not have testicles.

"No, ma'am. They're just mouthing off. We ignore them," Petersen said.

"So am I to get this dyspeptic event daily?"

"Yes, ma'am."

"Well, no one tried to take credit for all the deaths. I think we're through."

She ushered them out, and then she went into the bathroom and threw up. Luckily, she missed her clothes. She brushed her teeth, swished the taste of vomit, coffee, and eggs out of her mouth, and started the day again.

Abby asked Chaffee and Poppy to come in for a few moments. At least Logan Chaffee looked better than he did yesterday. His color was normal, if his manner was subdued. A sandy-haired guy in his forties, he was married to his job as President Harrington's Chief of Staff. Abigail could not imagine the depth of his loss.

Poppy McElroy, Abby's Chief of Staff in the Senate, was a well-known fixture on the Hill. She had short red hair in a spiky do, black trendy glasses and her fund of knowledge was huge.

"I'm used to working with Poppy, but you, Chaffee, also have the knowledge I need. If you could stay on, that would be a real honor. What would you think about working together as Chiefs of Staff?" Abigail asked.

"I'll give it a try," Chaffee said. "The Boss would want me to help you."

"I'm in. Why don't I manage you and the Hill while Chaffee does everything else?" Poppy even had things divvied up.

"Sounds like a plan. Have Wicker announce it. Oh, and I want Mikey appointed Special Counselor to the President," Abigail said.

"That'll tickle him pink," Poppy said.

Mikey Molloy, now in his eighties, was Abigail's Senate mentor, and she couldn't imagine this job without him nearby. He came in only a few hours a day, napped often, but was a walking political encyclopedia.

Even on a holiday when the President was supposed to be away, her schedule filled up with meetings. Poppy gave her a card with her schedule. *I have two years of meetings and panty hose. Could I substitute floggings?*

Funeral plans were first. *Thank heaven for O.T.*

O.T. Wagner, the White House curator, quietly marshaled everyone for 10 a.m. Abby met the White House historian, the protocol director, as well as Thomas Albright, the director of the White House Secret Service detail.

"Didn't you come to my sister's house?" Abigail asked. *At least his handshake wasn't a bone-crusher.*

"Yes, ma'am," he practically growled.

A tall thin guy in his fifties, he'd come back from a fishing trip in Cabo in the middle of the night. He looked tired and ragged with grief. He was kicking himself for not going to Colorado. *I could have stopped him from that damn fool heli-skiing. He listened to me about his safety. He would be alive right now, if I'd gone with him.*

Abby introduced Mikey as her Special Counselor. Most either knew him or knew of him. O.T. had a whiteboard to draft a timetable for the entire weekend.

"Can we get all five bodies into the Capitol Rotunda by 7 p.m. for families only?" Abigail asked.

"Yes, ma'am," O.T. spoke calmly. "The President's casket will be on the higher, center catafalque."

"If Mrs. Harrington is up to it, I'll go with her to visit the Rotunda. After the families come through, we'll open it to the public."

"I think that's the easiest way," O.T. said.

"Albright? What do you think?" Abigail asked.

"We'll get you there and back, but I'd like you to stay here in the complex until it's time for the funeral. Too much is going on, what with heads of state arriving."

"I can do that," Abigail said.

"I thought we'd have a diplomatic reception in the White House late Saturday afternoon," O.T. said. "That'll give Mrs. Harrington a chance to catch her breath beforehand. And you, President Adams, will have a chance to meet everyone."

"I agree," Abigail said.

"Press is going to be a nightmare," Wicker put in. "News will want wall-to-wall coverage, but this is a big football weekend, so there'll be some fights."

"We don't have a dog in that fight," Abby said. "So today's planned. Mrs. Harrington and I agree on a joint funeral at eleven on Sunday at the National Cathedral, assuming all families agree. Separate interments to follow. I know this is quick, but I want the country back to work on Monday. Maybe people will even shop on Black Friday if we don't have funeral events."

O.T. marked up the whiteboard by time, location and participants.

"We have two living Presidents with their wives. They automatically go to Trowbridge House," O.T. said. He was getting on in years, but his slow molasses drawl seemed to go with his chocolate skin.

Trowbridge House was one of the townhouses added over the years to Blair House, the official guesthouse for the White House across Pennsylvania Avenue. The Blair House complex has fourteen bedrooms and is actually bigger than the White House itself.

"I agree," Albright spoke up in his raspy growl. "Former Presidents at Trowbridge, it's the most secure. Getting this many heads of state into and out of one place in so short a time will take some work."

"How can I make it easier?" Abigail asked.

"Keep public details 'pending' as long as possible. VIPs use Andrews. Cancel all leave for White House staff, Secret Service, fire, police, and military in the district. All heads of state stay at their embassies. And I'll need a detailed briefing book as soon as possible."

Everyone looked at O.T.

"As soon as we finish here, my staff will have a briefing book and matching online info, in a couple of hours," O.T. said. "Mrs. Harrington is *en route*, and I want her approval of all details."

O.T. turned to Abigail, who nodded her head in agreement.

"She'll approve," Albright said. *He didn't want anyone doing anything stupid. A stupid decision had gotten them all here in the first place.*

"Nevertheless, I'll video conference with her on Air Force One," O.T. added.

"I agree," Abigail said. *A man of manners.*

"When does Mrs. Harrington arrive?" Abigail asked.

"Sometime around two," O.T. said.

"I think we're finished here for now," Abby said and stood. That was everyone's cue to leave.

"Mikey? A word?" Abby hugged him when the others left. "Thanks for coming in for me."

"Of course, my dear."

"Mikey, I'm, I'm…scared," Abigail said.

"Any sane person would be. This is an enormous job. That's why most countries have two people doing it: one as head of state and the other as head of government. You must simply put one foot in front of the other till the job is finished."

"But why me, Mikey?" Abigail asked. "I don't want this job."

"Maybe that's why you've been given it. But remember, you're standing on the shoulders of giants."

"Funny, that's just what Pris said."

CHAPTER THREE

THANKSGIVING AFTERNOON

Abigail called Duke and Regina on the back line.

"How're you doing, Sweet Pea?" Regina's voice was balm to her soul.

"I wish I was home," Abby said, biting her lip to keep tears away.

"It's so sad. President Harrington was so nice," Regina said, remembering the day the Harringtons visited Pris. His charisma flustered even Regina, who was unflappable.

"Well, now we have to do him proud," Abby said. "I need your help."

Abby started to tell Regina what to pack, but Regina cut her off.

"Laura Rowe is already here, packing for you," Regina said. Laura was a personal shopper at Neiman Marcus and had dressed Abby for the Senate.

"But it's Thanksgiving," Abigail said, shaking her head. "May I speak to her, please?"

"Good morning, Madam President," Laura said.

"Good morning, Laura. Thank you so much for doing this."

"It's easier this way. I've roughed out various outfits for various occasions and put them all together as we have done in the past."

"Could you make sure you put in my nightgowns, slippers, and a robe? I also need some soft, casual wear, like yoga pants and hoodies, for when I am alone."

"Certainly. And Andre came back from holiday to do your hair and makeup, so make sure you use him."

"Just give everything to Duke. He'll bring it over."

"Good, here's Regina."

"What are you guys going to do for Thanksgiving?" Abigail asked. Regina was a renowned cook, and Abigail was sad to miss her Thanksgiving meal.

"We'll go downstairs for the buffet," Regina said. "Duke is in an eating mood, and I'm not in a cooking mood, so that'll do us fine. How about you?"

"I think I'll eat in the White House Mess. Hey, Reege, do you remember that English, boiled-wool cape Pris brought back from England a few years ago?"

"Remember it? Lord, yes. I think I had ten moth holes rewoven."

"We kept it, didn't we?"

"Yes, it's here."

"Would you send that over? Along with the black cashmere coat. And my funeral hat."

"Sure."

"Reege?" Abigail said, feeling small. "I miss you, and I love you."

"We love you, too. Now get back to work. No rest for the weary," Regina said. Regina did not believe in self-pity.

Poppy buzzed her, "Your electronics are back."

"Great. Send him in."

Charley Garrett looked like a glum twelve-year-old with a goatee. He was in charge of all Presidential communications gear. He was one heavyweight in the IT world and had a staff of fifty, even though he was only in his early thirties. Abby felt ancient around him.

"Thanks for fixing my electronics," Abigail said.

"Sure thing," he said. "As President Harrington is gone, I figured he wouldn't mind that I put his ring tone on your phone."

"What is it?"

"'Hail to the Chief' for your calls. 'Ruffles and Flourishes' for your texts."

"Thanks," Abigail was touched.

The young man looked out onto the barren South Lawn. "He was over the moon when I did that for him. He called himself from his land line at least three times," he said wistfully.

"What a lovely memory you have of him," Abby said. "A story to tell your grandchildren."

He looked back at her.

"Yeah. You're right. That makes me feel a little better."

When he left, Abby went to her back line and dialed her Black-Berry. It did indeed play "Hail to the Chief." Then she texted Duke for his arrival time, and his reply triggered "Ruffles and Flourishes." Abby smiled for the first time in twenty-four hours.

Abby asked Hitch to join her in the White House Mess for lunch. Everyone in the room stood when they entered.

"As you were, please," Abby said. *I'd best get used to this. It's not for me, it's for the office I hold.*

They found a table with two empty seats. A young man and woman were sitting there.

"Mind if we join you?" Abby asked.

"Please do," said the pert young woman, jumping to her feet. The young man followed. "I'm Elaine Bennett, and this is Chris Hotchkiss, Madam President."

"Please, sit. So tell me, what do you guys do here?" Abigail said as she and Hitch sat down. She introduced Hitch to both.

A Navy steward appeared. "Any special requests, ma'am?"

"Dark meat only for me, please," Abby said. *Yes! I don't have to arm wrestle Duke for it. Though he lets me win half the time.*

"We're interns from the Kennedy School. Since it's a holiday, we can eat here."

"Great. I'm new myself. He's not," Abigail said, hooking a thumb at Hitch.

They tittered a bit.

"It's not often you see history made," Abigail said.

"This has been surreal," Chris said.

"Nine months ago, I was anonymous. Now? I go into the history books," Abigail said. "Go figure."

"I'd say you got off to a kick-ass start," Chris said. "Flipping off the Secretary of Defense like you did."

Elaine shot him a dirty look.

"What? What'd I say?" Chris asked with injured innocence.

"Language, Chris. This woman is the President," Elaine scolded him.

Chris reddened. "Sorry, ma'am."

"No problem," Abby said. *You should hear me in the hospital.* "So what's the scuttlebutt on that?"

"He had it coming for insubordination at least," Elaine said.

"Your citation of the Presidential Succession Act of 1947, as well as the Constitution itself showed you knew your stuff," Chris said.

Her meal came. "Ooh, dark meat. My favorite," she said to no one in particular. "Hey, I have an idea. How long are you guys here for?"

"Till May."

"How many interns are here in the building?"

"Maybe twenty? Lots more in the summer," Elaine said.

"I want a half hour with ten of you each week. I need your point of view. Elaine, you're in charge of getting it put on my schedule."

"Yes, ma'am."

Abby finished her meal. She and Hitch got up and left, and the entire room stood. *Weird.*

She'd also get O.T. to put together a group of adult "real people" for a once-a-week session. She would wither if all she got were massaged opinions from professional politicians.

She told Poppy to call a Cabinet meeting for tomorrow. Then Duke arrived with a wardrobe for her for the weekend, at least.

"Hey, am I glad to see you," Abby said, rising and taking some of the garment bags into the study.

He followed her. "Talk about ratty digs for the leader of the free world. I've had dorm rooms bigger than this."

"I'm fine in here, for now. Besides, that's a Mary Cassatt on the wall."

Who's Mary Cassatt?"

"Look it up."

"I hear you didn't have anything to sleep in last night." Duke was thumb-typing "Mary Cassatt" into his phone. He raised his eyebrows, and Abby knew the information would stick.

"Well, I do want my own things." If she told him about the tee-shirt, she'd never hear the end of it.

"Can you take these things back to Reege?" She handed him the shopping bag of dirty clothes. He saw the tee-shirt. *Damn. I meant to hide it from him.*

"Whose tee-shirt is this?" he interrogated her, with a smirk.

"None of your business. Just bring it back clean."

"Did somebody lose his shirt at cards?" Duke was enjoying embarrassing his aunt.

"Something like that." Abby slapped at his hand as he tried to pick it up. Having made her blush, he stopped teasing her. He'd won.

"Ms. Rowe said for you to see if she forgot anything. And here's that cape you asked for."

Abby went through things.

"Looks great. Though as soon as you leave, I'll think of something."

Duke pushed the rack into the Vice President's office to give her more room.

Mrs. Harrington landed on the South Lawn in Marine One about 2 p.m. with her son, Walter, Jr. Other members of the family were coming by car from Andrews.

Abigail walked out to meet them. The press was thick along the ropes; the air was cold and vicious. Many reporters called the women's names, hoping they would turn to the cameras. Neither acknowledged them.

"Welcome home, Mrs. Harrington," Abigail said.

The normally cheerful woman looked stunned. Her son took one arm, Abby the other.

"It's all starting to hit me," Evangeline said. Her voice quavered.

"A few more steps, then you can relax."

She looked like a new widow, who'd been up all night, and then crossed three time zones. Abby and Walter, Jr. did a good job of blocking her from the cameras.

"Yes. I'd die before I stumbled in front of them," she said of the press.

"That's the spirit," Abigail said.

The Harrington son shot Abigail a grateful glance.

After Abby helped Mrs. Harrington into bed for a much-needed nap, she spoke briefly with the son, Walter, Jr.

"Mom is insistent that we go to the Capitol Rotunda tonight. She'd like it if you went with us."

"Of course. After your family, the other families will visit. Then it will be opened to the public. But do you really think your mom is up to it?" Abigail was concerned.

"My mom hits her marks. Then she just dissolves. She'll go tonight and then stay in bed until the VIPs arrive on Saturday. Would you tell Albright she wants to leave about seven and be home no later than eight-thirty," he said.

"Sure. What can I do to make this all easier for your family?"

"Just let O.T. handle everything. He could run the world with his eyes shut," Walter Jr. said.

"I'm beginning to figure that out. Shall I send him over to talk with you? Your mom needs some serious rest."

After O.T. visited with Walter, Jr., he came to see Abby in the Oval Office. Abby was reading the manual on Presidential protocol. *I have to learn the pecking order, especially with heads of state arriving this weekend.*

O.T. had another stack of binders in his arms.

"Ma'am, you'll want to start on these. They profile who will be attending the services." He put them down on the desk. Abby could not see over them.

"Thank you, O.T.," Abby said, rubbing her temples. She asked a steward for drinks for them and invited O.T. to have a seat.

"I'm worried about Mrs. Harrington," Abigail said, sipping her tea.

"Well, from what I've seen of grief, I think she's about on track. Having the family around in the Residence will help her. She can hide out in her room or be with them. And she is on for a trip to the Rotunda tonight."

"I'm depending on you, O.T. Please promise me you'll tell me if I'm getting ready to mess up," Abigail said.

"That's part of my job. You have good manners and a good head on your shoulders. We've buried people before, so this is sad, but not new to the staff."

Abby indeed was reassured. O.T. thanked her for the tea and took his leave. *The man has five high-profile funerals to put on and is unfazed. What a pro.*

Abigail summoned Albright, the head of the White House Secret Service detail.

"Mrs. Harrington wants me to go to the Rotunda tonight. I have no idea what happens when I leave this building. I have not even put my head outside. I don't know the drill."

"You are at full liberty here on the eighteen acres," his voice sounded like someone had taken a cheese grater to his voice box. "However, you are safest on the part of the South Lawn with the berms."

"You can thank Jefferson for that. The lawn looks flat from the street, but isn't," Abigail said.

"I didn't know that," Albright growled. Abby was glad he was on her side. His body language said he was coiled and ready to strike a mortal blow in a nanosecond.

"If you want to leave the complex, the more notice you give me, the better. We will, of course, accommodate your desire to go with Mrs. Harrington tonight."

He explained the shifts and how they rotated. It sounded remarkably like the hospital.

"Most of our work happens before you go somewhere. Once out, please don't deviate from the plan. If your agent suggests a change of plan, trust him or her."

"What else?" Abigail asked.

"Don't be impulsive. And remember, your agents are there to protect you, not to chat with you."

"I'll do my best. May I have a female agent when I leave the complex? Makes bathrooms easier."

"Yes, you'll get some of Mrs. Harrington's female agents when she leaves. It'll all work out just fine," Albright said.

He did not tell her that her first-day threats were already running the highest of any President to date. It seemed that the nutcakes hated the idea of a white woman with a black "family."

By then it was dusk and Abigail was dead on her feet. However some leftover turkey and dressing helped. If Mrs. Harrington could go to the Rotunda, so could she.

"I'm headed home for some sleep, if that's okay with you," Poppy said. "I don't think Chaffee trusts you to be left alone yet. He'll stay. He says his sofa sleeps better than his own bed."

"Would you please arrange an informal meeting with the Congressional leadership on Monday in the Roosevelt Room?" Abby said. Poppy sent the email and left.

Abby changed clothes again, wearing an outfit Laura had put together.

When her phone played "Hail to the Chief," she smiled.

It was Cristo.

"Mission accomplished. All the caskets are at the Capitol Rotunda."

"Any surprises at autopsy?"

"None."

"President's cause of death?"

"Massive head trauma. A piece of a pine tree was embedded in what was left of his skull. I saw it with my own eyes."

"Sorry. At least there was never any hope. He didn't suffer…much. And the others?"

"All skiers had lethal wounds. The Vice President had total blockage of the L.A.D., whatever that is."

"The Left Anterior Descending coronary artery, also known as the widow-maker. When it occludes, it usually kills."

"She also had high-grade occlusions of all other coronary arteries. Her carotids were also almost totally blocked," Cristo said. "Whatever that means."

"Vice President Barker was a big smoker and drinker. She was also seriously overweight. Her death, either by heart attack or stroke, was a matter of when, not if," Abigail offered. "The Speaker of the House?"

"Had a two ounce piece of meat in this windpipe," Salazar said.

"Yes, well, that will kill you. Thanks, Cristo. You go home and get some sleep. And please bring me the camera in the morning."

CHAPTER FOUR

THE ROTUNDA

Thanksgiving evening

Abigail knew nothing of the elaborate preparations for a Presidential visit to the Rotunda, and it was just as well. It would unnerve her on her first foray out of the building. Abigail did not yet have a Kevlar vest, so made do with a borrowed one under her black cashmere coat.

She did her own makeup and hair and was ready to go at seven when a wan Mrs. Harrington appeared in the Oval Office. The older woman brightened at the sight of family pictures, undisturbed, on the credenza behind the desk.

"Oh, Abigail, my children don't understand my loss. I think you do because you just lost your sister," Evangeline Harrington hung onto Abby as if she were a life raft.

"They're probably just wrapped up in their own loss, ma'am," Abby said, patting her hand.

Abby was glad she brought an extra handkerchief for Evangeline. The two rode together to the Capitol. Her children followed in other limos.

"I am leaving for Colorado for good just after Margaret's Christmas Pageant next Friday. I'd go the day of the burial except for that," Evangeline said.

"I am going to cancel all other White House functions until the first of the year out of mourning," Abigail said. "If it is okay with you."

"Lovely gesture," Evangeline said with relief.

"This is awfully doctor-ish of me, but I checked. Your husband died of massive head trauma. He did not suffer, and he could not have been saved, even if we'd gotten to him immediately," Abigail said, taking Evangeline's hand in hers.

"Thank you, Abigail. That helps. That helps a lot."

In a few short minutes, they were in the Capitol Rotunda.

This time, no one had to warn her about the bright television lights or the cables snaking across the floor. Abigail would not need comfort; she was giving it. O.T. kept a gentle eye on Mrs. Harrington. Albright was vigilant, primarily about Abigail. Her personal safety was now his mission in life. He'd failed one President, he would not fail this one.

After Abigail and the Harrington family had walked past the five flag-draped caskets, Abigail and Mrs. Harrington said a few words to the family members whose loved ones flanked the President's casket. Todd Wilson's widow was about to burst, she was so pregnant. Abby tried to imagine a son's birth coinciding with the father's death and couldn't. Maybe that was why Mrs. Wilson looked so stricken.

By eight-thirty, they were back at the White House, and the public began streaming through the Rotunda and signing the condolence books. The Capitol would be open twenty-four hours a day until it was time to move the caskets for the funeral services.

For Abby, that night's tears were of sadness. Seeing flag-draped caskets would always remind her of the loss of Pris, just as seeing Texas bluebonnets would always remind her of her sister's life. After all, Pris's eyes were just the color of the bluebonnets.

CHAPTER FIVE

FUNERAL PLANS

November 24

Virtually everyone was at work on Friday morning, and at least Abigail knew what to expect at the PDB. No one seemed intent on interrupting the funerals, some fifty-three hours away. Abby was stuck with the Whore of the West moniker, which everyone shortened to "WOW," to Abigail's bizarre pleasure. Gallows humor helped, as it did at the hospital.

As Cristo was in the building for the PDB, they went to the Situation Room for a video conference with the commander in Afghanistan, General Woodfin, a lean and fit man in his fifties.

"Sir, can I do anything to make your job easier?"

"Not right now, ma'am, but I appreciate your offer," he said.

She was glad to take a video measure of him. Abigail thought he was fighting a losing battle but didn't tell him that. That could wait for another day.

She also viewed the autopsy photos of the President and returned the camera to Cristo.

"Let me check with the Attorney General. I will not see these photos on YouTube."

In a moment, Sam Sternberg, the Attorney General, was on the line, and Abigail told him what she wanted.

"Not a problem, ma'am. Kennedy's autopsy photos were sealed for decades."

"Good, you talk to Cristo and get it done. Also, I want you to rough out a commission to look into the deaths: bipartisan, at least one forensic pathologist as well as an expert in avalanches. Interim report in ninety days, full report in six months. Here's Secretary Salazar."

Abigail handed Salazar the phone and scrolled through the photos in the camera again. Lots of gore, but nothing looked criminal to her. She'd seen her share of mayhem, intentional and otherwise, and these looked accidental.

Human frailties had killed these people. The President's skiing party made a stupid choice to do back bowl skiing; the Vice President smoked, drank, and ate herself into an early grave; and the Speaker of the House couldn't even manage to cut his own food into bite-sized pieces.

Only the two Secret Service agents died a noble death, trying to protect their leader.

O.T. and the head of the National Cathedral planned the service. As all the deceased were Christians of one stripe or other, the bishop would do it.

The parents of the Vice President posed a problem, however. "They don't want 'her' anywhere near them," O.T. said of Jane, the VP's female partner of twenty years.

"Fine. Seat her next to me," Abigail said. "Next?"

"Then there is the question of transportation of the caskets to the National Cathedral," O.T. said.

Wicker liked the long cortege. "It's great video and very compelling."

"Too long a route to secure. One firecracker and we've got a problem," Albright rasped.

"O.T.?" Abigail said.

"I prefer removal of the caskets to the Cathedral in the wee hours of the morning."

"That's what we'll do," Abigail said. "Move the caskets in the middle of the night."

"Yes, ma'am," Albright said.

"Cathedral's security?" O.T. asked.

"A wedding on Saturday at six, everyone out by eight. We'll lock it down then," Albright said.

"How do heads of state get to the funeral?" Abby asked Albright.

"They all go independently to the Cathedral from their embassies. One of our agents accompanies them.

"So you have as much random movement into the Cathedral as possible. The Cathedral, not the route, is the primary target to secure?" Abigail asked.

"You catch on fast." Albright said. "Your route is secured, however."

"O.T., what about after the service?" Abigail asked.

"Each family has different plans. Mrs. Harrington has a reception here by invitation only. Harrington's body will go to Colorado that evening to be buried on Monday."

"On Air Force One," Abby interjected. "His family deserves that. And take their family and friends."

"Yes, ma'am, I agree," O.T. said. He liked Abigail's manners.

"Jane's hosting a reception at the Admiral's House for the Vice President's friends. The Vice President's body is going to New Jersey later that evening via train. The Speaker's wife has a reception arranged at their home in D.C., with burial in Ohio on Monday.

"The two Secret Service agents will be buried immediately after the service at Arlington," O.T. said.

"I'd like to attend, if possible," Abigail said.

"You might prefer to be at the White House with the heads of state and former Presidents," O.T. said.

"No, I will have met them all earlier. Albright?" Abigail asked, turning to him.

"We'd be honored, ma'am." For once, he wasn't gruff. If anything, he sounded proud.

"Please get me bios on the agents and their families. I've spoken with the widows, but would like more information," Abby said.

Albright nodded.

"O.T., the Barkers might act up if they go to the VP's residence after the funeral."

"I have given that some thought," he said with a twinkle in his eye. "And?"

"The Barkers are senile. I've appointed them a minder from my staff. She'll move them to Blair House today. Jane deserves her privacy. After the funeral, they'll rest until the minder puts them on the train, with the casket, later that afternoon. Their neighbor's son will meet them."

"Do give them a light meal before they leave," Abigail said.

CHAPTER SIX

THE CABINET

Friday, November 24

Her first Cabinet meeting wasn't until 3 p.m. Any time she had a moment, she wandered the rabbit warren that is the West Wing and asked everyone questions. She stayed out of the press area, lest someone ambush her for an interview.

She especially liked the Roosevelt Room, as it had no given function, but was centrally located near her office. A word with O.T. had turned it into a club-like room, where people could congregate, take things down a notch. As Regina would do, she asked that the room always have refreshments.

The Cabinet Room seemed self-important. Each Cabinet member's chair was oversized, leather, and had a brass nameplate on the back. As a result, furniture crowded the room before the people even sat down.

It's not as if they had endowed the chair, or worse, couldn't find a seat on their own.

Abby knew a few members already. Secretary of State Marilyn Chernosky and Cristo Salazar, whom she'd booted up from Chairman of the Joint Chiefs to Secretary of Defense. Most others returned from Thanksgiving holidays to be here. All sat with an aide behind him or her in a human-sized chair. The room would become stuffy if meetings lasted too long. *Short meetings are good.*

Abby entered the room at the third strike of the clock. Everyone stood.

"Please, everyone, take your seats."

Condolences out of the way, Abigail got right to the point.

"The country needs stability. If any of you wish to resign, now is the time. Letter on my desk by five, or I presume you will want to serve for the duration." Abby looked around the room. No one volunteered. All knew she had fired the Secretary of Defense.

"Thank you. I'm going to need all the help I can get."

Heads nodded. *Do these people not speak?*

"I need to name a Vice President as soon as possible. Please give me your suggestions by Monday. Party affiliation is irrelevant. I want someone who knows this government inside out and someone who can lead.

"Oh, and this isn't third grade. You may nominate yourself. All nominations will be anonymous."

She got a small chuckle. Abby paused and looked around the table. "What questions do you have for me?" she asked.

The silence was deafening. *This is not a good sign.*

Finally, the Secretary of the Treasury spoke.

"Are you going to run?"

For a moment, Abigail thought he was asking about jogging.

"It truly hasn't crossed my mind. I just want to get through the weekend. Let's adjourn to the Roosevelt Room for refreshments." Abigail smiled, stood, and led the way.

Once in the Roosevelt Room, the people loosened up. Topic One, of course, was the loss of the President. The Secretary of the Interior gave a good recap of avalanches. Abby told Sternberg to put him on the inquiry commission.

Then Abby realized no one in the room was in charge of the nation's communications, which had failed from overload. *Should the FCC be a cabinet-level position?* She shot Chaffee an e-mail. *If so, get a few kids on it. Geezers do not get technology.*

At three-fifty, Abby excused herself and went into her office to regroup. The icy reception of the Cabinet might well reflect displeasure with her, or it could just be grief. She had no idea. They did, however, improve with refreshments.

As Abigail reread the funeral briefing book, memorizing the names and faces of the heads of state and family members who would be visiting, the phone started ringing.

She spoke briefly with the two former Presidents, and each offered his help.

"Actually, I need your suggestion for a Vice President," she said.

Each offered one name, and the suggestions were identical. *That was easy, especially since he was her first choice anyway. Now if she could just convince him...*

"Poppy, please invite General Jerome Lafayette and his wife to dinner on Monday night. We'll dine in the private Dining Room here in the West Wing. Make sure the chef knows about any allergies. And serve his favorite dessert."

Abby went back to her briefing books.

Abigail was particularly interested in the Secret Service agents' families. One widow was particularly vulnerable. Rebecca Wilson, Todd Wilson's widow, had a four-year-old daughter and was heavily pregnant with a son. Abigail made a note to O.T. that she wanted to sit next to the four-year-old at Arlington. If nothing else, she could quietly engage the child.

Abby wasn't too concerned about the mother going into labor at the funeral. She could easily handle a term delivery, especially with an ambulance on site. *At least I know how to do one thing around here.*

Saturday dawned clear and cold. Abigail put on exercise clothes, attended the PDB in them, and then went for a brisk jog on the South Lawn. She—and her agents—needed the exercise. It cleared her head of all the venom she'd just heard.

The lawn was lovely, though barren. The Rose Garden had no blooms. The only splash of color was a bed of red and white cyclamen that ran along the South façade.

Abby worked up a sweat in no time. She was used to exercise, and hadn't gotten any for several days. She slowed to a walk and re-entered the West Wing.

"Thanks, guys," she said, as she peeled off to take a shower. Hitch was still sitting in the Oval Office with the football between his feet, while telecommuting to the Pentagon on another laptop. She wondered where the agents cleaned up, but not enough to ask.

She was free until the reception at four, though, of course, that meant that she had best get some rest. From dusk Saturday to dusk Sunday would literally be a death march.

For the first time since Wednesday, Abby stayed "unzipped" after her shower. She wore comfortable clothes, let her hair down, wore her glasses, and tried to relax. She unearthed her Kindle and read the trashy novel she'd been reading before her life went into a parallel universe.

Now where was I? Ah, yes, the heroine was on her way to Paris in First Class. Of course, she wore an Hermès scarf draped languidly around her neck. A handsome man, just graying at the temples and without a wedding ring, was sitting next to her...

CHAPTER SEVEN

PLAYING POTUS

Saturday, November 25

Abigail's rest allowed her brain to regroup. Though her conscious mind was on the book she was reading, the back of her mind was slotting things into places. She understood things better each day. She not only was the President of the United States, POTUS, but she had to play POTUS everywhere except in this tiny cubbyhole.

Bob Wicker had drummed this into her in her media training when she was a fledgling Senator. Even Andre Callas, her flamboyantly gay hair and makeup guy, drummed it into her.

"You are no longer a private citizen, baby girl. You are in the S-E-N-A-T-E, and you must play the part everywhere outside your front door."

He told her it was a "fashion felony" for her to appear outside her door anything less than "camera ready."

In a bizarre way, she felt like a new prisoner in an old jail. She had to adapt to it; it did not adapt to her. It was bizarre for a person with so much power, yet oddly balancing.

Just as her fear had subsided after her first night on call in the hospital without anything awful happening, her fear about her new job was similar. Sure, horrible things put her in this job, but since noon on Wednesday, she hadn't screwed up yet. Poppy's advice to "Stand up straight, smile and don't say the f-word" was still working.

Andre arrived at three to get her ready for the diplomatic reception. This time he brought a manicurist who kept Abigail's fingers busy while Andre worked from the neck up. He was his usual chatty self, and Abigail looked forward to this distraction. Until Mrs. Harrington left, she would not use the White House proper, so Andre was grooming her in the Oval Office.

He wrapped her face in icy cloths while he set up his wares and tools.

"You are looking tons better. Been playing with any of the boy toys around?" he asked, his blue eyes set off by guy-liner and a black Elvis pompadour.

"No. I went for a run this morning," Abby mumbled from under the towels.

"Oh well, a girl can only do so much." Andre shrugged as he unpacked his tackle boxes. "Still, you do need to keep those juices flowing. I hear the Italian leader's wife used to be a call girl," Andre went on, almost without taking a breath. "Governess? I think not. Pneumatic boobs, if I ever saw them.

"And as for the Queen, virtually all of her staff is gay. Maybe that's why she's so nice."

His patter entertained her while he did his work. Her comments were unnecessary, as he was always doing something that required her to hold still, be quiet, or both.

"Today we'll go with your hair up and in a chignon," he said, removing the towels.

"Why?" Abby asked.

"*Gravitas,* my darling. *Gravitas.* This is your coming-out party, so to speak. Of course, it is completely different from my coming-out party, but that's a subject for another day."

Abby missed Duke's clothes delivery today, as she was out for her run. In with the new suit was the washed and ironed tee-shirt she needed to return to the Marine.

Laura's choice was a deep purple wool crepe suit with an asymmetric neckline. It matched exactly her Ferragamo bow pumps. Laura accessorized it with an antique French gold pin and earrings left to her by her sister Pris, a collector of fine antique jewelry. With her watch and right-hand signet ring, she had just enough jewelry. Abby knew that her credit card must be getting a workout. Laura had offered her a twenty percent discount, but she declined.

I don't like White House moochers.

"Remember, if anyone asks who you are wearing, this is a Kim Tran," Andre said.

"Really?" Abigail said, delighted. "Did Neiman's pick her up?"

"No, but Laura had the shoes for you. She had Kim make the suit to match. You also have an outfit for tomorrow."

"But when did she find time to make it?" Abigail was astonished.

"She's been working day and night since Wednesday morning."

"I feel like a slave driver." Abigail knew how much work Kim put into a garment.

"For what you are paying, you should feel just fine." Andre was finished, and Abigail did indeed look regal.

"Now remember, this is Mrs. Harrington's party, but it is *your* show. Don't eat."

"Why not?"

"First, spillage. Second, photos of you stuffing your face. Third, a photo of something between your teeth. And no booze; it makes your eyes puffy. Only water. Welcome to being the most photographed woman on the planet. And you wonder why they all lose weight. See you tomorrow morning."

He blew her a kiss and was gone.

Abby misted on a touch of fragrance and put lip gloss in her purse. She felt odd not having to carry things like an I.D. or money. Launch codes in her bra? Yes. Keys? No.

The Marine Sentries looked pleasantly surprised when she left the office. Sgt. Thompson of the tee-shirt was on duty.

"Wait, I have something for you," Abigail said and returned to the little study. She scribbled a thank you on a sticky note and headed back out the door.

"Thanks so much," Abby said, handing him the tee-shirt. He turned red. With his white pants and navy blue tunic, he looked quite patriotic.

"Any time, ma'am." For the rest of his career, everyone called him "T-shirt Thompson."

Once the President reached the State Floor of the White House, the First Lady greeted her and took her into the Blue Room.

"Oh, my goodness, Abigail. You look splendid." Evangeline took both Abby's hands to admire her.

"Thank you, and you are looking much better yourself," Abigail said.

"I have an excellent autopilot. Let me introduce you. Now follow along, as I know the protocol." Mrs. Harrington took her by the hand, introducing her to people Abby knew only from the news.

She met the two former Presidents and their wives.

"You'll have some time with them later," Mrs. Harrington said, sweeping her along.

Then Mrs. Harrington introduced her to the heads of state, starting with the eldest, Her Majesty, who wore a well-tailored black dress and one of her famous diamond bow pins.

"How do you do, Your Majesty?" Abigail shook the Queen's hand and nodded her head a bit. American Presidents bow to no one. Abigail had to keep her jaw firmly shut at the sight of the glorious pin. The center of the bow was a diamond the size of a quarter. It threw rainbows on the wall.

"How do you do?" The Queen radiated warmth and good will.

"I am honored," Abigail said.

"And this is my husband," Her Majesty said.

"How do you do, Your Royal Highness," Abigail said.

The Prince offered a bony hand. "I'm jet-lagged and old, but one honors a fallen friend. And Walter Harrington was a friend."

"We're flattered you've come so far."

And so it went, down through the heads of state and their spouses. The French President's wife complimented Abigail on her pin and earrings.

"Oh, thank you. They're French, 1780, I think," Abigail said.

"I agree. Look at the length of that pin," Madame Latour said. "Women used them as weapons in the Revolution."

"The Secret Service wouldn't let this in the building on a guest," Abigail said.

"I should hope not," her husband put in.

Abigail took a glass of sparkling water from a passing waiter, held it firmly in her left hand, and sipped on it from time to time.

"You're doing great, Abby," President Fargo said when she next encountered him. "I couldn't be prouder."

"Thank you so much, Mr. President."

"You get to call me by my first name now."

"Thanks, but you'll always be worthy of your title to me."

Abigail went to the powder room. She felt the need to pinch herself. *This isn't my life is it? Did I really get to talk to the Queen?*

Indeed, it was her life, or so the drops of blood on her panties indicated. It was also her period. Abby opened her purse. No tampon. She searched the powder room. No tampon.

Mrs. Harrington can't help. I can't ask a male Secret Service agent. Poppy is home and would laugh her head off. The only time I pack my own purse, I don't remember the damn tampon. And I am entrusted with the launch codes? Going back to Oval Office will take at least fifteen minutes. There's gotta be someplace closer. A nurse's office?

Then Abby remembered the doctor's office downstairs. She slipped down there, and mercy of mercies, the weekend doctor was in.

"Good afternoon, Madam President. I'm Dr. Larson. What can I do for you?" a sandy haired man about her age asked as he rose to his feet.

"I, um, just need a tampon," Abby blushed.

"Sure," he said, handing her one from a drawer.

She was back in the reception before anyone missed her. That is, anyone except Albright.

"Where have you been," he hissed in her ear.

"Chick thing," she hissed back.

"Next time, please don't just disappear," Albright said.

"Sorry. Won't happen again." *Poor man. One president dead only three days and then I go off his radar.*

After the reception, she and the two former Presidents retreated to the Oval Office.

Ken Clutter, the White House photographer, had been all over the diplomatic reception and would photograph Abigail with her predecessors, so Abigail once more touched up her war paint and put in eye drops.

Surely, both former Presidents must have huge reservations about her inexperience, but both were complimentary.

"Great talk to the nation," President Wells drawled. "Even I liked it, and I hate television, unless it's sports."

She and President Fargo laughed.

"First rate," President Fargo put in with his Boston accent. "I felt you were very reassuring. I know I felt safer after I heard your speech than beforehand. And you did the right thing firing O'Neal."

"Thank you. I was shocked at his verbal assault." Abigail felt she could be candid.

"I'm not. He's a schemer of the first magnitude, though his defense expertise is quite strong."

"We three agree that General Lafayette should be the Vice President. The question is how do I get him to accept?" Abigail asked them.

"Win over the wife," Fargo said. "She has lupus and needs her life to be as stress-free as possible."

"She's also concerned about assassination," Wells said. "She was young when Martin Luther King was killed."

"Also, are you planning on running?" President Wells asked.

"Oh, heavens no," Abigail said, a little too swiftly. "Let me rephrase that. I barely know what I am doing next week. I am, as you might have noticed, an amateur at this."

"Well, that might make a difference to his wife," Wells said.

"Thank you, gentlemen, you've been a big help." Abigail stood up and so did they.

Both gave her private contact information, for which Abigail was grateful.

Abby got ready for bed, down to her flannel jammies and fuzzy socks. Overwhelmed and overstimulated, she lay on her back on the rollaway bed, the crossbar digging into her. *This bed is evil. Is it a leftover from the Spanish Inquisition?*

She did not want her job, yet she had fought for it against O'Neal. What could she offer the nation that other Presidents had not been able to give? And how could she do it in two years? Today she had met the Queen, two former Presidents, and the French President. *The world will look to me for leadership. And I can't remember to put a tampon in my purse?*

Suddenly, her eyes were flooded with tears. The proverbial busload of diabetics had gone off the bridge and come to her hospital. Not only was she the only doctor, but she didn't have the vaguest idea of what to do. Everyone had always relied on the protocol for injured diabetics taped to the nursing station window. Now, not only was the protocol gone, the whole window was missing. Once again, she cried herself to sleep.

CHAPTER EIGHT

SAYING GOOD-BYE

Sunday, November 26

The funeral day dawned clear and cold.

Abigail was again in her funeral suit, though Kim had spent the day before changing to it to accommodate a Kevlar vest. The manufacturer would come next week to make her custom body armor. *How reassuring.*

Abigail dreaded being back in the National Cathedral. The sight of five flag-draped caskets with President Harrington's up on risers and in the center was sobering. If nothing else, flag-draped caskets reminded her that her job was for keeps, just like medicine. *There are no do-overs in the presidency.*

The two Secret Service agents had died in service to their leader. Abby now had people willing to put their life on the line for her. *I've got to behave to keep them safe.* Even the honor guard rammed home the enormous responsibility of being Commander-in-Chief.

Every soldier, sailor, marine, airman, or coastie is some mother's baby.

Fifty minutes of known ritual was actually a respite for Abby. Jane, the VP's partner, sat next to her. She was a total mess: red nose, streaming eyes. Even her Hermès scarf was askew.

"Thank you, Madam President," she whispered. "I don't think I could have borne sitting in the back."

Abigail patted her hand and dug a handkerchief from her purse. Poppy had put in five. And a dozen tampons. *Cute, Poppy.*

"There, there," she whispered, giving Jane a fresh handkerchief.

During the service, the weather went downhill. The skies clouded over, and a damp north wind slapped at everyone leaving the Cathedral. Abigail was glad for a warm coat on the way to the car. Four separate motorcades formed up, Abigail's first.

Once Abby settled into her seven-ton armored personnel carrier that only looked like a Cadillac, she could relax a little. Poppy and Sally Gordon, her new Secret Service agent, rode with her.

Sally was tall and Nordic looking, and Duke would think twice before getting in a fight with her. Abby had read her file. Married, one daughter, aged two, Sally had been lead agent for Mrs. Harrington. She requested to stay in D.C., so Abigail inherited her.

"Just think," Sally said when Albright introduced them earlier, "I can tell my daughter I take the President to the potty."

"Hey, potty training's hard. Feel free to invoke me as a role model," Abigail said.

Other agents ringed the car, then most hopped into other vehicles once things started up. Albright himself entered her car at the last possible moment, diagonally across from Sally. He and Sally scanned the outside of the car, like lifeguards doing grid checks in a big swimming pool. They had totally different fields of vision, Abigail noticed.

Abby was glad she'd thrown her boots and old cape into the car. Boiled wool was impervious to everything. Besides, it had a certain panache. Remembering fidgety children would attend, she'd grabbed a couple of small flags off her desk as well as a White House snow globe paperweight. Those, as well as some pens and paper, were in her tote on the floor of the car.

"We've cancelled all social plans except for Margaret's Christmas pageant, but after the first of the year, I've got to start entertaining if I want anything from Congress. I'll have to entertain like Pris would do," Abigail said to Poppy.

"Do you know what you want from Congress?" Poppy asked.

"Not yet, but I have a few ideas," Abigail said. Abby had a thousand ideas. But since whatever was good for 99 percent of the people would be blocked by the lobby for the 1 percent, she wasn't optimistic on any of it.

"How much makeup have you bought just for the 'free gift'?" Abby asked.

"Too much," Poppy said.

"Well, let's think of some swag." Abby noticed the snow globe of the White House in her tote and began to think out loud. "Snow globes. Perfect. Create them of the White House in all four seasons. Snow; cherry blossoms; red, white, and blue confetti; and fall leaves. Each would play a different patriotic melody. They'd be lovely gifts when I entertain."

"We'll get with the East Wing people and make a calendar," Poppy said.

Abby thought of the Vice President's partner and her hangdog scarf. "Maybe we'll do seasonal White House scarves with magnetic pins that won't ruin the scarf."

"Kim can do those. Cherry blossoms, fireworks, that sort of thing. Ties for the guys," Poppy put in.

"Great idea."

"Oh, and Poppy, I need a meeting with the Attorney General. I want to fill all the vacant federal benches between sessions of Congress."

"Don't be so shy, Madam President, someone will think you are a girl," Poppy deadpanned.

The motorcade sped up and moved quickly toward Arlington National Cemetery. Once inside the gates, the pace slowed. The usual

Sunday afternoon visitors were out, even in the deepening gloom of autumn. Rain looked imminent.

Abigail touched up her make-up, wriggled out of her coat and shoes, and slipped into the warmer cape and boots. The hood would protect her hair if it rained suddenly. She picked up the tote and took it with her.

She offered condolences, then found her chair in the front row, and sat between the two families. She turned up the hood of her cape against the crosswind.

The chaplain began the service.

As Abigail expected, the four-year-old daughter of Todd Wilson was fidgety, so Abby patted her lap, and the little girl came and sat on it. Abby wrapped her in the cape.

"We have to whisper," Abigail said into the little girl's ear. "I'm President Abby. Who are you?"

The little girl lisped softly into Abby's ear, "I'm Samantha, but you can call me Sam." It came out "Tham."

The hugely pregnant mother thanked Abigail with a small smile.

When whispering stopped being a distraction, Abby reached into her bag and brought out the snow globe and, last, a small flag.

Finally, it was time to stand. Abby opened her cape, and Samantha stepped back inside it. Abby wrapped her in the warmth of the old thing.

Only Samantha's head and hands were visible. Her head, a riot of yellow ringlets, stuck out against the blue-black cape. They were almost a match for Abby's stray locks blown sideways by the wind. Samantha stuck one thumb firmly into her mouth, and with the other hand, she waved bye-bye to her daddy with a little flag from the tote.

Abigail put her right hand over her heart as Taps was played, and tears streamed down her perfectly made-up face.

The picture of Abigail and Samantha was the image of the entire horrible weekend. It was, as one broadcaster said, "the John-John moment, an iconic image."

CHAPTER NINE

FINDING A VICE PRESIDENT

Monday, November 27

The day after the funerals, the country was back at work. Anyone who wanted to see the burial services could catch them on cable news. Most citizens were glad to be back to normal.

Abigail faced her first full "normal" day on the job. *Whatever normal is.*

Today's PDB was especially gruesome. In Afghanistan, a roadside bomb killed two Marines on patrol. As fellow Marines attempted to recover their bodies, hostiles ambushed and killed them. By the time a third party went in, they found all hacked into small pieces. *Minced men.* The remains were deliberately heaped into a large pile. Animals made off with many of them during the night.

No wonder Abby excused herself and vomited up her breakfast. She brushed her teeth, rinsed her mouth, and returned to the Oval Office. *Perhaps I should schedule breakfast after the PDB.*

If anyone thought anything about her behavior, he had the good sense to keep quiet.

Immediately after the PDB, Abigail had time with Poppy and Chaffee.

"This is the time when we go over the President's schedule for the day," Chaffee explained. "Your day falls into several categories: standing appointments, such as lunch on Tuesday with the Vice President, meet and greets, message of the day, and open time."

Each had wirelessly linked laptops. The system was color coded. All military meetings (red) took place in the Situation Room for technology needed. Ceremonial events took place in the Oval Office (green). Meetings in the Private Dining Room were yellow.

"Harrington liked what he called the 'Shrink Schedule,'" Chaffee said. "Each 'hour' is fifty minutes, to allow leeway."

"I agree," Abigail said. Chaffee pulled up Harrington's schedule from three weeks back. It showed twenty 'meet and greets' with photos.

"You have got to be kidding," Abigail said. She wanted to use stronger language, but this was not a hospital.

"Nope, that's pretty standard. Donors, diseases, diplomats all want face time."

"Diseases?"

"Yes, lobbying groups for specific diseases want your support."

"Jeez. I feel like a wind-up doll. You have to lose the donors."

"Lose the donors?" Chaffee asked as if Abigail was talking of throwing them off the White House roof.

"Yes. I 'owe' them nothing, and I do not want them on my schedule. Period. Not negotiable. Full stop."

Chaffee and Poppy looked at each other. Poppy nodded, imperceptibly.

"Fine. We can do that," Chaffee said. She was committing political suicide. Without 'the big dogs,' she could never run.

"I do, however, want time with some of the interns—Elaine Bennett for one, as well as a rotating handful of the others. Thirty minutes, once a week. Also, I want some employees to be a group of 'real' people. Get O.T. to put together a list. Be sure to include naturalized citizens, as well."

"Why this sudden interest in the 'little people'?" Chaffee asked.

Abby cocked her left eyebrow at him, giving him Regina's Look. He would remove that phrase from his lexicon.

"I'll wither on the vine without input from real people. If all I hear are 'massaged' opinions, I'm useless. I need real people giving me uncensored opinions."

Abby looked at her notes. "What about this 'message of day'?" she asked, though she knew what it was.

"This is the White House's production of something in time for the nightly news broadcasts, something showcasing the President's agenda. Usually takes only about fifteen minutes of your time. The press people do the rest of the production."

Abigail grumbled.

"Ma'am. You need the country on your side. The 'John-John' photo yesterday is already an iconic image. Whether you like it or not, you are going to be the most photographed woman on the planet for a while. You must use that force to advance your agenda."

"You're right." *I just have to figure out what my agenda is.*

"Okay, guys. Here's the drill," Abigail continued. "I'll do what you have planned for me today. Dump the donors after today. Plead overwork. And lose half the diseases. I'll do the messages of the day. Clear them with Wicker. First one on infection control in offices."

Poppy, an excellent mimic, chimed in. "Stay home if you have a fever over 100˚, sneeze into your elbow, and wash your hands before and after everything."

Abby went through the motions of the day. She was near coma by lunchtime. Her face had frozen into a smile.

"Poppy, would you tell Albright that I want to go Christmas shopping one day this week?" Abigail said after her lunch break. "And I want to stop by Tran's store, but without Tran's knowledge."

"Okay, but why? You do your shopping online."

"A photo-op shopping. Mostly I want to see Regina. I hope I'm giving enough notice."

"Sure."

"Do we have the East Wing social planning scheduled?"

"Yep. I included Peggy Mellon for her expertise," Poppy said.

"Okay." *Great idea. Between Regina and Peggy, even the Queen would feel right at home.*

The Cabinet meeting was at three, and as usual, Abigail walked in at the third stroke of the hour. Everyone jumped to his feet. Most needed to lose weight. *Maybe I should enter the room a dozen times, just to get them moving.*

"Good afternoon," she said briskly. "Our first order of business is the vice presidency." Abigail looked through the names. General Lafayette's was number one.

"Thank you for your suggestions. I will take them under advisement," she said. "Now, I'd like your departmental reports."

Everyone said similar things. Too much work, too little money. The litany was long, the solutions few.

Not one person mentioned the long-term huge catastrophes looming: climate chaos, the national debt, or a population that was getting older and sicker, and fatter, by the day.

Health and Human Services thought fraud was its biggest problem. *Boy, have you missed the boat. Our biggest health care problem is not a broken system; it is no system at all. It's chaos.*

The lobbyists obviously ran the Hill. Seeing how many donors were on the President's schedule every day, they obviously ran the White House, too. They had even subtly made cabinet members look away from the long-term huge issues and focus on the now and narrow. *Very dangerous. No one was looking ten to twenty years down the road. Scary.*

The cabinet adjourned for the refreshments. She learned more as the people loosened up a bit. *Perhaps instead of cabinet meetings, we should have cabinet strolls.*

"Mr. Attorney General, a word, please?" Abigail said.

She took Sam Sternberg into the Oval Office and offered him something to drink. A small, dapper man who smelled faintly of citrus aftershave, he possessed a first-rate legal mind.

"Do you mind if I call you Sam?" she asked.

"Certainly. Just not Sammy. That sounds like a baseball player."

Abigail smiled and took a seat across from him.

"Sam, I have a bad feeling about something. I think it might fall under your jurisdiction."

He began to take notes in precise printing on a fresh yellow legal pad.

Abigail gave him copies from her files and told him the brief story of John Lafferty, the Secretary of Defense, and the Mockingbird missiles. "The Secretary of Defense stonewalled not only me, but also my sister fifteen months earlier. I think that odd."

"But he is no longer in office."

"No, but if he was committing a crime, it bears looking into."

"Could you be more precise?"

"I think, but cannot prove, that he and Lafferty Weapons Systems were skimming and splitting the difference."

"I see."

"A worse scenario is they have diverted enough parts of missiles to build four of their own. We cannot 'lose' shoulder-fired nuclear weapons. They'd be worth a fortune to terrorists."

"Chilling."

"Before I could pursue this, I ended up here. So now, this is your problem. If O'Neal is a bad guy, nail him. If not, do not embarrass him further. I did fire him rather publicly."

"Ah, yes, the Great Turkey Shoot," Sternberg smiled.

"So it has a name, does it?" Abigail had to chuckle.

"Oh, yes. The picture of you and the little girl captured the public's heart, but the Great Turkey Shoot established your Presidential chops inside the Beltway."

"The second thing I need for you to spearhead is a search of candidates to fill the open federal benches between sessions of Congress," Abigail said neutrally.

"President Harrington was already well into that process when he died," he replied. "Chaffee and I have almost a full slate, all well vetted."

"Great, but I have a little different take on that."

Abigail explained that she wanted a slate that represented the party ratio in the Senate.

"But I want to be blind to party affiliation. That way, the Senate can't whine," she said.

"Ma'am, that's awfully, um, aggressive."

"Perhaps, but the benches have to be filled. If people have to work day and night, then pull in help. That is why God created interns. Besides, they are so computer savvy, they can spot a porn addict long before you or I could."

Sternberg laughed.

"I sat on the Judiciary Committee and saw what Senator Whitman tried to do to Justice Hirsch. It's a wonder we have any judges at all."

"This could be interesting. May I get help? Like from the American Bar Association and law school deans?" Sam asked. "We've got some excellent U.S. Attorneys ready for the bench."

"Certainly. I plan on announcing just before Christmas."

"I'd best get cracking," Sam said.

"Not even a squeak of a leak," Abby said.

"Yes, ma'am. I like my job." *Sternberg was a fast learner. Maybe I should offer him a bench.*

After Sternberg left, she peeked at the closing numbers on Wall Street. The markets were broadly up, though modestly. Trading volumes were normal.

I want to do the happy dance. I want to do the happy dance.

Somehow, the financial markets had taken the bizarre change in leadership without a hiccup. No poll number in the world could beat that one.

She was so relieved, she could cry. But her day was not through. She had to convince a very reluctant man to become Vice President.

He didn't need the job. He had been a general, then Chairman of the Joint Chiefs, and finally retired to the lucrative speaking circuit. He commanded fifty grand per speech and gave forty speeches a year. Moreover, his two books had been bestsellers. Most importantly, his wife did not want him to take the job.

Jerome Lafayette and his wife, Lynne, arrived on the dot at seven.

He was chocolate skinned; she was much lighter. Both had the bearing Abby would have expected. Mrs. Lafayette looked perfectly healthy in a pink Ralph Rucci suit, but Abigail knew that looks were deceiving, especially where lupus was concerned.

"May I offer you refreshments?" Abigail asked.

The steward mixed a bourbon and water for the general. Mrs. Lafayette and Abby had sparkling water.

"Please, have a seat. I, for one, have had a long day."

"They are just beginning," General Lafayette put in.

"Long days are my norm. I work hard, always have. However, I always reward myself at the end of the day with a good book," Abigail said.

"What are you reading now?" Lynne asked.

"You'll laugh. I'm reading Penny Royal's latest romp," Abigail confessed. *Surely, no one as elegant as Lynne Lafayette would even know about such trashy novels.*

"Really? Have you gotten to the part about the Frenchman on the plane?" Lynne's face lit up.

"Just last night," Abigail said. "I was sorry I couldn't read the next chapter."

"You're going to love it. It is her best ever." Lynne smiled a Cheshire cat grin.

"Who is Penny Royal?" General Lafayette wanted to know.

The women just looked at each other and rolled their eyes.

"Never mind, dear. Let's just say she's not your kind of writer." Lynne turned to Abigail. "He likes what I call 'guy romance' novels, where things explode every few pages."

"Nothing's wrong with a little Ram Vince now and again," he said defensively.

"Nothing at all," Abigail concurred. Mrs. Lafayette just smiled indulgently.

The three had dinner in the President's dining room, followed by Jerome's favorite dessert, lemon meringue pie.

"How is Mrs. Harrington doing?" the general asked over coffee.

"Doing better than expected, I'd say."

"But aren't you cramped living and working in the West Wing?" Lynne said.

"I'm used to little spaces. I've spent many a night in a hospital call room. So no, I'm fine. I try to get out every day and get some fresh air. I'll probably rattle around in the White House itself. After all, it'll just be Regina and me living there."

"Who is Regina?" Lynne asked.

"She was my guardian from the time I was a baby," Abby started in on the story.

"Oh, yes, yes, I remember. The patchwork family," Lynne smiled. Abby could tell she approved.

"It's worked well so far. Duke is a third-year in law school at Georgetown. *Law Review.* He's the apple of my eye. But I didn't ask you here to talk to you about my family.

"I want you to become Vice President, sir." Abigail looked at Jerome, who looked at his wife.

"I'm very flattered, Madam President, but I think you know my answer will be no," the general said plainly, putting down his coffee cup with a soft clink.

"Lynne, I think I understand some of your concerns. Tell me, how's your lupus?"

"Doing well. It's been a while since I've had a flare, primarily because I fly below the radar. I'm still on all my medications. Mostly, there's just less of me to go around."

"As a doctor, I commend you for living within your limits. What if we made accommodations?"

"Like what?" General Lafayette asked.

"Like no travel for you, sir, home for dinner every night, barring a disaster. You would be home more than you are now. Plus, no entertaining for you, Lynne."

"How would you arrange that?" Lynne asked.

"Well, Marilyn Chernosky would travel in my stead, not you. She loves her travel." Abigail said. She could tell that the Lafayettes were at least interested.

"And Lynne, I'd do all the entertaining. You need to do nothing. You would always be included in invitations, but you could decide at the last minute whether you felt like coming. You could always leave early. You'd be the only person in Washington who could blow off the President," Abigail laughed.

The Lafayettes knew nothing in the White House was ever last minute or loose. This type of casual approach was a tremendous compliment and a rare perk indeed.

"And if you wanted to bring your daughter, Lynnette, instead of Lynne at the last minute, that'd be fine. Every girl likes to get dressed up to go out with her dad."

The Lafayette's adult daughter was a beautiful young woman, though mildly autistic. She was perfectly fine in social situations. The only clue to a casual observer was her almost robotic speech and lack of eye contact. She lived in a group home in D.C.

"I'm still worried about Jerome's safety," Lynne said.

"Of course you are. But remember, he will not be out and about. You, sir, would be primarily here, in the building, as my mentor, as my teacher. This place, I need not remind you, is a fortress. I need you desperately, and however much I need you, the country needs you more."

"That is true," Lynne said. "And now that I am better, I'd like to be more of an advocate for lupus, and for autism. I've resisted the 'poster child' mentality, but quite frankly, unless someone does it, illnesses are ignored."

"I asked both former Presidents for recommendations and both suggested you. And you were the Cabinet's overwhelming favorite." Abby was giving it all she had.

"We'll think about it. But my lady, here, she gets the final vote," General Lafayette patted his wife's hand.

"You, sir, are a very wise husband."

The Lafayettes left holding hands.

Abby crawled into bed at nine and enjoyed every steamy, silly page of what happened with the Frenchman on the airplane.

CHAPTER TEN

OUT OF THE CAGE

Sally Gordon was a good agent for Abby. As well, Albright assigned a second female agent to Abby's detail. Debbie Taylor was the young woman who came to Pris's house with President Harrington. She was as petite and redheaded as Sally was tall and blonde. Ideally, she would need at least four, but two were better than zero.

Abigail would have liked both women as friends, but remembering Albright's words, she did not befriend the women. You don't ask a friend to take a bullet for you. Just as she had to play the role of POTUS, she also had to play the role of protectee, Goldilocks, not the friend.

Abby was heading to Franklin Towers to do some photo-op shopping and see Regina. Abigail's outing inconvenienced virtually a quarter of Washington. Streets closed, traffic signals slammed to red for inordinate periods, and taking the short way was taking the stupid way. The President's movements should always be unpredictable. No one would know in which vehicle the President would ride. Debbie Taylor wasn't a look-alike, but wearing a strawberry blonde, curly wig, sunglasses, and sitting on a phone book, she could, and did, pass for Abigail behind the bulletproof glass in the second car. This time, it seemed, Abby would go in an ambulance. *Oh well, it isn't my first ambulance ride.*

Abigail never thought to argue with Albright because he was trying to protect her. Mikey drilled into her that she absolutely and forever lost her privacy and freedom when she took the oath of office. Abigail usually followed the rules, so it hurt less. But it still hurt.

Besides, arguing with Albright would have been like arguing with Regina. Words might pass between them, but there would be no meeting of the minds, only the crashing of skulls.

Franklin Towers had a secure underground entrance for VIPs. Abigail unfolded herself from the back of the ambulance and stepped into the designated elevator. She whizzed to the service entrance of the penthouse and was thrilled to smell the ginger cookies Regina made near Christmas.

Home.

Regina was there to greet her, and Abby clung to her for a long time, feeling the comfort of familiar arms holding her tightly.

"I've made you guys some cookies and such. Help yourselves," Regina said as they passed into the kitchen. "The advance guys had a head start, so you've got some catching up to do."

Regina had set up cookies and spiced cider in the living room for the two of them, and Abigail ate and drank ravenously. She wanted to gorge herself on the familiar.

"Slow down, girl. Those cookies aren't going anywhere," Regina said.

"I'm just so glad to be home, Reege," Abigail said, bursting into tears. Abigail put down her teacup sat as close as possible to Regina. If she could have climbed onto her lap, she would have.

"I know, I know," Regina cooed. "I've been missing you, too."

Regina dried Abby's tears with a tissue from the coffee table.

"You're doing good, girl. Everyone I talk to says so. And that phone's been ringing off the hook."

"Who's called?"

"Who hasn't? Everyone and his brother. I've got a list somewhere."

Abby looked around the penthouse. Only a few days away and she'd forgotten things. She'd been so busy; the world outside her office had disappeared. It was like being a medical intern, only worse.

"Here's the list." Regina offered a steno pad filled with calls.

"So what do you tell them?" Abigail asked.

"I tell them that there's no telling when, or if, anyone will return their call."

Abigail flipped through the list. Some of the names were vaguely familiar; others were complete shots in the dark. John Lafferty had called, twice. He would not get a call back.

"Hey, I need for you not to watch the news tonight," Abigail said.

"But I keep up with you on the TV. I think you are doing great. The press loves you."

"Right now, maybe. But if I as much as fart, they'll turn on me," Abigail said.

"You watch your language, Ladybug. I do not want to hear talk like that from you." Regina was still boss. *There is hope for the universe, after all.*

"I'm shopping for your Christmas presents," Abigail said.

"Well, I guess I'll record my stories and watch them during dinner."

Abigail was suddenly sad at the thought of Regina eating alone in front of the television.

"Reege, I want to talk about your moving into the White House with me."

"Mrs. Harrington isn't even gone yet, is she?"

"No. But she'll go next weekend," Abby said mildly. "Moving into the White House is your decision, not mine. I want you and Duke with me, but only if you want it."

"But what would I do?" Regina asked. "I have to have a purpose."

"When a President is unmarried, a female relative traditionally serves as Official Hostess," Abigail said.

"That sounds like a restaurant job," Regina scowled.

"And Jackie Kennedy said 'First Lady' sounded like a good name for a saddle horse."

Regina laughed. "You know, it does."

"Reege, the work as head of state and head of government overwhelms me. I need you desperately for the entertaining part."

"Well, your sister certainly trusted me with all of that." Regina's wheels were turning. "And I can't leave you there all by yourself to mess up menus and put up with bad flowers."

"Well, you could, but I'd be awful lonesome." Abigail was dialing up the pity factor.

"I don't think Duke would come, though. He has to be the star of his own life," Regina said.

"Yes, I suppose, but he can have a room there," Abigail said.

"Well, I'll pray on this," Regina said.

"If I invite Naomi to the first State Dinner, will you say yes?" Abigail said. Naomi was Oprah's heir; therefore, she was Regina's favorite talk show host.

"I think my prayers have been answered."

CHAPTER ELEVEN

SHOPPING

Abigail walked through the penthouse and mentally surveyed the furnishings in the elegant five-bedroom home. She couldn't picture what to take or what to leave, as she'd barely been in the White House living quarters, but she knew she didn't need to buy anything. If anything, the penthouse had too much furniture in it.

She opened her own closet. Her Houston clothes seemed to mock her. All were comfort things she'd worn while tending her sick sister. Her clothes in Texas were little better. After all, she'd been paying off student loans for med school until just recently. She'd lived frugally well into her thirties.

The woman who wore the clothes in the closet no longer existed. The groomed and coiffed woman with launch codes in her bra had replaced her. She was different, inside and out. She would never lose the bearing she had acquired in the Chief Justice's office. The Oath of Office transformed her, pulled her head a little higher, and straightened a spine bent by grief.

Abby depended on her medical training to see her through. Act in the best interest of the patient, assess the problem, gather information, weigh choices, make a decision, implement it, check up on how well it is working, change course if necessary, always going back to the beginning of the circle: the best interest of the patient. The loop was a complete one.

Her patient was now the nation. Just as her patients looked to her for care, comfort, and reassurance, the nation would look to her for the same. And just as the interests of the patient came first, the interests of the nation came first.

She had lost a lot. That was true. Privacy was gone. Forever. Anonymity was gone. Forever. Her name had changed. From Abby or Abigail, to Madam President or ma'am. Dr. Adams had morphed into President Adams. She had worked hard for one title; the other had dropped into her lap.

But people lost things all the time. One minute they are fine; the next they've lost a treasured item, or worse, a hand, or an eye or, heaven forbid, a child.

She could cope with the losses the presidency brought. She had to. Also, the job came with some incredible perks. She'd yet to cook a meal or go to the grocery store. She would live in a museum and could wander it at night, probably. Anyone on the planet would take her phone call. Anyone would come to her house for dinner.

It was too soon to tell if she would like the job. Like it or not, she had to do her best. She'd taken an oath. She was stuck with it, unless of course, some whack job got to her. Having Regina in the Residence would help a lot. Regina never wavered and had no use for self-pity.

Abby shook off her reverie and walked into the kitchen. All of the agents stood.

"Hey, relax. Finish your coffee. I'm ready to shop when you are. I want to go to Tran's first."

"We just wandered through. All looks okay," Debbie Taylor said.

"Does he think I'm coming?" Abigail asked. Surely, Kim had told her father that she'd done work for the new President, hadn't she? And her motorcade had gone right past the store.

"I got no hint of that."

"Good. Tell Albright I'm going with my hair down, glasses on and in a ratty, red parka."

Abby went to her sister's closet and took out the parka, changed her contacts for glasses, and put her hair under a knit cap. She looked like a generic nobody, especially if she slumped a bit. The Kevlar vest bulked her up even more in the parka.

She and Sally went out the service entrance. Agents had unobtrusively checked out Tran's store. Other agents loitered along her one minute long walk. She and Sally walked side by side in the brisk December day without incident. Sally got the signal that Tran's was empty, and Abby entered. Sally followed her in and headed for the other side of the shop.

Abby had forgotten the lovely jingle of the bell above the door and the scent of freshly cut ginger root.

"Hey, Missy. Long time no see." Tran's eyes lit up as she approached.

"Yep, been busy. How are you?" Abby said as she looked for something, anything, to purchase. She decided on a couple of quarts of eggnog, Regina's favorite.

"Oh, been better," Tran said. He didn't try to up-sell her.

"What's the matter?" Abby asked.

"It's Kim." He shook his head with bewilderment.

"What's the problem?" Abigail asked with genuine concern.

"She have boyfriend," Tran said flatly.

"A serious one?" Abigail asked.

"Yes." Tran looked like he'd lost his best friend.

"Have you met him? Do you not like him?" Abby had never seen Tran so sad.

"He okay," Tran said, his voice was flat. He rang up the purchase.

"Does he have a job?" Abby asked.

"Finish school this year. Have pick of jobs."

"Is he good to Kim?" Abby asked. "Would he run into a burning building to save her?"

"Oh, yes. Good man. Polite. Always bring flowers to Kim and to mother."

Then the penny dropped.

"But he's not Vietnamese," Abby said softly, putting a twenty on the counter.

"Kim is Vietnamese. Husband should be also." Tran was firm.

"I understand. But real love is hard to find, and Kim is a sensible girl," Abigail said softly.

"You have point." Tran handed her the change and package. Abby turned to go.

"Good luck," Abby said.

"You come back soon, Missy. Old Tran like you."

"I like you, too."

Abby was sad leaving the store, but she and Sally were back at her apartment at Franklin Towers within a few minutes. Albright could take his cares down a notch. Likely, his blood pressure would follow.

Once back at the penthouse, Abby again dressed as POTUS, popped into Regina's bathroom, and rooted around for her powder. The Estée Lauder compact did not have the shade on it, so she pocketed the whole thing.

She appeared at the appointed hour ready to shop. As an example to others, she was paying cash. *Thank goodness, the West Wing had an ATM.*

A scrum of reporters and photographers greeted her when she came out of the elevator on the shopping mall level. The stores were all high end, their windows lavishly decorated for Christmas. A pianist played holiday tunes on a grand piano. Even Abby felt festive at the scene.

"Hi, guys," Abigail said cheerfully.

She fielded a few softball questions, and asked for a favor.

"I'm shopping for gifts for my family, so don't spill the beans."

She went to a luggage shop and bought Duke a wallet. She looked at high-end briefcases, snapped a photo of one tag with her phone. She'd call back to order and monogram it.

Next, Abby went to the Estée Lauder counter in a department store. Women shoppers were shocked to see the President browsing. Abby waited her turn. The saleslady showed her this year's assortment of compacts, Abigail chose one and had the date engraved on it, and the woman put the correct shade into the tray. For Regina's bigger gift, Abby would order an Hermès scarf online.

On a whim, Abigail stocked up on the Bulgari Green Tea as an indulgence for herself. Abby paid cash for everything.

"I hate to face the credit card bills," she said to the press. *Hint, hint, people.*

Abby went into a cashmere shop. Poppy was the fussiest human being on the face of God's green earth, but Abby saw two items that caught her eye. One was a red muffler, which she bought; the second was a red cashmere throw she'd order. It would go nicely in Poppy's apartment.

Her last purchase was the most fun.

"I'm going to Margaret Harrington's Christmas pageant. I can't go empty handed.," she said to the press as she went into a card shop and bought twenty silver Christmas bell ornaments already engraved with the year. "The kids will love them, but the parents will want to throttle me."

Back at the penthouse, she replaced Regina's compact and asked her what she'd like to bring to the White House.

"I especially want my iron and ironing board," Regina said.

"Reege, you don't have to iron there," Abigail was fairly sure of that.

"Has it occurred to you that I actually might like to iron?" Regina said.

"I know you do. I grew up with ironed sheets and pillowcases. And to this day, I can't put on a blouse that isn't ironed." Abby did not say she dutifully touched up the next day's clothes before she went to bed. However, Regina's ironing board was not essential to the functioning of the nation.

"Love me, love my ironing board and iron," Regina said.

"Okay, okay." Abigail knew to pick her battles.

Her desk phone rang. "Lafayette on one" popped up. *Please, oh please say yes.*

"Good afternoon, General," Abigail said pleasantly.

"I wanted to tell you again what a lovely evening Lynne and I had with you."

"The pleasure was all mine." Abigail was getting used to niceties, but they were time-eaters.

"I thought I should get back to you in a timely fashion," Lafayette said.

Abigail's heart sank. *He is going to turn me down, and I don't have a second choice.*

"Lynne and I have looked at this thing from every which way and think it is something we can and should do. I accept your invitation."

"I am deeply honored and very grateful," Abby said. *I want to do the happy dance. I want to do the happy dance.* "I'd like to announce it tomorrow, if possible. I look forward to a speedy confirmation. Do you have any accommodations we need to make?"

"Like what?" General Lafayette asked.

"Well, do you want to move into the Admiral's House at the Naval Observatory? If it is too big a move for Lynne, you can stay in your own home."

"We've talked about that, but believe it or not, she wants to move."

"Well, I'll make it as easy as possible. As an Army officer's wife, she's a veteran at white-glove inspections with moving, but the only thing she'll have to do is point and it will get done."

"Funny, she uses that system with me very effectively," he chuckled.

"Shall we say noon in the Oval Office? We can have lunch, then announce it at the one-thirty press briefing. In the East Room," Abby said, all but giddy with relief.

"Yes, ma'am."

"Oh, and please bring your kids and grandchildren. They need to see where you'll be working."

"My son would love it, as would my grandchildren. There is one thing I'd like to say."

"Of course."

"Thank you for including our daughter." His voice was husky with emotion.

"No thanks necessary."

Abigail hung up and buzzed Wicker.

"Lafayette said yes." Abigail whooped for joy. *Finally, I'll have someone around who knows what he's doing. Everyone needs backup, especially an accidental President.*

Her other line rang when she finished with Wicker.

"Yes, Mrs. Harrington, what can I do for you?"

"First of all, stop with the 'Mrs. Harrington' bit. My name is Evangeline," she said good-naturedly. "Secondly, I'd like to show you the Residence later this afternoon."

They fixed a time, and Abby ordered a small bouquet of flowers from the White House florist to take with her. White roses with some holly and red berries arrived shortly. Before they brightened Evangeline's table, they would cheer up her desk.

While she was at it, she ordered a weekly bouquet for her desk, and Poppy's, every Monday. *Guys might swoon over Air Force One, but I'm tickled pink to have flowers on my desk.*

"Nothing ostentatious, just something pretty," Abigail said to the White House florist. "And red for Poppy's desk."

"Yes, ma'am. We've already figured that out."

CHAPTER TWELVE

MEET THE PRESS

Holiday decorations engulfed the White House. Abigail saw barely one inch spared as she walked to the Family Quarters. *Ick.*

Evangeline Harrington looked as well as anyone could who had just buried a husband. She brightened at the small bouquet.

"Thank you so much just for being there for me," Evangeline said, hugging Abby.

"No thanks necessary."

The women sat in the West Sitting Room, bereft of sun this time of day. Abby accepted a sparkling water.

"So tell me, Madam President, what do you think of the Christmas decorations?" Evangeline asked with a small smirk.

"They're certainly enthusiastic." Abigail tried to be diplomatic.

"Actually, they make me gag, but the volunteers who do this take their mission very seriously."

"Ah. I see," Abigail said. *It looks like they have carpet-bombed a Christmas store.*

"But I didn't call you in to talk about the 'SWAT team in panty hose.' I need to show you around as I am moving home after the pageant on Friday," Evangeline said.

"Are you sure? I don't want you to feel rushed," Abigail said.

"I need to be in my own home."

"I understand. How can I help?" Abigail asked. "Of course, I'll want you to use Air Force One."

"If you think you won't need it…" Evangeline knew she had no "right" to it.

"I have a spare, or so I'm told," Abigail laughed.

"Thank you. I will get with O.T. tomorrow. I thought I'd give you a tour."

The women took their drinks and wandered around the floor.

"The Family Quarters take up two floors. This one is largely ceremonial, but quite nice if you and Regina want to live here. This hall is too big for anything except entertaining," Evangeline said. Abigail could feel the older flooring underneath her feet. Some boards squeaked, and it had the hollow feel of old floors.

"The Yellow Oval Room is as close as you come to a living room, but it's too big. Most recent Presidential families have lived on the upper floor, which they decorate to their taste and privacy."

"This floor has both the Lincoln Bedroom and the Queen's Bedroom, which are traditionally for guests. And if Duke came to spend the weekend, there's plenty of room, as well as a full kitchen and dining room."

The upstairs floor held no charm for Abby. It did, however, have an unused workout room. *Ah, normal people do live here. Maybe I'll use it. Yeah, right.*

"So what's your favorite spot?" Abigail asked, as they returned to the lower floor.

"East Sitting Room. Very cozy."

Abigail was no decorator, but she could visualize some of her sister's furniture here. "I think we'll live on this floor. No sense heating two floors for two people."

At noon the next day, the entire Lafayette family dined in the President's dining room. The grandchildren, a boy and girl, ten and twelve, behaved perfectly, in part because Lynne seated herself between them, and a parent on either end.

The son, a history professor, was the spitting image of his dad. Lynnette, the autistic daughter, lit up around her sister-in-law, a pre-school teacher.

"I am thrilled with the Infants First Act, Madam President," the teacher said. "I'm so glad you 'get it' about the first few years."

"Thanks," Abby said. Monthly parenting classes at the local elementary school were a big hit. They paid for themselves in decreased abuse and accidents.

After pictures and lunch, they moved to the East Room for the press conference. Everyone popped to his feet as Abigail and the Lafayettes entered.

"I am proud to announce that General Jerome Lafayette has consented to be Vice President. He is more than qualified. Indeed, he was the first choice of the Cabinet and both past Presidents. I look forward to his swift confirmation."

Much to everyone's surprise, the press gave him a standing ovation.

Abigail's next foray with the press wasn't nearly as pleasant. She appeared the next day in the Brady Press Room to start random appearances.

Abby began with a statement. "The First Lady has decided she wants to be in Colorado and will be leaving over the weekend. We will all miss her. Her last official appearance will be at Margaret's Christmas pageant, which is tomorrow. I've asked my childhood guardian, Regina Temple, to live here as my Official Hostess. I also asked my nephew,

Duke Temple, a student at Georgetown Law School, to join us, but he declined. No doubt, the Secret Service and I would cramp his style."

That got a small laugh.

The dean of the press corps, Bob Shorter, stood and led off.

He stood. "What is your plan for Afghanistan?"

"Good question. To paraphrase Malcolm X, I didn't fall on the White House, the White House fell on me. So I didn't come in here with an Afghan exit strategy, but I am working on one.

"Next?" She pointed to a man she didn't know.

"Billy Wheaton. MSNBC. Tell us about your social life, Madam President."

"It's pretty minimal. I work a long day and study at night. I have a weekly standing dinner with one gentleman, a Mr. Michael Molloy. I'm not sure he wishes to be linked romantically with me, as he is quite the man about town. After the New Year, I will entertain more. Next?" Abigail pointed to a young woman in the middle of the pack.

"Marie Joseph, *L'éclair.*" She had a malicious grin on her face by the time she was standing.

"Madam President. Briefs or a thong?"

"Clean. Inappropriate question," Abigail said, giving her one of Regina's cocked-eyebrow looks. No one would venture there again.

"Jason Dudley, *D.C. Courier Times.* Don't you think it's inappropriate for you to move your maid into the White House and call her your Official Hostess?"

"Whoa, there, Mr. Dudley," Abigail said, making sure to keep her face pleasant. "Ms. Temple did start out as my family's housekeeper, before I was born, but she was my legal guardian from the age of one. She is the closest thing I have to a mother. No one, and I mean no one, shows disrespect to her in my presence.

"One of the many times my dad was busted flat as a wildcatter, he couldn't pay her wage. So she bartered herself a share in an oil well. It hit and she was finally headed to college, her dream. Then we were orphaned. She saved us from going into foster care. Later she took in her own nephew.

"She could have gone on her way, a young, wealthy, single woman. Instead, she did a noble and selfless thing. She's produced a Senator, a doctor-turned President, and a Phi Beta Kappa *Law Review* student so far."

Abigail paused, almost overcome by love and fury. *Hold it together. Be polite.*

"This country is lucky to have her as its Official Hostess. She is a woman of great intelligence, charm and backbone." Abigail's smile was indulgent, one she would give to an errant toddler. "Besides, if I did the entertaining, we'd have pizza and beer."

She got a big laugh for that.

"I apologize," he mumbled and sat down promptly.

"Do you have a follow-up?" Abigail asked pleasantly.

"Uh, no, ma'am."

"Then I'd like to invite you to interview Regina, with her approval, of course. She really is a remarkable woman," Abigail said.

"Uh, thank you."

"You're welcome. That's it for today. See you guys later," Abby smiled, turned on her heel, and left the room.

Margaret Harrington, aged four, thought she had a lock on the Virgin Mary role because of who her grandpa had been, so Mrs. Harrington decreed that her pay grade ended at angel.

The pageant was upstairs in the schoolroom. The children had done the work. Their painted palm trees were quite abstract, and the hay in the barn was scattered with artful abandon even onto the chairs for the parents.

When Abby arrived at six, things were running late. The parents milled around and made small talk as teachers tried to get the children in place and ready. It was like herding wet cats.

The Virgin Mary kept fiddling with Baby Jesus, who was supposed to stay under the elastic in her outfit until his "birth." Joseph had a hook-on beard that kept falling off one ear, but he seemed not to notice. One of the shepherds was quite intent on something up his left nostril. Only live animals could have completed the chaos.

In short, it was delightful. Soon the adults were seated and quiet. The music started.

The children sang "Silent Night." Well, they sang about half of it. Kids were looking everywhere except at their teacher who was conducting them.

The Angel of the Lord, Margaret Harrington, was not given to subtlety. She marched down the aisle and started her line at full volume.

"Behold. A babe is unto you," she said. The adults tittered, and that threw her off. *Had she said something wrong?*

"Peace in earth," she shouted. Then she stopped, panic-stricken, her eyes welling with tears. She looked at her grandmother, who smiled reassuringly and whispered, "Take your time, dear."

"Peace on earth…to men of good will," Margaret said loudly, with an emphatic nod.

Abigail's jaw dropped open at the wisdom of the mixed-up saying. *Perhaps that is the correct translation.*

Then Margaret waved her star on a stick and whacked poor Mary on the head, just missing an eye. Mary didn't cry, though. She put one hand up under her dress, pulled out Baby Jesus by a leg. Mary plunked him, fully dressed, into the manger, and ignored him. *So much for maternal feelings.*

The three wise men brought in their gifts, though only one could remember what he'd brought. He called it "Frank's cents." The shepherds gathered around, one still mining his left nostril, and everyone sang "Away in a Manger." Mercifully, it was over. They were greeted with thunderous applause.

Peace on earth…to men of good will. Out of the mouths of babes.

Everyone trooped downstairs for refreshments. Apple juice and ginger cookies for the children, eggnog and holiday munchies for the adults. The children careened around the White House hall on a sugar high.

By seven-thirty, the first tantrum started, signaling it was time for Abigail to leave. Abigail gave them all silver bells, knowing full well that the noise would drive everyone crazy until the parents could safely put them away as an heirloom.

After she left, the others could corral their offspring and head into the cold night.

Abigail came to see Mrs. Harrington lift off the South Lawn in Marine One the next morning, her possessions already aboard Air Force One. O.T. worked fast. The next day, the staff did a thorough cleaning of the Family Quarters. Abby and Regina would move in on Monday.

CHAPTER THIRTEEN

MOVING IN WITH GIANTS

December 11

Congress would adjourn after Lafayette's confirmation, their last business for the two-year session. No doubt, he would be confirmed; the only two questions were by what margin and when?

The Senate would debate on December 12 and a vote on December 13. The House would take the next two days. By December 15, Abby would have a VP. Till then, she felt she was on her own in a job she didn't understand.

Senator Cordelia Laurus publicly said the Senate needed more time. "This is totally out of keeping with the deliberative nature of the Senate."

Leave it to Cordelia to be sour. Louisiana's tall, Afro-Asian senator was nothing if not imperious. No doubt, she thought the job should go to her.

Tonight, Abigail would sleep in the Family Quarters for the first time. That was good, as the study was starting to smell like dirty clothes. Another night on the evil bed might tempt her to bomb someplace.

Abigail had mastered a lot in three weeks. With minimal fuss, she kept herself camera ready from 7 a.m. until she retired for the night. Curse words no longer leapt from her mouth. Regina would be pleased that she kept a clean hanky up her sleeve every day.

As to her learning, she had developed a system. She instructed Poppy and Mikey to prepare a briefing book on a given subject. Then Abby mastered it. One night she learned all the names, capitals, and politics of all former Soviet Union "-stans."

Another night, she did the same with Africa, including which countries were headed by the biggest thieving dictators, the "kleptocracies."

She vowed to get those dictators off the U.S. gravy train. We sent aid; the dictators sold it and put the money in a Swiss bank account. Our money was gone and the starving people had long since died.

Santayana was right: "Those who cannot remember the past are doomed to repeat it." She might not remember it, but she could darn well learn it.

Mikey was therapist and tutor. He read widely and well and clipped a variety of articles for her. She read them at night and filed them by subject. She had a current, insightful dossier on almost any topic.

His presence near the Oval Office comforted her, even if he was in just a few hours a day. Their dinners were a treat for them both, even if Mikey did have a curriculum planned for her. He focused on leadership, and the bigger the tome, the better he liked it. Luckily, Abby was a fast reader.

Abby had also mastered her schedule. It had taken some work, but Poppy and Chaffee had dumped the donors and lobbyists, put ceremonial things in the morning, leaving her afternoons for substantive work. Her day ended at six, and then she ate and studied. She was short on exercise, but maybe she'd start using the workout room.

Tonight, Regina and she would sleep in the White House Family Quarters. As predicted, Duke chose a guest room, but lived in his own digs. O.T. assured them both that their rooms would be livable. *Right, I'll be looking for stuff for months.*

When her day ended, she walked to the Residence. *Great commute. Of course, this means it'll be harder to separate work from life. Guess that goes with the territory.*

She walked in on an argument between Regina and O.T.

At least it sounds like home.

"I cook on a gas stove," Regina declared in no uncertain terms.

"Miss Regina, you have a chef," O.T. said.

Abby saw Regina cock her left eyebrow at him, but he did not back down. *The Look did not work. This is a first. Maybe I ought to call Duke.*

"I don't call room service for scrambled eggs." Regina had her hands on her hips. *Now that is a serious sign. Maybe O.T. is not as smart as I thought he was.*

"Well, Miss Regina, we like to minimize open flames to protect the building," O.T. said, refusing to take her head on. "You'd hate to be the woman who burned down the White House, wouldn't you?"

"You have fires under George Washington all the time. I see them on the TEE-vee." Regina was not giving an inch. She seldom did.

"Please just try it. Just for a week. If you don't like the induction cook top, I'll put you in a gas stove my very own self," O.T. said.

"I guess I can try it," Regina said. "But I'm too old to learn new tricks."

"From what I hear, your cooking is so good, no new tricks are needed," O.T. sweet-talked her.

"I thank you for that. But if my cooking isn't up to snuff, that thing goes." Regina pointed an imperial finger at the evil cook top.

"Deal," O.T. said.

"I see you two have met," Abigail said pleasantly.

"Miss Regina and I were discussing her trial of the cook top," O.T. said.

Regina stomped off to her room to direct the movers where she wanted certain things.

"Madam President, may I show you your room?" O.T. asked, an unusually large smile on his face. "I've put you in the former Prince of Wales suite. It has a lovely southern light. Under either of the porticos, your room can get dreary."

Abby looked around. It was a mixture of furniture from various rooms in Pris's apartment, but it was a perfect bedroom for her. As well, it had a sitting room configured as a dressing area. Its view of the South Lawn was leafy. *My own tree house.*

She could hardly draw breath at the art O.T. had chosen for her from the National Gallery. In her very own bedroom, she had the 1771 John Singleton Copley portrait of Mrs. Thomas Gage, a beautiful and pensive woman in a coral silk dress. *I've come a long way from the ratty futon I had a year ago.*

"You do know that Copley left the colonies and went to London in 1776. He was a loyalist," Abigail said.

"We try to keep that a secret," O.T. replied. "Keeps the value up."

Abigail laughed. She felt at peace in the room. O.T. was thrilled to have an art lover as President. He had stopped many a President from touching the paintings.

"In here is your dressing room. Has good natural light."

Indeed, it did. It also had a professionally lighted vanity for her makeup. Even her clothes were all put away.

"May I open a window?" she asked, knowing the answer.

"I'm afraid not," O.T. said with a sad shake of his head. Abby loved to sleep with a window cracked in almost any weather.

"O.T., you've outdone yourself." Abigail was enthralled with her surroundings.

"We do this for a living, ma'am. Here's your panic button." He pointed beside the bed. "This will summon the cavalry."

He showed her the other rooms for Regina, one for Duke when he visited, as well as the Lincoln Bedroom and the Queen's Bedroom and dressing room.

"Would you like the rest of the tour now or later?" O.T. asked.

"I think later, if you don't mind. May I prowl around at night?"

"Any place you want."

"I'll probably stalk the halls if I can't sleep," Abigail said. "I'd also like to meet the chef, please."

O.T. took her to the basement kitchen. The chef, a burly German man with sausage-like fingers, was busy preparing her dinner. She complimented him on the reception he'd done the first night.

"Ach, nothing. I hope you entertain a lot. I like to keep busy," Chef Dahm said. "And you, what do you like to eat?"

"I'll eat most anything. Low salt for Regina's blood pressure. Please keep me under about fifteen hundred calories a day," Abigail said.

"Ya, ya, I can do that."

"You do know that the woman who raised me will be living here? She is known for her Southern cooking." Abigail wanted to warn him about Regina and food.

"We've met. I've asked her for some lessons. We start tomorrow." *Even the chef was smart.*

"I can't wait to get a mess of greens one day," O.T. said, rubbing his hands together in glee.

"That, fried green tomatoes, chicken fried steak, and lemon chess pie for dessert," Abigail said, ticking off a few of her favorites.

"I've died and gone to heaven," O.T. declared.

Later, Regina and Abby had a simple meal, their first in the White House. Abigail thought it was perfect, but Regina thought it a bit bland. *That's because I've cut out your salt.*

The Secret Service agents and Hitch or Dabaghi were as unobtrusive as possible, and Abigail supposed she would get used to their presence at the stairs. Unless Regina and Abby shouted, the agents couldn't overhear them.

"Well, so far, what do you think, Reege?"

"I am a little scared, to tell you the truth," Regina said.

"You? Scared? I've never put those two words together."

"Oh, it's just so much change in a year. First Pris, now this incredible luck, and she's not here for it."

"I understand." Abby could see that Regina had aged a lot in the last year.

"And Duke, he's up to something. I can just feel it," Regina sounded suspicious.

"He's up to finishing law school," Abby said.

"But he's getting that money soon. I hope some woman doesn't break his heart to get at it."

Pris had died a wealthy woman, and it would come to them as soon as the estate settled after the first of the year.

"Regina. You raised him right. He'll cope. He'll have a life different from ours. That doesn't mean worse," Abigail said, her hands on both of Regina's shoulders.

"I guess."

"You're going to have a ball living here. A million invitations a day come in here. You can go out on the town every night, if you want. You're going to entertain, like when Pris was alive, just bigger. The Mission Ladies will be pea green with envy. This is the most famous home in the world, and it is yours."

Abigail was near tears. She was so grateful to be able to give this to Regina. She wanted so much for Regina to like it.

"Well, since you put it that way," Regina hugged Abby, "I'd best go get my beauty sleep. I have a cooking class to give tomorrow. Oh, and I've already invited the Mission Ladies for January 1."

"That's more like it," Abigail said. "I'm going to go do my homework."

Abigail got ready for bed, finding everything in a proper place. She laid out her clothes for the following day. Then she prowled for a place to study. The Yellow Oval Room was too big. The Lincoln Sitting Room was too spooky. Finally, she ended up in the East Sitting Hall.

Like Goldilocks, it was just right.

The Secret Service already called her Goldilocks, and while Regina didn't merit protection, she was definitely Mama Bear.

CHAPTER FOURTEEN

TEARS AND FEARS

Abby didn't cry often, but this had to get out. Otherwise, she'd be up half the night.

First, she wept in the shower, and then into a cold washcloth. Finally in bed, she continued to weep into her pillow, hoping no one would hear.

Is it fear of failure? What if I make a wrong decision? People could die. That's not new; I'm a doctor. I've held lives in my hands and known I was playing for keeps, but the number of people at risk is enormous.

Is it the nukes? I hope no one would be crazy enough to play nuclear chicken with me, but I can't control that.

Am I scared for my safety? No. I live in a fortress with snipers on the roof. I'm safer as President than as a private citizen.

Am I afraid of the press? No. I once told a woman that her husband murdered all three of her children. After that, anything is easy.

So what was spooking her?

It had to be the White House itself.

On this very floor, some in this very room, every President since John Adams had put down his cares for the night. Until the early twentieth century, the West Wing did not exist, and the President did all his work in the White House proper.

To live where Jefferson lived, where he answered the front door in his robe and slippers was an enormous burden. No, it was overwhelming. She was bright, she knew that, but Jefferson's intellect was mythical in size and scope.

Her "ancestor" Abigail Adams had been the first woman to live in the building, and now she was the first woman President. What would that Abigail think?

If she were less of a history buff, the ghosts might recede.

But she could see Lincoln battered by war and a crazed wife. He must have paced this long hall. He watched one of his sons, Willie, die of typhoid while Tad lay ill with it down the hall. All while trying to keep a warring nation together.

Next to them, she was a total lightweight, of no more substance than a feather.

Churchill stayed here a lot during the war. She could almost smell his cigars as he and Roosevelt worked and drank here. Churchill helped save the Western World with words and little else.

She had so little to offer, and the country needed so much.

I am standing on the shoulders of giants…and I am a gnat.

She wailed even louder.

Then she started on the losers who had been President. Wasn't Warren G. Harding "not bad, for a bum?" Andrew Johnson made a mockery of Lincoln's view of peace. Taft was so fat, he had to have a custom-made bathtub. Hadn't Grover Cleveland fathered an illegitimate child?

No, the country survived some real losers.

I think the country can stand me. At least I hope it can. At least I'm honest. And I try.

That thought let her sleep. She prayed the phone would not ring. Miracle of miracles, it did not.

At shift change, the Secret Service reported the President had cried herself to sleep. Otherwise, it was a quiet night.

The PDB the next morning showed nothing new on the horizon. She was looking forward to the day General Lafayette would be Vice President. Lafayette would kick up the President's Daily Briefing a notch, pointing out discrepancies that slid through. She needed him.

Abby had her social calendar powwow in the East Wing with Regina as Official Hostess; Liza Taylor, the head of the East Wing; Marilyn Chernosky, Secretary of State; Senator Peggy Mellon as hostess *extraordinaire,* as well as Kim, Poppy, and the chief of protocol, Ellen Mather.

"I prefer to read, but to get anything done in this town, I have to entertain. I want this house hopping. I want it to be the best invitation in town. I want this effort to be bipartisan, fun, and roughly three events a week, minimum."

Everyone loved the idea of the snow globes, scarves, and ties available only as a gift from Abigail personally. In a city where a politician never paid for anything, they would have greater cachet.

Liza Taylor volunteered for the snow globes. "I know a buyer at the Smithsonian gift shops. She'll have a source for me."

Kim Tran, Abigail's dressmaker, volunteered to design the scarves for free. "But I don't know about production."

"The Children's Art Project at M.D. Anderson does scarves," Regina said. "Liza, if you call them, they'll give you a vendor."

Peggy Mellon pointed out that presentation was everything. "I suggest navy blue boxes with the Seal of the United States on it in gold. And the scarf box must be the same size and texture of an Hermès box."

"Brilliant," Abby said. "An American Hermès. Let's do four designs this year and four next."

Kim nodded. "No problem for me, but please mix in other designers if you wish."

"Now, as to the events themselves, who has what ideas?" Abby asked.

Liza Taylor spoke up. "Our national holidays are all points for entertaining. Not all are happy, but…"

So they roughed out plans for the various holidays. Many were parties.

"I'd like to showcase American artists from all media one night a month. That'll take some doing, but would make careers," Abigail suggested.

Everyone liked that idea.

"The head of my hospital did a monthly birthday party. If I did one for Congress, that would be what, eighty people a month?" Abby said. "If they have kids or grandchildren, they could come, too. Make a memory."

Peggy Mellon loved that idea, "Especially if we did things like pin the tail on the donkey or the trunk on the elephant. Make it a weekend afternoon party with families, complete with ice cream and cake."

"I know I'd kill to eat Regina's food," Poppy said. "I think you ought to have Regina's recipes for small dinners, maybe every Thursday night. Eighteen people max, casual, and if it's on a weeknight, people won't want to stay too late."

"The food's gotta be good. I won't have my reputation sullied by some cook who doesn't know a crawfish from an *etoufee*," Regina harrumphed.

"The real key is how we rotate the invitations," Abby said. "I want everyone included except lobbyists. None of the K Street crowd."

The room went silent.

"You want to tell us why?" Poppy asked.

"They have too much influence as it is. I want to deal them out. If I am entertaining two or three times a week, I don't want to be with lobbyists. Period," Abigail said.

Peggy Mellon suggested goldfish bowls full of names: one each for the House, Senate, Supreme Court, Cabinet, Military brass, media, cultural people, diplomatic corps, celebrities, and wild cards.

"Grab a handful from each bowl, and, *voila*, you have a guest list," Peggy said. "Or some youngster can make a computer do the same thing."

"Who are the wild cards?" Abby asked.

"Any newsmaker, like the pilot who glided the plane into the Hudson. They really add spice," Peggy said.

"Oh, and do a bowl with my real people and the interns. This is their house, too. And can we plan something for Bastille Day, Chinese New Year?" Abigail asked. "We should celebrate our melting pot."

Liza put those dates down as well.

"I want a State Dinner honoring Mexico and Canada. ASAP. They're great neighbors," Abby said. "Liza, can you start on that?"

"Actually, that comes from me, from the State Department," Marilyn said. The Chief of Protocol nodded.

I hope they can get things moving quickly.

"Regina, as Official Hostess, you're in charge," Abby said. "Peggy, will you help with the State Dinner?"

"Of course," Peggy said indulgently.

"When can I expect a roughed out calendar?" Abigail asked. "I want to start entertaining just after the first of the year."

"Then we'd best get busy," Regina said. "You'll have a calendar before Christmas."

Abigail needed some political capital, though she had no idea what she'd spend it on.

CHAPTER FIFTEEN

NEW FRIENDS

The Senate was debating Lafayette's appointment. Someone asked a question. Lafayette answered. Someone else asked virtually the same question, so Lafayette rephrased his answer to avoid repeating himself. At the end of the day, they stopped.

They would vote tomorrow. Abby ordered an intern to count the questions. She counted no more than ten questions, all asked differently. The House would do the same. Only then, would Lafayette be confirmed.

I need a Vice President NOW, and Congress flaps its gums for the cameras.

The trial soul food dinner was that night. Peggy Mellon was delighted to come, as were Laura Rowe, Wicker, Mikey Molloy, Poppy, Chaffee, the Salazars, Marilyn Chernosky, Regina, Duke, and O.T. They dined in the family quarters, and Regina was pleased that the chef was learning her techniques. After the first dinner, they'd get a lot more important.

They had drinks in the Yellow Oval Room, looking over the South Lawn. The national Christmas tree on the South Lawn was a visual delight. Regina had an open bar, but also a seasonal beverage, as they'd do in the real dinners. *I'll bet Reege shuts the bar after dinner.*

Abigail felt relaxed. Regina was the hostess; Abigail only came to the party. Regina could fuss over flowers, dishes, and silverware, as Abby was totally ignorant about entertaining, and Regina's natural charm always infused a party.

Of course, the over-the-top Christmas decorations still disgusted Abby, but she couldn't do a thing on earth about it.

Regina put people at two tables of six in the center hall. Red table-cloths and the Truman china, with its green border, were lovely. Low pots of red and white cyclamens nestled in winter greenery, and fake votives flickered in and around the flowers.

"O.T. can't complain about any fire danger," Regina said trium-phantly about her fake candles.

Abigail was the last to arrive. She'd let the meeting with interns run long. They thought up tiers of cell phone users. At the lowest end, one could call 911 and one family member in a declared communi-cations emergency. Easy to do with phone software. Great idea. Abby would pass it along.

Everyone had a drink in hand in the Yellow Oval Room, while Abigail freshened up in her suite. She put on soft, black wool pants and a simple red, cashmere, cowl-neck sweater, touched up her makeup, and stepped into the warmth of friends.

The only person she didn't know was Secretary Salazar's wife, a petite blonde who was pushing sixty, but built like a fifteen-year-old. She wore a short dress and high heels. Susan was in such wonderful shape, Abby saw every muscle in Susan's lower legs.

"I'm Susan Salazar," she introduced herself. "I hear Poppy is look-ing for a trainer for you."

"Why, yes she is. You are in great shape. I want your trainer," Abigail said.

"Well, actually, I am a trainer of sorts."

Just then Cristo piped up, "She was the head of martial arts at West Point."

"But you can't weigh more than 110 pounds soaking wet," Abigail said, almost spluttering her champagne.

"Martial arts are more up here," she said, pointing to her head. "The body is less important."

"I'm really just looking to get fit," Abigail said. *I'm too tall, too flabby, and too wimpy for this woman.*

"I also have certifications in yoga, Pilates, and as a personal trainer," Susan offered pleasantly. "We start where you are, in your comfort zone, not in mine."

"I guess you're the woman for me, unless of course, you won't like the hours. I'm planning on doing it at five-thirty in the morning and paying your going rate."

"I can do that. Let's start tomorrow."

"No time like the present," Abigail replied, raising her champagne flute. *This woman's going to kill me.*

The menu was inspired. Fried chicken, black-eyed peas, collard greens, sliced hothouse tomatoes, cheese grits, and lemon meringue pie. All served family style.

Some White House parties are about the sparkling repartee, the super A-list attendees. This one was all about the food. During the meal, Abby didn't think anyone said anything more important than "Pass the salt, please."

The chef had cooked for twelve, which meant closer to eighteen. The serving dishes were bare, not a morsel of anything remained. Abigail noticed that O.T. grabbed a crumb off the empty fried chicken platter as a steward reached to take it away.

People waddled to the sofas for coffee and had the pleasant talk of the truly sated.

The party broke up early, as it was a school night. Everyone hugged Abby and Regina as they left. Abby was in bed by ten and did not cry herself to sleep that night. She was too scared of the next morning.

Susan's going to kill me.

Abby couldn't decide which was going to be harder: the workout or getting up for it at five-fifteen.

Susan was in the upstairs gym, smiling and wide-awake, when Abby arrived, bleary-eyed at 5:30 a.m.

"Today I want to assess your fitness level: cardio, strength, flexibility, balance, and the like," Susan said pleasantly.

Even if it was "just" an assessment, Abigail worked up a sweat.

"You're more fit than you realize, but increasing your fitness will improve your job performance. Also, I'm going to get you boxing. Every President needs an outlet for aggression."

"You mean I can pretend to punch out the people who tick me off?" Abby was smiling at the prospect.

"Yes, ma'am, as long as it isn't me." Susan had a lovely laugh.

CHAPTER SIXTEEN

A HOLOCAUST OF ONE?

December 14, 2 a.m.

Abby always caught the phone on the first ring.

"Ma'am, Collins in the Situation Room. Kidnapped American reporter in the Middle East," the duty officer said. Abigail was wide awake.

"Get the team in. NSA, CIA, Salazar, Chernosky, even Wicker, for starters." Tech staff was always there.

Abigail hurried into knit pants, a hoodie, and fleece-lined moccasins. No time for contacts, she put on her glasses and walked swiftly to the Situation Room, two agents in tow. The walkway was dank, and all the heat in the world could not warm her up for a middle of the night emergency.

"Talk to me," Abigail said as she entered the room. She poured herself a coffee that had been on the burner too long, and filled it with sugar and cream. *I need caffeine and sugar. This god-awful taste is irrelevant.*

On the screen was video from Al Qaeda. A young female hostage held by an Arab-appearing man.

"Katherine Stuart, reporter for the *New York Times*," Collins said.

"When did we get this video?"

"Just now, 9 a.m. local time."

"How?"

"We pulled it off the Al Jazeera feed."

"Get me the editor of *The New York Times*," Abby ordered. *The White House operators could hunt down anyone, any time.*

Aides scurried to make these things happen.

"Gershman, *NY Times*, Line one," an aide said.

"Sorry about your reporter. What do you know?"

"Nothing yet. Our scanner people just saw it. Her name is Katherine Stuart and she was on assignment in Israel."

"Are the local police involved yet?"

"Don't know."

"Where was she staying?" Abby twiddled her pen. The caffeine was starting to kick in.

"The King David. Probably." Abby made a note.

"Fine. Do you have full access to your internal website where you are?"

"Yes, ma'am. I'm logged in."

"I'll give you to Colonel Busby. Tell him everything and e-mail everything. Next of kin, personnel records, everything. Is she Jewish?"

"It'll take me a few minutes."

Abby transferred the call to Busby, who nodded and picked up.

"Get me Prime Minister Meyer of Israel," Abby ordered. *Maybe he knows something.*

"Meyer on two."

"Sorry to meet like this," Abigail said.

"Same here."

"What do you know?" Abigail asked.

"Damned little just yet."

Abby transferred Meyer to Marilyn, who had arrived and settled in.

By two forty-five, everyone was there. Abby needed Lafayette, but the vote was later today. *Damn the Senate for its blather.*

Everyone watched the video. It was short, under two minutes. On it, the young woman's voice wavered. She was shaking and crying with fear; her eyes, hands, and feet were bound. She sat on the floor, a nondescript beige blanket nailed to the wall behind her. A masked guard stood beside her with a large knife on his belt and an automatic weapon slung over his shoulder.

"Please, please, believe me," Katherine Stuart said. "These people are going to kill me. All because I am an American. America has done horrible things in the Middle East, and I am to be beheaded for those misdeeds."

Then they watched it without sound. Next they listened to audio only. Finally they watched it in slow motion.

"We know her name and where she was working. We don't have the vaguest idea where she is now," Abigail said. "Here's the drill. Each person will work his area of expertise. Talk to me, not among yourselves. Every thirty minutes we all re-assess."

"Yes, ma'am," the room chorused.

"Wicker, you work the press. Get staff to help you," Abigail said. She went through every assignment: Chernosky was to work heads of state and the "dark" diplomats; Salazar, the military. Abigail took Katherine's family.

Just before the next assessment, the press section gave her contact info for Katherine's family. Abby called them with the bad news. *I'm good with bad news.*

After she convinced Mr. Stuart who she was and what the situation was, she said, "I didn't want you to see it on the morning news."

"Oh, my god, my god," the man moaned. She could hear his wife in the background asking what was going on. "It's Katherine. Kidnapped," he said.

The mother was almost hysterical.

"The video is on CNN now. Tell me, sir, is your daughter Jewish?"

"Yes. Her grandmother survived Auschwitz. And now this?" Sobs punctuated his words.

"Well, I will move heaven and earth for Katherine. May I speak to your wife, please?"

Abby could hear the mother gulping back her sobs, "Hello?"

"Mrs. Stuart, we are in early hours. I will do my best for your baby girl, but you both have to be strong. For Katherine." *The last thing I need is for one of them to have a heart attack.*

"We'll do our best."

"I'll speak with you again. Do you have family nearby to be with you? Or perhaps your rabbi could come."

At the re-assessment, everyone watched the webcam video again several times, with and without sound, as well as audio only, even slow motion.

Abigail reported that Stuart was Jewish. Busby said she was doing a piece critical of the Israeli behavior in the West Bank. Marilyn reported that the fixer had his throat slit. Stuart's room at the King David was undisturbed.

At 4 a.m., Wicker reported that several Middle East reporters found out that the video went via Internet to Al Jazeera. "The reporters at Al Jazeera knew it could be them, so they are helping us. They report both sides, and have been threatened and even killed."

"We need the IP address of that computer," Abigail said.

Wicker again spoke to his source. Wicker had to promise him, and his girlfriend inside Al Jazeera, jobs at Wicker Washington, his media-consulting firm. The IP address came in ten minutes later.

Charley Garrett was rousted out of bed and asked what he could find out about the computer.

"That sounds like a Cameron Computer address," he said sleepily.

"Great, thanks."

Abigail got Michael Cameron on the phone at his palatial home in Hawaii and brought him up to speed.

"I'll get with my wizard if you can hold on," he said.

Abby drummed her nails. People stared at her, so she stopped.

Cameron was back on the line. "Great news, it's a machine with a GPS in it. Here are its coordinates." He rattled off the exact location of the computer. Salazar ordered a geosynchronous satellite to stay above the site.

Cameron then gave them payment and shipment information. It went to an Ali Jabar in the metro DC area. Abby sent the FBI out to pick him up.

Abigail feared that Stuart would be a female Danny Pearl. *A holocaust of one.*

By 5 a.m., Chernosky and the CIA reported that this was a kidnapping of opportunity. Her abductors sold her up the food chain. She could be anywhere. Word was, she would be beheaded on a live feed during American prime time via Al Jazeera. A girl Danny Pearl for the first female President. Abigail excused herself and barely made it to the closest bathroom before she threw up the night's coffee and bile.

I hate this job.

She was back in the room in moments, reaching for a ginger ale.

Wicker couldn't talk to either the head of Al Jazeera or American media without compromising the operation. That would likely trigger an immediate execution. Their only hope was to stop the execution due later tonight.

The FBI knocked on the door of one Ali Jabar in southern Maryland. He flew an American flag by the door. He was a naturalized U.S. citizen who had shipped the computer to his brother-in-law, Mahmood Abbas, Um Qasra 15, Basra, Iraq.

The agent texted the address to the Situation Room. It matched the GPS co-ordinates of the computer. Exactly.

Even better, it was only 20 kilometers out of town from the sprawling U.S. Consulate in Basra. That place was all but a walled American city unto itself, complete with a hospital as well as live-in covert ops teams. *What an incredible piece of luck. Or their stupidity.*

"It is for my nephew who is going to college," Jabar said, rubbing the sleep from his eyes. The FBI took Mr. Jabar, who ran a successful coffee shop, into custody and showed him the video during his interrogation.

"Oh, no. That is my nephew. See the birthmark on his left hand? That floor looks like my brother-in-law's house," he said, weeping openly.

"How can I help? I am not a man of violence." He confirmed the address and prayed his life in America was not over.

At 7 a.m., Wicker released a generic statement, intimating that the President was doing everything to obtain the release of Ms. Stuart. All options were open.

"We have twelve hours. Cristo, what are our military options to get her out alive?"

Salazar had flashed up satellite photos of the house and its environs from a few minutes earlier. It was broad daylight, 2 p.m. in Iraq.

"The satellite will stay above the site, giving us pictures. The house is relatively isolated and lightly guarded."

Abigail saw incredible detail. Only one vehicle parked near the house, and the nearest road was some distance away.

"I want confirmation of how many people are in the house, especially if there are any children or infants in there. Can we do that?"

"Sure. Thermal imaging. Give us an hour."

Abby was drumming her nails. She noticed that people were staring at her.

"Sorry." She stopped. Again.

"We must put everyone in the house down so they have no ability to kill Stuart. Then we extract her and bring them into custody. If they resist, kill them," Abigail said. *Please resist.*

"Get Billy Finn on the phone for me," she said. "I think he's at Fort Detrick."

"Who the heck is Billy Finn?" Salazar asked.

"A crazy anesthesiologist I went to med school with. Now he's with the Army at Fort Detrick."

"Using biologic weapons is against international law, ma'am," Salazar said sternly.

"I'm a doctor, and I'm going to prescribe some anesthesia. Billy's just crazy enough to have some delivery system up his sleeve. Or up his nose."

The White House operator found Finn within a matter of minutes.

"Billy, this is Abby. I need your help."

"Sure, Abs, I mean, Madam President," he replied.

She recapped the situation for him.

"Got just the thing for you." He described in detail a mixture of two inhaled anesthetic agents that could be "oozed" into the house. Abigail was familiar with both.

"The only danger is in dosage. Give me the size of the house and the weights of the people in there, and we can do it. The only kicker is if a baby's in the house. Could be lethal to a baby. Any military hospital should have more than enough."

"And how would we do it? These people aren't going to put on masks and inhale it."

"I've been tinkering. I put it in a plain nebulizer, like for asthma treatments. I put animals into sealed cages and turn on the neb machine. They are out in seconds. The trick is to get the weights of the patients and the volume of the house right."

"Great, stay on the line. I'll need dosages from you shortly."

Abigail turned to the room.

"Anyone have a problem with the plan?"

They shook their heads. Abby watched the clock as the seconds ticked by.

"It's 3 p.m. in Basra. I want to go as soon as it is dark there. However, we must be ready to go ASAP," Abigail said. "Tell these lying bastards anything they want to hear to keep her alive till dark. What do you think, Marilyn?"

"I can go back channel and say you are willing to consider ransom for her safety. This will eat up time. This was a sell up, so if you offer five million, they may keep her alive," Marilyn said. "Of course, they won't like being duped."

"I don't care. I also do not want any survivors except Katherine. The only thing terrorists understand is brute force."

Tech staff reported sunset would be at 6:50 p.m. local time. Abigail wanted to go in full darkness, so she ordered the launch for 7:50 local time. Ten minutes to one in D.C.

The pieces of the puzzles came in slowly. Four adults were in the house. No infants. Salazar calculated the volume of the house for Finn.

"How do we get the window open without alerting anyone?" Abigail asked.

"Begging your pardon, ma'am, but they *are* Special Forces. They can take out a circle of glass silently," Salazar said.

Duh. "It's time for breakfast. Let's get some down here," Abigail said.

While people in the Situation Room had a hot breakfast, The Consul ordered a Red Cross helicopter to the roof of the building. He then marshaled needed men and supplies for a briefing with Secretary Salazar. Salazar briefed the ops teams in detail.

Abby briefed the doctor and he stripped the infirmary of anesthetic agents. Techs hastily converted nebulizers to battery power. They checked and packed an oxygen tank, tubing and masks, as well as camo gas masks for the team and hostage.

The doctor grabbed his bag, added some reversal agents, and a few other emergency tools. He would go with the team.

After a hearty breakfast, *diet be damned,* Abigail went to the Residence and got dressed for her day. *I would rather work out with Susan than be in the Situation Room. That's pitiful.*

Wicker gave a live statement for the morning news shows that basically said nothing, but did so with poignancy and hope.

Abigail talked with the parents again.

"What exactly are you doing?" the father wanted to know.

"I'm sorry. I can't tell you that." *I'm just waiting for the sun to set.*

At noon in D.C., 7 p.m. in Iraq, the field commander reported via code, "All ready."

Everything was ready at the Consulate. The team had checked and rechecked everything. According to the satellite, no one had entered or left the house.

"Go," Abby ordered at 7:50 p.m. An armored delivery bay opened, and a beat-up, dusty van with Iraqi plates pulled out.

Radio silence from the field began. Everyone in the Situation Room went quiet. Even the movement of the second hand on the clock seemed to come forward over the background noise of computers. Seconds stretched. Minutes were eternal. It was the worst sort of waiting.

People sat, knowing the end, one way or the other would come within two hours. If, at three, they had no communication, they could assume defeat, and while they could "see," the night images weren't great.

Abigail, remembering Eisenhower, drafted a statement of defeat, as Ike had done for D-Day. So many things could go wrong. She took full responsibility for the loss of Katherine Stuart's life. *God, please let me never need this.*

In Iraq, it was a moonless night, and a brisk breeze and night noises covered the almost silent operation. The van had easily a quarter-million dollars of special equipment in it. The men slipped out in night vision goggles.

Some of the team rapidly approached the house and snapped the guards' necks soundlessly. Another group, all chewing gum, crawled through the brush with nebulizers strapped to their backs. One went to each side of the square house. They simultaneously signaled each other to start with clickers that sounded like crickets.

Silently, they cut holes in the windows just big enough to insert the tubing. They heard two men talking, but no other sound. They put an inch or so of clear tubing in and caulked around it with their chewing gum.

With luck, Katherine Stuart was still alive.

Each ops member donned a gas mask to ensure he inhaled none of the anesthetic. With another set of cricket clicks, they started the flow of anesthesia.

The small hissing of the nebulizers went unnoticed amid the other night noises.

Billy said the effect would be instantaneous, and it was. All sound and motion in the house ceased within seconds. The clock was ticking. They had three minutes before respiratory depression might set in for the lighter weight woman.

A third team, also wearing gas masks, went in, silently cutting out a back window and slithering through it. One picked up Katherine while a second opened the door. He carried her to the van, and she was already starting to stir when he handed her off to the doctor.

"You're safe now," the doctor said to Katherine as she gulped oxygen from the proffered mask. The ops guy in his camo gas mask headed back to the house.

When the team shut off the anesthesia, the men started to stir. One man, Ali, began to rub his eyes. *Why was a space creature in his house?* The creature had a huge desert camouflage snout where his face should be. Ali took a drunken swing and would have fallen down, except the ops guy grabbed him and snapped his neck.

The team did the same to the two others as they awakened. Then they picked up all the evidence they could find and wrapped it in the blanket: computer, video camera, guns and knives. They ripped off their masks and ran to the van. Each broke into a smile to see Katherine awake, if a little dazed, as they piled in with the blanket full of evidence as they slowly pulled away.

The house was barely disturbed. There were four tiny holes in windows and a pane of glass sitting up against the back wall. The men inside looked asleep. For eternity.

The bearded driver took his time back to the Consulate. He didn't want to get stopped for speeding by an Iraqi cop.

"Package is safe," the Consul broke radio silence fifty minutes later, once Katherine stepped out of the van, safely inside the Consulate.

The room exploded into applause, tears, hugs, and more tears. Wicker let Clutter in and he was clicking away.

The doctor and Consul hustled Katherine to a waiting Red Cross helicopter atop the building. The doctor rode with her to a hospital in Kuwait City.

Abby wanted no Consulate fingerprints on this, in fear of reprisals.

Once in the air, Abigail spoke to her.

"Katherine? Did they hurt you in any way?" Abigail asked, after identifying herself.

"Physically, I'm fine. I'm just so grateful to be alive," the young woman said, and then burst into tears.

"You'll get a physical in Kuwait City, and then we'll get you straight home."

"Thank you so much, President Adams."

"Would you like to talk to your parents?" Abby asked.

"Sure," Katherine said through her tears.

"Hang on, let me see what I can do."

Within moments, the room listened in as parents and child were electronically reunited. People wept openly.

Wicker tipped off CNN in Kuwait City, which captured the first video as Katherine exited the helicopter under her own steam.

"Hi, Mom, hi, Dad. I'm fine, really. Just a little shaky still. The guys who came to get me were awesome," Katherine said, waving to the camera.

Al Qaeda learned of Katherine's release from U.S. television. The idiots who bungled the kidnapping were lucky to be dead. The higher-ups decreed beheading and then feeding them to the jackals.

The story was the lead on every news station on the planet. Abigail asked for and got airtime that evening. She sat calmly in front of the fireplace, this time in a green turtleneck sweater, a simple gold chain, and black pants, her hands resting in her lap.

"As you know, for the last eighteen hours, hundreds of people have been working to free Katherine Stuart, a *New York Times* reporter kidnapped by the worst sort of terrorists. I'm glad to report that she is free, physically unhurt, and on her way home.

"I thank everyone who helped with Katherine's release. You know who you are.

"We lost no American lives in this effort, and incurred no innocent casualties. The men who held Katherine are all dead. Details of this operation are classified and will remain so. No one will discuss it."

Abby turned to camera two, which focused in tightly on her face.

"Recently, I attended a Christmas pageant here at the White House preschool. Margaret Harrington, aged four, was the Angel of the Lord. She flubbed her big line. She meant to say, 'Peace on earth, good will to men.'

"Instead, she said, 'Peace on earth to men of good will.'" That has stayed with me.

"My message is a simple one. If you are people of good will, you will have peace from the United States. If, however, you act as these men did, I will bring the terrible swift swords of the United States of America down on you."

The cameras cut back to a wider shot with camera one.

"Look at the places where hatred rules. Women die in childbirth. Children die of preventable diseases. Old people don't have medicine for their aching bones. They can't get their eyes fixed so they can see their beloved grandchildren.

"Put down the burden of hatred. Use that energy for clean water, decent medical care, and good educations. If you live in an area of hatred, begin to change yourself. Today, nod to your neighbor, tomorrow, greet him. Make the choice to raise your children without your hatred. Not only can you do it, people have already done it.

"The people of Northern Ireland did it. The people of Europe did it after World War II. Americans of different races have done it. And the people of South Africa are doing it.

"So this holiday season, I want to remind you of the wise words of Margaret Harrington, aged four.

'Peace on earth to men of good will.'

"Good night."

CHAPTER SEVENTEEN

A CHRISTMAS ABROAD

The next morning, she had an interview and photo shoot with *Time Magazine*. She was thankful for Andre, as being up all night wasn't good for pictures. She would be their Person of the Year. *Better me than some weirdo rock star.*

The interview was straightforward, and the photo shoot simple enough. She steadfastly refused to discuss the Stuart matter, so they would probably spank her on the hand for that in print. *Oh, well, I prefer feedback from the real people.*

As soon as the shoot was finished, she got word Lafayette was confirmed. The Chief Justice swore him in that afternoon, and he was in the Oval Office for the PDB in the morning.

"I cannot tell you, General, how reassuring I find your presence," Abigail said.

"Well, you did an excellent job on the Stuart case. Very important first international move. Showed terrorists you won't put up with them."

"Why, thank you." *I was just trying to get the girl back alive.*

Abby had a "real people" meeting later in the day, with snacks, of course. Brownies and milk were the favorites, but the Rice Krispy snacks were running a strong second.

"Glad you didn't tell anyone how you did it," a gardener said, of the Stuart matter. "You might want to run that play again." *I hadn't thought of that.*

"I'm glad we don't have to spend any money on those creeps that took her," the florist said.

"We're really happy with Lafayette. He's always been a stand-up guy," the plumber said.

"Yeah, Harrington practically begged him to the take the VP slot," an electrician added.

I didn't know that.

🇺🇸

By virtue of her office, she had box seats to virtually every cultural event, and during the holidays, a blizzard of invitations hit the East Wing.

Abby instructed Regina to decline all out of respect to the late President. In reality, she was too busy just getting her feet underneath her.

"But if something appeals to you, go," Abby said. "You should have some fun."

Job One for Abigail was to fill empty federal benches.

She brought Lafayette up to speed and enlisted him to interview half the candidates.

"Ma'am, how'd you get this done without a leak?" Lafayette was impressed.

"Can you say 'P.J. O'Neal'?" Abby said. "It's like the father who shoots the daughter's first boyfriend. After that, the rest behave."

Sternberg dug out Harrington's pre-vetted partisan list and added in a correct number of names from the other side. All were qualified and willing to serve. Many were U.S. Attorneys who had FBI checks already done. Abby neither knew, nor cared about, their party affiliations.

She had eighty benches to fill in the judiciary. She took the appellate candidates and half the district court positions, leaving the rest for Lafayette to interview.

She briefly looked up landmark cases and asked a few softball questions about everything from *Marbury vs. Madison* to *Gideon v. Wainwright*. Most candidates explained cases simply. She struck off the list anyone patronizing or huffy. *If a federal judge would speak down to me, what would he do to a citizen, the guy who pays his salary?*

It took marathon interviewing, but they got the job done. Before she announced her appointments, she had Charley Garrett grab a couple of his staff to check the appointees out on the Internet. They would pick up quickly on anything kinky.

She offered Sam Sternberg any bench he wanted, but he declined.

"It's really nice to have the pick of the litter, but I'm happy here," he said.

The evening Abigail went over the final list of appointees, Regina attended one event, a Christmas Gala at the Kennedy Center. Neither Abigail nor Duke was available, so she asked O.T. to be her escort.

Reege changed clothes three times before O.T. called for her.

Abby was almost finished with the appointment list when Regina came home just before eleven.

"How was your evening?" Abigail asked mildly.

"Fine. That's all I'm going to say," Regina declared and headed for bed.

Abby wanted to jump for joy. *Reege has a boyfriend, or as Regina would say, a gentleman caller.*

The next morning, Evangeline Harrington called from Colorado; she sounded sad.

"I'm working on Walter's library—it helps time pass. I'll have a few of Walter's things picked up from the White House after New Year's, if that's okay."

"Certainly," Abigail said. Abby had already boxed up the photos from the credenza.

"Your handling of that kidnapped reporter was fabulous. You're a media natural, Abigail. And including Margaret's remarks was spot on."

"That's so kind of you to say."

"You think with your head and act with your gut. That's what Walter always used to say."

"Best advice I've gotten in a while," Abigail said. "Give my love to Margaret."

The next day at the press briefing, Abigail walked in unannounced. Wicker had packets ready for everyone. Abby wore a red suit and her highest power heels. She was commanding, if somewhat in pain.

"Under the Constitution, I am allowed to make appointments between sessions of Congress. The Senate has a year to say 'yes or no' to them."

"First, I am appointing Cristo Salazar Secretary of Defense. Up until now, he was Acting Secretary.

"I am filling eighty empty federal benches because it is my Constitutional responsibility. The vacancies slow dramatically an already slow process. The Senate has the right within a year to throw out anyone they do not want.

"President Harrington had started on this. I have tweaked it a bit: the pool from which I've chosen has the same party ratio as the incoming Senate. I, however, neither know, nor care, what party affiliation anyone has.

"I have chosen men and women of legal excellence. The Chief Justice will swear them in January second. I am deeply humbled that people would leave lucrative careers to serve their country for life. Questions?"

"Why are you subverting the right of the Senate to advice and consent?" one conservative reporter asked.

"Read Article II Section 2. I'm on firm Constitutional ground according to the Attorney General."

"Ma'am, what would you say to critics who will call this high-handed?" Bob Shorter asked.

"First, it's my Constitutional *duty*, as well as the Senate's, to keep the benches filled. Even if the Senators do not do their job, I still have to do mine.

"Second, the Senate has turned federal appointments into the worst sort of political theater for the cameras, as happened with Senator Whitman's 'outing of a seventh grade Nazi.' Excellent candidates do not wish to have a bare-naked televised rectal exam and have it called a 'Senate confirmation.'

Third, I have included members of both parties. I think even-handed is more like it.

"I hope you all have a nice holiday," Abigail said, turning and leaving the room. Wicker passed out the packets on all the new federal judges and justices.

She figured on some bitching and moaning, but she wasn't running for office and had no need to pander to anyone.

That night at dinner, Abby asked Reege what she'd planned for Christmas.

"Well, I think it'll pretty much be low key. You, me, Duke, maybe Poppy and Chaffee, maybe O.T."

"Anybody like dark meat besides Duke and me?" Abby asked, just to hear the usual response.

"If so, you just keep your mouth shut. I didn't raise you to be a greedy pig. Sharing is good for you."

"Yes, ma'am." Abby pretended to be chastened. *If Regina invited O.T., she was sweet on him. She liked having strays for Thanksgiving, but Christmas was for family.*

Abigail read a lot about Muslim women. She was convinced that when the American forces left Afghanistan, the Taliban would crack down, hard, on all the women who had literally shown their faces.

"I want to do something to help the women of Afghanistan," Abigail said to Marilyn Chernosky the next day. "I fear for them when we leave."

"Madam President, billions of lives need saving. We can't save them all," Marilyn said.

"I'm a doctor. I know that." Abigail was blunt, almost rude. "But we invaded their country, told them we'd get rid of Taliban. We haven't. When we leave, the Taliban will go on a rampage."

"I agree," Marilyn said.

"It may not be a smart thing to do, but it is the right thing to do," Abigail said. "I need you to tell me how to do it."

"I'll look into it," Marilyn said.

"Look fast. I have some ideas of my own in mind."

"Uh-oh."

Christmas was fast approaching, and Abby was starting to hit her stride. Her workouts were paying off, she was beginning to tame her schedule, and the New Year looked good. Abigail decided at the last minute to visit the troops in Afghanistan. The only four people who knew were Salazar, Albright, Lafayette, and Colonel Barnett, the commander of Air Force One. Lafayette would tell Regina on Christmas morning. *So much for a peacetime job for him.*

Abby asked Salazar, "What can I take them?"

"Well, we got about ten thousand phone cards from some charity."

"Good, can you get them aboard Air Force One?"

"No prob."

"What about equipment? Aren't they still waiting for up-armored Humvees?"

"Yes, due for shipment just before the first."

"Great. Can you get the vendor for me?"

Within moments, the supplier's CEO in Fairfield, Ohio, was on the phone.

"Mr. Burns, this is the President. I want a date certain for delivery of the up-armored Humvees to Afghanistan," Abigail said.

"We are shipping December twenty-sixth."

"How?"

"Rail to Mechanicsburg, per our contract."

"I'd like to get them to Wright Patterson on Christmas morning. We'll start flying them out. They'll be a great Christmas gift for the troops."

"But my guys will have to work on Christmas Eve."

"Gee, so do our troops." *What a whiner.*

Abby called Cristo back. "They'll be at Wright Patterson on Christmas morning. I want them in the air behind me."

"Yes, ma'am."

My two favorite words.

Luckily, the pilot of Air Force One, Col. Barnett, had done this run into Afghanistan before. All Abigail had to do was show up in the middle of the night at Andrews Air Force Base with a single duffle made heavy by her custom-made Kevlar vest. She even had her own full desert camo uniform, from helmet to boots. She loved the outfit and was proud to wear it.

Abby decided that no press would accompany her. Period. Clutter, the White House Photographer, who was single, could go. *Better to ask forgiveness than permission.*

Air Force One is a cross between a flying Situation Room and a five-star hotel. It also had an incredible stash of Air Force One swag, complete with sheepskin-lined Presidential flight jackets. It was cold in Afghanistan, and she would be glad to have one. At least she'd thought to bring silk long underwear and gloves. And tampons, of course. *"Tampons. Never leave home without them."* Maybe I'll be their spokesperson after this is all over.

Abigail's heart raced as the plane lifted off. Within minutes, she was deep into her newest read, *Infidel*, another book about the intolerable abuse of Muslim women.

I need some chick book to read. She thought about downloading something to her Kindle, but decided it would be poor form to screw up the avionics on Air Force One for a romance novel.

She called Salazar, who sounded like he was in the next room. "Sorry to disturb. I had an idea," Abby said.

"No, you can't divert to the North Pole," he said, sleepily.

"Do any of the people on base have a birthday on Christmas Day?"

"Don't know, but I can find out," Salazar said.

"Get me their sizes, too, and leave the info with the duty officer."

"Yes, ma'am."

"Give Susan my best."

Abby had a nice shower and got ready for bed. She climbed into a queen-sized bed, complete with its own extra-long seat belt, put on an eyeshade, and was asleep in moments.

About an hour before landing, the female attendant woke her with a ginger ale.

"You'll want to dress quickly and drink this, ma'am. Then buckle up," she said. "We're coming in corkscrew for security reasons."

Then she smiled and handed Abigail a barf bag with the Presidential seal on it. *This is not a good sign.*

Abby freshened up and dressed in her full uniform, down to combat boots. She strapped herself into a seat, alone in her cabin.

Abby had heard of this type of landing, but not being a fan of roller coasters, she was in total denial. Her denial turned to terror. It was like doing doughnuts in a car in a parking lot, but in an airplane going five hundred miles an hour while pointing down toward the earth, a scant six miles down.

She was shocked, surprised, terrified, and nauseous. She screamed the entire time. If the plane blew up, it would be a mercy. She knew the wings were coming off. She would be a smudge on the ground in Afghanistan any moment.

Just before final approach, Barnett pulled the nose up hard and popped the air brakes, slamming Abby back into her seat. Mercifully, she did not wet the only pair of panties she'd brought.

However, she was safely on the ground for about ten seconds before she barfed the Presidential ginger ale into the Presidential barf bag. She freshened up quickly and, still dizzy, asked for another ginger ale and some crackers.

"I thought you'd need one," the flight attendant said. "Most of us do."

As she prepared to de-plane, she spoke to Colonel Barnett, a bear of a man who no doubt had wrestled the plane onto the ground with his bare hands.

"Thank you for a lovely flight. Are the wings still on?" she asked pleasantly.

"I haven't checked. Sometimes they come off," he said with a wink. *Alas, he's wearing a wedding ring.*

Abigail laughed and wobbled off the plane like a drunk, clinging to one stair rail with both hands. The steps were canopied. The less sight-line people had to her, the safer she was. Her armored vehicle was at the end of the canopy, and she saw only a peep of daylight as she was hustled inside. Still, she could feel the bone-numbing cold of an arid mountain winter. They headed for the mess at warp speed.

She entered, smelled turkey and dressing, and felt right at home. She took off her helmet and shook out her hair. When the personnel got sight of the tall blonde with the long, curly hair, cheers broke out. She bounded to the podium and took the microphone.

"Merry Christmas, Bagram," she said, doing her best imitation of Robin Williams in *Good Morning Vietnam*.

She was greeted with thunderous applause.

"You know, I wondered what you'd think about having a female Commander-in-Chief. Then I remembered that you all have mothers. And if your mom is anything like the woman who raised me, you are used to taking orders from a female." Lots of hoots and hollers.

"And since it is Christmas, I brought you some presents. I pulled a few strings. I had to pull rank to get your big present. That shipment of up-armored Humvees due to arrive after the first of the year? It's in the air behind me. You won't have to drive your tin cans anymore."

The crowd was jubilant.

"I've also brought a stash of phone cards, something like ten thousand of them."

Abigail was pleased to see smiles on the young people's faces. And she was appalled at all the gray hair in the group. *That's the cost of sending the reserves.*

"And now, if PFC Chang would come up here? Chang. On the double," she ordered.

A baby-faced kid no more than twenty vaulted himself up onto the six-foot high stage. The XL jacket would fit him nicely.

"I hear it's your birthday, Private."

"Yes, ma'am." He looked pretty pleased as Clutter's camera flashed.

"Well, I brought you a very special gift," she said alluringly.

More hoots and hollers.

A steward from the plane handed her one of the jackets.

Abby held it for him as he put it on.

"An Air Force One leather flight jacket, complete with shearling lining. They are specially designed to be worn over Kevlar vests," she said, opening her jacket.

Then he turned and saluted her. She returned his salute and shook his hand.

"You make me proud, Private Chang. You make the whole country proud," She had to all but yell into his ear, the crowd was so loud.

She gave away two more jackets, one to a female sergeant who loved the jacket, even if it was a little big. "I've never had a leather jacket before."

Abigail imagined a life where a leather jacket was an incredible luxury. She was humbled, once again, by the incredible luck of her existence. *There but for the grace of Regina, go I.*

She stood on the food line and served dressing for a few minutes.

"The bad guys have probably figured I'm here, so I gotta leave. You make me proud to be an American. Merry Christmas and God speed." She blew them a kiss and bounded out the door.

She visited the wounded at the base hospital. She took a stack of phone cards with her, and most of the soldiers were happy to see her. Having a "babe" for a Commander-in-Chief was fun to them. Visiting with them was easy, as hospitals were her home turf. *At least I know how to work a room of maimed people.*

The women's ward had only one occupant, a young woman lying in bed and staring into space.

"Hey, lady," Abby said, sitting down and taking her hand. The male doctor hung back.

If she knew who Abby was, she gave no sign. The woman did not make eye contact.

"Looks like no one's done your hair," Abby said, still holding her hand.

The woman shook her head.

"May I?"

She shrugged.

"Can you sit up?" The woman swung her legs over the bed and sat up. She slumped and stared into space. The woman's comb and brush were in the bedside table. In a few minutes, Abby had worked out the tangles. Abby had a couple of extra hair elastics in her flight jacket.

"A pony tail above each ear works best in the hospital," Abby said.

"Oh."

Soon the woman had her two pony tails and was lying back down.

"I have to go, now," Abby said, squatting down to look her in the eye. "I hope you feel better soon."

Abby pulled the doctor aside to inquire about the shell of a woman.

"PTSD. Saw her best friend raped and killed. Then they raped the corpse."

"Sweet Jesus. Let me guess. They made her watch but deliberately left her untouched."

"Yep. And if a male with facial hair comes into her line of sight, she freaks."

"What's the plan?"

"I'm waiting for a bed in Ramstein in Germany. They do the best with these women."

Abby scribbled her back line number on her card. "Call if you need help."

Abby left with a hole in her heart the size of Afghanistan. She was airborne, air sick, and out of Afghan air space in less than twenty minutes.

She had hoped to get a firsthand view of the godforsaken terrain, but all she saw was the inside of her barf bag. She figured they were comparable.

CHAPTER EIGHTEEN

JET LAG

Christmas Night, Washington, D.C.

It was dark when Abigail returned to the White House. Abigail knew Regina's mood would be darker. Flying fourteen thousand miles, doing doughnuts in Air Force One, both into and out of Afghanistan, wasn't fun, but it was worth every minute to Abigail. *It might even be worth Regina's wrath.*

Before Abigail could drop her duffel and hit the shower, Regina was in her face wearing her red Christmas robe, pink foam curlers, and fluffy pink slippers. Abby wanted to laugh, but dared not.

"You could have told me, girl. I know stuff about people that no one knows." Regina had her hands on her hips. *Bad sign.*

"I knew you'd worry. This way, you had less worry time. By the time you found out, I was almost home."

"And now you're lying."

Abigail was too tired to remember the First Commandment: Thou Shalt Not Lie to Regina.

"I'm sorry, Reege. I was not on my way home when you found out."

"I didn't raise you to get your fool ass shot off." Regina was angry. Words like *ass* were normally not on her vocabulary list.

"Well, if it makes you feel any better, I threw up right after landing and again after takeoff from Bagram," Abigail said.

"Serves you right," Regina said, and then she stomped off. *Regina got the last word, so all would be well.*

The following morning, she did her workout, but even Susan went easy on her. She cut her lunges in half. "Lots of water, some sunshine today. No caffeine after noon," was her jet lag recipe.

Abby must have drunk five cups that morning and still felt her head was full of cobwebs.

Wicker was a little miffed that she hadn't taken any reporters, but she told him, "Live with it. It's over."

At the one-thirty daily press briefing, Wicker announced he'd posted the photos. Then he briefly recapped the President's trip.

"How did the President do with the corkscrew landings and take offs?" one veteran asked.

"No comment," Wicker said, beaming.

Abigail was starting to want her bed about two that afternoon, but Sam Sternberg asked for, and got, her naptime. After the first few minutes, she had to stop him and drag in half the alphabet soup in the government: the VP, the DOD, DIA, CIA, NSA, FBI, and Homeland Security. The list sounded like the Seven Dwarfs. Oh, the Secretary of State made eight. *Too many for the dwarfs.* While they assembled from their various outposts around D.C., Abigail went to the Residence to ask Regina a favor.

"Hey, Reege, am I forgiven?"

"Of course you are, until the next time." Regina looked up from a newspaper she was reading.

"What's that?"

"Oh, it's an article in the *D.C. Courier Times* that young man wrote. It's okay. He does point out that I didn't go to college. Hmph. I was the valedictorian of my high school. In my neighborhood, going to college was like going to the moon," she sniffed.

Abby picked it up and scanned the article. It was a valentine of the first magnitude. Abby was pleased.

"How's the reception coming for the new Congress?

"Already scheduled. Invitations went out before Christmas."

"Any chance we can lose the Christmas decorations by then?"

"Nope. The volunteers leave them up until Twelfth Night. Besides, the Mission Ladies are coming New Year's Day for three days. They'll be impressed."

Let's see, I can tell Air Force One to fly me halfway around the world, but can't get the White House Christmas crap down. What's wrong with this picture?

Her BlackBerry told her that everyone was in the Oval Office.

"Back to work…" Each step on the way back felt heavier than the previous one.

"Good afternoon, everyone. I think it's afternoon, anyway," Abigail said to the roomful of people.

"I asked the Attorney General to look into something." She recapped the problem with Lafferty and O'Neal. "I wondered if they were money-skimming. My biggest worry was the possibility of their owning four shoulder-fired nuclear weapons. I'll let Sam take us from there."

Sam sat and briefed them from his notes. "I think both men are involved in both schemes. John Lafferty is worth nearly one hundred million dollars, all in Lafferty Weapons Systems in California. His wife left him recently, taking his twin sons back to England. Her alimony is substantial. He has a high burn rate for cash. He owns a Gulfstream-650 as well as an ocean-going hundred-foot yacht."

Abigail took a big sip of her coffee. She needed all the fortification she could get. "Please be specific."

"Yes, Lafferty was paid for weapons that weren't delivered. The plan was simple. We took delivery, paid Lafferty, and then O'Neal said some small percentage of this or that was defective. He cleared nuclear invoices and could easily alter them on the computer. The secretary shipped the 'rejects' back, followed by a check." Sam paused and looked around the room. "Only two hitches. They weren't rejects, and the money was split between them."

"How much?" Abigail clenched her jaw and frowned.

"Without warrants, we can't get that information," Sternberg said.

"So what about the more dangerous scenario?" Abigail asked.

"In a munitions plant, especially a nuclear munitions plant, only two people know the whole manufacturing process, sort of like knowing the recipe for Coca-Cola®. Lafferty and one other, the nuclear engineer would know it. Manufacturing is incredibly fractured and deliberately disorganized. No worker has any way of knowing what any other worker does."

Everyone nodded. *Sensible.* Then Sternberg continued.

"Finally, the missile needs some electronics like a SIM card for a phone. The U.S. government supplies them from a vendor. And O'Neal had chain-of-command access to those.

"In auditing Lafferty's production records submitted to the DOD, he had enough nuclear material to make four more warheads than we actually have."

Abby's heart did a flip-flop. *Four loose nukes in a world with lots of bidders.*

"How would that happen?" she asked.

Cristo explained, "I've been in munitions plants. Randomly, pieces are removed for spot inspections from various places along the line to make sure they meet specs."

Abby picked up the thread of thought.

"So eventually he culls enough 'defective' pieces and DOD 'rejects' enough pieces to make four complete shoulder-fired nuclear weapons." She glanced around the room. Every face was ashen.

"How do you get those missiles out of the plant and into the hands of a bad guy? Jerome? Any thoughts?"

"Ocean-going yachts get the least scrutiny."

"Lafferty has a yacht of that category," the Attorney General put in. "He's entertained Members of Congress on it."

That thought hung in the air until Abigail spoke. "Who can do what?"

"We can find out about the engineer," the head of the FBI said.

"I'll get all passport information on Lafferty, his engineer, and O'Neal," Marilyn offered.

"I can get the info on the yacht and G-650's travels," the Homeland Security director said.

"Do we have any evidence that the missiles have been sold?" Abigail asked.

No one seemed to know the answer to that.

"Then let's buy them," she said, putting her palms down on her desk. She turned to CIA Director Spooky Petersen. "Can you set that up?"

After some thought, Petersen spoke. "Yes. We can do that."

"Okay. I want to get Lafferty, O'Neal, the four devices, all in U.S. jurisdiction," Abigail said.

"It might be best to go to spy court to get warrants for wiretaps," Jerome put in.

"Spy court?" Abigail asked. "I've heard of it, but don't really know how it works."

"FISA is the Foreign Intelligence Surveillance Court, the D.C. court that can authorize electronic surveillance of suspected foreign intelligence agents in the United States. It sort of works as a grand jury in matters of espionage," Sam put in. "They basically will give us the authority we need if they see probable cause."

"This is clearly a matter of national security and does involve the Cayman Islands," Abigail said. She had tried to stop this plot in the Senate, to no avail. Then it dawned on her. *If I'd kept pushing, I might be dead. Men like this don't play nice.*

"We must be meticulous. If we get shut down by FISA, we can't go back again," Sam said. "They don't give fishing licenses."

"His wife divorced him and took his twin boys back to England virtually without a fight," Abigail said. "That's very bizarre for a rich man. She may have dirt on him. She might give us probable cause for our FISA warrant."

"We can likely get around spousal privilege," Sam was thinking out loud. "One, she is out of the country. Two, she is a British subject, and three, they are divorced. We just need to find someone to talk to her. Maybe wear a wire. Do you know anyone in England, ma'am?" the head of the CIA asked.

"Only the Queen. Lovely woman."

CHAPTER NINETEEN

THE SPY WAS TOPLESS

"Madam President," Marilyn put her hand in the "stop" sign.

"Her Majesty is head of state, not government. If we want to query the Brits, we talk to the prime minister."

Abby let the rest of the group leave with plans to reconvene. "Two days? Same time?"

As the others left, she turned to Marilyn. "You know him. Would you join me in a call to him?"

"Of course." Marilyn glanced at her watch. "He's a notorious night owl."

Christopher Highgrove was a portly man with an encyclopedic knowledge of British politics, past, present, and presumably future. He kept moving up because he stayed just one step ahead of the British public. Two steps would be radical. One was leadership.

Pleasantries aside, Marilyn briefed Highgrove on the situation.

"Dreadful. Of course, we'll help," he said.

Abigail told him about the wife, and Highgrove took detailed notes.

"I'll ring you in a day or so, either way."

Abby was grateful that most people on the planet were gone between Christmas and New Year's. Her schedule was empty and her jet lag, severe.

The Queen meets with her Prime Minister every Tuesday at 6 p.m. Their conversations are always informal, without minutes, and private. Her Majesty, however, is an astute observer whose opinion is usually correct.

She and Highgrove discussed the American situation. Her Majesty promised to think on it. She did more than that. She called one of her younger sons. Every single woman of means sets her cap for him eventually. If he didn't know Jemima Lafferty, he'd know someone who did.

Abigail was in the office when the Queen called on the back line. Abby was slogging through end-of-year paperwork.

"Good evening, Your Majesty," Abigail said, calculating the time change.

"I do hope I am not disturbing you, Abigail."

"No, ma'am, not at all." *I was about to go face first onto my desk from boredom and jet lag.*

"I have information on Jemima Lafferty. Lovely girl, climbing the social ladder now that she's home." *Is there any higher rung than the Queen's?* "Luckily for us, she's been climbing the wrong ladder," the Queen said.

"How is that, ma'am?" Abigail said.

"She's become good friends with a former daughter-in-law, Annabelle, Duchess of Eton. Right now, Annabelle is Jemima's guest in Mustique, on holiday in the Caribbean." The Queen was not amused. "We're in a recession, and as usual, Annabelle is topless somewhere."

"I see," Abigail said, though of course, she didn't.

"I am not sure that you do. Annabelle spends her days smoking, drinking, and socializing. She mooches all she can, but is in debt up to her Botoxed forehead. I've given up on Annabelle. She wants two things desperately. First, money, which I can produce. The second is my affection, which she has lost. We've given her an opportunity to get, at least, the first."

"How?"

"I've made Annabelle an offer. If she will help our intelligence people, I will cover her debts—this time. Two stipulations. She must get some nugget of professional misconduct by Mr. Lafferty. I think you Americans call it 'wearing a wire.' Of course, she'll have to sunbathe wearing more than just a bikini bottom," the Queen snickered.

"And the second?"

"No press leaks. If the press gets wind of this, I'll strip her of her title and throw her in the Tower. We can do the first. Unfortunately, we can no longer do the latter."

"Does she know what we are looking for?" Abigail asked.

"Oh, dear no." The queen sounded shocked. "The woman's a sieve. Our intelligence people will be in Mustique by morning. On another matter, I do hope you had a happy Christmas."

"Yes, ma'am, I did."

"I so envy you." The Queen sounded wistful.

Now that's a line for my memoirs. "Why, ma'am?" Abigail asked.

"Two things. One, you get to vote, and I don't. And two, age prevents me from visiting our boys in Afghanistan."

"They know you love them, ma'am," Abigail said. *Have I overstepped?*

"I do. I also remember being at war at their age. There is something noble about being involved in a cause bigger than you are, however unpleasant. Ah, well, I must run. We'll be in touch."

When she put down the phone, Abby turned to the pardon requests that piled up annually. They were quite the anachronism, as if she were a queen. Many were requests from Harrington cronies involved in white-collar crimes. She denied them all. They knew better. One, she put aside to consider.

A small-time hooker in Laredo had played in the big drug leagues to get money for the care of her disabled daughter. The feds had collared her, but the big drug guy walked. She refused to testify against him in fear of her life. *Maybe she can be salvaged. Probably not, but maybe.*

CHAPTER TWENTY

PLANS

The back line rang again.

"Aunt Abby, do you have plans for New Year's Eve?" Duke asked.

"I'm either going to oil my cuticles or organize my sock drawer. I haven't decided which. Why?"

"I'd like to bring someone by to see the White House."

"Who?" Abigail asked. *Duke never brings anyone by.*

"A girl I've been seeing." Duke sounded proud.

"Why, of course. What's her name? Tell me about her."

"All in due time, Aunt Abby. All in due time. Shall we say about seven on New Year's Eve? After that, we are headed out."

"Sure, we'd love to meet her. Have you told Regina?"

"Uh, I was hoping you'd do that for me." Duke sounded meek.

"Uh, I don't think so. Time to man up," Abby laughed.

"I knew you'd say that."

Abigail smelled the bacon cooking when she walked in the door, and by the look on Regina's face, Duke had probably called her.

"I felt like breakfast for supper, and so help yourself to bacon and eggs," Regina said.

Everything was perfect.

"You did this on that cook top?" Abigail asked.

"Yep. Just took a little practice."

"Did Duke call you about tomorrow?" Abigail asked.

"He did. I assume she'll be the first in a parade," Regina said.

"I'm staying in and going to bed early," Abby said.

"You need to. You've had a hard Christmas. I told him we'd open presents when he came."

"But he's bringing a girl," Abigail said. "We should have presents for her."

"Oh, I hadn't thought of that," Regina said, knitting her brow. The women came up with generic gifts, a black cashmere muffler and a red Baccarat butterfly. Regina, of course, could get out to buy them. Abby was beginning to chafe under her virtual house arrest.

That settled, Abigail asked about Regina's plans.

"I'm resting up for the Mission Ladies on the first. O.T. and I are giving them a private tour."

"They'll love it." Abby imagined a veritable sea of church lady hats bobbing around the White House. *They'll look like floats in a hat parade.*

Abby was glad that Regina was blasé about Duke's girlfriend. Maybe she was realizing he wasn't a five-year-old with training wheels anymore. Abigail still wanted romance for herself, but her biologic clock had stopped when she took the Oath of Office. Sure, she could still find a man, marry him, and reproduce, but the odds were slimmer than the odds of a Senator's sister becoming President.

Happiness is not getting what you want; it's wanting what you have.

She slept hard and dreamed of women in burqas floating away from Afghanistan, shedding their fabric cages, and smiling.

Abby awakened on New Year's Eve with a clear idea about Afghanistan. It was risky, but still a classic idea: *Lysistrata* turned upside down.

An army runs on its belly, and without the slave labor of Taliban wives to feed them and wash their shorts, the Taliban would likely be hobbled. If she could get those women out of Afghanistan, the Taliban would collapse. *This idea has promise.*

After the PDB, Abby huddled with Marilyn and Salazar about her Taliban idea. Both were initially skeptical, but could see the benefits.

"It could end the war," Abigail stressed. "But we'd need help from Muslim women around the world. Someone to take them in, mentor them."

"I know just the person. Layla Farid," Marilyn said. "She's American born, and the widow of a wealthy Saudi banker. She knows every Muslim woman who is anyone."

"Great. You talk with her, please. See if she'll be willing to undergo a background check. If so, then we can see if she's interested."

Marilyn wrote herself a note.

"Oh, and on another subject, Her Majesty called me. She's getting Annabelle, the Duchess of Eton, to wear a wire. Seems she and Jemima Lafferty are pals."

"Oh, good grief, I hope this doesn't make the tabloids." Marilyn was fearful.

"The Queen said if it did, she'd strip her of her title and throw her in the Tower," Abigail laughed. "Besides, Annabelle does not know the nature of the dirt we want."

The full working group on O'Neal/Lafferty met later in the day. The FBI reported the chief nuclear engineer was clean.

The Defense Intelligence Agency reported that O'Neal was living pretty high, traveling back and forth to the Caymans, likely visiting his money. Divorced for several years, he has been seen sporting some high-priced arm candy.

"Marilyn?" Abigail asked.

"I can place O'Neal and Lafferty in the Caymans three times together in the last three years, and as you know, the Brits are on board, looking for dirt on Lafferty."

Homeland Security said Lafferty's boat had stayed in port, and Lafferty blocked the tail number of the G-650. "We can get around that with a warrant."

"Okay, we can ask for a FISA warrant as soon as the Brits get us enough for probable cause," Abby concluded.

Abby stood. The meeting was over. She wished everyone a happy New Year as they filed out.

"Poppy, can you come in here?" Abigail had tea and cookies sent in, and the two women curled up in front of the fire.

"Are you having fun?" Abby asked.

"I'm good. I'm very good. Chaffee and I have a good relationship. I manage you and the Hill. He manages everything else."

"I need a minder?" Abby asked.

"Not often. After the Afghan trip, you couldn't remember your name. But overall, you've come a long way in a few months." *High praise, indeed.*

"I think of you two as one." Abby was fishing, and Poppy knew it.

"Funny you should mention that. We have a date tonight," Poppy said, looking pleased.

"A 'date' date?" Abby was impressed. "One where he picks you up, he pays and sends you flowers afterwards? Do you have a new red dress?"

"No. Green. Short, no cleavage, but DDG." Poppy was quite proud. Abby looked puzzled.

"Drop. Dead. Gorgeous."

"Would you like to wear Pris's emerald earrings?" Abby asked.

"Oooh. That'd be great, but they're treasures," Poppy said.

"And so are you. Besides, they're insured."

Abigail was glad that a second person in her posse was finding love.

"Duke's bringing a girl by tonight," Abby said.

"It's about time. I do hope she's good enough for him." Poppy too adored Duke.

"Let's go get your earrings."

The two women walked to the Residence, flanked by agents.

Poppy and Regina had a chat while Abigail rummaged through her sister's good jewelry box. She found the emerald earrings and Poppy immediately put them on.

"Oooh, girl, you do look good," Regina said, giving Poppy a big hug. Poppy, usually the porcupine, even gave Abigail a hug also. "Thanks. I'll take good care of these."

"Actually, they're spy cams. I want a full report," Abby said. *Maybe one day I'll have a date, too.*

CHAPTER TWENTY-ONE

A GIFT FROM DUKE

Duke was on time, as usual. He looked great in black tie.

Kim Tran was on his arm in a little black dress, an Asian Audrey Hepburn.

"Hey, Aunt Abby," he said, "you remember Kim?"

"Of course," Abby said, kissing her on the cheek. "I didn't know you two were seeing each other." Abigail motioned them into the East Sitting Room.

Kim dipped her head. "We wanted to be sure before we said anything, Madam President."

Just then, Regina appeared. She stopped for a moment, looked at the young couple, and burst into tears.

"Oh, my goodness," she said, bawling. Regina grabbed a tissue and started patting at her face. Duke went to comfort her. Regina realized there would be no parade of girls. Duke was serious.

"I thought you might want to see this," Duke said, proffering Kim's left hand. She was wearing an oval-cut diamond solitaire, not too big and definitely not too small.

Everyone admired the ring. Kim blushed, and Regina started crying again.

"This calls for champagne." Abby retrieved a bottle of chilled champagne and four flutes. Regina was delighted that Kim would be the mother of her grandchildren.

"To love," Abigail said. "May your happiness grow each year."

All four raised their glasses. Abby saw the gleam of tears in every eye.

"So how come I didn't know about this?" Regina asked.

"I saw Kim in her dad's shop a few times. She said 'no' the first five times I asked her for coffee. I was glad I asked a sixth time," Duke said.

"I hated going behind my father's back, because he did not approve."

"Have you told your parents yet, Kim?" Abigail asked.

Again, she dipped her head.

"I have tried. My father respects Duke, but thinks I should marry someone Vietnamese," she said sadly.

"I've done my best with him, Aunt Abby," Duke said. "I've told him I'll take good care of her, but he is a tough nut to crack. We've decided if we have to marry without his blessing, we will."

"This is America. I get to choose my husband," Kim said.

"Your dad's view doesn't surprise me," Abigail said. *He said the same to me.*

"But you do not mind that Duke marries outside his culture?" Kim asked Regina and Abby.

"We're thrilled you've chosen each other. I'll invite your parents to dinner. Maybe that will help," Abigail replied.

"Dinner at the White House is very persuasive," Regina said, nodding sagely.

"Oh, would you? You are very kind," Kim said, truly surprised and pleased at the suggestion.

"I'll go you even one better," Abigail said. "We'd like to give you a White House wedding. That is, if you want one here." *Don't push.*

Duke and Kim looked at each other. "That would be quite an honor," Kim said.

Regina started to cry again. A White House wedding like this would be so very American, not society snooty, but a real American story.

"Let's just open our Christmas presents," Regina said. "Then maybe I'll stop crying. I'm just so happy."

"But I did not bring you gifts," Kim said, embarrassed.

"You brought our Duke happiness," Abby said. "That's the greatest gift for us."

"Thank you, Madam President."

"Kim, please, I'm Abby, or Aunt Abby."

"Yes, Aunt Abby."

Their small, delayed Christmas gift exchange was happy for everyone. Regina loved her compact, complete with the correct shade of powder, as well as her new Hermès scarf. Duke liked his briefcase with the gold monogram, and he needed the new wallet she'd put inside it. Kim was thrilled with her shawl and butterfly.

Duke gave Regina an impressively long strand of pearls with a diamond pavé ball clasp.

Regina all but fainted, but revived when Kim showed her all the ways she could wear the strand.

"I wish all the pearls were diamonds, Auntie Reege," Duke said.

Abby was always the last to open her gifts. She liked to watch everyone else.

Duke and Regina pondered what to give Abby. She and Duke had gone through the past year's digital photos and had an online service put them into a book. Some came from Clutter, but most were Duke's.

The book was titled *The Accidental President: Abigail Adams*.

"This was your year of years, girl," Regina said, as Abby looked through it.

The first picture was of Abby in sweats, at the penthouse, drawing up medicine for Priscilla. The last was Duke's picture of her being sworn in as President. Duke had quietly caught sweet photos of her with Pris,

Regina had put in one of her with the Harringtons, and there were snaps from Abby's Senate swearing-in. Even of her scratching her name in Sam Houston's desk.

"Wow," Abby said, giving Regina and Duke each a big hug.

Kim and Duke left for their fancy party. Abigail was happier than she believed possible. She was also asleep in less than ten minutes, luxuriating in the knowledge that Susan was taking tomorrow off.

At morning shift change, the Secret Service reported that the President had finally stopped crying herself to sleep.

New Year's Day dawned with a brittle cold, but Abby was snug in her bed. She luxuriated in bed, stretching and napping until she finally felt rested. She padded into the kitchen and made herself a pot of coffee. Surprisingly, she remembered how.

Soon Regina appeared, glad to have someone pour her coffee for a change.

"So how are you this New Year?" Abby asked.

"I'm real happy with Kim for Duke," Regina said, stirring her coffee three times, as always.

"Do you think the Trans will come around?" Abigail asked.

"For a White House wedding? They'll come around, all right. Vietnamese refugees are very patriotic."

"And you? What do you think of the cultural differences?" Abigail asked Regina. "They'll have different assumptions about marriage."

"That'll keep things lively."

"Well, I'm turning the wedding over to you. Get the parents in here for a dinner ASAP."

"I'll get it on the schedule. By the way, you're to appear at three to say hello to the Mission Ladies."

"Yes, ma'am." Abigail would rather read, but she knew a command when she heard one. Even the President has a boss. Regina had been her boss her entire life, no reason to stop now, just because she was the POTUS.

CHAPTER TWENTY-TWO

A NEW YEAR

Abby's jet lag was finally gone by New Year's Day. The PDB was later that morning, and it didn't bother her that much. *Is that good or bad?*

Just once, since it was a holiday, Abby did the thing she vowed not to do: she read her own press. She was *Time* magazine's Person of the Year, so she read the article.

They emphasized her trend setting. Curly hair was "in." Straight hair was "out." Capes were everywhere, as were pinky rings with one's initials and baroque pearls. Hat sales soared. "Abigail" was suddenly the 'in' name for baby girls.

The head of her hospital gave her high marks. *Nice, considering my abrupt departure.*

Even an ex-flame said nice things about her. At the time, he dumped her because she didn't have "enough time for him." The operative word was "him."

An old roommate said, "She could be a slob, but she was a smart slob." *Yeah right. That girl alphabetized her mail by return address before she opened it.*

Yes, Katherine Stuart was alive, but *Time* didn't know the level of Abby's involvement in her rescue, as details were secret. *I was off getting a pedicure, you morons.*

She chose an excellent Vice President. *Hell, I got a saint to change his no to a yes.*

Time was ambivalent about her intersession appointments; some thought she was packing the court, and others thought her blind picks were a good idea. *Hell, I got the job done, didn't I?*

Time concluded, properly, that it was too soon to know about her agenda. *I don't know where I want the country to go. How can I take it there? Anything that would make sense for 99 percent of the people would be blocked by the 1 percent's lobby.* Special interests contributed heavily to both parties, so they owned whoever won—in advance.

Abby remembered the maxim, "The best politician is the one who, once bought, stays bought." *That's corruption on a grand scale.*

Abby shut the magazine. She had a more immediate problem.

The Mission Ladies were due at three. She had to be in full church attire, including a hat, one of the three she owned.

The ladies all but levitated around the White House. Regina gave Abby many a grateful glance, and O.T. gave a lovely tour. He told amusing anecdotes and kept people moving. Abby was glad Regina had included the Family Quarters. Abigail's bedroom door was closed with stanchions in front of it. She remembered Walter Harrington's remark about only having privacy in the bathroom and he wasn't so sure about that.

During the tea in the Yellow Oval Room, which included Texas Caviar, cold, marinated black-eyed peas, for good luck, one of the women asked O.T. about his career.

"When I first started here, the staff was all Negro," he said, with the emphasis on the word *Negro.* The ladies tittered.

"We were the cream of Washington's Negro society. My mother was a cook here, and I started as a bootblack after high school. She insisted I graduate, but some children started earlier. I kept the President's shoes shined, but I also vacuumed, mopped, and waited table. And of course, I polished enough silver to last me a lifetime."

The Mission Ladies laughed loudly in sympathy with that.

"But I kept reading about the house itself, and I worked my way up to Chief Usher. Then one First Lady really surprised me. 'Mr. Wagner, you are a walking history book,' she said. 'You need to be the curator, not the usher. Though you are a fine, fine usher.'"

"Well, the retiring curator was annoyed at putting a black man with no formal degree in his job, but she prevailed. He left me a cubbyhole office, which is still full. If I as much as sneeze, I am buried by paper."

"O.T. is being very modest," Abigail said. "He is the glue that holds this place together."

To spare him embarrassment, she didn't mention the ten books he'd written or the museum exhibits he'd curated.

The Mission Ladies were gone by five.

"Even Bessie Brooks couldn't find any fault with today, and she would nitpick St. Peter himself," Regina said, sitting down heavily and kicking off her shoes.

"Well, she'll be on her way to Houston in two days."

"Yes, we have private tours at the Smithsonian tomorrow and Mt. Vernon the next day."

"When's our reception for the new members of Congress?"

"Sunday brunch. The Trans come the night before," Regina said.

"Any news on the State Dinner for Canada and Mexico?"

"Liza says she can't nail it down."

"I'll call them."

Abby took off her hat and walked over to the Oval Office. She was surprised to find Logan Chaffee in his office. She wanted to know about his date with Poppy, but dared not ask.

"Paperwork," he said.

She called the White House operator and asked for a conference call with the Canadian prime minister and the Mexican President. Chaffee came in and disapproved. "The President of the United States does NOT get put on hold."

"Oh, don't get your panties in a wad, Chaffee," Abby said as she punched on the speakerphone to give her two hands free for the computer. "I'll just play Free Cell like everyone else does on hold." Her patience was rewarded. She won two games and was on her way to a third win when the two men got on the phone.

"This is Abigail Adams. Happy New Year, gentlemen."

The Canadian prime minister was momentarily speechless. Not so the Mexican President.

"*Si, si, si, Presidente*," Mexican President Lopez said. "I am happy to talk with you both."

"Yes, well, delighted here, too," a reserved Pierre LeDuc said.

"Our staffs can't schedule the State Dinner honoring the two best neighbors on the planet, so I thought I'd call directly."

Both were a bit shocked at the compliment.

"You guys need to help me, though. I've not done a State Dinner before," Abby said. *Might as well be frank.* "I hear they can be a real chore."

LeDuc spoke first in all seriousness. "The key to a State Dinner, Madam President, is to remember that it is only slightly less pleasant than a visit to the dentist."

"No, I think it is worse," the Mexican President said. "At least if it is a Mexican dentist."

"Oh, great. I hear men aren't big on white tie," Abigail said.

"I feel like a lost pianist in search of a Steinway," LeDuc said.

"And I feel like a penguin," Lopez said with a laugh.

"Ah, well, that won't do. How about a compromise? Women do like dressing up. It's a chick thing. How about just tuxedoes for the men but long dresses for your wives?"

"Very wise, madam," LeDuc said. "We're free the third weekend. Lopez?"

"Count us in also," Lopez said.

Abby could hear the relief in their voices as they said their goodbyes. She won the third game at Free Cell.

"See, Chaffee? I can talk on the phone by myself," Abby said playfully. "You need not have interrupted your football to come in."

"My team was down thirty in the fourth quarter. It was a mercy to get away."

American-born Layla Farid was tall and dark with turquoise eyes. She was an exotic beauty even as a grandmother. The widow of a prominent Saudi banker, she had grown children flung across the globe, each successful. She lived in upstate New York and supervised the care of her failing parents.

Upon her marriage, she became a devout Muslim and, thus, would never marry again. Her faith was not just for show. She was well known throughout the Middle East.

Layla dashed for the ringing phone. Her parents were napping. She was shocked to find it was Marilyn Chernosky, an old friend.

"I think you'd be a good adviser to the President on Muslim women, but anyone in the President's inner circle must have a security clearance. Would you be terribly offended at a background check?"

"Not at all. If I can help my Muslim sisters, I will."

"As soon as it comes through, she'll invite you to the White House. Very informal."

"I am honored."

Abby looked at her calendar. Her evenings and weekends were filling up: Mikey tonight, then the Trans, Sunday brunch with the new Members of Congress. *Be careful what you wish for.*

She and Mikey had an early dinner in the President's private dining room. It was the closest she came to having a date for New Year's: dinner with a dear old man on January 1.

"Ah, my dear President," Mikey said. "How did you and Winston get on this week?"

William Manchester's *The Last Lion* was a doorstopper, literally. She'd skimmed it and used the second volume to prop open her sitting room door. Things sag in a two-hundred-year-old house.

She didn't tell Mikey that she'd learned a lot from Wikipedia.

"Churchill was wonderful. I wish I'd known him," Abby said.

"Well, I did, but I was very young, and he was very old," Molloy said. "I asked him for advice."

"What did he say?" Abigail was enchanted.

"'Words, my dear young man,' he said in his gravelly voice and punctuated things with this cigar. 'Words are the greatest weapons we have. And their power comes from ideas.'"

"This from a boy who flunked English," Abby replied.

After their meal, she brought up the State Dinner.

"No one can fault you for having the neighbors to dinner," Mikey said over English trifle, his favorite dessert. He suspected Abby was buttering him up for something, serving something so sinful for his cholesterol.

"Would you please be my escort?" Abby asked. "I'd be honored."

"Oh, no, dear girl, I'm much too much of a rake. I'd ruin your reputation," he replied with a twinkle. "I'd be much better escorting Marilyn." The Secretary of State's husband had Alzheimer's, which prevented his going out. Mikey would be a good escort for Marilyn.

"So do I go alone? Do I have a military aide escort me? What do I do?"

"Well, if you knew some presentable young man…" Mikey said with a shrug.

"Everyone in this town has an agenda. You know that."

"Well, Washington has some good walkers," he offered.

"Walkers?"

"Yes, dear. Gay men who enjoy a fancy night on the town."

"No. No walkers."

"Hmmm. Perhaps my baby sister's boy. Attached to the United Nations, presentable enough…" he trailed off.

"No criminal record? Manners? Straight? Single? Tall enough?" Abigail needed to be picky, as he too would reflect on the nation.

"Let's see. No criminal record that I know of. Mannerly enough, I suppose. Straight, I assume. Unmarried. I think he'd be tall enough. Named George Michael after me…" He kept talking, but Hitch's distinctive three abrupt raps on the door distracted her.

"Excuse me, please," Abigail said abruptly, walking to the door to speak with Hitch.

Then she briefly returned to the table.

"I apologize, an emergency. Your nephew sounds fine. Please inform the East Wing? I have to run."

Abby was out the door.

"Ma'am, I have to leave the White House. Procedure dictates you take the football and wait in the Situation Room until my relief arrives," Hitch said, flustered as they headed downstairs

"Is your wife in labor?" Abigail asked.

"Yes and I need to hightail it to the hospital." The normally cool Hitch was antsy.

"Go, go," Abby waved him out the door of the Situation Room. Traffic slowed Dabaghi, so Abby pestered the technical people about what they did. They liked it that someone took an interest in their work.

By the time Dabaghi arrived, Mikey was long gone.

Abigail went to bed and slept well. Those five-thirty workouts came awfully early.

Susan was ahead of her; Abby noticed she had the stair machine on the highest setting and hadn't broken a sweat. *I want to be you, but I hate you.*

"You're ready to step up your workouts," Susan said. She decreed an increase in lunges after warming up.

"You're killing me," Abigail said as she did her lunges. "Assassin."

"If you whine, you get twenty more," Susan said sweetly.

"Thanks, Miss Susan," Abby panted in a child-like voice. "I'm really enjoying this, Miss Susan."

As a reward for lunges, she got to box. That really let her vent. Susan started by having Abby hit mitts that Susan wore, but Abby's fists were hard and fast. One slip and Abby would rearrange Susan's face. She ordered a heavy bag, and Abigail beat it mercilessly.

Even as President, everyone was constantly telling Abby no.

No, I can't get Congress to ban excessive credit card interest rates. The financial services lobby would protect their loan shark rates. Wham, wham, she pounded away on the heavy bag.

No, I can't get everyone on board to increase mileage standards for cars, it would increase the price of a new car. What's the bigger danger? Inflation or global warming? Bam, bam, bam.

No, I can't get us out of Afghanistan, which costs us two hundred million dollars a DAY. That's over two grand a SECOND. It would look bad. And having our country go broke would look good? Wham, bam, bam,

No, I can't cut drug costs twenty percent just by returning to the rules banning advertising prescription medicines to the public. The drug lobby would see to that. Wham, wham, more punches on the bag.

No, I can't get a law passed mandating both equal bumper height and damage-resistant, impact-absorbing bumpers. The auto repair lobby would crash that. Wham, wham, wham, wham.

No, I can't get rid of cigarettes that kill a thousand people a day, the equivalent of three jumbo jets crashing every damn day. But Medicare has to pick up the tab. Jab, jab, jab.

No, I can't walk on the North Lawn, I'd be too exposed. Why don't they just put in an electric fence and a shock collar on me? She really beat the bag hard on that one.

I can start a nuclear war, but cannot get the Christmas crap out of the White House for another week or more. Bam, bam, bam, bam.

I can't even get my own date to a State Dinner. Mikey has to get me a pity date. He'll probably have bad breath and no chin. Wham. Wham. Wham. Wham. Wham.

After a few minutes of this, Susan said, "Okay, ma'am. Time to stop and hit the shower."

Abby ignored her and punched the bag harder.

"Madam President, stop." Susan's tone was commanding.

Abigail stopped.

"Training means doing as I say. Otherwise I will quit," Susan said softly.

"Sorry," Abigail said, peeling off her gloves, huffing and puffing, sweat rolling down her face. She bent over, bracing her hands on her knees.

"Training involves discipline. It will improve your job performance, but only if you listen."

"You're right. As usual."

CHAPTER TWENTY-THREE

WHERE'S THE RUG?

January 2

It was snowing heavily when Abigail left for the office. Abby grabbed her old cape and boots and walked outside. Snow gave her childlike joy. She loved the quiet it brought. The White House lawn looked like a fairyland. Abby wanted very much to share it with someone, preferably an unattached male who thought the world of her. Oh, well, a snowy day was what she had, and she would make the best of it.

Abby greeted her Marine Sentries and then Poppy.

Poppy, resplendent in a new red suit, looked somehow gentler today.

"Good morning, Madam President," Poppy said, popping up from her chair and dropping the emerald earrings into Abigail's hand.

"Happy New Year. Anything I need to know?" Abby asked.

"No, nothing," Poppy replied with a large smile.

"Well, we have big news. Duke's engaged to Kim Tran," Abigail said joyfully. "And Hitch's wife is in labor. Be sure to interrupt me as soon as we know something."

"Hmmm, Duke was always real quiet when Kim's name was mentioned," Poppy said. "Now we know why."

"It went right past me. Sure you aren't CIA?" Abigail asked.

Abigail walked into her office. The floor was completely bare. She was bewildered.

"Poppy. Where's the rug?" Abby yelled out the door.

"I assumed it was off being cleaned," Poppy said as she walked in. The bare wood floor was an intricate inlay of alternating light and dark rays starting in the center of the room. Very expensive, but also distracting and over the top.

"Get O.T. in here, please."

O.T. appeared within moments. He was usually the first person in the building.

"Where's the rug?" Abigail asked.

"Mrs. Harrington had it picked up last night for the Harrington Library. She said you knew," O.T. replied. Abigail recalled Evangeline saying his "artifacts" would be picked up.

"I didn't realize the Oval Office would lose its rug. What do we do now?" Abby asked.

"Well," O.T. bent his head, scratching at his thatch of snowy hair. "Usually a President's inner circle has a rug custom made, like Harrington's did. That's why his had WH in the center. They were his initials."

"Silly me, I thought it was for White House," Abby said. "My posse's Regina and Duke, and they aren't about to pony up for a rug. Besides, it'd take months. Isn't there some other oval rug somewhere?"

"I'll check the database."

"Thanks."

Abby had to laugh. *Only I get the rug pulled out from under me as soon as I get my feet on the ground.*

Dabaghi was on hand for the PDB. Apparently Hitch's wife really was in labor.

The PDB again tried to ruin her day. In Afghanistan, a baby girl in her mother's arms was stoned to death along with the mother. Why? The child was a product of rape; therefore, the woman was an adulteress. They would have spared a baby boy.

Once again, Abigail felt the need to vomit, but her anger was greater than her nausea, and she vowed to do something to get rid of the Taliban.

Poppy stuck her head into the Oval Office.

"Hitch's wife had a baby girl. Eight pounds of perfection, named Madeleine," Poppy announced happily.

"Please send an enormous bouquet from all of us."

Everyone was grateful for the brief respite of good news.

As most of the people in the PDB were involved in the O'Neal/Lafferty investigation, they segued into that topic when the others left.

Marilyn led off. "Prime Minister Highgrove reports the wife blabbed to Annabelle that Lafferty was skimming. I've heard the tape and have the original."

"How about the money trail?"

"Waiting to get a FISA warrant. This will give us probable cause," Sam said. "The Cayman banks will honor those."

"How about the sting?" Abigail asked.

"We have operatives who can pull it off as Chechens," Petersen from the CIA answered.

"So how do we get Lafferty, O'Neal, and our stingers in touch?"

"Very carefully," Petersen said.

"Duh. Tell me something I don't know, Spooky," Abigail said, chuckling. *Smart aleck.*

"We'll approach Lafferty. O'Neal might have some shred of patriotism left. We'll contact him in London around his kids. That'll spook him. We'll also approach and avoid a couple of times. That'll keep him off guard and he'll blab more to O'Neal for the wiretaps," Petersen said.

"I have one reservation. Lafferty needs to be hard up for money to take the bait," Jerome Lafayette said. "He isn't, yet. I don't want him to turn us down."

"Then let's make him poor," Abby said. "You, dear Secretary of Defense, stop doing business with him and cease paying his invoices."

"On what grounds?" Salazar asked.

"The Attorney General can come up with something abstruse, arcane, and completely incomprehensible, can't you?" Abigail asked Sam.

"It's what lawyers do, ma'am."

Abigail continued, "So he sues us. That eats up tons more of his money. At his burn rate, how long will it be before he is desperate?"

Lafayette was the first to speak. "He's not liquid. No cash flow in and extra legal fees out? He'll be desperate in three to six months. Once he starts shedding hard assets, like the plane, we'll know he is on the ropes."

"Any idea where the nukes are?" Abigail asked.

No one knew.

"Any ideas where O'Neal has the electronics?" Abigail asked.

No one did.

"So what are we using for money?" Abigail said. "Electronic transfer would have to involve the Cayman banks. Too bad bearer bonds have gone away."

"Well, some are left, but not in the denominations we need," Sam put in, gloomily. Then his face brightened. "Wait a minute. We can print our own fakes if we like. Better than Monopoly money."

"Brilliant, Sam," Abigail said. "The Bureau of Printing and Engraving can make us bearer bonds that 'haven't been redeemed.' The 'Chechens' could have stolen them during the break-up of the old Soviet Union."

"So do we have a plan? One: Make Lafferty desperate for cash. Two: Approach and avoid a couple of times, then demand a buy with bearer bonds on U.S. soil with both men present?" Abigail asked.

Everyone in the room nodded.

"Are we on safe grounds to get FISA warrants?" Abigail asked.

Everyone agreed they were.

Sam said, "I'll get them going. O'Neal and Lafferty will be under electronic surveillance 24/7 within a day or so."

Abigail wanted these nukes secured and Lafferty and O'Neal in federal prison for life.

A rug appeared at noon.

"Where'd you find one?" Abby asked O.T.

"In the Yellow Oval Room in the White House."

"So basically, you took the living room rug and put it in here."

"Yes, ma'am."

"Oh, well, at least it didn't cost the government any money."

"Well, it did, sort of. Miss Regina told me to find one for the Yellow Oval Room or she would have my hide," O.T. said, with a wide smile.

"At least you know who's boss around here," Abby said.

"I figured that out the first day."

The reception for incoming Members of Congress was a success. It was exciting to see optimistic and energized people. *Soon enough, you'll learn how little you can do, and how long that almost nothing would take.*

Lawson and Lorena Gray looked very happy. Lawson was particularly pleased with his office. As soon as Abby became President in November, he quite properly took her seat. With his "early check-in" he got to keep Pris's office. A freshman Senator with a senior office.

It was nice to see him back among the living.

Abigail explained the deception about Kim's family to Albright, who, for once saw the humor in a situation. As head of the White House

Secret Service detail, he had precious little cause for laughter. And anything resembling a practical joke had to go through him.

When Duke brought the Trans to the White House, Mr. Tran got very excited. "Does your father work here?" Tran asked, as everyone went through security.

"Not exactly."

Upstairs, Mr. Tran looked suspiciously at Abigail, who looked like his friend, Missy, minus the glasses.

"Hello, Mr. Tran," Abigail said, extending her hand. "Welcome to the White House."

"You are Missy?" he said incredulously.

"Yes, Mr. Tran, I am your Missy." It took a while for him to figure out how she and Duke were related. Once he learned Kim's future in-laws lived in the White House, his resistance melted. Regina and Abigail met Kim's mother Vee, who was quite lovely. Abby could see where Kim got her poise.

When the photographer showed up to take pictures, Tran was ecstatic.

"I love America. When I was in grade school in Vietnam, I had to walk over dead bodies to go to school. Then America saved me when I was just a young man, at sea in an old boat. To think my daughter will marry here in the White House is beyond a dream." He had tears in his eyes. Abby looked around. So did everyone else.

Tran would blow up photos for the shop window. Business would be up twenty percent.

The following Tuesday, all of the women involved in the wedding, plus Liza Taylor from the East Wing, got together. The sooner Kim realized that Regina ruled the White House the way a great white shark rules a baby pool, the better. Kim, as always, was most polite, as was her mother.

Abby chose the East Sitting Room for the meeting. The day was bright and the women excited.

"Thank you for your kindnesses. My father has put a big picture of you and him in the shop window. I hope you do not mind," Kim said with the characteristic dip of her head.

"I expected he would," Abby laughed. "We were pretty tight when I lived at the penthouse."

"Well, nobody bothered to tell me anything," Regina added.

"You don't have to know everything, Regina," Abby said, teasing.

"Since when?" Regina scowled.

"I'd like all the plans in place before the announcement, if that's okay. And you two need an afternoon with Wicker," Abby said.

"Why is that, Aunt Abby?" Kim asked.

"You need to know the basics of handling the press." *I still don't know.*

"As you wish," Kim said.

"Sometimes I feel like the African tribe that thinks the camera steals your soul," Abigail said. She put in a call to Wicker Washington and scheduled a half day on Thursday.

"The East Wing of the White House is the social side. Liza Taylor reports to Regina, who is the Official Hostess. I'd like Liza to be your wedding co-coordinator. Is that okay with you?" Abigail asked.

"That would be most welcome," Kim said, and Vee nodded.

Liza said, "I can do all the invitations, RSVPs, help you with menu planning, reception details. But President Adams says I am to give you what you and Duke want."

"That sounds wonderful, Liza," Kim said.

"Now, as to the wedding itself, what would you and Duke like?" Abigail asked.

As Abigail expected, Kim's first thought was the dress. "This is the dress I am making," she said, passing around the sketches and swatches of a tea length gown that would set a new trend.

Abigail remembered her sister's Edwardian, five-strand "dog collar" of pearls. She'd hoped to wear it on her own wedding day, but this dress cried out for it.

"Wait, wait," Abby said. She got up, went into her bedroom, and returned with the pearls in their original case.

"Please take these from your Aunt Pris," Abigail said, with tears in her eyes.

"I am very honored," Kim said. Abby put them on her, Kim piled her hair atop her head, and the effect was stunning. Everyone agreed the pearls would be perfect.

"Duke has suggested the pastor of Mt. Zion Church to marry us," Kim said.

"An excellent choice," Regina pronounced. The Mt. Zion Church was the oldest African-American church in D.C. It had been the bedrock of Georgetown after the Civil War, when the area was largely black.

"Kim, what Vietnamese wedding customs would you like?" Abigail asked. *Please don't make me eat anything weird.*

"Please visit our home, so Duke and I may serve our elders tea, to show respect," Kim said to Abby. *I can get a hall pass for that.*

Everyone left the rest to Kim and Liza, who had everything done before the day was out. Kim and Duke spent their allotted afternoon at Wicker Washington.

The next day the White House announced the engagement. Within days, every media outlet in the country and half the outlets around the world wanted interviews.

Doing photo shoots and interviews were fun for them. Luckily, both were sensible, and life had a way of humbling them. The week that they appeared on the cover of *People* magazine, neither could enjoy it. They had a stomach bug and both were home running to the bathroom. Kim was glad she was living at home. *If Duke and I were living together, we'd have only one bathroom.*

CHAPTER TWENTY-FOUR

BEQUESTS

By banning donors and most lobbyists, Abby had more time than Harrington had. Living as a cardboard cutout in a zillion pictures a year was bizarre. *Something's wrong with anyone who wants this job.*

The skeleton of Abigail's schedule left enough room for her to think, and work, during the day. Job one was to write the State of the Union address. The American people deserved her words, not the mass platitudes of the professional speechwriters.

Abby didn't like her speech. It was mushy. Besides, she'd only been in office two months. What could she say? "I haven't screwed up yet?" She didn't have answers for the biggest problems, at least not as long as God let lobbyists live.

The State Dinner was also looming several days before the State of the Union speech. Last weekend, she hosted the first birthday party for Congress, and a senior Republican Senator won a snow globe for pinning the trunk of the elephant on the hind end of the donkey. The American Arts Night, featuring New Orleans musicians, would close out the month.

Layla Farid joined Marilyn, Salazar, and Abigail one Tuesday to ponder what to do about Afghan women after American troops left.

Abigail feared the Taliban would take serious revenge on any women who had literally shown their faces.

Abigail was impressed with Layla's poise and passion for oppressed Muslim women.

"Islam means 'submission.' Just as the wife must submit, the husband has a moral obligation to care for his wife's safety and happiness. Any man who enslaves his wife or beats her is not a good Muslim," Layla explained.

"As well, Afghanistan is a signatory of the U.N. Declaration of Human Rights, which prohibits slavery, honor killings, as well as wedding ten-year-olds to men the age of their grandfathers."

Finally, a Muslim woman more incensed than I am at the plight of Afghan women.

"The Taliban has roughly fifty thousand members. Al Qaeda is but a few thousand. When we leave, the Taliban will go on a rampage," Abigail said.

Marilyn, Cristo, and Layla agreed. Abby went on.

"If we allow wives and children of the Taliban to flee, two things will happen. One, without their wives to feed them and wash their shorts, they will be kneecapped. Two, we can attack the Taliban without killing innocents. I think these women want out. As for Al Qaeda, there is major jostling going on for leadership. If we could know where Al Zawahiri is, not to mention the cadre of jostlers, we could get rid of them. Get rid of these two groups and we can leave Afghanistan with a clear conscience. I've run the numbers, and depending on where they go, a five-year stipend is far cheaper than this damn war."

Abby took a deep breath. "Okay, now guys, let's kick this around."

And kick it around they did. At the end of the discussion, the four decided it was doable, but just barely doable.

Layla was concerned. "These women cannot be in the presence of men. That's my first concern. Secondly, I must get a network of women to help with resettlement. Thirdly, I am concerned the stipend would be stolen by their host countries."

"I'll get a cadre of U.S. military women trained to be their shepherds," Cristo said.

"As for the stipend, we can do direct deposit into a bank of their choice like we do with retirees abroad," Abigail said. "This is hard cash coming into a country. The countries will want these women."

"You know, of course, that if a man's wives all leave him, he'll simply take more," Layla said.

That clinched it for Abby.

"Not if we attack them in their beds, they won't," Abigail said. "I had hoped to root them out at our convenience, but we'll move swiftly."

"I've been a refugee twice," Marilyn said. "The least I can do is find them a place to wait for placement."

One problem remained. They had to wait for winter to be over. And it had to be a moonless night. Cristo looked at the calendar. June 6. D-Day. That should give them enough time to plan. Barely.

Abby was executrix for Pris's estate that settled easily, thanks to the hard work of Marston Mills, Pris's lawyer. Uncle Sam took his mega-share, but an enormous amount remained. The largest assets, Logan Ranch and Logan Oil, were in some complex corporate structure for tax reasons. Still, Abby, Regina and Duke were the "owners." Marston divided the liquid assets as instructed: 51 percent to Abby's blind trust, 49 percent split between Regina outright and into a trust for Duke. As well, he gave Abby the checks for Poppy and Mason Ingram, the ranch manager.

Abby knew she'd added some zeroes to her name, but was too busy to spend much money, except on snow globes, scarves, ties, and clothes. She also remembered her sister's admonition, "Those who need not work must yet serve."

Mason Ingram was surprised to get a certified letter from the White House. He was even more surprised at the check and the letter from the President. He knew hard work paid off, but he'd never thought of it paying off like this.

Abby got O.T. to take Regina on an outing while she gave Poppy and Duke their checks.

On a snowy Saturday afternoon, Abigail asked Poppy to come to the Family Quarters at two. Abby handed her the envelope with the check in it.

"Pris gave you this as a bequest. I'm her executrix," Abby said. "She wanted you to have a nest egg."

Poppy looked at the check, and tears overflowed down her cheeks, a sight Abby never expected from Poppy. Of course, tissues were at hand.

"I can't believe this, not after giving me a mink coat," Poppy sniffled.

"You meant a lot to her, Poppy. You mean a lot to all of us," Abigail said, squeezing Poppy's hand.

Duke came at four. When she gave Duke his first distribution from the trust, he was flabbergasted. "Not in my wildest imagination," he said, shaking his head. "I knew you all loved me, but I can't imagine this on top of everything else," Duke sighed.

"You can stop paying my tuition, Aunt Abby. I think I can handle things with this," he said, holding up the check.

He moonlighted for a law firm to buy Kim her ring and Regina her pearls, and he almost had enough saved for their honeymoon. This would let him focus full-time on studies.

"Pris believed that those who need not work must yet serve. I hope those words will guide you," Abigail said to Duke.

Abigail asked the White House doctor to be available when she gave Regina her check, lest she have a heart attack. Regina was just back from Sunday church, and Abby invited her for a cup of tea.

"Just the thing. It's cold outside," Regina said.

"Here's your distribution from the estate," Abigail said.

"I can understand passing money down, but really, passing it up?" Reege said.

Regina opened the envelope and looked at the check for a long time.

"Reege, say something—you're scaring me."

"For my first thirty years, I pinched pennies till they squealed. Then, when that well hit, I was pretty sure I could take care of you without having to clean white people's toilets. But this? This is hard to take in." She shook her head and wiped a tear from her eye.

"Perhaps you'll think of it as a smidgen of your worth as a person," Abby said. "All the dollars on the earth couldn't equal your value."

They both had a good cry, primarily over how much they missed Pris. Abby was useless the rest of the day.

CHAPTER TWENTY-FIVE

CINDERELLA ALL BALLED UP

Peggy Mellon helped Regina with the State Dinner. Her contact database spat out guests from all three countries. From financiers like Carlos Huerta, one of the richest men in the world, to an obscure Canadian writer whose first novel won a Nobel Prize, they had a socko guest list. Also included were some of the press, including Thad "T.J." Jackson, a sexy and very single war reporter. As well, Congressional members with direct ties to either country attended, as did each country's ambassador.

"And who will escort you?" Peggy asked.

"Oh, Mikey Molloy's nephew, Michael something, named for Mikey. I didn't catch his name. I'm sure he gave it to Liza," Abigail said.

"Ah, yes, here is a single "Michael Something" on the list. Must be him," she said.

The chef and sommelier really came through at the tasting dinner. Everyone agreed the food was sophisticated without being odd. Blending cuisines from three cultures was not easy. Abby stepped up her workouts to make sure that her dress would fit and that the spandex undergarment would be just an insurance policy.

Andre gave her instructions two weeks before the party. A week before: haircut and waxing. The day before: shampoo. The day of, mani and pedi.

"Day-old hair is easier to style," Andre said. "Your dress is cut on the bias, right, baby President?"

"Yes."

"Well, even with spandex, you'll have a pooch if you don't do a colonic."

"What? An enema? NO." Abigail was genuinely aghast.

"Why do you think the women look so good on the red carpet? They all go that morning and get all flushed out."

"Andre. Stop. No. Full stop. No. Not now, not ever." Abigail was horrified.

"Well, avoid anything carbonated or gas producing for at least forty-eight hours. No broccoli, no prunes, nothing like that."

"Oh, for crying out loud, I do two hundred crunches a day. My belly is just fine."

Andre also suggested a fake tan, which she nixed.

"I don't look good in orange."

Sometimes, she just wanted to smack him, he was so outrageous.

Laura Rowe sent over silver peep-toe platforms and a silver clutch. Abigail was getting excited about her Cinderella moment. Kim and Duke were attending, so Kim could help her into the dress.

The day of the party, everything was ready. Abigail did a walk-through of the dining room. The Fargo china sat on yellow, watered silk tablecloths, and the low centerpieces were primarily yellow and coral flowers with a generous amount of greenery. Tall candelabra with a dozen fourteen-inch coral tapers lighted every table. Every woman looks better by candlelight.

The menu cards were on the plates, and each attendee had a hand-done place card in gold ink. Everyone would take them as souvenirs.

Protocol dictated that each plate be equidistant from its neighbor. The White House kept knotted strings to place around the table depending on table size and number seated. If someone dropped out, the staff re-set the entire table with a different knotted string to assure each plate was still equidistant apart.

Protocol also dictated that Abigail and her party be the last to arrive (so that she waited on no one) and that she be the first to leave (lest anyone appear to walk out on her). Both were fine with her.

However, for the arrival of the heads of state upstairs, she must be ready to greet them. She could not have them wait on her.

Abby gave herself extra time to get ready. Most times, she got dressed at a dead run. Regina was downstairs tending to something, so she had peace and quiet.

Winter always gave her lizard skin. She had a shower then slathered on baby oil onto her damp skin. She was practically glistening from so much extra moisture. She patted herself dry and fished out the spandex, backless slip from the accessories bag. Her sparkly red toenails were supposed to be seen, so she did not need panty hose. *Yes!*

Andre was due momentarily, so Abby pulled the slip over her head. Well, she tried to anyway. Somehow, it wouldn't go down. She contorted herself, and one arm shot out through an armhole, like a stone from a slingshot. She was starting to sweat. *I must look like a perfect idiot.*

She wrestled the other arm into its armhole, but it was even harder. She got it in, somehow. By now, sweat was streaming down between her breasts.

The spandex monster took on a life of its own and settled in the real estate between her breasts and her armpits. She could barely breathe. The underwires poked her, and one pointed ominously toward an eye.

Don't panic. Just push the panic button. Help will appear.

She was not going to summon armed men to see her naked, sweaty, and being squeezed to death by an overgrown rubber band. She had no female agent today. There had to be a better way.

I'll cut this off. Where were the scissors? Regina had them downstairs. *Okay. What about a knife?*

Don't be ridiculous. She couldn't walk across to the kitchen to get that chainsaw thing for the turkey. *Besides, what if I cut myself?*

She sat down on the bed and got control of her emotions. She wasn't blue. She could breathe. Sort of. This thing had to go back up over her head, or it had to go down.

At first, she tried to pull it down. That didn't work.

Judging from the discrepancy between the small size of the tube and the relatively larger size of her body, back over the head was the most likely way to extract herself.

She crossed her arms, her right hand grabbing the wad under her left arm and vice versa. She exhaled to make her chest as small as possible and then pulled with all of her might.

Nothing.

She tried it again.

Nothing, still. She was sweatier, but that didn't count as progress.

She would rest and try a third time. If that didn't work, she'd wrap herself in a robe and send an agent for scissors. She'd do whatever it took to silence them. *Probably a case of some rare, single malt Scotch for each. Cads. They'd blab anyway. She'd make Secret Service history.*

The third time, the garment came off with a giant plopping sound. Abigail inhaled lungs full of nice, clean oxygen. She looked at herself in the mirror. Her face looked like a wet beet, and her hair was in full frizz.

At least I didn't break a fingernail.

Andre knocked at the door.

"Just a second," she said, hastily throwing on her robe.

"Madam President, baby, what on earth have you been doing? You look horrible," Andre gasped and put his hand to his mouth.

"Oh, well, you know." Abigail waved her hand vaguely. "I'll pop into the shower and be out in a sec. Just start setting up."

Andre was suspicious until he saw the garment snake on the bed.

"Ah-hah! You tried to put a spandex slip on over your head, didn't you?" he all but cackled.

"No comment!" Abigail yelled from the bathroom. She showered quickly and did a quick rinse of her sweat-laden hair. She didn't want to smell like the workout she'd just had.

Andre worked in record time.

Abby wore her hair in a loose French twist, with "charming escapees."

Just as Andre finished, Kim knocked softly on the door.

"Aunt Abby, would you like me to help you with your outfit?" she said sweetly. "If you have dusting powder, it will make things go more easily. I tried to bring some in, but the Secret Service would not let me."

"That would be lovely, Kim," Abby said, trying to absorb Kim's calmness.

Andre blew her a kiss and stole away.

"First you must be completely dry, no oils or anything. Then put on a lot of dusting powder. Then you step into the slip and pull it up. You may wear a thong, but the dress works best with just the undergarment," Kim said, demurely turning her back for Abby's privacy.

Great. Now she tells me.

Abby considered putting on a thong, but with her luck and this thing, she'd likely have the Mother of all Wedgies at a State Dinner.

Abby skipped the underwear and dusted herself with scented powder. She stepped into the spandex creature. It behaved perfectly. Abby fiddled with the underwires and straps for a moment, and then all was well. She put the launch codes and thumb drive into the bra part.

"I think I am ready for the dress now, Kim," Abigail said, looking into the mirror. Her tummy was flat from crunches and spandex. The drape of the neckline would cover the launch code hardware in the bra part of her undergarment from hell.

Kim helped her into the dress and zipped up the side zipper. The side slit went nearly to the bottom of the zipper. The dress felt like a liquid silk, and Abby gasped at herself in the mirror.

I feel like the most beautiful woman in the world.

The midnight blue silk crepe draped beautifully at the wide neck-line. If it were an inch wider, it would fall off Abigail's shoulders. The dress was all but backless, with a true back cowl. Kim took out the dou-ble-sided tape.

"This way, nothing will show," she said, putting the double-stick tape in strategic locations.

Abigail put on her watch, signet ring and Edwardian shoulder-duster diamond and sapphire earrings. Everything was from Pris who called her antique jewelry "sparkling history."

Abigail again looked at her image in the full length mirror. *If you could only see me now, Pris. Perhaps, just perhaps, I can forget the Spandex Strangler and enjoy myself.*

"You are very lovely," Kim said. "Mr. Aston will be amazed."

"You made me lovely. The talent is all yours. And who is Mr. Aston?"

"He's your escort? Michael Aston? I met him on my way up. He is even handsomer than in his movies."

Abby all but stopped breathing. *Is Mikey's nephew "with the U.N." really my Hollywood fantasy lover inside the camera?*

Mikey Molloy, I swear, I swear I will get you for this one. Only you would send me on a blind date to a State Dinner with this year's Sexiest Man Alive.

CHAPTER TWENTY-SIX

THE PITY DATE

Kim went out into the Family Quarters. Abigail stood still, breathing in deeply through her nose and exhaling slowly through her stained and glossed mouth. She did this three times and opened the door. She should have been five minutes earlier.

"You cut that too close," Regina said. "The heads of state are on their way up."

Before a State Dinner, the President always receives the honorees upstairs for introductions and drinks. Abby had her family, plus O.T., Kim, the Lafayettes, as well as Marilyn Chernosky and Mikey with her. The group was just coming up as the protocol officer opened the door for them. The LeDucs, the Lopezes, and Michael Aston all entered.

Kim was right. If anything, Aston was better looking in person.

The protocol officer made the introductions.

"Welcome to the White House," Abigail said warmly to everyone except Aston. Her tone with him was chilly at best. Shaking his hand made butterflies flutter deep below her belly button.

She spoke French to Prime Minister LeDuc, who was from Quebec, and Spanish to President Lopez, and as little as possible to Mr. Aston.

"You look lovely tonight, Madam President, from the top of your head down to your sparkly red toenails. In Hollywood, you'd be called

'Oscar®-ready,'" Michael Aston said sincerely. *Of course he sounds sincere. He is an actor.*

"Thank you, Mr. Aston. I can really see the resemblance to your uncle," she said, lying through her teeth. Michael bore no resemblance to his elfin, once redheaded uncle. Aston was six-feet, four-inches of male grace, with hair graying at the temples and big brown eyes.

"Really? Uncle Mikey's my idol," Aston said. "That's a real compliment. And please, call me Michael."

The first ladies of Mexico and Canada, as well as Lynne Lafayette, were aflutter over Michael. This infuriated Abigail. She, in turn, was as flirtatious and charming with the heads of state as decency would allow, which was not much.

Lynne took Abigail aside and said breathlessly, "Don't you think he'd be wonderful as the Frenchman on the airplane in that Penny Royal book?"

"No, not really. He's so obviously American." Abby again was lying. He was the embodiment of the luscious man in the book. *What is the matter with me?*

"He is such a hunk. I cannot tell you how glad I am that I let my husband take this job," she giggled, returning to the other women clustered around him.

Mikey broke away, went to Abby's side, and kissed her fondly on her cheek.

"My dear, I fear I caught you off guard. I thought you knew who my nephew was," he said.

"I didn't hear his last name. Hitch called me out of the room. It will be fine."

This will put me in the tabloids. The last place I want to be.

"I just wanted you to have an escort worthy of you," Mikey said.

"You are a dear, Mikey. What would I do without you?" Abigail asked with an indulgent smile.

"Probably spend the evening with a drab man in a fancy uniform."

Abigail had to laugh.

Abigail asked Regina what she thought of being the prime mover of a State Dinner. She looked regal in a plum velvet gown.

"Folks can get used to 'bout anything. If my great, great grandmother could get used to being a slave, I guess I can get used to being the Official Hostess of the White House."

"And an excellent hostess you are," O.T. put in.

The White House photographer took a series of pictures upstairs. Lynne Lafayette looked like she might swoon at any moment when standing next to Michael. Abigail posed stiffly beside him and nearly jumped out of her skin when he placed his hand on the small of her back. His touch on her bare skin was electrifying. Thank goodness, he put his hands in front of himself in the next shot.

The problem was not the pictures upstairs; the problem was pictures downstairs. As Abigail was the first single female President, she did not want her escorts to appear in the pictures with heads of state. She might have different escorts for every party, and that wasn't very Presidential. *Actually, I don't want to look like a Presidential slut.*

The protocol officer communicated this to Mr. Aston, who graciously complied. "If I never see another camera, that's fine." He hung back as the five principals went down the stairs for the official photos.

The Marine Band played "Ruffles and Flourishes" and then "Hail to the Chief."

The five headed downstairs. Madame LeDuc all but yelled over the music, "Michael ees an international treasure. We must have heem in zee pictures," she commanded, reaching up and grabbing him by an arm.

Madame LeDuc was poured into a dress fit for a starlet. Unfortunately, she was old enough to be the starlet's grandmother. She was determined to have her moment of international fame in pictures. So Abigail bent to the will of her guests and smiled regally for photos of the six of them, not the five she thought proper.

National anthems out of the way, Abigail and Aston made their way into the East Room for cocktails.

"May I give you back to Mikey? He can introduce you around. I have a room to work and business to do," Abigail said. *I have got to get away from you.*

"Of course. I'll find you in time to escort you into dinner," Aston said amiably and disappeared. Abigail let her breath out and plunged into the crowd, her sparkling water in her left hand. No canapés for her, she couldn't risk spillage.

One of the first people to put himself in her path was T.J.

"Wow. You clean up good," he said. He reached for an air kiss, which she uncharacteristically allowed, even laughing.

"You're no slouch in a tux, yourself," she said flirtatiously. He quickly introduced his date, his aunt. She was a famous Canadian domestic diva. Feathers and sequins were her favorite things. Tonight, she managed to wear both.

"I'm so happy to be here, Madam President," she said with a square smile that showed most of her thirty-two teeth. "I told T.J. that if he brought one of his bimbos, I'd cut him out of my will."

"T.J. and I had quite a Middle East adventure when I was in the Senate. Unfortunately, it is still the 'Muddle' East," Abigail said, giving T.J. a conspiratorial smile.

"He said you were very impressive," his aunt said.

"Then I am truly flattered. T.J. is a hard man to impress," Abigail said, all but fluttering her eyelashes at him. *Why am I flirting with T.J.? We have no vibe.*

"So how 'bout sitting for an interview one day soon?" T.J. asked.

"I'm time-famished, but talk to Wicker. If you'll excuse me?" Abigail said, flashing them both a quick smile.

Then she turned clockwise to the next group. She chatted with Carlos Huerta about his favorite parts of Mexico.

"My sister loved the Costa Careyes," Abigail said.

"Lovely yes, but I think Quintana Roo has some beautiful beaches. The water is almost lavender off Playa del Carmen," he said.

Another turn and she saw Regina talking with Naomi, the talk show host and her husband, as if all were the best of pals. Abby said hello and then worked her way to the next group. She enjoyed the Canadian novelist. She'd worked her way through most of the guests when the dinner chimes rang, and Michael appeared at her side and offered her his arm.

"Madam President, may I have the honor?" he said, offering her his arm. She took it unwillingly.

I walk the halls of this house daily on my own, thank you very much, without the aid of an arm.

Then, as luck would have it, she caught a heel on a wrinkle in the red carpet. She faltered and stumbled slightly into him. His strong grip steadied her. She liked the feel of those biceps, but was mortified that her breast was the contact point.

Pride goeth before a fall.

Regina had done a spectacular job with the dining arrangements. Regina seated people with like interests from the three countries at each table, and their partners, elsewhere. People admired the candlelit room and found their seats easily.

The toasts were easy.

"To the two best neighbors on the planet. Welcome to the White House," Abigail said easily, lifting her flute of California champagne in the direction of the two leaders.

Each responded. Lopez's toast was warm; LeDuc's as warm as his chilly demeanor allowed.

The food was spectacular, but Abby pushed it around her plate. Somehow she wasn't hungry. Dinner went without a hitch, which was easy because Michael sat between the two first ladies at one table and Abby was between the two men at another table. Once Michael caught her eye and smiled at her. On impulse, she winked at him. *I winked at him?*

To cover her gaffe, she took the handkerchief and mirror out of her purse, and flicked away the nonexistent eyelash. When she looked back at him, he was still gazing at her. She took a long, long drink of ice water, hoping to quell one of her blushes. It didn't work very well. Her neck was quite warm.

President Lopez was funny and buoyant while LeDuc was reserved. However, by the time the entrée came, they were inviting each other for visits.

"You come to the Riviera Maya in February, escape the snow," Lopez said.

"And you can come to the Canadian Rockies in July to cool off," LeDuc countered.

"Hey, what about me? Don't I get an invitation?" Abby said with mock indignation.

"You can come, but you gotta leave that man, Aston, here," Lopez said. "My wife will leave me for him, and I won't be able to remember the names of my grandchildren. Without her, I couldn't even remember how many I have."

Abby told them the story of her blind date with the Sexiest Man Alive, and each thought it was hilarious.

"At least he didn't send a nephew with no chin," LeDuc said. "I once had a blind date who said not one word all night long." The three laughed heartily. North American relations were off to a good start.

"I wish I could have a date with the Sexiest Woman Alive," Lopez said wistfully. "Of course, my wife, she would kill me, and then I'd be back to the problem with the grandchildren."

Ten members of the Naval Academy Chorus entered unobtrusively and moved among the tables. They sang "Oh, Shenandoah," an American folk song, gliding easily into five-part harmony.

The guests clapped delightedly. Their next number was "Nessuna dorma," and the crowd went wild at opera, not only *a capella*, but completely surrounding them.

They closed with "Singing in the Rain," with two young men singing, and the other eight making the sounds of instruments from the cello to the bass to snare drums. Somehow, they even sounded like rain.

The heads of state asked to meet the singers, and Abigail was delighted to introduce them. She would send letters of commendation to their files at Annapolis.

Abigail and Michael led the group into the East Room for dancing. She excused herself and touched up her makeup. She did not want to dance with Michael Aston, but she couldn't figure out a way to get out of it. She headed back to face her fate.

Oh, well, there are worse things than dancing with the Sexiest Man Alive. I could dance badly. And likely, I will.

"Ah, here you are. Would you honor me with a dance, Madam President? I've never danced with a President before," Michael said.

"Mr. Aston, I am a terrible dancer," she said, all but wringing her hands. "I can start an intravenous line on a premature infant, and even a war, but dancing eludes me."

"Is that a 'no'?" he asked gently, his big brown eyes looking down into her baby blues.

Abigail took a deep breath.

"It's more of an 'I'll-try-but-only-if-the-floor-is-crowded-and-the-song-is-slow,'" Abigail said in a rush.

He laughed and smiled down at her. He had one dimple in his right cheek. *What causes dimples?*

"Then we share something. I trained for two months for a dance sequence in a movie. I was so awful, the crew was laughing out loud. The scene ended up on the cutting room floor," he said. Then he bent closer to her ear and whispered, "We can dance badly together."

Far from being relieved, his whisper sent goose bumps down that side of her entire body.

They took to the dance floor when the band played "Unchained Melody."

"Did you know this song was number one twice, twenty-five years apart?" she asked a little too brightly as she moved into his arms.

"Shhh," he pulled her closer. "I have to listen to the music, or I'll just start walking on your feet."

Abby shut up.

Without talk, sensations overtook her. The goose bumps, the feel of his toned body, the scent of a freshly groomed man, his thumb rhythmically rubbing the bare skin at the base of her back-less dress. Abigail's heart was pounding, and a million butterflies flitted below her belly button in a rhythm she'd never felt. She hoped he couldn't tell. Their bodies fit together perfectly, at least most of the time.

"Oops. Sorry. I stepped on your toe," he said.

"My fault. I always try to lead," she replied.

"Appropriate for a President," he said softly into her ear.

And then the song was over. Michael waited a moment before he let go of her hand.

Next Abigail danced with President Lopez and then with LeDuc. Abigail did not trust herself to stay any longer. She must, by protocol, leave first. Now was a perfect time.

She walked to the microphone.

"Thank all of you so very much for coming to the North American Block Party. Please stay, dance, and enjoy yourselves. Drink America's best wines. Tonight's a school night for me, so I'm going to say good night, *bonne nuit,* and *buenos noches.*"

"I'll see you gentlemen in the morning," she said to Prime Minster LeDuc and President Lopez.

"Ladies, I hear Regina and O.T. have a fun day planned for you," she said to the wives.

"It ees a shame Michael cannot join us," Madame LeDuc pouted.

"I'll be in sunny California. Otherwise, I'd be delighted," Michael said graciously.

"Good night, Mr. Aston," Abigail said. She offered her hand to shake.

"Thank you for including me in a State Dinner," he said. *His hands are so warm.*

When she turned toward the stairs, he followed her. She stopped.

"Shouldn't I at least see you to your door?" He was not going to let this woman get away.

"Thank you, no. The Secret Service does that." *Tongues would wag furiously if he went upstairs with her.*

"I'd like to see you again," he said.

"I'm on the news most nights," she said with a shrug. She started walking again. He walked by her side.

"Okay, let's try another tactic. May I send you flowers?" he asked.

"You have about as much chance of getting flowers into this building as getting a convent full of naked nuns into the Sistine Chapel," Abby replied, deadpan.

He laughed heartily.

"Okay. May I call you?" They were by now nearing the bottom of the stairs.

"The switchboard wouldn't put you through."

"You must have a private number." Abigail turned to face him directly. *Oh, are you gorgeous or what?*

"Please, Mr. Aston, don't think me rude, but my job takes all my effort and more. I truly don't have time for anything except work." Her tone was sincere, as was her statement. "I do hope you understand."

"Well, when…and if…you have the time, here is my card. My cell is on the back." He took a card from his pocket. She slipped it into her purse. Hopefully, no one noticed.

"Good night," she said, her Cinderella moment over long before midnight. Her agents indeed walked her up the stairs.

Keeping the presidency out of the tabloids is the right thing. But sometimes, doing the right thing sucks.

She was mentally writing lines for Wicker's use with the press corps by the time she kicked off her shoes.

The next morning, the three leaders met over coffee in the Oval Office. The first five minutes were a photo-op, and all three were having a good time. The cameras left, and the business started.

"Gentlemen, how can the United Stated be a better neighbor?"

She got an earful. Luckily, she had a pad and pen at hand. President Lopez led off.

"Your nation's appetite for illicit drugs is destroying my country. We are on the edge of anarchy, all because your people want to smoke marijuana and use cocaine. Then when my poor, honest people come to the U.S. to do honest work, you treat them like criminals. And most of the weapons the drug lords use come from the U.S.," Lopez said. The jolly man of the night before was long gone.

"I agree the money Mexican nationals send home is vital. I do not want to destabilize Mexico further. Remember, I am a Texan, so part of my soul is Mexican," Abigail said.

"Before, the Mexican government turned a blind eye to drugs for a small fee. I won't. We desperately need Americans to stop buying drugs. As well, the billions that come home from our people in America is the only thing keeping us afloat. We don't take jobs away from Americans— your people don't want them." He all but spat out the words.

"I agree."

"If Mexico becomes Colombia *norte*, you will have anarchy cross your border. It is ugly. We know. We live it daily."

"So what would you suggest?"

"Spend money on treatment of addicts, not interdiction. And make people ashamed to do drugs. Let them know they are killing my country with every joint they smoke. And when my country is dead, yours will be next."

Abby was taking copious notes. These pearls were going into the State of the Union message.

"Monsieur LeDuc, I would ask you the same question."

"Our border has always been porous and peaceful. What good is peace if we have to live like we are at war?" He too, was all business.

As predicted, Michael Aston was Topic One at the daily press briefing. Wicker kept it simple.

"President Adams's escort was the Academy Award® winning actor Michael Aston, who happens to be the nephew of her mentor, Mikey Molloy. The President thanks Mr. Aston for helping to make the evening such a success. No follow-up meetings are anticipated."

The story would not die. Their picture made the cover of *People* that week, and the article gushed at what a gorgeous couple they made. The only redeeming feature of the piece was that Kim was mentioned as her dress designer.

What's next? Composites of what our babies will look like?

Each day, someone asked if Michael Aston had called Abigail. Each day, Wicker gamely said the same thing, "He, like most of the attendees, wrote a lovely note."

The next week, one tabloid put their pictures on the cover under the banner headline, "He Hasn't Even Called."

Mikey was due at dinner that night. Abby hadn't seen him since the State Dinner and valued his input, even if he was complicit. This was a distraction, and Abby disliked devoting time to trivialities.

"Oh, dear Madam President, I fear I opened a can of worms for you," he said, bussing her on the cheek.

"It's not your fault, Mikey. I didn't catch his last name."

"He's quite smitten with you. He said he couldn't take his eyes off you all night."

Abby felt a sensation; those butterflies deep below her belly button were acting up again. *So that wasn't my imagination. Every time I looked at him, he was looking at me.*

"Mikey, I don't have the time. You of all people should know that. Besides, didn't he have a girlfriend who was a cocktail waitress?"

"Didn't you tend bar in med school?" Mikey asked.

"*Touché*," Abigail said. "But he would never have noticed me if I was just a doctor."

"Trust me, he would have noticed you," Mikey said, withdrawing an envelope from his jacket. "He asked me to deliver this to you."

The flutters reappeared. *Go away, whatever you are.*

"I'll open this later. Right now, I want to talk about the State of the Union speech. I'm thinking short and punchy, but I have been having some ideas."

"Remember, my dear, Americans get bored after three ideas."

Before Abigail got ready for bed, she put Michael's note on her nightstand to read just before she went to sleep. She was snuggled in and ready to open the note when someone rapped on her door three times.

"Ma'am, you're wanted in the Situation Room."

There goes the night.

Abby slid into the warm comfy things she kept for nights like this and was out the door in under sixty seconds.

CHAPTER TWENTY-SEVEN

ON THE BORDER

"Two Mexican drug cartels are having a shootout," the duty officer said.

"And how is that news?" Abigail asked, stretching sleepily.

"It's on our side of the border, ma'am."

"Oh. That *is* news." Abby grabbed water from the fridge.

"Downtown Laredo. Five Laredo police officers are dead, three Border Patrol dead, and no end in sight."

Abigail felt a stab of sadness.

"Screen up on Texas governor and Laredo mayor. Patch in Mexican counterparts. Who needs what? How can I help you?" Abigail asked as various video screens lit up with pictures of the Texas governor from his command center and the mayor in the emergency preparedness center in Laredo. The governor spoke first.

"I'm calling out the National Guard. That is, the units that are not in Afghanistan," the new governor said. *Another reason not to use back-up troops in a war of choice.*

"I'll declare a state of emergency in Webb County. I'm ordering the border sealed twenty miles in either direction of the International Bridge," Abby said.

Two phone trees activated. One automatically called all guards-men and the other ordered all border patrol personnel to appear and close border traffic.

"And you, Mr. Mayor? How can I help you?" Abby asked.

"We need all the firepower we can get. At least fifty guys are on each side, many with automatic weapons. They skirmish and then disap-pear into light industrial buildings all over the city."

"Governor, what about adding the Air National Guard? Nothing like a few helicopter gunships to ruin a crook's night," Abby said.

"So ordered," the new governor said. Another phone tree lit up. The closest ones were in San Antonio, less than an hour away.

"Better warn the news outlets. We don't need a midair helicopter collision." Abby couldn't ground them. *They'd go up just to fly their First Amendment rights.*

An aide to the mayor had all the news outlets on speed dial into the scanner rooms that monitor fire and police emergency radio traffic 24/7. They already knew what was up, but appreciated the safety warning.

"Let's talk with our Mexican counterparts."

Within a few moments, the mayor of Nuevo Laredo and the gov-ernor of Tamaulipas were patched in via audio. The President of Mexico appeared moments later, also on audio.

"We need to keep everyone off the streets," the mayor of Nuevo Laredo said.

"I'll do an emergency broadcast alert in English and Spanish," the mayor of Laredo said.

"Everyone okay with telling civilians to shelter in place?" Abigail asked. Everyone was.

"Oh, and tell them to stay off the phone, except in emergencies," Abby interjected, remembering the meltdown of her first day.

Something niggled her about drugs and Laredo. Laredo and Nuevo Laredo were really one city separated by a shallow river of economic opportunity. The Rio Grande was no barrier to the drug trade. Believing that drug violence was only a Mexican problem was a serious misjudgment by the United States.

It wasn't *if* the violence would cross the border, it was *when*.

Tonight was the night.

Abby suggested that police fall back until backup appeared. *Let the bastards kill each other until we can overwhelm them.*

Abby remembered the pardon request. She went up to the Oval Office and grabbed it. *Yes.* The woman was from Laredo. She hustled back to the Situation Room with it.

"Please get Maria Hernandez. She's in the women's federal prison in Bryan, Texas," Abby said to an operator.

In a very few minutes, a young Hispanic woman was on a video conference from the warden's office. She looked old for her years.

Abigail identified herself and told Ms. Hernandez she was on video in the Situation Room. "I'll consider your pardon, plus the witness protection program, for information," Abigail said, bringing her up to date.

Everyone was all ears, on both sides of the border.

"I'll tell you everything, but I need two things first," Maria said. "Get me out of this building. Two, get my mother and daughter in San Marcos someplace safe. Otherwise, we'll all three be dead before dawn."

Tough cookie.

"I can do that." Abby ordered the night warden to take Ms. Hernandez immediately out of the building.

"Okay. Where?" he asked. *Good question.*

"Take her to the governor's mansion in Austin. It's a two-hour drive. Make sure the phone in the car works."

"She can't come here," the governor spluttered. "I can't shelter a federal inmate here."

"Oh, relax. She won't be the first crook to ever spend the night in the building. The FBI will get her in the morning," Abigail said, laughing, and hoping she hadn't offended Maria.

The governor shook his head in defeat. Everyone else laughed, especially the Mexicans.

"Maria, give me your mom's address."

She rattled it off.

"Call her. Tell her the sheriff will be there within minutes. He'll take them to the governor's mansion in Austin."

Abigail watched as Maria called and spoke in rapid-fire Spanish. She was indeed telling the mother what Abigail said. *Nice being bilingual.*

The Texas governor gave the order to pick up the grandmother and child for the "felony sleepover."

"Leave now and call me from the car," Abby said, giving them the number. "You'll be patched through."

In five minutes, Maria called.

"There used to be one cartel for the Laredo market and supply line. Then they split."

"How do you know?" Abigail asked.

"One of the gangs is my brother Jorge's. The other is Jesse Hernandez's, my ex-boyfriend. There are cameras all along the border with pictures on the Internet. So my brother and my ex-boyfriend, when they were partners, came up with a system of tunnels that are outside the view of the cameras."

"But what about the river?"

"They found an engineer who could make a tunnel under the river itself. Like the Chunnel, about five feet in diameter. Several land tunnels feed into the river part."

"I see," Abigail said. *That wasn't cheap.*

"They kidnapped his family and returned them when it was complete. To make sure he didn't talk, they cut off one of the wife's fingers with a machete." People in the audience gasped. *Body parts are persuasive.*

"You know how old clotheslines work?" Maria continued. "On a continuous loop and pulley? That is how the drugs go across on a rolling platform. Guns go the other way."

Maria then listed six addresses on each side. Almost all tunnels went to and from warehouses, so truck movements wouldn't arouse suspicion.

"And the warehouse people?" Abigail asked.

"They know," she all but snorted. "If they say anything, their families die. Cooperate and they are paid in drugs, which they convert to cash. No one cares. Drugs come north. Weapons go south. Simple as pie."

Everyone was writing like mad. When the gunships arrived, the drug guys would forget about shooting each other and run back across the border.

Abigail spoke with President Lopez while Maria was being grilled further by people on the scene and in Austin.

"President Lopez? How are you with all this? I think they'll all head for Mexico."

"We call this a 'roach stomp.' You turn on the lights—they all scurry. You stomp as many as you can on your side. We stomp them on ours." He sounded weary and resigned.

"Good plan," Abigail said. "I don't know how many we will apprehend on our side."

"Apprehend no one, if you're smart." Lopez was blunt. "If they survive, they have their friends murder the judges, the jurors, the prosecutors, anyone else they like. This is their first incursion. If you do not show massive strength, they will only grow bolder."

"I see." Abigail knew that only three federal judges had ever been murdered in the United States. In Mexico, drug cartels murdered over a thousand police and judges in recent years; thirty thousand people in all had died in the drug wars, many "collateral damage."

Abigail relayed Lopez's remarks to the governor and mayor.

"Christ, that's brutal," the governor said.

"What is? Killing the drug guys or having judges, prosecutors, and jurors killed?" Abby asked of the mayor and governor on video conference.

"Both," the governor said.

"Mr. Mayor?" Abigail asked.

"The Mexican President is right. The best outcome is to chase them into the tunnels and let the Mexicans deal with them."

"I'll back you up on whatever plan you have. Governor?" Abigail said to the two men.

"Let's draw the line here. We'll order people to surrender once in each language. If they don't, we'll shoot to kill. As well, any fire will be returned with lethal force," the governor said.

The mayor concurred. So did Abigail.

Abby heard the gunships arrive at the warehouse locations. They gave one warning in rapid-fire English and Spanish to drop the weapon and surrender. If they did not comply, guardsmen shot to kill. Many men headed back into Mexico, where the *federales* mowed them down as they emerged.

The bulk of the warfare was finished by 5 a.m. Those who hadn't heard the raging battle awakened to bloody but peaceful streets.

No sense going to bed, so Abby went to dress for the day.

Michael's note was still waiting for her. She'd forgotten it. *At least some sweetness followed a bitter night.*

He had made a greeting card. On the front, he had drawn a bouquet of yellow roses. *Hmm, well done drawing.* She opened it.

"I am sending you flowers the only way I can. Michael."

CHAPTER TWENTY-EIGHT

STATE OF THE UNION

Abigail dressed and returned to the Situation Room.

The fighting long since over, now they were assessing the damage. By ten, the numbers were in.

U.S. fatalities included one Air National Guardsman killed by hostile fire, as well as five Laredo police officers and three border agents. Forty drug cartel members died on the U.S. side, forty-seven on the other. Perhaps autopsies would shed light on who killed them. Maria's brother and ex-boyfriend were among the dead. According to Maria, each group limited itself to fifty members. So somewhere, thirteen men were still at large. No doubt, they would pick up the business where the others left off.

The two nations confiscated one hundred tons of drugs, a million dollars in U.S. cash, and four thousand weapons, mostly automatics. All Laredo warehouse owners were in custody. Abby would throw the biggest book she had at them. She and President Lopez agreed to fill in the tunnel system with cement. It was too risky to leave it open.

Maria, her mother, and daughter had a tearful reunion at the governor's mansion, where the governor's wife treated them as her guests.

"They've been up most of the night. Let them get their sleep," she told the FBI agents when they showed up at seven. Then she smiled, "But I've got homemade biscuits and coffee in the kitchen."

The nation saw Laredo as a dramatic gun battle, straight out of the Old West. The right wing cheered the massive show of force. No one discussed turning a U.S. city into a war zone. Abigail was incredibly sad at the loss of life and at the violation of U.S. territory by such despicable people. *If we buy it, they will come.*

Abigail decided her State of the Union Speech would be on Laredo. She kept the speech simple and short with references to the website for greater detail. No one had seen the speech, and she took the copy for the teleprompter with her.

On Tuesday night, she dressed purposefully for the occasion, now without even thinking. She chose a dusty blue, shawl-collar suit accessorized by an antique eagle pin on her right shoulder. She wore blue baroque pearl earrings. She packed her bag perfectly. Regina and the others had gone on ahead. She would travel only with the Secret Service, tonight in the lead car but sheltered from view. Her look-alike rode two cars back and waved a black-gloved hand to any bystanders in the frigid night.

The Secret Service inserted her into the House of Representatives with military precision. Albright even planned a stop in the ladies' room before she went into the House chamber.

Oddly enough, she had never been in the House of Representatives. To walk in as a leader, to speak to the Supreme Court, both houses of government, and a packed gallery gave her enormous focus.

She didn't choose this, but she must do her duty.

"The President of the United States," the sergeant at arms said loudly.

As usual, the aisle hogs were jostling for television coverage. Cordelia Laurus greeted Abby like an old friend for the cameras. Everyone was standing and applauding. Abby reminded herself that they were applauding the office, not the woman in it.

She looked up into the gallery. She saw Regina, Duke, Kim, and OT, as well as Poppy and Chaffee. Mikey looked as pleased as punch.

She thought that she caught a glimpse of Pris, but when she blinked, her sister was gone.

You are standing on the shoulders of giants. Take your place. This is no accident. Her sister's voice was clear as day.

Abby quieted the crowd and began simply.

"Article II, Section 3 of the Constitution requires that the President give Congress information on the state of the union from time to time. I have been in service to you, the American people, for only two months. You have been patient and kind, and I thank you for that.

"I am only your servant. The true power is within all three hundred million of you. Whatever enough of you want, it will happen. Your power is enormous. I am but your servant.

"As I learned in the practice of medicine, we are more alike than we are different. Most people want the same things: peace, a better life for our kids, and a fair shake in life's dealings. Someone once said that America is not a place, it is an idea. And this wonderful idea is threatened not only from without by terrorists, but from within by our appetite for illegal drugs.

"Tonight I want to concentrate on Laredo and how we need to change our national focus on illicit drugs."

Abigail recapped the events. Then she read the names of the dead peace officers and showed their pictures. The audience was suitably grave at this.

"Days earlier, President Lopez of Mexico told me that only three federal judges in the U.S. have ever been killed. In Mexico, a nation with a third our population, it's a thousand. One town in Mexico has no police force because the drug lords killed so many officers, the rest resigned.

"In Laredo we confiscated one hundred tons of drugs and over four thousand weapons, many automatic or semiautomatic, and all made here in the U.S. of A.

"Where drugs are concerned, Mexico is not the problem—*we* are the problem."

Abby expected and got an audible gasp.

"Drugs are a demand business. If demand ceased tomorrow, the drugs would stop the day after. Ponder that for a moment. Everyone close your eyes. Imagine your neighborhood untouched by drugs.

Smash and grab burglaries virtually disappear. Why? Those thieves are stealing to support a habit. Look, too, at serious crimes. Many of those are drug related. Remove the demand for drugs, and that crime vanishes. Your tax money can go from prisons to parks.

"Imagine you fall and break your wrist. You have to go to the emergency room. Thirty percent of ER visits are drug related. Remove the demand for drugs, and you won't have to wait in the ER.

"Imagine drivers who are high. Remove the demand for the drugs, and innocent people get home in one piece instead of going to the grave.

"If every current drug user spent that time helping his community, imagine your neighborhood park. It would be full of children playing and old people reading the paper. And the only person to suffer would be the drug lord.

"Finally, imagine all the family dinner tables without an empty chair. Imagine those lost to overdoses, to drugged drivers, to drug-related murders, to incarceration, to drug-related drive by shootings."

Abby paused to let that comment sink in. People opened their eyes, and saw the problem with them.

"Lately, the idea of legalizing drugs has resurfaced as a way to raise taxes and remove the criminal element. I respectfully disagree. This is not your father's border. These drug lords are shadow nations unto themselves, complete with armies, and with economic clout greater than many real nations. If you think they'll meekly fill out tax forms and give the IRS money, you are smoking some serious stuff."

That too got a good laugh.

"Marijuana is more potent and addictive than ever. Frequent marijuana users often don't have much get up and go. Many work just enough to pay for their habit. And if there weren't millions of them, why would we have movies about stoners?

"How many of you know a family in which someone has a drug problem? Go ahead, raise your hands." Abby saw a sea of raised hands. "Do you really want it easier for them to stay stoned?"

Abby was shocked by a loud and vehement "NO."

"Marijuana is a gateway drug for many. Heroin comes from opium poppies. Opium poppies grow in Afghanistan, and much of that money goes to the Taliban and Al Qaeda, our enemies. We pay the people who want to destroy us. Do you really want that?"

"NO." the chamber said in unison.

"Our use of illicit drugs is a threat to our national security.

"One thing our current system has done is truly despicable. When rich white kids get into trouble with drugs, they go to rehab. When poor minority kids do the same thing, they go to prison. That's despicable."

She got a standing ovation. The first people on their feet had the darkest skin.

"So if you do drugs, your behavior was behind the deaths of those peace officers in Laredo. How many more people will die for your high? Take home that message and drum it into your children. Teenagers pretend not to listen, but they do.

"Mexico is teetering. If we cut demand, Mexico can make it. If we don't, we will push them into anarchy. The other night, anarchy crossed our border. Keep up our demand, and anarchy will move in permanently.

"The tunnel under the river was built by an engineer in Mexico. The cartel didn't pay him. They kidnapped his family until he finished the job. Then the cartel leader made him watch while he cut off the wife's finger with a machete to keep him silent. You really want guys like that here?"

She got another resounding "NO."

"So the drugs flow north, and the guns go south. We are arming the cartels. How crazy is that? What can the government do?

"I'm ordering the ATF to review how guns in this country are accounted for as they move from manufacturer to end user. We will stop the flow of arms to cartels. We will tighten and enforce laws against illegal export of guns. Oh, federal prisons don't have parole, so gunrunners, be afraid. Be very, very afraid.

"The same system that controls marijuana and heroin, also controls selling controlled substances to recreational and addicted users.

"I am ordering the FDA to strengthen auditing controls, so that controlled substances cannot get diverted from manufacturer to illicit use. I will ask Congress for legislation if necessary.

"In 2010, we spent fifteen billion dollars on the war on drugs. Interdiction alone doesn't work. Everything the government does is a drop in the bucket compared to what you, my bosses, do.

"We, as a nation, must cut demand. If you use any recreational drugs, stop. Go flush your stash. Delete your dealer from your speed dial. Otherwise, the bad guys with the automatic rifles will be at your door eventually. Stopping recreational use decreases your chances of addiction. Want to kick back after a hard day? Try meditation, learn yoga, read a book or volunteer somewhere.

"Parents, clean out your medicine chests, as this is where most kids start on drugs. Tell everyone living in your home that it is *your* home and it *will* be free of illicit drugs. Advise your teens, even young adults, that you are going to go through their rooms and the cars you own, so they'd best flush the stash before you find it. Give them an hour and don't let them leave the house. Then follow through. We even have a "hidey-hole" check list at www.drugs.gov. It will help you in your search.

"Secondly, don't be an enabler. Stop making excuses for the drug abusers in your family and neighborhoods."

Applause again broke out.

"Since the beginning of time, life's been hard. That's not an excuse.

"I am not naïve. I know addiction is real. We'll explore ways to increase addiction treatment. If an addict wants help, he or she should be able to get it easily and cheaply. Treatment is far, far cheaper than either continued use or incarceration.

"If you can't quit, get help. The drugs.gov website lists treatment options by zip code. Don't have a computer? Go to the library and look it up for free. See a doctor, join a twelve-step group, get involved in your community. Busy people don't have the time for drugs.

"Boycott the work of entertainers who use drugs. You're financing their habits, and their habits endanger our national security.

"This is your country, and what you do matters. I am just your servant.

"I will leave you with the words of poet and wise woman Maya Angelou, 'When you know better, you do better.'

"Please, don't let the deaths of the good men in Laredo be in vain. Good night."

CHAPTER TWENTY-NINE

THE CHARM OFFENSIVE

Abby feared she sounded like a scolding nanny, but she smiled through the thunderous applause. She vetoed any idea of an after-party. Poppy showed her only negative reviews. The folder had two in it, and they weren't major papers.

Good. At least the major papers didn't hate it.

Her Real People's Cabinet liked it. "About time shame reappeared for screw-ups," the florist said. "I'm sick and tired of hearing excuses about my neighbor's son's multiple run-ins with the law, all fueled by drugs, alcohol, or both."

The Intern Cabinet liked it. "We'd never seen recreational drug use as bad. Sometimes dumb, but not morally wrong."

Mikey scanned the Mexican papers. "If you don't want to be POTUS you could be POM." *President of Mexico.*

President Lopez called her with thanks. "Finally, someone gets it. But you must watch your back—the drug lords do not like your words."

"Thank you." Abby passed that on to Albright. He added them to his ever-growing worry list.

The Charm Offensive was going well. At the reception for new members of Congress, each had to supply a baby picture. Regina put together booklets of ten pictures. The first person to identify all ten correctly got his or her choice of gift.

People peered into each other's face looking for the baby inside from decades earlier, not seeing a Republican or a Democrat. The most macho new Senator was an infant in a dress and ringlets.

Washington parties are a notoriously dull extension of a dull day. Not so after the Congressional reception. When people left, they were happy and relaxed, having started on friendships begun in nonpolitical laughter. Abigail was thrilled.

The gifts, too, were a hit. The winter scarf was a work of art. Kim painted snowy tree branches with cardinals on a navy background. The magnetic pin was a red fabric camellia. The winter snow globe played "My Country 'Tis of Thee." And the tie was American Flag Red with tiny bald eagles all over it, one row looking right, and the next, left.

Everyone knew that Abigail paid for the gifts, and in a town where no public servant ever picked up a tab for anything, that gave them real cachet.

Of course, the pins carried a warning for pacemaker wearers. It would be poor form to kill a voter. A stickpin could puncture a lung, but no one ever worried about old, well-known risks.

The soul food nights were the most coveted invitations. Every Thursday night, Abby, Regina, and the Lafayettes had ten lucky people up to the Family Quarters for the menu of Regina's choosing. Regina picked the guest list from the goldfish bowls.

This was no free lunch. At least three people had to enter the talent contest.

People would do virtually anything for Regina's friend chicken, fried okra, black-eyed peas, and lemon meringue pie, so people stepped forward.

A White House correspondent could type with his toes. One snow globe went home with him. The head of the NSA could play the spoons on water glasses. That went poorly, in large part because Abby squirted vodka into the water and the pitch was all wrong. He got a tie just for being a good sport. And the Senate Majority Leader, Chuck Schwartz, played a mean harmonica. His wife insisted on a scarf, which she wore home.

Once a month, they had a New American Artist night. The artists submitted samples of their work, and a committee from the National Gallery and the Kennedy Center chose the artists. The artists got twenty invitations. The goldfish bowls produced another eighty, and soon the White House merited its own column in *American Art*. Careers took off.

Abby had less time for herself, but she projected an image of youthful vigor. It was apparent that she required no man at her side to have a good time. She jogged in all sorts of weather, played tennis, and continued her workouts. She gave in to Wicker and became a poster child for physical fitness and a healthy lifestyle.

In late January, Layla, Marilyn and Cristo joined Abby in the Oval Office for another meeting on Operation Women in Flight.

Layla had scheduled her entire series of conferences on Women in Afghanistan. She'd already done two, one in Jordan, the other in Turkey. A thousand women registered at each, giving Layla a roster for later helpers. She was ready to go in countries ranging from Algeria to Indonesia.

"My friends tell me virtually all of the women in Afghanistan are clinically depressed. Many literally have no identity. Your legal name might be 'Billy's Mom.' And when you plunge them into poverty and fight a war around them, they are overwhelmed. Plus, the Taliban insist they 'submit.' These women are slaves to their husbands and in-laws, both of whom beat them at will. The men might not mind losing their daughters, but losing their sons would be an incredible insult."

"Wow, don't sugar coat it," Abigail said.

"And if their wives flee, they'll enslave new ones."

That did it for Abby. She'd kill them in their beds. They were a legitimate enemy of the U.S. military. All wives of Taliban and Al Qaeda, as well as female children, would be encouraged to emigrate.

The four agonized over taking boys. Young ones would be welcome, but no country wanted older boys who might already be on the path to extremism. Finally, the four settled on taking boys seven and under. Any boy eight or over would have to be left behind. This tore at Abby's heart, but it had to be done.

"Once they are out, where can they go?" Marilyn asked. "Would men in progressive Muslim countries allow their wives to help?"

"In progressive Muslim countries, women have plenty of power. They are just very selective in how they use it," Layla said. "If they want to take in the Afghan women, they will make it happen."

"With the President's permission, I approached the Aussies. They've wanted to stick it to Al Qaeda since the Bali bombings," Marilyn said. "They've offered a base in Northern Australia. We'll get it ready. They know only that it will be crucial to the destruction of Al Qaeda and the Taliban."

"Fantastic. That simplifies the air operation." Cristo gave Marilyn a high five. "I need numbers, though."

Abigail spoke up. "There are maybe two thousand Al Qaeda and fifty thousand Taliban total. Assume three wives each, that's one hundred and fifty thousand women. Assume each brings two children, we're talking roughly a half a million people. Very roughly."

Cristo had time to stockpile jet fuel. He could also produce enough women from all the services who were Muslim, Arab-American or olive skinned to be "shepherds." More importantly, he could give them language and cultural training for a mission "unspecified."

"Good. The easiest way to spread the word is on market days. The shepherds can blend in at market, starting a month before D-Day," Layla said. "They shadow the vendors who travel from town to town. They can give the women a different message each week."

Cristo started rough calculations, "A half-million in seven days, with five hundred passengers per plane, is six take-offs per hour, round the clock.

"We can do it," he said, pausing, "if we borrow a few planes from the Aussies."

The women breathed deeply. That many people in one plane was possible, but not ideal. *Think flying sardines. Of course, the women wouldn't have flown before...*

"We have a hundred C5 Galaxies total. I'll order passenger conversion kits for those without them. We'll put them in Diego Garcia and around Afghanistan the week before," Cristo said. Abigail agreed.

"No question the logistics will be tight, but we can do it," Cristo assured the women.

"Now, about their stipend. We've settled that it will go with the woman into her bank account, but where do we get the money and how much should we give them?" Abby asked.

"I'm having trouble with figures, so I'm estimating five thousand dollars per woman per year for five years if they go to a poor country. That's roughly $1.25 billion over five years. The war is costing us two hundred million a day. That's six days of warfare. At twenty grand, that's twenty-five days of warfare."

"That's a helluva bargain if it will end the war," Cristo said.

"If it doesn't, it's at least given slaves their freedom. Beats forty acres and a mule," Abigail opined.

"Don't forget that my women will come through also," Layla said.

"Can these women support themselves after five years?" Marilyn asked.

"I think so," Layla said. "Even as widows, they can work as hairdressers, seamstresses. You forget, some women in Afghanistan were pharmacists, doctors, teachers. Many have skills."

"Do you really think progressive Muslim countries will take them if we, the infidels, have lured them out?" Abigail was playing devil's advocate.

"Yes, I do. The entire Muslim world is afraid of the Taliban and Al Qaeda. Moderate nations would love for someone else to destroy them both," Layla said.

"As well, we have nearly three hundred thousand Afghans in the U.S. I predict they'll sponsor many after the operation is complete," Marilyn said.

"We cannot speak one word to any man in Afghanistan, or this operation will turn into a bloodbath," Abby said. "Marilyn, call the people in Houston. We took in a quarter of a million Katrina refugees with one day's notice. I know they made a playbook for future use," Abigail said.

They had just over four months.

CHAPTER THIRTY

AWAY ALONE

As February neared its end, Abigail felt the sad anniversary of Pris's death. She might have visited her grave, but could not in good conscience put Air Force One in the air for that. A one-day turnaround would cost the taxpayers something like two million dollars, over seventy grand an hour just for Air Force One's fuel. That was just for the first plane. A second plane flew in with the limo, helicopter, etc. *Ridiculous.*

Instead, she wanted a weekend at the penthouse. She needed to be a bum, and that was hard, even in the family quarters of the White House.

"You want to go alone?" Regina asked.

"Yep, I think I do," Abigail said.

"Well, then that is exactly what you should do," Regina said. "Let General Lafayette take your calls for a weekend."

"I hadn't thought of that. Reege, you're a genius," Abby said.

"You are a slow learner if you're just now figuring that out," Regina said with an indulgent smile.

Hitch, the football and launch codes went with Abigail. She did the PDB via teleconference. She would return to the White House if Lafayette went to the Situation Room. With Marine One, she could come and go in ten minutes.

The Lafayettes spent the weekend at the White House with Regina. Abby went home for a rest cure on Friday night.

Hitch and the Secret Service camped out in the utility room and the kitchen. They locked the front elevator. Abby ordered in enough junk food for a week for everyone and insisted they get whatever they wanted from room service. Who wanted room service when Abby stocked the place with chips, dips, Twinkies, Ding Dongs, and Little Debbies?

The guys loved their two-day poker marathon. It would have been better with beer and cigars, but they were on the clock.

Abby would pad to the kitchen in her jammies and robe. She thought it was funny that her kitchen contained armed men playing poker. Of course, guys rotated in and out, but hey, a shift away from either the hive of the White House or the chores at home was a great gig. Funny, neither Sally nor Debbie Taylor asked for a shift.

"I'm not getting out of my robe and pajamas. So deal with it," she said on one of her forays into the kitchen. "I'm eating junk food, sleeping, and streaming chick videos to my room."

"Hey, 'bout time," one agent said. "My wife does this one day a week. She says God commands her to take a day off." Then he chuckled. "But let me try it …"

Abby had the new Penny Royal book on her Kindle. Poppy smuggled in the latest tabloids, her closest approach to a true vice. *I'll shred them before I leave.*

For dinner, she had two root beer floats and was asleep by eight. She slept through the night. Her eyelids popped open at five for her work out, and then they gently drifted back down when she realized she had two whole days when Susan could not torture her. She awoke for good about 9 a.m., feeling like a new woman. The PDB didn't bother her, in part, because she was eating a root beer float for breakfast and seeing it via video conference. She was visible from the neck up as she was still in her pajamas *I know as much in my pj's as I do in a suit.*

She decided to indulge herself. Instead of her usual two-minute shower, she dry brushed her skin to rid it of dead winter skin, then used up a whole tube of body scrub, and then rinsed in the shower. Finally, she soaked in her sister's jetted tub for a good long while. She thought of having a massage, but that was "off plan." Albright would have a cow.

Instead, she put conditioner into her wet hair and left it. Then she slathered herself with cream and read the latest Penny Royal book. The Frenchman on the airplane figured prominently in this title too. *Damn. She didn't need to be reminded of Michael.*

Her BlackBerry rang at two. It sent a jolt to her heart. *I've been caught. I just know someplace has been invaded.*

"Abigail, my dear, I do hope I am not disturbing you," Mikey said.

"No, not at all. What's up?" Abigail said.

"Would you consider joining an older man for dinner? I am feeling rather low."

Abigail thought quickly. Going to Mikey's was too much trouble. A cross-town jaunt ties up traffic for an hour. Plus, it's too late to schedule with Albright.

"Anything special making you low?" Abigail asked. *I hope he's not getting sick.*

"No, this is my wedding anniversary. I know it's a sad time for you, too. I thought we could commiserate."

"Sure. But let's do it here, if you don't mind getting out in this weather. We can play some Scrabble. Shall we say seven?" Abby felt guilty either way. Either she would tie up traffic or send an old man into an icy, snowy night. *I hate this job sometimes.*

"Seven it is." Mikey rang off, wondering whether Abigail would kiss him or kill him.

Abby had little to do to get ready except wash out the conditioner, dry her hair, order some flowers for the house, and pick out something to wear. Casablanca lilies had been a favorite of her sister, so she had the florist send up a generous bouquet for the entryway. They would please Mikey.

It had started to snow as Abigail dressed. She had brought nothing appropriate, but found a set of cornflower blue cashmere sweats and matching slippers that Pris gave her their last Christmas. Perfect for a winter's night indoors. And almost a perfect match for her eyes.

The utility room refrigerator held plenty of wine, even champagne. She pulled out the champagne and put it into a champagne bucket with ice. It needed drinking. Champagne does not improve with age. *No sense wasting it.*

"Sorry, guys, none for you. Mikey's coming at seven," Abby said.

"That's fine with us," Hitch said. "I need my wits about me. I'm down two hundred bucks." The guys even kept the kitchen halfway clean, emptying the trash when it filled up with junk food wrappers.

The sleet changed to fat snowflakes, and Abigail felt a real sense of peace. She was wrapped in clothes from her sister. She was doing a job her sister would be proud of, and she was luxuriating in the home her sister made. Somehow, she felt grief falling away from her.

Just before seven, she spritzed on some perfume and brushed out her dry hair, parting it the way Andre had showed her. It actually behaved. She put on earrings and a little makeup. She found the Scrabble game and set it up on the game table.

The agents alerted the reception desk to send up the penthouse guest, and they unlocked the front elevator. The front desk created a single-use key. They put the guest in the elevator and barred anyone else from entering. The guest whisked to the penthouse, alone.

The Secret Service agent checked his identity, logged it into his book, wanded, and patted him down in the vestibule. He also inspected the flowers from the building's florist.

Then he allowed the guest to ring the doorbell.

Abigail was coming from the kitchen, wiping her hands on a dishtowel.

"Hi, Mikey," she said, smiling widely and opening the door.

Michael Aston stood in the doorway, holding a large, gorgeous bouquet of white roses.

He had snowflakes in his hair.

CHAPTER THIRTY-ONE

THE SWITCH

"Gee, nobody's called me Mikey in a while," he said with mischief in his eyes. "But you may, if you like."

Abigail stood glued to the floor, speechless. At the security lapse. At Mikey. At the raw good looks of the man in front of her. At the extravagant bouquet of white roses. *When was the last time a man brought me flowers?* She couldn't remember.

She opened her mouth to say something, and then having nothing to say, she shut it again. *I look like a goldfish having a drink.*

"May I come in?" Michael asked, looking down into her baby blues with his big browns.

Abigail took a deep breath.

"Yes. Yes, of course, do come in," she said, stepping to the side of the doorway.

"These are for you, though the white lilies in the entry are gorgeous," Michael said, handing her the flowers and flicking the snow out of his more-pepper-than-salt hair.

"Thank you," Abby said, taking the flowers and inhaling their fragrance. "These even have a scent, rare in flowers from a florist."

"Yep, it seems that they do," Michael said, now fully a foot inside the apartment. "I've deceived you, and I'm sorry, but I couldn't wait until you left office. I promise I'm tame. Your Secret Service guy patted me down." He opened his top coat to show he was unarmed. Underneath he was wearing charcoal flannel pants, a white shirt, and a yellow cashmere V-neck sweater. He'd even shined his tassel loafers. *I'm a sucker for tasselled loafers.*

"I'm not big on surprises," Abby said. *What? The most gorgeous man on the planet shows up when I look and feel fantastic?*

"Please don't be mad at Uncle Mikey. I put him up to this. I've wanted to see you again."

"So now you have." Her voice was flat.

Michael raised his hands in surrender. "If you want me to leave, just say so. I'll go." He was sincere. *I can't let this man go.*

"No, no, please, let me take your coat," Abigail said, remembering her manners.

She kicked the door to the vestibule shut as she put his coat in the closet. *I am going to own these agents. They let a perfect stranger into my home. Well, he has better face recognition than I do. Still it was a breach… unless, of course, they were in on it. Those rat bastards.*

"I was going to open some champagne. I can't guarantee it's still good," Abigail said, heading toward the kitchen with the flowers. Michael followed her, admiring the back view. *This woman is in shape*, he thought.

The poker game stopped while the guys stood and introduced themselves to Michael. Abby felt like she had four armed and dangerous older brothers for chaperones.

"I'll just put these in water," she said. "Let me go get a vase."

One more agent was in the utility room where she kept the vases.

"I hear the wrong Mikey showed," he said. "You okay with that?"

"Yeah, I guess. If he's half the gentleman his uncle is, I'm fine," Abigail said.

"Don't forget the panic button in your left earring. Tug it and the nearest agent comes running."

"I had forgotten," she tugged it and the agent's beeper vibrated and pulsed with red lights.

"See?" he said.

Abby retrieved a vase and filled it with the flowers and water. She carried the vase and flowers into the living room, while Michael took the champagne and glasses.

"I'll open the champagne," Michael said, rolling up his sleeves and sweater. *Damn, this man looks good. He even has handsome forearms. And his hands are gorgeous, not hairy. Clean, trim, but not manicured.* He twisted the cork, and it popped loose with a sigh. He poured them both a glass two-thirds full.

She tasted it. "It seems fine to me."

Michael sipped his. "Still wonderful. Has another two or three years in it yet."

"Nice to know I don't have to drink it all in a few days," she laughed.

She put the roses in the middle of the coffee table. They had arranged themselves into a lovely bouquet. *How do they do that? Grocery store flowers don't.*

She offered him some simple appetizers she'd already set out, along with some monogrammed cocktail napkins. Michael raised his eyebrows at the letter "L."

"My sister's. This was her home until she died of cancer. Last year, about this time."

"I'm very sorry," Michael said simply.

"Her death changed my life."

"I know," he said.

She stiffened. *How dare he presume to know my feelings?*

"I lost my little sister to leukemia," Michael continued. "She was six. I was ten."

"Oh, how awful for you." Abigail was genuinely shocked. And at that moment, Michael Aston stopped being the Sexiest Man Alive and started being her friend.

"Yes. It still is. I have this fairy-tale life, and she didn't even get to finish first grade. All she ever got to be was my little sister."

Abigail raised her glass, her eyes brimming with tears. "To absent sisters."

Their glasses touched, and they drank to their shared history.

"Would you like the tour?" she asked, to break the moment of sadness.

"Sure. I'm betting this is the living room, right?" he asked.

"I think so. I can't be sure, but we've been in the kitchen and through the dining room, so I think you're right." She showed him around the apartment, but wouldn't let him see her room.

"Why not?" he teased.

"It's a mess," she said, blushing. *The tabloids are out on the bed. I'd die if you saw that I read them.*

"Besides," Abby continued, "it's really just a guest room. Pris's room is the pretty one." She took his hand and pulled him toward Priscilla's domain. She liked the feel of his hand. He was pleased she had touched him. He knew to let her come to him.

"Ooh, a Corot," he said of the painting over the bed. "One of my favorites. He actually did an etching of my home in Italy, but I've never been able to buy it."

"He liked to paint in Italy, didn't he?" Abigail asked.

"Yes, but mostly northern Italy and France. Sargent loved all of Italy and did a ton of watercolors there. You're something of an art buff, I hear." Michael turned the conversation back to her.

"Who wouldn't be, living in the White House?" Abby asked. "John Singer Sargent painted Teddy Roosevelt's White House portrait."

"Well, I can name a few Presidents who wouldn't know that."

"Their loss," Abby said.

"Mikey says you are incredibly diverse in your intellect," Michael said.

"I'm a trivia buff. Thanks to Mikey, I'm actually learning, though he wants me to read tomes. I'm using *The Last Lion* about Churchill to prop open my bathroom door."

"Yeah, sounds like Mikey. Me? I just did an internet search on Churchill and faked it," Michael said.

"Really? Me too," Abigail said, throwing back her head and laughing.

He reached over and whispered into her ear. "If you don't stop laughing, I'm going to have to kiss you. And we haven't even had dinner."

He was perilously close to the panic-button earring.

Again, the goose bumps ran down that side of her body. And a blush crept up from her neck to her hairline. She was all of a sudden very, very warm in her cashmere sweats. The butterflies were rioting due south of her belly button.

"I'm going to crack the door to the balcony," she said, slipping away from him.

She opened the door, and they watched the fat, fluffy flakes fall through the soft night sky. Michael was standing behind her, and she dared not turn around.

"Michael, would you back up a little, please?"

"Sure." He did. Abby turned to look at him.

"My life is not my own right now, Michael."

"I know," he said. "I'm hungry. I thought you were going to feed me."

They ordered from room service. Michael disappeared when room service brought up the order. Abigail signed for it, and when the coast was clear, he came out of the powder room.

"I feel bad hiding and making you pay for dinner," he said. "I'm not that kind of guy."

"You *should* feel bad. You weren't even invited," she replied, laughing.

They talked of various subjects over dinner. Normal things, current events, books they'd both read, favorite artists, what they liked to do for fun.

"I don't have a lot of fun right now," Abigail said. "Don't get me wrong. I do some neat things. They're just not play. Unless of course, you count boxing."

"You box?" he said, putting down his fork in surprise.

"Yes, with my trainer in mitts or on the heavy bag. It's great for a bad mood."

"Well, I'll be damned. Here I was thinking you were some sort of girly girl and you box?"

"My trainer is a woman who is five-foot-three and taught martial arts at West Point."

"Whooh. Remind me never to tick you off," he said with admiration.

"And you, what's fun for you?" she asked.

"Oh, during the day, I like to be outside. I play lots of hoops, touch football, tennis, love to take the boat out, or in winter, I ski. Do you ski?"

"Yes, but not now," Abigail said. "A skiing accident put me here."

"After dinner, I love to read. I can't function without my Kindle," Michael said.

"Me, too. I was antsy when the White House IT guy took it away for a day."

Neither could tell you what they had for dinner, but both thought it was delicious.

"Mikey said something about Scrabble. Are you up for a game?" Michael asked after dinner.

"Sure," Abigail said, grateful for something that would keep him here, but not too close.

They agreed to play with a timer and the dictionary. Michael could tell she was a serious opponent.

He trounced her, in no small part because he had a seven-letter word that ended on a triple word score.

"You've done this before," Abigail said with a laugh.

"I was weaned on Scrabble. My mom and Mikey are both cutthroats."

"You outplayed me," Abigail said graciously. "I lost fair and square."

"May I ask you something?" he said, taking another sip of the champagne. Abigail noticed he was not much of a drinker. *That's good.*

"I might not answer, but you may ask."

"Would you please come with me to the Oscars®?" he said. His gaze was steady on her face. "I'm nominated for Best Director, and if you were sitting next to me, I wouldn't be so nervous."

"It's an enormous production, right?" Abigail asked.

"Monumental," he confirmed with an eye roll.

"That's me if I go to the drugstore. My attendance would be very disruptive. Getting me there and back would cost the taxpayers well over two million dollars. I would adore going with you, the invitation is lovely, but I can't," Abigail said.

"Okay. Then I'll take my mom. She loves going." Michael was cheerful. "And she's a cheap date. Give her a couple of glasses of champagne, and she sleeps in the limo while I go to the after-parties."

"I'm sure she'd appreciate hearing that," Abby laughed.

Soon the time had come to end the evening. It could end two ways. Each knew how their bodies wanted it to end, but each knew their brains would make the decision.

"Thank you for having me to dinner, even if I appeared under false pretenses," he said as Abigail went to collect his coat. "You were a delightful hostess. You not only gave me dinner, you even let me win at Scrabble."

"I most certainly did not," she said. "You beat me fair and square. Thank you for the beautiful flowers and the invitation to the Oscars®," Abigail said, handing him his coat.

He took it and threw it on the back of a chair. He cradled her face in his hands and held it as if she were made of the most delicate crystal on earth. He loved the feel of her skin and hair in his hands. He gently tilted her face up and looked at her for the longest time before he kissed her.

His kiss was soft and lingering. He dared not let anything other than his hands and lips touch her, or they would end up in the bed. Both of them knew that. The kiss became more passionate, and Abigail's butterflies again rioted deep below her belly button.

When at last the two of them could bear to break away, he spoke, his voice raw and husky with desire, "For heaven's sake, woman, will you at least give me your phone number now?"

CHAPTER THIRTY-TWO

PHONE DATING

Abigail slept in.

Wow, what a man. What a kiss.

She luxuriated in her memories of Michael and then ordered breakfast and the papers. She, for once, skipped the news and read the fluff. She even read her horoscope, nonsense that it was.

Romance and danger loom.

Well, they got the first part right.

She knew parting was right last night. She smiled at the prospect of becoming lovers. *Have I ever felt this way about a man?* The answer was a resounding, "Never."

Abby had no idea where it would lead. Life, she had learned, is simply not predictable.

Abigail was back at the White House by late afternoon. It felt like home. Looking out her window, the city was blanketed in soft, peaceful snow.

The next morning's PDB contained good information about the Mockingbird project.

The NSA reported, "The wiretaps are all in place and all legal."

"Where are we with the bonds?" Abigail asked.

"They're printed and aging in the lab. They aren't fakes," Petersen said.

"Is there any chance they could be cashed?" General Lafayette asked.

"No, they're duplicates. No bank would redeem them," Spooky Petersen said.

"So what happens next?" Abigail asked.

"We wait for Lafferty to go broke. At his burn rate, I think May," Petersen said. "Meanwhile, he's under surveillance, as is O'Neal."

The head of the FBI stayed behind, giving Abigail a handwritten letter from the woman in Laredo that she pardoned. The FBI had scanned it for everything from anthrax to radiation.

"Dear President Adams, Thank you for a second chance. I will not let you down. I am sorry for those good men who died in Laredo. I was sad to lose my brother, but he'd become so bad, I no longer knew him. I have started beauty school, my daughter is in a special needs program, and my mother can finally get some rest. We are happy together. You make me proud to be from Texas and America. Maria"

Abigail bit back the tears. "May I keep this?"

"Sure."

Michael brought home another Oscar®, this time for Best Director. Abby, watching in her pajamas, jumped up and down with joy for him. As promised, his mother was on his arm. Abby swore he mouthed, "Hi, Abby," and blew her a kiss after his acceptance speech.

He called her from the limo.

"Congratulations, Michael. I'm so excited for you."

"I'd name this one for you, but he's a guy," Michael said.

"So where are you going now?" she asked.

"The *Vanity Fair* party, then the Governor's Ball, then home," he said. "You want to say 'hi' to my mom?"

"Sure, unless she's asleep," Abigail said.

"Your son is a vicious Scrabble player," Abby said when she came on the line.

"He's only beaten me twice. He's never beaten Mikey."

"Then I don't feel so bad," Abby said. Michael took back the phone.

"Don't worry. She knows I'm smitten, but keeps her mouth firmly shut. Oops, we're here at *Vanity Fair*. I'll call you tomorrow?"

And he did, every single night about ten o'clock, her time.

Abby settled into a work routine.

She had frequent short news conferences, and Americans seemed to like that.

Wicker engineered the Message of the Day, and she did as directed. In one piece, she stressed the need for citizens to change their spending patterns from frills to important things. "Save first, and then buy what you need. If anything's left, get something you want." *Keep money flowing, but stop buying crap.*

She was also big on physical fitness. "Birthdays happen, so add a new health habit every year. You can't help getting older, but you can get healthier."

Regular troops were replacing reservists, and that cheered the country.

Her "Workfare Bill" was fast-tracked and passed easily. It, too, captured the interest of the voters. It was simple. After six months of receiving federal unemployment compensation, you had to volunteer twenty hours per week in your community to qualify for extended benefits.

"Everyone's gotta give back," Abby said at the signing. "Besides, your community needs you."

Cash-strapped communities loved it. Volunteers who cleaned parks or worked in senior centers were heroes. One man, out of work for six months, felt working at the food pantry was the least he could do.

"Working here beats sitting home and feeling sorry for myself."

The press fell all over this program, and many a closer on the news was a story of someone whose life had changed because he'd been made to volunteer.

The Infants First Act was paying its own way. The decline in child abuse and postpartum depression paid for the cost of the program.

Abigail stayed away from Middle East peace talks.

"When they want peace, they'll give it to each other. If we get involved, we get blamed for the failure. No thanks." Abby was blunt with the press. The American people agreed.

Abby made sure Marilyn told the Arabs to behave. If anyone attacked the Israelis, Abby won't muzzle them the way the U.S. did in the first Gulf War. Saddam was lucky that Baghdad didn't glow in the dark after his SCUD missile attacks.

Arabs took Abby seriously after the Katherine Stuart and the Laredo cases. Abigail understood force and was not afraid to use it. And the Middle East runs on force.

She looked forward to Michael's nightly calls. Topics were all over the map, from favorite books, to junior high school mortifications, to silly things that happened that day.

She told him about how her family came to be. He told her about his family after the death of his little sister.

"My dad was head of the hospital pharmacy where my sister died. When Emma died, he sort of did, too. Going into the building every day took its toll. He fell into a bottle and lost his job. Mom went back to nursing, and dad drank. Finally, she divorced him, and we moved in with Uncle Mikey and his wife for a while. I was angry for a very long time," Michael said.

"Of course you were. You were alive and deserved a dad." Abby could only imagine how much that must have hurt.

"Then, about the time I could make peace with things, he died of colon cancer."

"I bet that hurt, too," Abby said.

"Yes, but my life experiences helped my career. I was 'discovered' playing Frisbee on Venice Beach. I was visiting a buddy before my senior year at Georgetown. A guy with a big, greasy nose walked through the sand in street shoes and a suit to give me his card.

"'You got an agent? I need a second lead that can play Frisbee,' he said in a thick New York accent.

"'No thanks,' I said. 'I'm not an actor.'

"So he takes the card back, scribbled two names on the back, and said, 'Call these guys.' Then he heads to a red Ferrari. The two names were big stars, and the red Ferrari got my interest. I called the guys that night. Both said the same thing.

"'Call him, kid. He'll make you rich beyond your wildest dreams.' And Arnold Schwartzbaum is still my agent."

"Great story. I'm impressed," Abigail said.

"Don't be. Acting's just pretending. And my first character had an alcoholic dad. How hard was that?"

"So what happened next?" Abby asked.

"Well, I won an Oscar for my first film. Which meant I had to do a second to make any money. So I lived like a student, took courses toward my degree, and looked for a good part. My second and third films did well, so I bought Mom a condo in LA. After a few more, I bought the house in LA, and two years ago, the house in Ravello. Everything else, I pretty much sock away. Today's heartthrob is tomorrow's hemorrhoid."

Abigail laughed.

"Besides, I like my work with the United Nations on human rights."

"Tell me about that."

"Well, my face opens doors, and I can highlight things the world wants to ignore."

"But you don't lobby me," Abigail said.

"When I'm around you, I'm thinking about you."

"What about your degree?" Abigail asked. *Oh, don't be a snob.*

"Uncle Mikey was on my case. Memorizing lines while typing a paper on the GDP of Botswana was not fun. But Georgetown gave me my degree in international affairs when I finished my hours."

"So you have a degree in international affairs from Georgetown? You do realize you're more qualified to be President than I am. Of course, that's not saying a lot," Abigail laughed.

She loved their phone calls. It was lovely getting to know him without lust getting in the way.

One night he called from Italy. He'd gotten up in the middle of the night to call her.

"I know it's short notice, but I'd like to see you this weekend," he sounded sleepy.

"Oh, are you on the way back to LA?"

"No. I'd just like to see you."

She pulled up her calendar.

"I have an arts night Friday, but I could be at the penthouse about nine."

"Good. Very good."

Abby dreaded telling Albright.

"Um, I'd like to go to the penthouse after the Arts night on Friday. For the weekend," Abigail said to Albright. She knew he'd want details. He was a detail kind of guy.

"So Mikey's nephew's working out, huh?" he swallowed his smile. "Well, don't do anything I wouldn't do."

So he had been in on it at the beginning, after all. Between Mikey and Albright, Abby didn't stand a chance that snowy night.

She had to laugh out loud.

Telling Regina would be worse. She'd wait until later. The Lafayettes were coming for a bridge marathon with her and O.T.

Abby's agents brought Michael in through the VIP/service entrance, and all were glad to see him. When they were alone, he wrapped her in his arms for what seemed like the longest time.

"Michael, what is it?" Abigail asked.

"I just needed to hold you."

She led him to her bedroom, the one place denied to him before.

"You know, being the Sexiest Man Alive is a something of a burden, the tiara, the sash. Before things go further, you might oughta know about Shorty. He might not be up to Presidential standards."

Abigail smiled from ear to ear. *Humble to boot.*

They sat on the bed, and she laughed as he pulled her sweater over her head.

Finally.

Then the sweater snagged on her left earring, and she shrieked. She fled from the bed in a panic, half blinded by the sweater and trying to reposition the snagged sweater to cover her bra.

She peeked around the door as the agent came running.

"False alarm. Caught my earring," she said, blushing.

"No problem, ma'am." He swallowed his smile. It was about time that lady got lucky, and Aston seemed like the real deal to the guys.

"What was that about?" Michael asked, bewildered.

"My left earring is a panic button. Snagging the sweater activated it."

"Then take the damn thing off, woman, and get back in this bed."

There they stayed for the better part of the weekend. Occasionally, one would make a foray into the kitchen for provisions, or room service would send up something. Mostly, they spent their time intertwined with each other.

As new lovers, they went through the imprinting process, learning the nuances of the other's responses, finding their unique style of lovemaking.

"Michael," Abby said on Sunday morning as their time drew to a close.

"Hmmm?" he said. He rolled over and propped himself up on one elbow. He was looking into her eyes. She rolled to face him. *Damn, he's was even better looking than in his photographs.*

"I don't think you ought to call him Shorty," she said.

"Really?" he smiled.

"Trust me on this. I'm a doctor."

CHAPTER THIRTY-THREE

ROMANCE

Abigail and Michael knew they could not allow themselves to get outed.

I wouldn't trust a starry-eyed ingénue President living out a romance-novel plot.

A few days after her weekend with Michael, Regina nailed her. They were awaiting guests for Soul Food night. They were in the Yellow Oval Room, and Abby poured herself a glass of sparkling water.

"Okay, baby girl, I raised you. Only one thing makes a girl this happy. What's his name?" Regina had her hands on her hips, and Abby knew better than to lie.

"His name is Michael Aston," she said, sipping her drink.

"Ooh. You sure can pick 'em. He is one gorgeous man," Regina said. "But I don't want you getting your heart broken."

"That's always a risk," Abigail said, with a shrug of one shoulder. "No risk, no reward."

"And don't you even think about giving up this job for him, you hear me?" Regina was finger-wagging.

"I took an oath. He knows I have a prior commitment," Abigail replied.

"Good. And when he wants to marry you, he has to ask Duke as well as me. Got that?"

"Yes, ma'am." *Marriage? We've only been together one weekend.*

Regina waved her away; the audience was over. Abigail left her own living room. *I wonder if the American people have any idea who's the boss in this house?*

Michael loved the story about Regina, especially Regina's dismissal of Abby in her own home. Abby edited out the bit about marriage.

Abby told General Lafayette and Lynne about her involvement with Michael.

"You have a need to know," she said. Well, Jerome did, and Lynne would be thrilled for her.

"If he makes you happy, we're happy," Jerome said. "Besides, we enjoy our time playing bridge with Regina and O.T. Keeps us on our toes."

"I still think he'd be perfect for the Frenchman on the airplane," Lynne said. Abby just smiled. *He is so much better in bed than the Frenchman could ever be.*

March 6, D-Day Minus Three Months

Everything was on track for Operation Women in Flight.

Salazar reported that he had all the jet fuel required in Diego Garcia, Afghanistan, and Australia. The C-5 conversion kits were ready and awaiting installation.

"Too early to convert them. They have other jobs to do," Salazar said.

The women "shepherds" were ahead of schedule in their training. Not only were they learning language skills, learning to wear Afghan clothing, underwear and shoes. Soon they would start eating Afghan food and stop wearing deodorant, so they would smell like an Afghan.

Layla organized three conferences a month. "I'm following up personally with widows at liberty to travel. They will end up working in Australia—they just don't know it yet."

Marilyn reported the camp would be ready, including a U.S. Passport Office. "They can't get Afghan passports before they leave, and they can't enter other countries without passports, so we've got to give them U.S. passports."

Abby felt badly for people banging on the doors to get into America.

"But if we lure them out, we have no choice," Abby concurred.

Michael asked her what she wanted for her birthday.

"I'd love an entire weekend at Camp David."

"I'd prefer to take you to Paris, but Camp David, it is."

He was working on a movie, a romantic comedy with Kendra "The Body" Wallace. The director didn't like shooting around him. But Michael couldn't tell him the truth about his weekend off, so he pled "personal reasons."

Early spring always reminded Abby of a newborn baby, just opening her eyes and looking around. Fully formed, but still most comfortable swaddled tightly, a human bud. She loved the neon green of the new leaves, the crocuses, and the daffodils coming up.

Sure, Camp David could be really dreary, as everything was wood: floors, walls, and ceilings, like a Maine camp. On a gray day, it was grim, but they had privacy and access to the outdoors.

For her birthday, the weather cooperated. The air was clear and sweet, the breeze usually from the south, redolent with the moisture and the warmth of spring. They took a long walk each day. Finally, she was in fresh air. In winter, the White House air felt stale: over-baked air in some rooms, dank and chilly in others. *Ah, the joys of an old home.*

"Do you know what this is called?" Abigail asked as she held up a bloom she picked for a dinner table bouquet.

"No, but I bet you do," Michael replied, kissing the end of her nose.

"Actually, I am a loser when it comes to plant names."

Abby picked more.

"Me too. Paolo, the gardener, keeps the yard full of bougainvillea. I wish you could come visit, meet my friends."

"Me, too. Hey, do I need to be jealous of 'The Body'?" Abigail asked as casually as possible.

"Nah. She smokes like a chimney. Besides, everyone knows her body is all plastic," he said with a chuckle. "Yours is the body I want."

Later that evening, after they had a simple dinner, they snuggled up in front of the fire and drank hot chocolate. Abigail actually made it without scorching it. She'd learned to warm milk slowly, something that went against the grain of her personality. The bouquet she picked looked pitiful at best.

"Oh, damn," Michael muttered, hurriedly getting up and walking off down the hall.

Abigail hadn't the vaguest idea what he was upset about. He came back with a large black box with a pink ribbon wrapped around it.

"Happy birthday," he said, plopping down beside her.

Abby couldn't decide whether she was glad or sad that the box was big. *You moron, the man of your dreams is giving you jewelry. Besides, it's too soon for a little box.*

"Aren't you going to sing 'Happy Birthday' to me?" Abby teased.

"I can, but you will fall over laughing, hit your head, and pass out."

"I'm not going to open it until you sing," Abby pouted.

"Okay," Michael said. He snatched the box back and hid it under his arm.

"Not fair," Abby said, reaching for the box.

They tussled a while, and then Michael gave her back the box, which she opened with glee.

"Oh. My. Goodness."

Glee turned to shock.

Inside was an Edwardian pearl choker with an enormous Burmese ruby clasp to wear in the front. Platinum and diamond spacer bars held the five perfect strands of pearls in marching order.

"Michael, this is beyond my wildest dreams," Abigail said.

"May I put it on you?" he asked.

"Of course." Abigail lifted her hair, and he fastened it expertly.

"It took me forever to learn how to fasten it," he said.

Abby's eyes filled with tears. "I gave Pris's pearl choker to Kim. Now you've replaced it tenfold."

"Good. I'm glad you like it," Michael said.

"No, I like the flowers we picked this afternoon. This I adore, though not as much as I do you." *She was perilously close to the L word.*

"Done," he said, clasp secured. "I just want to see you in a bed wearing only that." He stood, offering his hand. She followed him into the bedroom and granted him his wish.

When their passion was spent and she lay in his arms, he played with her hair.

"Abigail?"

"Hmm?"

"I love you," he said, kissing her forehead.

"Ummm. I love you too, Michael."

Mother Nature smiled for Duke's wedding weekend.

By Vietnamese custom, Abigail, Regina, and Duke went to the Trans' house the evening before the wedding. For once, Abby didn't care if her motorcade impeded traffic.

The Trans lived over the shop, which had closed early. Their apartment was spotless, and the décor, spare with Vietnamese adornments. Duke took Kim six lacquered boxes covered with red silk.

In one of the boxes were betel nuts; in another, fine silk fabric; and the rest had jewelry, including Kim's wedding ring and various pearl items.

Duke and Kim served their parents tea as a sign of respect.

The parents each gave advice to the couple.

Mrs. Tran said, "Never go to bed angry with each other."

"Girl, you're going to have some late nights," Regina said. Everyone laughed.

Mr. Tran said, "Say 'I love you' every day."

Abby said, "Being happy is better than being right."

Regina had lots of advice. Editing was her dilemma.

"Let Kim have the last word."

Everyone laughed at that one.

Their outdoor ceremony took place beneath the oldest magnolia tree on the South Lawn. A bower of spring flowers covered them. A hundred guests attended, mostly friends of bride and groom.

Regina had her oldest two friends from Houston come and stay at the White House. Mary Frances and Lovey were thrilled. They flipped and Lovey won the toss for the Queen's Bedroom. Mary Frances didn't pout, but announced at breakfast that the Lincoln Bedroom was haunted.

Regina, Abby, and Vee Tran were all dressed in shades of a pinky plum and carried nosegays of orchids. Regina, Lovey, and Mary Frances, of course, wore hats. Mrs. Tran chose traditional Ao-dai, the sheer, floor-length tunic, in a deep shade of plum, wearing it over pants and a fitted top in pink satin.

Duke stood under the magnolia tree, handsome and proud. His best man, John Beamer, a law school buddy, had been to many a fancy wedding, but never one at the White House.

The officiates wore their robes and vestments. A chamber music group from the Marine Band played the wedding music.

At six precisely, Kim's maid of honor appeared to strains of Vivaldi and then Mendelssohn.

Elaine, a classmate in couture class, wore the same basic dress as Kim's, but in one layer of fuchsia silk with crinolines beneath. She carried cherry blossoms.

Next, Kim appeared on her father's arm. Tran looked so proud. Abigail could not stanch her flow of tears. *What a life story for a refugee: he'd gone from walking over bodies on the way to grade school to walking his daughter down the aisle at the White House.*

Kim's gown was perfect. Tea length, its full skirt was layers of pale pink tulle, interspersed with a few layers of starched white lace. The fitted bodice had a scoop neck and cap sleeves. It had three layers: pale pink silk, white lace, and pink tulle. Pris's pearls glowed on Kim's neck, and her bouquet of cherry blossoms was perfect. Her veil was short pale pink tulle.

Abby looked at Duke, and she had never seen such a look of love and adoration on his face.

The Reverend Harcourt gave a short homily on marriage. He stressed that commitment was the key ingredient.

"Sometimes you will not be able to stand each other. But you are committed, and those times of friction will pass into times of even greater love." *I wonder if that will happen with Michael and me.*

The Chief Justice performed the actual ceremony, in part because Duke was going to clerk for him as soon as school was out. Duke kissed his bride but did not embarrass her. He was jubilant and triumphant walking back down the aisle. Abby and Regina held hands and wept. Until this day, he'd been a baby boy who happened to be six-five.

The wedding banquet was fun, with many toasts and lots of laughter. The food was wonderful, the wedding cake a work of art, decorated with fondant cherry blossoms by Chef Dahm. Then everyone adjourned to the East Room for dancing with music by the Marine Band.

Duke was taking Kim to a chic resort in the Caribbean for his school's Easter break. Later, between graduation and starting his clerkship with the Chief Justice, he would take Kim and her parents to Vietnam.

Abby gave up about ten and went to her room, leaving the guests to enjoy themselves. She called Michael and, oddly enough, got no answer. She hung up before it went to voice mail.

CHAPTER THIRTY-FOUR

DARK DAYS

April 6
D-Day minus two months

The PDB was awful.

The Taliban had beheaded four baby girls in front of their mothers after someone in the extended family spoke out against the Taliban. Spending two hundred million dollars a day waiting for the weather to change would annoy anyone. Adding atrocities put Abigail beyond anger.

The sting for Lafferty and O'Neal was moving at glacial speed, normal for this phase. Lafferty had to go broke; otherwise, he had no incentive to sell.

Marines in Helmand Province took the heaviest casualties of the war when they were trapped in an ambush. Fifty men had perished in the firefight. Abby personally wrote each family a letter, quoting Lincoln's letter to Mrs. Bixby.

"I pray the Heavenly Father may assuage the anguish of your bereavement and leave you only the cherished memory of the loved and lost."

Dressed from head to toe in black, Abigail met the plane at Dover Air Force Base when the bodies returned. Saluting fifty flag-draped caskets hurt her soul. *I hate this job.*

She cried herself to sleep that night. Michael's silence did not help. The deaths cast a pall over the country. Abigail despaired. She had no good news to give. D-Day was still two months off.

▰▰▰

Michael had not called in five days. Perhaps he backed off because declaring his love had scared him. She knew he was alive. If he had died, the world would have known. Maybe it was Kendra. After all they worked together all but naked.

On the tenth night, he called and acted as if everything was fine at his end. He commiserated over the loss of the Marines.

"Michael, I haven't heard from you lately. Is something up?" *I don't want to hear about Marines. I want to know about us.*

"No. I've been incredibly busy," he sounded evasive.

"We're both busy, but we've always talked," Abby tried to sound neutral.

There was a long pause on the other end of the line.

Okay, here it comes. Be a lady. You started this job an old maid. It was a great fling. One day it will be just a memory.

"I think we should talk in person about this," Michael said.

"Very well, when?" she said. *At least he's man enough to do it in person.*

"I'm on my way," he said and hung up. She had no idea where he was. For all she knew, he could be in Italy.

Luckily, Regina and O.T. were out of town. Both were tired after the wedding. They'd be home in time for the Easter Egg Roll on Sunday.

She called Mabel. "Mr. Michael Aston will be arriving at some point. Please make sure he is admitted."

"Yes, ma'am."

He did not show that night.

The following morning's PDB was no better. *At least it was no worse.*

Easter was late this year. Abby stood in for Regina with the East Wing people to go over final "EER" plans. The Easter Egg Roll is to the White House what the Thanksgiving Day Parade is to Macy's. The East

Wing had things firmly in hand. All Abby had to do was hit her marks on Sunday. Even the weather forecast was perfect. Abigail returned to the Oval Office, wondering when, or even if, Michael would ever show. She had the Edwardian pearl choker in her desk drawer to return if all was indeed over.

At noon, Michael was announced. She let him wait while she freshened her makeup, slipped into the four-inch power heels she kept under the Resolute desk, then let the Marine Sentry open the door for him. She stood behind her desk, her fingertips on it.

She would look him in the eye. In a pink suit.

At least he wore a suit into the Oval Office.

"Wow," he said, looking around the room. "I know you're the President, and I know this is your office, but this is the first time I've actually put the two together."

Abby emerged from behind the desk. Michael went to hug her, but she stepped out of reach.

"The windows are bare," she said. *And if I am getting dumped, there will be no touching.*

"Have you had lunch?" she asked.

"Nope. Do you know a good sandwich place?" he asked, jingling the change in his pocket.

He was nervous. Good.

"PBJ or tuna fish?" Abby replied, with little warmth and a neutral face.

"Anything's fine with me."

Abigail leaned across the desk, to hit the intercom. Michael got a good look at her long legs and her toned rear end. "Poppy, please ask the Navy stewards to serve lunch for two in my private dining room. And please hold all non-urgent calls."

Michael was as enchanted with Oval Office as Abigail had been the first day she saw it. It annoyed her that he got to come in here to dump her. All visitors were logged in and that log was public information. Their affair had been private. *The least he owes me is a private break-up.*

"Great art. And intimidating as hell."

"Walter Harrington called it his 'golden cell.' Please, have a seat. May I offer you something to drink?" Abigail asked.

"Sure, I'm thirsty. I took the red-eye from L.A. I'd love a glass of water," he said.

Michael knew Abby was too composed. *This was not going to be easy.* He had his water and sat on the sofa, while Abby perched upright in a wing chair. She was beautiful in a pink suit, unbearably so right now.

"I came to tell you why I didn't call you."

Abby said nothing and moved not a muscle. Her neutral face was pleasant. Inside, she was a roiling mess.

He repositioned himself. He leaned forward, put his elbows on his knees and talked to the floor, "I, um …had some …um bleeding and it took a while to see the doctor," he said.

Abby again felt the world crack underneath her.

"Long story short, I've been waiting for biopsy results and thinking."

"And the results are?"

"Two polyps. Negative. This time. But you know my dad died of colon cancer at fifty-six." He glanced up at her.

"I'm relieved. Polyps in jars never get cancer. So what did you learn in your thinking?" Abigail asked. *No Kendra Wallace, just a guy afraid of commitment.*

"I needed time to think things through, either way. With cancer or without. I love you so much, I decided to break things off if I had cancer. I wouldn't put you through another loss."

Abigail erupted into tears. *Where was a tissue when she needed one?* She forgot the hanky in her sleeve. Michael produced one for her.

"Let's go into the study," she said, needing privacy for her tears.

Once in the little room, he wrapped her in his arms and placed tiny kisses all over her face and hair.

"I was so frightened, Michael," she said.

"I was, too. But I was more frightened for you. You just lost your sister last year. Now I realize that whatever the future holds for either of us, we must be together."

Then he kissed her tears until the earth's crack healed. Michael waited while her flood of tears stopped. She had thoroughly soaked him and his handkerchief. He felt like a cad for making her cry.

Michael pulled a small black box tied with a pink satin ribbon from his jacket. He got down on one knee. Abby sat down, hard, on the love seat.

"Abigail Adams, would you do me the incredible honor of marrying me?"

He looked beseechingly into her face, box in hand.

Abby wasn't ready for this. *Five minutes ago, she was ready to return to her celibate cell.*

"Michael, I don't know what to say. It's all so fast," Abigail said, gulping back sobs. "Only a few months. And then you just disappeared."

"I'm so sorry about that. Please, Abby, please take the next step with me. We get engaged so we don't have to hide. Then, when you're ready, we marry. Maybe while you are in office, maybe after. Or if you decide to break my heart and ruin my life, you can break the engagement. It's all your choice."

Abby was nearly catatonic. *Say yes, stupid.*

"Maybe if you looked at the ring?" Michael started to pull the bow off.

"No, no, no." Abby waved her hands in front of the box. "I mean yes. You don't have to show me the ring."

"You're a little hard to follow. Was that a yes or a no?" he said asked with a puzzled look.

"Yes. Yes. Yes. It was a yes."

He got up off the floor and drew her up to stand in his arms, kissing her for the first time as his fiancée.

"You're hard on a man's knees, you know that?" He handed her the box, and she pulled on the ribbon slowly.

"This will only happen once in my life," Abigail said, looking into his eyes.

It was the ring of her dreams: an emerald-cut diamond, flanked by slightly smaller rubies. He slid the platinum ring onto her finger. It fit perfectly.

"How did you know my size?" she asked.

"You aren't the only one with spies, woman." He kissed her sweetly, and then each felt the tug of passion.

"Not here, Mister. Never in here."

"Okay, Missus."

The two went into lunch. The steward had been and gone. Abby and Michael didn't care that their lunch, whatever it was, was cold.

Abby looked lovingly at the ring and was all smiles during the meal. Then she remembered her job.

"Michael, could we keep this private for a while?" she asked.

"May I ask why?" he said.

"I have some things I can't talk about. An engagement announcement would be very distracting."

"Okay. Sure you're not just punishing me?"

"Yes, I'm sure. But next time you need some time alone, please warn me. No reason required, just a warning."

"Deal. And we'll announce the engagement when you're ready."

"Thank you, my love."

After lunch, Michael returned to L.A. and a movie that was behind schedule yet another day.

Abigail put the ring in her bra. It was getting crowded in there with the launch codes and thumb drive. She'd find a chain and keep it close to her heart.

On Sunday, Abigail enjoyed the Easter Egg Roll and realized why it took nearly twelve hundred volunteers to put it on. She enjoyed it even more when it was over. Children's laughter was lovely for an afternoon, but the silence afterward was priceless.

CHAPTER THIRTY-FIVE

STINGERS

London, April 28

John Lafferty took his twins to Regents Park. People were out, turning their faces to the feeble sun. The boys ran wild; their noise was deeply offensive to proper Brits.

"Stay on this patch of grass," he said, "If you're good, we'll go to McDonald's."

John had brought a bag of toys. They went through them all, twice. They fought over them all, twice. John was frazzled and tired when they got to McDonald's. Forking over the equivalent of forty bucks for their execrable meal only worsened his mood.

He dropped the boys off at their mother's. He was steps away when two scruffy men fell into step with him and muscled him onto a bench. He felt a gun in his side.

"Lafferty?" one said with a thick Eastern European accent.

"That's me." His armpits ran with sweat.

"We want Mockingbirds," the other said, also in a heavy accent.

"You sell to us, only. We call you."

Before he could speak, the two men walked off in different directions. *Christ, these goons know where my kids live.* He sat, paralyzed with fear. Finally, he went to his hotel and called O'Neal.

"This is great. We can sell these puppies and retire," O'Neal all but crowed.

"I'm scared shitless, and you think this is great?" Lafferty shrieked.

"What did they offer?" O'Neal asked.

"Nothing yet."

"Then stay put. They'll be back."

There went another chunk of change to stay in London. Even his fleabag hotel was a hundred dollars a night. The Russian oligarchs moved in and drove up prices, just as the Arabs had done a generation earlier. People called it "Londongrad" for a reason.

John saw his boys every other day. He even spent the weekend at Jemima's house so she could have a weekend away. That saved him two hundred dollars. At least the nanny stayed with the boys. John ate and slept, taking them for a daily outing.

Back in Washington, the O'Neal/Lafferty group had good news for Abby.

The FBI reported that Lafferty would be flat broke shortly, so the sting should pick up steam rapidly. He'd unloaded his G-650 a week earlier at a huge loss and was trying to sell his boat for pennies on the dollar.

May 9
D-Day Minus Twenty-Eight
Afghanistan

Salazar's "Shepherds" had finished their training. They were now wearing Afghan clothing, from burqa to Afghan shoes. They even used Afghan toiletries, such as they were. None liked the scanty bathing and lack of deodorant. They ate Afghan food so their clothes would smell "right." They were fluent enough in dialects of Pashto, Dari, Uzbek, and a few others.

Each day for seven days, they went to markets in seven sectors. They whispered, "Your Muslim sisters all over the world want the wives of the Taliban and Al Qaeda to be free. They will take in you and your children. You'll have money of your own for five years. You may bring your daughters, but leave behind boys eight and over. Tell no one. We will tell you more as the night draws closer."

Women, fearing for their very lives, said nothing. Not even to their best friends.

London, May 9

One of the men appeared, again, just after John had dropped off the boys.

"We talk," the man said, once again beckoning him to another a park bench.

"Who are you?" Lafferty asked.

"Grigory."

"Who do you work for, Grigory?" Lafferty asked.

"Is important who I work against," Grigory said, glancing around nervously. "We are against Russia. Here is my number. Call me."

He handed him a phone number and walked away quickly.

Lafferty again called O'Neal.

"You need to wrap this up. Get a price, for fuck's sake," O'Neal ordered.

O'Neal wanted that cash. He had a new girlfriend, one with bigger boobs. O'Neal thought she loved him for his personality. He had one, but it resembled that of an underfed buzzard. Her interest was strictly financial. She was hot to get married, to live higher and faster so O'Neal would kick off sooner.

"O'Neal, they haven't made an offer. We have to have a price and a plan."

Lafferty could use some quick cash. Ever since that bitch, Abigail Adams, had fired O'Neal, his defense contracts had dried up. Then DOD stopped paying him for work already done. He had sued them, but that's like suing God with lawyers that charge like the Devil himself.

Lafferty Weapons Systems spent lavishly all over the Hill, only to have a woman who stumbled into the presidency shut him out. He'd had an affair with Poppy and wanted to bag Abby, too. When he saw her last, at the White House on the Fourth of July, she shut him out. *A beauty. And a bitch.*

Jemima took virtually everything when she and the twins went home to "Mummy and Deddy." She knew about the skimming, but didn't want her sons' father in prison, so he kept the money coming and saw the boys whenever he could.

Every month he lost another zero off his net worth. In days, he'd be flat. He'd bought the house in Brentwood for nine million and sold it for four. Handing over five million at closing hurts. Jemima had vaporized another five million "getting settled" in London.

He'd taken a bath selling the Gulfstream 650. The broker was blunt: in a bad economy, jets are the first to go.

Forget selling the yacht. He'd be lucky to scuttle it in a storm for the insurance money. He was in arrears on marina fees. *When you can't pay marina fees, you need to lose the boat.*

He figured these guys were Chechens. *Better than jihadists.* He called the number on the card.

"Yes?" Grigory growled.

"For the right price, we're in. Where and when?" he said.

"We'll let you know." Click.

He gave up and caught the next flight back to L.A. Coach. For someone used to a Gulfstream 650, flying First Class is a come-down. Coach was worse than Greyhound; it was paid hitchhiking. After twelve hours in the air, he felt like soured milk. He wanted a large Scotch and a shower, in that order.

"Grigory" was in a CIA plane right behind him, sleeping soundly in a flat bed.

Once inside the door of his cheap apartment, John knocked back a stiff Scotch and shed his travel clothes. He poured a second Scotch and was headed for the shower when Grigory called.

"We want see merchandise."

"Twenty million for each bird." Lafferty was too frazzled to play games.

"No. Too much. Your boys, very cute." He chuckled.

Lafferty felt his bowels loosen.

"We pay thirty for all."

"Forty. How will you pay for them?" Lafferty said, beaten.

"Bearer bonds."

"Christ. Those went out in the late eighties." John rolled his eyes. *Oh-puhleeze.*

"We 'liberated' bonds when we left KGB," Grigory said.

Lafferty was suspicious.

"Scan one to this number." It was O'Neal's number in Cayman. "Then I'll call you back, Grigory."

"One hour, max. I'm hurry."

Jeez, these guys can barely speak English.

O'Neal had been at Treasury in the late eighties and confirmed that they looked real. "I can tell for sure when I feel them," he said. "Like tits."

Lafferty called Grigory back within ten minutes.

"You may see the birds. They are in L.A." Lafferty hoped that would tick off the London-based Grigory. At least he could grab some much-needed sleep and food. The Scotch was starting to hit his jet-lagged brain.

"I call Mikhail. Your office, two hours. If he like, I come."

John wanted to weep from fatigue. At least it was after hours. He would have to drive to the office, pick up the company van, go to the marina, load the birds, and be back at the office in two hours. He could do it, but just barely.

Between jet lag and two Scotches, John was amazed that he could even make it to Lafferty Weapons Systems.

"Hi...Frank," he said, reading the man's badge. "I need to use the van for a while."

"Sure, Boss," he said, pleased that Boss had remembered his name.

John got the van to the marina in one piece. He manhandled each of the four lockers from down below. Each weighed eighty pounds, and getting them up two sets of skinny stairs to the aft deck wasn't easy. Carrying them down the rickety aluminum gangplank at dusk was harder.

With the last locker, he wobbled badly but caught himself. He was sweating from fear, fatigue, and muscular exhaustion. *Dropping a nuclear weapon into the harbor was lunacy.*

He neared the office and remembered the guard. *Oh crap, I gotta get him outta here before the goon arrives.*

"Hey, Frank, I could barely get this van to start. When I've unloaded it, I need to you take it to an auto place. Get it a new battery."

"I don't know, Mr. L. ...leaving the gate unattended?"

"Frank, I own the place. If I say it's okay, it's okay." Lafferty handed him two one-hundred-dollar bills. "This should cover the battery, as well as a little something for the hassle."

Lafferty drove the van to the service entrance, got a dolly and hauled the lockers from the truck into the service elevator and up to his office. He was trembling from exhaustion. He still had to take the van to the guard.

"I'm leaving it running for fear it won't start. New battery, for sure," John said. "And have them look at the brakes. They're mushy."

Within minutes, an old gray Volvo pulled up to the gate. A scruffy guy with an accent cranked down the window.

"I'm Mikhail. You?"

"Lafferty. Park around back." The car looked, and smelled, like Mikhail grew some sort of fungus in it. Lafferty walked behind it.

They said nothing on the way up in the elevator. Mikhail smelled like his Volvo looked. Lafferty hoped his fear did not show.

"I see now?" Mikhail said when they entered Lafferty's spacious office on the top floor.

John opened the lockers, and Mikhail saw the weapons. Then he went to touch them.

"See, not touch," Lafferty said, with a smile.

Mikhail slapped him across the face. Hard. Lafferty staggered, but stayed upright.

"I touch what I like," he said menacingly, his face in Lafferty's. His breath was fetid.

Lafferty's jet lag, fear, and the physical assault were adding up to sheer terror. He said nothing.

"We buy. Tomorrow. Here. Seven in night. Grigory bring bonds."

"The software's on the East Coast," Lafferty said, as pleasantly as possible.

The man slapped him again, this time a backhand.

"What, you don't know FedEx?"

Lafferty agreed. *I hope to hell I can find O'Neal.*

Mikhail left. Lafferty locked himself in the office and called around until he found O'Neal in Grand Cayman.

"The deal is on for tomorrow at seven, here in LA."

"I can't get the software there in time."

"When I said that, he slapped the snot out of me, twice. These guys are dangerous. They know where my kids live, for Christ's sake. Charter a jet, but get it here," Lafferty shouted.

O'Neal was pissed. Penelope was ready for another round, but he was out of the mood. He couldn't see his dick for his belly, so if he had anything left, it wasn't much. And it was too early for another pill.

"Gotta go to work, babe," he said, smacking her on the bottom. "I'll be back a rich, rich man."

Penelope blew him a kiss and watched him walk away. *An old man's ass is a sorry sight.*

O'Neal booked a jet in the Caymans and flew straight to D.C., glad he kept the software at home. He didn't want to think what the trip was costing him. Chartering a jet and keeping it waiting while he snaked through D.C. traffic was particularly painful. At least the rental car in L.A. would be cheap.

When the two men met at 5 p.m. at Lafferty's apartment, both looked awful. Lafferty hadn't been able to sleep for the fear. He had great gray circles under his eyes and jumped at the slightest noise. O'Neal was red-eyed and cocky at the thought of so much money.

They reviewed the plan. They would take separate cars. O'Neal would take the SIM cards. They'd give the guys the weapons and SIM cards, get the money, and split. Neither would tell the other where he was headed.

Lafferty called the guard shack and asked who was on duty.

"It's me, Frank, sir," he yammered on about the car repairs.

"Hmm. I have some gifted software-design people coming after work. Software guys can look real weird. If I get caught in traffic, just wave them in and show them up to the office, okay?"

"No problem, Boss. I've got keys."

O'Neal was the first to arrive, and then Grigory and his friend Mikhail. O'Neal didn't like the look of either of them. He hoped Lafferty was behind him.

Lafferty hit every red light between the apartment and the office. He was running late when some idiot in a Suburban ran a red light T-boned him, hard, on the passenger side. Lafferty was shaken up but unhurt. His cell phone, however, was shattered. The cops were summoned as both cars were wrecks.

Lafferty descended into a mental fog. He could do nothing except go along. The cops figured he was shaky from the accident, wrote up the other guy, and summoned the wreckers.

Lafferty sat on the curb and saw his life fracture into shards. *Great. O'Neal will sell the Mockingbirds and disappear with all the money.*

The three men waited for Lafferty. O'Neal called him. Twice. Both calls went to voice mail.

"No Lafferty. Oh, well, no problem. I have the software, and here are the weapons." O'Neal smiled his sneer.

"You show how," Grigory said with a grim face.

O'Neal put in the software, wrong. Then he flipped it around, and the display lit up.

"See? Piece of cake."

"Here is money." Grigory handed over a battered briefcase.

O'Neal looked inside. He had done his homework. The serial numbers were from the late eighties. He felt the paper. They were, indeed, old bearer bonds, and they were as real as the Rock of Gibraltar. He would get them out of the country before Lafferty showed up.

"Nice doing business with you gentlemen," O'Neal said, extending his hand.

Grigory took his hand and cuffed it.

"Patrick John O'Neal, you are under arrest for attempting to sell nuclear weapons illegally," "Grigory" said in perfect and unaccented English. Then he slipped off his fake teeth, and smiled his American pearly-whites at O'Neal.

He told O'Neal his federal rights and transported him to the Federal Detention Center in L.A in the back of the fungus-smelling Volvo. "Mikhail" stayed behind in case Lafferty showed.

O'Neal was catatonic.

Meanwhile, the cop who wrote up the accident scene offered Lafferty a ride.

"I was on my way to the office. It's only about five minutes from here." Lafferty wondered what had happened in his absence.

They turned up into the canyon and were headed toward Lafferty's office, when John saw the fungus Volvo coming the other way. O'Neal was in the back seat. Judging from his posture, Lafferty supposed he was in handcuffs. In any event, Grigory was driving.

"Mine's up a ways."

He thanked the cop and got out at the next complex. When the cop left, he called a cab from the security desk and headed to Los Angeles International Airport. With a little luck, he'd be on the first plane out before alerts could be issued.

He boarded the first outbound flight. It was to a red-eye to D.C.

Abigail Adams has ruined my life. I'll find some way to ruin hers.

CHAPTER THIRTY-SIX

REVENGE

May 13
D-Day Minus Eighteen

In Diego Garcia, Air Force personnel camouflaged the converted C-5s as they arrived. Since no civilians lived there, they could be seen only from space. Abby was still antsy having so many planes there. She remembered Battleship Row at Pearl Harbor. Planes were also in Afghanistan and Australia. Abby was antsy anyway.

In Afghanistan, the shepherds again visited markets in all seven sectors. "You need only walk into the night, away from your Taliban or Al Qaeda husband, with your children. Your sisters in the world are doing everything else."

In Australia, Marilyn reported that the base was nearly finished. The place had a fresh coat of paint, and supplies arrived daily, including several crates of playground equipment. The GI's would wait till D-Day minus one to assemble it.

On the French Riviera, Layla was making her compound of houses ready for the widows who had accepted her invitation for the summer. They would arrive tomorrow. "I'll have their tickets for Australia waiting for them, but we'll spend the first two weeks training."

Abby was as nervous as a long-tailed cat in a room full of rocking chairs.

May 13, Washington, D.C.

Lafferty went to his twin brother's house in Silver Spring, MD. He rang the doorbell and hoped Tim was home.

Tim and he looked nearly identical, but were fraternal twins. John had blue eyes, but Tim's were brown. John was straight. Tim was gay. John didn't ask, and Tim didn't tell. For twins, they had remarkably little to do with each other.

"Hey, bro, great to see you," Tim embraced him. "Come in. I'm having a sandwich. Want one?"

"Sure."

When Tim went into the kitchen, John sprinted silently up the stairs. Tim had kept his wallet on his dresser since they were kids. John quickly switched out their driver's licenses and helped himself to half the cash in the wallet. Luckily, Tim always sported a lot of cash.

He was back downstairs by the time Tim showed up with a pastrami sandwich and a beer.

"How are the boys?" Tim asked.

"Good. Great if you like noise." John wolfed down his sandwich. *When did I last eat?*

"And Jemima? How's the divorce going?" Tim asked.

"Good, good. I give her all my money. I get to see the boys whenever," John said.

"Sorry."

"Hey, you mind if I crash here tonight? I'm whipped."

"Fine. I'm headed out, so help yourself," Tim said.

John wondered where Tim was off to, but not enough to ask.

"I'll be gone by noon. Catching a plane to the Caymans."

"Whatever."

When Tim left, John called Cordelia Laurus. She was the biggest money whore on the Hill.

"Halloo," she intoned.

"Hey, Senator, John Lafferty here. What have you been up to lately?"

"Oh, just doing the work of the people," she said.

"I need a favor, Senator."

"What kind of favor, Mr. Lafferty?" Her tone was always condescending.

"I need to have a word, face-to-face, with the President."

"I suggest you call her."

"No, I'd like to see her less formally, like at a party."

"Tomorrow is the monthly birthday party, and I am invited."

Finally, something breaks my way.

"I'd love to be your escort." John tried to sound flirtatious.

Cordelia didn't like Lafferty, but she was up for re-election and needed money.

"That would be fine."

"Oh, my license says my first name is Timothy, so you'd best use that name."

"I didn't know you were a 'Timothy.' I had an Uncle Timothy."

Like I care.

"What time shall I call for you?"

"Please pick me up at one. It's a barbecue. Casual attire. And do bring me a present, 'Timothy.' It is my birthday party. I'm registered at Tiffany."

Cow.

Weapons did not get into the White House. It was a barbecue, so perhaps a steak knife would be at hand. John knew his plan was unhinged, but if he was going to rot in a federal prison for the rest of his life, he was going to take Abigail Adams down with him.

John slept fitfully. He showered, shaved, and dressed in an outfit of Tim's. The man had taste; John gave him that. John wore a white, long-sleeved, Ralph Lauren dress shirt, navy slacks, and a red cotton sweater draped over his shoulders. *So very perfect for the White House.* Tim was still asleep when he left at eleven.

The car service charged extra for going that far out of the Beltway. *So what?* He went to Tiffany in Chevy Chase. Everything on Cordelia's list cost over five hundred dollars.

"What the hell?" He charged an oversized crystal brandy snifter. He remembered fondly being able to walk in and buy anything he wanted. *That bitch, Adams, took it all away. If it weren't for her, I'd still have my gig, maybe even my boys.*

He was spot on time to fetch Cordelia. She was notorious for her tardiness; however, she deigned to appear at the appointed hour for the White House.

She had added "Timothy's" name to the East Wing list that morning. It was a bit unusual, but nothing alarming.

Social functions entered through the East Wing Entrance. John walked in with his brother's driver's license, as Cordelia did with her Senate ID. They passed through the body scanners without difficulty.

Stanchions directed them to a bar set up on the South Lawn. The spring afternoon was just right for a Saturday afternoon barbecue, rare in a city known for its mugginess. John looked around. Perhaps eighty to a hundred people were present. The atmosphere was casual, and kids played impromptu games of tag.

"May I get you something from the bar, Senator?" he asked Cordelia.

"Yes, I'll have a perfect Manhattan, please," she said, and wandered off.

It took the bartenders a few minutes to make the drink, and John sipped at a soda. He wanted a clear head. In fact, he was on his second soda when he finally found Cordelia to give her the Manhattan.

"Oh, thank you, John," she said, and then she turned away from him, as if he was merely a servant.

John wanted to slap the bitch silly.

Abigail was mingling with her guests about fifty feet away, and John scoped out the Secret Service agents and their positions. Everyone looked pretty relaxed. Picnic tables dotted the lawn. They were set with red checked tablecloths, blue bandanas for napkins, and, yep, steak knives. He could smell the barbecue cooking and considered waiting until after lunch. He was getting hungry. Instead, he nursed his soda.

John slunk back into the shadow of a large magnolia tree and stood with his back to it, one foot braced on the trunk. The blossoms perfumed the air. There was no sign of Poppy. She'd get him tossed, for sure.

Abigail looked good, really good. The presidency agreed with her. She had her hair in a ponytail and wore a white skirt, chambray shirt, and a Concho belt. Something niggled at him. She wore the same outfit the last time he saw her, when she snubbed him.

She won't snub me today.

Abby was in animated conversation with some stranger and was unaware of John's gaze.

He walked away from the tree and traced his hand down the edge of one of the tablecloths. He glanced around. No one was watching him. He palmed a steak knife and slid it up his sleeve, point downward.

He meandered toward the President, stopping every few feet to pay attention to something else. He touched the daisies on the tables, smiled at a couple of small children running helter-skelter, anything to keep himself under the radar but moving toward his target.

Abigail caught a glimpse of him out of the corner of her eye. She tugged on her left ear lobe, hard. John felt her fear.

Time stretched, as it is wont to do in moments of great import. Lafferty closed the gap between himself and Abigail, the knife poised to come down into her chest.

Tom Albright, the head of the White House Secret Service detail, launched himself, weapon drawn, between Lafferty and Abigail. Abby heard the knife crunch into the bones in Albright's right chest. He wailed like a wounded animal. He dropped his weapon as he went down under the force of the attack.

His fall knocked Abby to the ground. She grabbed for the Sig Sauer as it went down and scrabbled to get control of it. *Damn, it was heavy.* She looked up. Lafferty had the bloody knife in a two-handed hold, high in a strike arc into her. She prayed the gun's safety was off. She pointed the gun at the mass of his chest and squeezed the trigger. Hard. The sound nearly deafened her and the recoil banged her head against the ground. A single round went into the middle of his chest. Blood spewed from his chest onto Albright and into Abby's face. Lafferty staggered backward and fell.

Sally appeared, and other agents tried to get Abby to safety. Abby kicked them away viciously.

Abby's sole concern was Albright. She ripped his shirt open to get to the wound. Bright red blood was spurted rhythmically out of his chest. The knife hit an artery. *Damn.* As well, air bubbled in the blood. Lafferty had also punctured the right lung. *Double damn.* It collapsed a little more with each breath.

She knelt beside him and fished inside her pocket for the ever-present tampon and opened it.

"I'm sorry, Albright, this is gonna hurt," she said, pushing the tampon firmly into the wound. She had to get it past the chest wall if it was going to do any good. Albright turned his head away. He must be in agony, but he only gritted his teeth and moaned. She wanted to stop the bleeding and reseal the chest. The tampon filled the deep chasm, and blood expanded it. The blood flow slowed, but not enough. She repeatedly kicked backwards at agents who tried to get her away from Albright.

She ripped off her white cotton half-slip, folded it into a thick hand-sized pad and knelt over Albright, holding it firmly in place over the wound. His arm was already limp, a sign Lafferty might have severed the delicate web of nerves that run the arm and hand. *Triple damn.*

"Just stay with me, Albright. I'm right here. I'll take care of you," she said to Albright. "Help's coming."

Then in her most commanding tone she started barking orders to her Secret Service agents.

"GET THE AMBULANCE. CALL GEORGE WASHING-TON HOSPITAL. TELL THEM WE HAVE A STAB WOUND TO THE RIGHT CHEST. HAVE A GODDAMN VASCULAR SURGEON AT THE DOOR. AND A FUCKING NEUROSUR-GEON TOO."

In moments, the doctor and ambulance crew were there on the South Lawn. They started to load a moaning Albright into the ambulance. Abby never took her hand from the pressure bandage that was now sopping with bright red blood. Abby tried to climb in with him.

She wanted precisely the right amount of pressure on the wound: just enough to stop the bleeding. Then easing a bit every few seconds to let oxygenated blood and clotting factors in via any small collateral circulation that wasn't cut. Too much pressure and the arm would be damaged further, too little, he'd bleed out.

Sally grabbed her from behind, around the waist and tried to pull her out of the ambulance. Abigail again kicked Sally so she could ride with Albright. Three extra agents, plus Sally, managed to get her out.

"This guy has a pneumothorax, an arterial pumper, and nerve damage," Abigail yelled to the White House doctor in the ambulance. as the four agents pushed her head down and carried her into the building.

"Ma'am, you can't go with him. We have no idea what is going on."

Sally later said it was like a bullfighter trying to pull the bull out of a ring with just a bear hug.

Abigail was stunned. She caught a glimpse of Lafferty, lying immobile, face up on the South Lawn. He looked as if someone had poured a quart of bright red blood all over his chest. It was seeping into the lawn.

Red blood means I hit the left ventricle. He's dead for sure.

I just want Albright to live with two arms, not one.

CHAPTER THIRTY-SEVEN

AFTERMATH

Four agents muscled Abigail into the bunker deep below the West Wing.

"Where's Lafayette?" she demanded as she sat down on the bed and wrapped herself in its wooly blanket.

"In the Situation Room," Sally said.

"Good. He can handle things. I need to make a phone call. My phone's probably on the lawn." Abby got the shakes.

"Ma'am, you need to stay quiet. That's why there's no phone." Sally said.

"Get me a goddamn telephone. That's an order," Abigail barked at Sally. Abigail had blood all over her, even in her hair. Somewhere along the way, she lost her belt and one shoe. She didn't look commanding. She looked like the patient, not the doctor, in the emergency room.

"No," Sally said. "You need to rest."

Abigail got up and opened the door. Two Marine Sentries stood outside it.

"Marine. Get me a cell phone. Now. That's an order."

He handed her one from his pocket. She stared at Sally and smiled sarcastically. She tried to call Michael, but she was shaking too badly to use the phone. Finally, she handed it to the Marine and told him the number. Michael was on the line in seconds.

"Hello, Michael?" she said, making scooting motions to Sally, who stepped just outside the open door.

"Hi. Whassup?" he could hear something weird in her voice.

"I need to tell you I'm fine. When you see the news, don't worry. I am just fine." Abigail's voice was shaky.

"What the hell happened?" Michael sounded panicky.

"Someone tried to stab me, but Albright took the hit. He's probably in the OR at GW by now. He'll survive, but I hope he doesn't lose an arm."

"Oh, my god. How horrible. You're sure you're all right?"

"Shocked, but intact."

"And what about the guy with the knife?"

"I, um, killed him." Finally, Abigail's voice had settled down.

"How?" Abby's calm tone was scarier than her flustered one.

"Albright dropped his weapon when he was stabbed. I picked it up and pulled the trigger," Abigail reported.

"I didn't know you could shoot."

"Michael. I'm from Texas. I was born knowing how to shoot," Abigail said in exasperation.

Michael laughed. *Abigail would be just fine.*

"I'm leaving now."

"If Regina catches you in my room, we're both toast."

Abigail ended the call. She was overwhelmed with fatigue and cold. She wrapped the blanket tighter.

"I want to shower and go to my own bed," she told Sally.

"They want you upstairs first, and then you can clean up."

The Situation Room was a hive. Lafayette sat in her chair, definitely in control. When she appeared from the bowels of the building, everything in the room came to a stop.

People jumped to their feet, and gasped.

The President was alive and walking under her own steam. But she had blood head to toe, her hair was a mess, to say nothing of her mussed and bloody clothes. She had on only one shoe.

Lafayette got up and offered her his seat. Abby sat down, scared her legs would no longer hold her.

"General, I trust you've been minding the store? Would you continue until tomorrow?" she asked, then turned to Sally and asked her to retrieve the blanket she'd left below.

"Yes, ma'am."

The computer spit out the appropriate documents to temporarily transfer power. Abby and Lafayette signed them. Somehow, she smudged blood on the document. *Who cares?*

Abigail gave the second in command of the Secret Service a detailed statement. She told him everything she remembered. It only took a few minutes. By the time he was finished with the photos, Sally was back with the blanket. She wrapped herself up, as she was starting to shiver.

"And Lafferty?" Abigail asked Lafayette.

"Dead."

"I thought so. Albright?"

"Still in surgery. Lung will be fine, but they have to do microsurgery on his branilla pectus?"

"Close. Brachial plexus."

"Only one thing doesn't add up. His ID said he was Timothy Lafferty from Silver Spring."

"Oh," Abby said, distracted. *I want to know about Albright.*

She sat down and picked up a phone. "Put me through to a human at GW." *At least my teeth aren't chattering.*

When the call connected, she said in her standard doctor mode, "This is Dr. Adams. You have patient Thomas Albright in surgery. Connect me to the posting desk for that suite."

In a few moments, a nurse came on the line.

"Posting. Markham."

"This is President Adams."

"Yeah, sure, and I'm Lady Gaga," the mouthy nurse said.

"Sorry to burst your bubble, Gaga, but I really am Abigail Adams and I was wondering if you could stick your head in and give me report on patient Albright, the stab wound to the right chest."

"Oh, we all know who he is. I'll be back on the line in a moment, ma'am. And I apologize…"

"No need." Abby held for about a minute, sleepier by the second.

"Dr. Hasani is closing now. Said all went well. He anticipates a full recovery. He'll call you when he's out. He asked that I get your number."

"Great," Abby said, giving her the main number. "Ask for the Situation Room."

"Oh, and ma'am?"

"Yes?" Abigail said.

"We're all real proud of you," she said. "Dr. Hasani said your quick thinking saved his life."

"Thanks, but I was just doing my job. You'd have done the same thing, Gaga," Abby rang off and turned to the room with a smile of relief.

"Albright's going to be just fine," she said.

Then she burst into tears. Sally and three other agents accompanied her to the Residence. Two put protective arms under her blanketed arms, lest she collapse.

Regina was waiting for her with an anxious O.T. It took Abby a few minutes to assure both that none of the blood they saw was hers. She was stunned and tired, but mostly in need of a shower. She left the bloody clothes in the corner, in case anyone wanted them.

The warm shower helped, as did flannel pajamas and socks in May.

Regina hugged Abby as they sat on her bed.

"I couldn't lose you, not after Pris." Regina was crying. Abby could not remember tears like those in a long time.

"Reege, I'm fine. Really. Just shaky," her teeth were again chattering.

The White House doctor, the one she thought of as Dr. Tampon, was at her side in a few minutes.

"I just got back from GW, ma'am," he said. "Mind if I look you over?"

"Fine," Abby said.

He did a set of vital signs on her and a brief exam.

"You're stunned and need some rest, this kind of thing takes a while to sink in," he tried to be reassuring.

"Yeah, I know."

Regina inspected her ever more closely, like a mother counting fingers and toes on her new baby.

"I'm hungry and really thirsty," Abby said.

"I'll go get you a sandwich."

Reege headed for the kitchen.

O.T. took a seat in Abby's room.

"Regina was in quite a state," O.T. said. "I'm glad I was here for her."

"Me, too. I sometimes feel like Teddy Roosevelt and his daughter Alice. He said he could run the country or run Alice, but not both."

O.T.'s chuckle seemed far away.

Abigail felt like she was winding down to zero.

Regina returned with a grilled cheese sandwich and a glass of orange juice. She had her fiery face on.

"Were you two talking about me? You know how I hate people talking about me behind my back."

"No, Miss Regina, we were talking about Teddy Roosevelt," O.T. said with the best poker face Abby had ever seen. Abby ate a few bites, drained the orange juice, and suddenly felt cold and terribly, hopelessly sleepy. She crawled under the covers, asked for another blanket, and was asleep before Regina covered her with it.

Down in the Situation Room, the Attorney General, Secret Service, FBI, and Lafayette put together what they knew and what they didn't know.

"One. Our victim's ID said he was Timothy Lafferty from Silver Spring."

"Two. O'Neal's in custody in California, but John Lafferty never showed up for the buy. His car, however, was T-boned in the vicinity. The officer who wrote it up is away fishing for a few days," the head of the FBI said.

"Well," Lafayette said, "we need a positive ID. Get the FBI and Secret Service out to the Silver Spring address and sort this out."

"You want them to play nice?" Sam asked. "That'll be a first."

"Yes, I do. The Secret Service is stressed and needs backup."

"Three. Cordelia Laurus brought the guy to the party. We need to interrogate her," Sam said.

"She'd better not pull any separation of powers voodoo or claim she can't be detained," Lafayette said. "If she does, refer her to me."

"Sir, Dr. Hasani is on line 1," Chaffee said to Lafayette.

He, too, confirmed what Abigail had said.

"Thank you so much, Dr. Hasani. I'm sure the President will want to talk to you tomorrow. We've given her an evening off."

CHAPTER THIRTY-EIGHT

HOME SAFE

Regina watched Abby for a long time. Finally, she slipped away. O.T. was still up, and he would stay in the Family Quarters to watch over these two women so dear to him.

"How are you doing, Miss Regina?" he asked.

"I don't think I could have lost them both," Regina said, bursting into tears. O.T. gave her a handkerchief and an enveloping hug. He patted her gently. Having O.T. hold her allowed her to cry even harder.

In Silver Spring, FBI and Secret Service agents pulled up in front of Timothy Lafferty's home in two cars. While FBI agents took the rear, Secret Service rang the doorbell. In moments, the clone of the man dead on the White House lawn answered the door.

"Hey, what can I do for you?" Timothy Lafferty said.

Agents Pierce and Prose flashed him their badges and asked if they could come in.

"If you like. What's up?" he said, his voice betraying only curiosity.

A high-end sound system played classical music. Tim turned it down.

"I kinda get lost in the music, you know? So how can I help you?" He looked from one to the other.

"Could you tell us your name please?"

"Sure. I'm Tim Lafferty," he said pleasantly.

"Do you have any identification?"

"Sure. I'll get my wallet. It's upstairs."

"We'll accompany you."

Timothy thought this odd, but complied.

His wallet sat atop his dresser.

He opened the wallet and looked at his brother's driver's license.

"This is odd. This is my twin brother's license."

"May I see it please?" Pierce asked.

Lafferty handed it to the agent. He held it by the edges. Different names, addresses, and eye color. Same date of birth.

"Do you have any other photo I.D.?"

"My passport. It's is the other drawer."

The agent opened the drawer. Timothy Lafferty's passport was inside.

"Could you fill me in?" Timothy sounded concerned.

"When did you last see your brother?" Pierce asked.

"Not in months, we're not close. Then last night he drops by to crash for the night. I gave him a sandwich and a beer, and then I left. I got up late, and he was gone."

"Did you leave him alone at any time with your wallet?"

"Let me think. When he came in, I made him a sandwich. I was alone in the kitchen. Then he was here all night. I was asleep when he left this morning, so yes, he was alone with my wallet. Why?"

"Mr. Lafferty, we think your brother has passed away, and we need you to identify the remains."

"Oh, how awful. How did it happen?" Tim went pale.

"First, let's just make sure the man is John Lafferty."

"You're right, first things first." Tim knew to go with the feds with-out a fuss.

The guests at the barbecue gave individual statements and were long gone. Only one remained.

Secret Service Agent Franklin Merriweather walked into a small utility room, where he'd purposefully left Cordelia Laurus to stew in her own juices.

"Why have you detained me in this manner?" she demanded, standing up. "I'm a member of the U.S. Senate and we are not detained. Read the Constitution."

He ignored her, "Sit down."

Cordelia remained standing.

"Why did you bring the assailant to the party?" he asked, sitting down.

"My invitation said 'Senator and guest,' so I was well within my prerogative," she said. She sat down to humor the odious little man. Her nose pointed slightly upward, as if she were avoiding an unpleasant smell.

"When did you invite him?" Merriweather said.

"He called me. Last night. I planned to go alone, but he's a pre-sentable enough escort. He's been a big supporter of my campaigns, so when he said he wanted to see the President socially, I called and added him to the list this morning," she said. "End of story. May I leave?"

"If he was John Lafferty, how did the name Timothy get onto the list?" Merriweather sounded bored, but was anything but.

"He volunteered his given name was Timothy. I just assumed he went by his middle name. Now may I leave, or shall I have to have you formally reprimanded?"

"Did he give you anything of monetary value to induce you to bring him?" Merriweather said sharply.

"No, but today is my birthday, so he showed up with a gift for me. Just a brandy snifter. From Tiffany," she said with a small smile. She didn't say it was oversized and cost north of five hundred dollars. And she made sure to say "Tiffany." "Tiffany's" is so déclassé.

"Did you have any indication that he meant to hurt the President?"

"Oh, don't be absurd. He was a presentable escort, and that's all." She began gathering her things to leave.

"We are not finished," Merriweather said. "Were you aware that he and the former Secretary of Defense were targeted in a sting?"

"No. A 'sting' about what? This sounds like a bad movie." She made a small, dismissive wave.

"Ma'am, you need to cooperate."

"It's 'Senator' Laurus to you. And U.S. Senators do not get 'detained,' if you've read the Constitution lately."

"They do when they are implicated in an assassination attempt," the agent said without emotion.

"Please stand and put your hands behind your back."

"You are making a grave mistake. Do you have any idea who I am, young man?" Cordelia was livid.

"Yes, ma'am. You're the a-hole that brought the man who damn near killed my boss, a man who's like a father to me. You brought the man who tried to assassinate the President. Now stand up."

Cordelia remained seated. He grabbed her by her arm and yanked her out of the chair. She slapped him.

"You've also assaulted a federal agent. That, too, is a federal crime," he said, his face smarting.

Cordelia Laurus finally had the good sense to shut up.

Sometime in the small hours of the night, Michael appeared at the White House complex.

"The President is expecting you, sir."

Michael willingly went through more searches than ever before. "Please, do whatever you need to do."

Once inside the Family Quarters, agents directed him to the President's bedroom. He'd never been there before.

He knocked softly, and getting no answer, he stepped into the room. His eyes adjusted to the glow of a nightlight. He put down his bag and sat next to Abigail's bed, watching her breathe. Then, fatigue and anxiety overwhelmed him, too. He stripped down to his shorts and tee-shirt and crawled in next to her. She murmured something unintelligible and fell back asleep in his arms.

She awoke at five, aware that Michael was enveloping her in his arms. She relaxed and went back to sleep.

By seven, she was awake, wearing leggings and a long shirt, and ready for breakfast. Michael stirred and opened his eyes.

"Sorry to wake you," Abby said.

"No prob. What time is it?" he asked, sleepily.

"Seven my time—four, yours. You sleep. I'll have breakfast with Reege and O.T."

"Gimme five," he said, heading for Abigail's bathroom. Indeed, he reappeared clean, shaved and bright eyed. He grabbed his jeans and a fresh shirt, slipped his bare feet into Italian loafers and went out to breakfast with her.

Three of the people who valued Abigail the most had met only once before, and Regina was in a quandary. She did not like hanky-panky under her roof, but would make an exception this time. It wasn't really her roof, and Abigail had barely escaped death yesterday.

However, she wielded the coffee pot with authority.

"Coffee, Michael?" Regina said.

"I'd sell my soul for a cup about now," he said, smiling up at her.

She filled his cup. He took a long smell and exhaled in pleasure. Then he sipped it. "This coffee is fantastic. Where do you do get it?"

He expected it to be a Starbucks Presidential blend.

"I get it at the grocery store," Regina said, as if Michael was a total moron.

"I asked for that," Michael said, enjoying the joke as much as anyone.

Abby asked if Regina and O.T. would give Michael a tour of the Family Quarters only.

"I think the country's had enough news for one day."

"Michael, a word?" Abby said, indicating that he was to come back into her suite.

"I thought we could have a few minutes alone while I get ready for work."

Michael sat in a chair and watched as she quickly laid out all her clothes, from lingerie to outerwear. Then she added jewelry to the pile, plus a couple of odds and ends. She opened her purse, rummaged through it, and added a clean handkerchief and a tampon. At last, he'd found a woman who didn't dawdle getting dressed.

She peeled off her clothes and stepped into the bathroom, shutting the door. Within a few minutes, she returned, clean, groomed, coiffed, and wrapped in a towel. She dressed quickly.

"You wear a suit to the office on Sunday?" Michael asked.

"I'm going to visit Albright. I never leave the building without dressing as POTUS."

"Cameras everywhere," Michael said.

"Your ring was caked with blood yesterday," she said, offering it to Michael to fasten around her neck. "That really bothered me."

He bent down and gently kissed her neck.

"Ooh, no you don't. Regina is listening at the keyhole. Besides, I have to go to work."

She put on her watch and earrings. She held up the her left earring back/panic button. "Remember this?"

"That was a speed bump on the road to romance," he said.

Abby put a thumb drive and small plastic card into her bra.

"What are those?" he said.

"Nuclear launch codes," she said, pecking him on the lips. "Lunch? Noon? Here?"

General Lafayette was in the Oval Office when she walked in.

"Good morning. Thanks for babysitting. I was exhausted. But I'm ready to go back to work."

They both signed official control back over to Abby.

"Anything happen overnight?" Abby asked.

"Not really. Looks like Lafferty did indeed use his brother's ID. Brother seems clean. Cordelia Laurus brought him here, at his request. Of course, she slapped a federal agent who was questioning her, so she has a few problems…"

Couldn't happen to a nicer woman.

"So where did you sleep?" Abigail asked.

"O.T. sent in a rollaway bed." Lafayette stretched and tried to unkink his back. "And to think I bitched about a tent in Vietnam."

"I slept on it for weeks. I thought the Geneva Convention prohibited things like that. We'll order a new one."

"Any chance I can visit Albright?" she asked.

"Who can tell you no? Albright's in the hospital," Lafayette said with a chuckle.

"I'd love to take him flowers, but he'd hate it."

"How about a cactus?" Lafayette suggested.

"Brilliant. How was the PDB?

"Nothing new. Amazing, isn't it? Lafferty almost got you, but he wasn't on the radar. We knew we were chasing him in L.A., but we never thought he'd double back for you."

"It's always the wild card."

CHAPTER THIRTY-NINE

ALBRIGHT

Poppy came in on Sunday morning to eyeball Abby, who appeared as if nothing had happened to her. She walked with her to the motorcade exit under the West Wing. The in-house florist had no cactus, so Poppy made a note to get some with very long thorns tomorrow morning for Albright.

"Perfect. He'd hate flowers," Abigail said.

Abigail hugged a surprised Poppy. "You are very dear to me, Poppy." Then Abby entered the appointed vehicle.

The hospital had a secure entrance with a swift elevator to the Presidential area.

The area had enough floor space and outlets to bring most of the hospital to the President. The suite had plenty of room for security personnel, as well as bulletproof glass and Kevlar in the walls. When the President was not using it, it was sealed and locked.

The doors swooshed outward with a rush of air. The room contained ultra-pure air under pressure, so hospital germs wouldn't waft in.

"Wash those hands," she said to her agents at the sinks. They complied, watching Abby for technique.

She went to the nursing station.

"How was his night?" she asked the burly male nurse, who appeared to be in this forties. Larry was charting and not expecting to see the President.

He went to salute and then, remembering his civilian status, dropped his arm.

Abigail asked, "Where'd you serve?"

"Afghanistan, ma'am," he said.

"Thanks, Larry." She handed him a card with her semiprivate number. "If the VA hassles you, call me, okay?"

"Yes, ma'am." This time he did salute. Abigail returned his salute.

"Now, about Albright's night…"

"He did great. Already on room air, extubated, still has a chest tube, of course. He's using nothing from his morphine pump."

"I'm surprised he hasn't ripped it out. That man's tougher than rhino hide."

Larry laughed. "He didn't even flinch when I did gases after extubation." Arterial blood gases are very painful. "His wife was here all night. Sorry you missed her."

"I'll catch up with her."

"I'll page Hasani."

Abby went through the anteroom. A couple of off-duty agents were sitting in vigil.

They sprang to their feet when they saw her. Both needed a shave, but would not leave until relieved. Abby's agents stayed with them.

"Hey, thanks for helping our boss, ma'am," one of the agents said.

"I was ticked I couldn't ride with him to the hospital," Abigail said.

"No, about, um, packing the wound. Hasani said that saved him."

"Well, he saved me. It was the least I could do. Of course, he got the knife. Twice."

Hospital habits die hard. She rapped twice on the door and walked in. Luckily, Albright was decent and sitting up, a scrumptious breakfast of green gelatin and apple juice in front of him.

"Hey, you are a sight for sore eyes," she said, wiggling his big toe under the blanket. He smiled.

"G'morning, ma'am," he said, his voice even raspier from having a tube down his windpipe for eight hours. He had a "trapeze" over his bed so he could use his good arm to move himself. His right shoulder was heavily bandaged, his arm was carefully positioned on a bolster, and his fingers were pink.

"Can you wiggle your fingers?" Abby asked. He did. She smiled from ear to ear.

"I have flowers coming later."

"No pink," he croaked.

"Oh, phooey, and I sprang for a teddy bear and balloons, too," Abby feigned hurt. "I have a case of your favorite Scotch for you back at the office. How's Evelyn?" Abigail asked.

"Fine, as always," his voice was breaking up.

Abby gave him a big spoonful of ice chips. "Tilt your head back and let these slide down."

They did this twice. "Better."

"Albright, this is hard. No one's ever offered his life for mine. Thanks."

"It's my job. You die? I'm Mudd," he managed to growl out.

"Do you know who Dr. Mudd was?" Abby asked. He shook his head. She filled him in on Dr. Mudd, the conspirator/doctor who helped John Wilkes Booth after the Lincoln assassination.

"Who are you?" he asked in bewilderment. Some of his bosses didn't know jack.

Abby shrugged. "Just a trivia buff."

Abigail cast an expert eye on all the medical things around Albright. He was on track in his recovery.

"I better go back to my day job," she said.

"Thanks."

"Wild horses couldn't keep me away."

Her agents slipped in for a quick hello while Abigail greeted Dr. Hasani.

Each was pleased to shake the other's hand.

"The nation is in your debt," Abigail said.

"Just doing my job. Though I do have a problem…" he said reluctantly.

"What's that?" Abigail asked.

"They're trying to revoke my J-1 visa. If I go back to Iraq, I'm dead. They killed my dad, and he too was a surgeon."

"I'm so sorry. You're married? What does your wife do?"

"She's a neurosurgeon from D.C. Our daughter's two." *Smart family.*

"Oh, good grief. You are not going back. Give me your Social Security number, date of birth, something."

He scribbled away.

"Thank you, ma'am," he said, looking relieved as she took the paper.

"No, thank you. I'm glad you brought your skills here. I'll get the Secretary of State on this STAT."

CHAPTER FORTY

ALL EYES ON ABBY

Abigail took the rest of the day off, as it was a Sunday. She had a quiet couple of hours with Michael.

"I've got to get back to the shoot. I have a 5 a.m. call. We're already behind," he said as he cradled her in a hug. "I wish I could stay."

"I'll be fine. Knowing you'll be in my life forever makes everything okay," she said, aware at once of how short 'forever' could be. *Concentrate on Michael's warmth. Do not cry.*

Abigail was incredibly fatigued. She napped under the watchful eye of Regina or O.T. She did call Wicker about five p.m. and have him set up a press conference for ten a.m.

Michael called to tell her good night. Before she went to sleep, she called GW to check on Albright. She called again as soon as she awoke.

The PDB on Monday morning was routine. There was no chatter that implicated anyone other than John Lafferty in Saturday's events. Of course, the Taliban was thrilled with his effort and sad he did not succeed, but Abigail would expect nothing less from them.

The Secret Service reported that Timothy Lafferty was not criminally involved in the events on Saturday. Cordelia Laurus did require a disposition, however.

"While she wasn't a co-conspirator, she did slap a federal agent," the Attorney General said.

"Yes, well, that is unfortunate, but I think the sooner we put all this behind us, the better. I'll send Agent Merriweather a nice case of single-malt scotch," Abigail said. "Cordelia is probably allergic to apologies."

"I agree," the Attorney General said. "We have other fish to fry."

The only unusual part of her morning was Poppy asking for five minutes after the press conference. For the press appearance itself, Abigail made sure she looked ultra-perfect. Navy suit, power heels, pearls and the gleaming Great Seal of the United States pinned onto her left shoulder.

She ramrodded her posture and walked into the Press Room. The journalists sprang to their feet and gave her a spontaneous standing ovation.

No one should be applauded for killing another human being.

"Please, sit down. I wanted everyone to see that I'm in one piece and back at work. Your briefing materials contain all the details.

"I visited Secret Service Agent Albright. He's doing better than expected, in large part due to the work of an Iraqi-born cardio-vascular surgeon, Dr. Habib Hasani. Dr. Hasani trained at Johns Hopkins and did his cardio-vascular fellowship at Harvard. His wife is a neurosurgeon from D.C. and they have a little girl who is two.

"The federal government, in its infinite wisdom, is attempting to deport him for no other reason than he left a country where terrorists exist. His father was murdered and he fears for his life if he returns. The loss of this man would be a loss for our community, and a loss for common sense. I'm ordering a review not only of his case, but of the J-1 visa issue as well. If smart people want to come here as doctors, we should be smart enough to welcome them.

"I want to express my deepest thanks to Agent Albright for putting himself between me and a knife. I doubt I would have survived the knife headed down toward my chest. We'll have a full review of the incident, and its report will be forthcoming. Questions?"

"Madam President, we have heard that you saved Albright's life. Is that true?" Claire Bellows from CNN asked.

"I rendered aid appropriate to my level of training."

"But in doing so, didn't you expose yourself to more danger by remaining on the scene?" she asked as a follow-up.

"With all due respect, if Agent Albright was your dad, you wouldn't be asking that question. Next?"

"Frank Pierce, BBC. We've heard you were quite incapacitated after the incident and that Lafayette took over for you."

"Yes. As an emergency physician, I knew to expect physical and emotional aftershocks. I asked him to assume the presidency. He did a splendid job. We signed the appropriate documents. As usual, the Constitution worked well."

"What do you have to say to the family of your would-be assassin?" he followed-up. Abigail steeled herself not to cry, and offered instead the standard platitude.

"My heart goes out to his little boys, his brother, and to others in his family."

"Pierce Clive, BBC. Madam President, how does it feel to kill someone?" *What an ass.*

"You never, never want to know that feeling. I've spent my life saving lives. For once, I have no words." *And if I did, I wouldn't tell them to you.*

"Ma'am, we hear this was all part of a sting involving nuclear weapons. Would you comment on that?" CBS's White House correspondent asked.

"It's in your briefing materials. The weapons were never armed. They are secure now."

"And how was this discovered?"

"It's in your briefing materials."

"What charges will be filed against O'Neal?"

"The full force of the law will be brought against him."

"Senator Cordelia Laurus is also in custody. What was her role in this?"

"We do not believe she was criminally complicit. She still has one charge pending of assaulting a federal agent. Thank you, that's all." *I'll let her at least stew publicly for a while.*

She turned on her heel, leaving Wicker to deal with the rest.

Abigail beckoned Poppy into the Oval Office when she returned from the Press Room.

"Okay, Pops, you have my full attention." Abby kicked off her power heels and put on comfy navy pumps.

"I want to talk to you about John Lafferty."

"Do we need law enforcement?" Abigail asked.

"No. It's a chick thing."

"Then we need some mint tea." Abigail asked a steward to bring some in iced tea and cookies.

"Oh, I got Albright a cactus garden. It needs water once a month, max," Poppy said, as the steward brought the refreshments and left. "I specified the biggest thorns possible."

"He'll love it," Abigail said.

The women laughed. Poppy fell silent. Abby sipped at her tea and waited.

Finally Poppy spoke.

"John Lafferty and I were involved. You knew that." Poppy still sounded ashamed.

"These things happen, Poppy. No one is in any position to judge."

"When I disappeared to a spa to nurse my broken heart? I didn't go to a spa. I had an abortion." Her voice was totally flat.

"Oh, Poppy, were you all alone during that?" Abigail asked.

"I wanted to be alone," Poppy said. "I feared I'd never have another chance at motherhood, but I didn't like that man and I didn't want his baby."

"And now we know why. You knew, instinctively, what no one else did. Lafferty was a sociopath, and ones who are successful in business are hard to spot. What a wise, wise woman you are, Poppy," Abby said.

"I'd never thought of it that way," Poppy said, looking up into Abby's face. Abby could see the guilt leave Poppy's eyes.

"Oh, Abby, thank you so much," she said, tearing up.

Abby fished out a clean hanky from up her sleeve and put it in Poppy's hands.

"I'm honored that you would confide in me," Abigail said.

Poppy cried, and then it was over, done, gone from her mind.

"I have happier news, too," she said, sniffling. "Chaffee and I are talking marriage."

"Can I do another White House wedding? This could be better than the wedding chapels in Las Vegas. I could get an Elvis impersonator…"

"Funny, we're thinking of doing it in Vegas."

"Your choice."

Abby was home by noon for a bite to eat and a small nap.

Regina appeared as Abby was finishing her lunch.

"We're going to have to talk about something, baby girl," Regina said, hands on her hips. *She's going to tell me I can't sleep with Michael under 'her' roof.*

"Reege, I hate to be the one to break it to you, but we live here because of me. This isn't my house, but I do have some say in the house rules." *Let's have it out, right here and now.*

"So what are your thoughts about a single woman spending the night in the same room with a single man?" Regina asked archly, folding her hands in front of her.

"I assume both are of age?" Abigail asked.

"Yes."

"Then it is not my business," Abigail said.

"Good, then I think O.T. and I will move into one of the suites upstairs. That way, we can all have our privacy," Regina said, turning around and heading for the stairs. "I do hope we can take a number of our meals together, though," she called down from the stairs.

Abigail opened her mouth to speak and then shut it. *When you've won, shut up.*

Abby had a sandwich and iced tea. She knew if she went to sleep, she'd be gone for the afternoon, so she returned to the office. By two, she felt like she'd been up all night. She plodded through the rest of her day.

The West Wing seemed too crowded and too loud. She felt more conspicuous than usual. The attempt on her life was Topic One everywhere. Mikey and Wicker kept a close eye on the coverage, and a closer eye on her. It seemed every television was on. She'd escaped death, killed her attacker, and saved her agent. The media was enraptured.

Chris Stacy, an ABC investigative reporter, made one phone call to get the back-story. He called the head of the Senate Armed Services Committee, one of the handful of people who could honestly outplay him at golf. The chairman was anxious to bare his soul.

Abby labeled O'Neal as a bad guy, and his committee had let it slide.

"I should have listened. I blew her off because she was just so damn young," he told the reporter, ruefully. He agreed to sit for an interview, but only if the President agreed.

"That's the least I owe her," he said.

Luckily, no video coverage of the actual attack existed, except from the fixed security cameras deployed all over the White House grounds. In several shots, Lafferty meandered closer to the President, but the assault itself took place in the corner of one camera's eye.

The only flaw the Secret Service could see in their response was allowing Abby to assist Albright. All agreed an Abrams tank would not have kept Abby away from helping him. Sally was black and blue where Abby had repeatedly kicked her away.

Abigail spent most of the day reassuring world and national leaders that she was, indeed, just fine. The call from Her Majesty was one of the firsts.

"Hello, Your Majesty," Abby said with a smile in her voice. *I like this lady.*

"Oh, my dear, I am so glad you weren't physically hurt," she said warmly.

"Thank you, ma'am. I'm just glad my agent will recover. His actions are very humbling."

"Indeed. But he wasn't just protecting you."

"I don't understand."

"As President, any attempt on your life is an assault on your nation's stability. You are the symbol of that."

"Oh. So that's why I needed to be perfect in front of the press."

"Yes. And if you need to be a weepy mess in private, that's what privacy is for." She used the British pronunciation, "priv-uh-see."

"Wise words, ma'am, wise words."

"Why thank you, my dear. Over here, I can't give advice, even after sixty years at the center of things."

"How are Jemima Lafferty and her boys?"

"She'll land on her feet. Her father's quite well to do. She'll likely take back her maiden name. Good or bad, the father will fade for the boys. Do keep in touch." And she was gone.

One of Abigail's calls was from the chairman of the Armed Services Committee.

"Good afternoon, Mr. Chairman," Abigail said pleasantly.

"This is all my fault. All my fault. I should have listened to you." He sounded quite distraught.

"Climb down off the cross, Mr. Chairman. The committee, not you, ignored me. I do not hold you responsible," Abigail reassured him.

"I knew you were right, but you were so young. O'Neal was a smart Secretary of Defense. I knew he was mean. I just didn't think he was a crook."

"Neither did I. I just thought he was arrogant. Doing the right thing sucks—that's why we sometimes skip it."

The chairman laughed.

"So how come you knew this and I didn't?" he asked.

"I practiced medicine. The first time I didn't do the right thing, someone died."

CHAPTER FORTY-ONE

TURF WAR

Two days later, Michael called and asked if he could come for the next night. "We rearranged the shoot schedule a bit. It's just for one night, but…"

Abby was tremendously complimented that Michael would again cross the country to spend one night with her.

She and Michael wandered around the White House that evening. He was in awe of the building. She showed him nooks and crannies she'd discovered on her late-night rambles. She hated having the Secret Service clear a path for them, but their romance could not get out.

"I cried myself to sleep for weeks when I first came here. Some mornings I even threw up, I was so scared," she said.

"And you're not more scared now?" he asked.

"Michael, I can't function if I'm afraid. Albright was hurt, but I walked away. Sad to say, but the system worked. We were chasing Lafferty, but we didn't think he'd walk in the front door," she said.

They got ready for bed like an old married couple. Each took a quick shower. He slept in clean boxers and a tee-shirt; she put on a lightweight gown.

When they were ready for bed, he asked politely, "Which is your side of the bed?"

"The one with the phone," she said. "Occupational hazard."

"I should have known that. You know, we might, just might, think about putting the phone on the other side." Apparently he had a favorite side of the bed. *First turf issue.*

"Can't tonight. It's hardwired and a secure line."

"Then I'll just get in on the other side," Michael said.

"I am counting on that, yes," Abby said with a smirk.

When she was snuggled on his shoulder, he spoke, "We can't get outed, Abby dearest."

"I know," she sighed.

Once again, Abigail felt her world crack. She did not move a muscle. She waited for him to speak.

"I love you. We'll be together forever. But I've learned the depth of your prior commitment," he said earnestly. "I didn't get it until Lafferty came after you."

Abigail remained mute. She didn't trust herself to speak.

"Now come here, woman. I think you need some loving."

Indeed she did. He was gentle and slow with her, afraid she would feel attacked anew. If anything, she was greedy. She needed the life-affirming act of sex to reclaim her hold on life's loveliness. If this was their last night for a long time, she was going to make the best of it. And their best was magnificent.

When she awakened in the morning, Michael was a bundle of smiles, a kid on Christmas morning.

"I've figured this out," he said.

"And how is that?" Abigail asked.

"My production company will rent an apartment in the Franklin Towers. Then I'll visit you in the penthouse on weekends, or longer if I'm not working. You can chopper over without giving Albright a coronary. We'll 'come out' when the time is right."

"Michael, you're brilliant."

"Our lovin' shook loose a pretty good idea last night."

Abby was thinking how she could spend nights at the penthouse and be back for the PDB. She'd drop her 5 a.m. workouts. She and Michael could work out horizontally. Those were more fun, anyway.

May 23 D-Day Minus Fourteen

Again, the shepherds went to all seven sectors on seven market days. "If only Taliban or Al-Qaeda are left in your home, your home will be destroyed. If you cannot send away your sons eight and over, your husband will be hunted down on foot. No children will be hurt. Get enough pills for everyone in the house. You need only do one thing for freedom. Leave. Your Muslim sisters have a place for you. Tell no one."

Abigail tried to cook at the penthouse, but each effort resulted in dinner in the trash and a call to room service. Michael could do breakfast and lunch easily. Finally, after a cooking attempt involved the use of the fire extinguisher, Michael put his foot down.

"My darling, it's no problem paying twice for any dinner. But if you set this place on fire, our gooses are cooked."

"Bad pun, Mister."

"So, Missus, I'll cook and you can help. I imagine you are trainable. Whether you have talent, I don't know," he said, kissing the tip of her nose.

Abigail laughed and became a *sous* chef. She got quite proficient at chopping, mincing, dicing, and the like. She actually went on line to learn how to boil an egg. She had to watch a DVD, twice, to learn to run the espresso machine. *Being President is way easier than running the espresso machine.*

They cleaned up together and found that domesticity suited them, especially when it landed them in bed.

Their nicknames, Mister and Missus, stuck, and this pleased them enormously.

Near the end of May, Michael announced that he needed to leave for work.

"You, my dear, are not a cheap date, and if I'm going to keep you in the style to which you are accustomed, I gotta make some money. Being First Gigolo is fun, but it doesn't pay for beans," he said.

"I thought movies took a while to get going," she said.

"Normally, yes. But their lead had a car accident, and they're desperate. So I told my agent to see how much extra he could get out of them."

"Is that really necessary?" Abigail asked. Two references to money in one conversation set off an alarm. She didn't want to marry a man who lived beyond his means. Texans had a saying for people like that: all hat, no cattle. Abigail couldn't respect that.

Michael laughed harder than she had ever seen him do.

"Honey, I couldn't spend all the money I have in a zillion years. You'll never want for anything," Michael said. "I never touch my capital. I only live off the income."

She decided it wasn't time to tell him she did the same thing.

CHAPTER FORTY-TWO

RUN-UP TO D-DAY

May 30, D-Day Minus 7

The shepherds told the women, "It will be soon. Bring nothing. Wear two sets of clothes. Wear good shoes. Dress the children warmly. Count how many pills you will need, one for everyone left behind. Plan where to send your sons eight and over. If you have dogs outside, get pills for their food."

Salazar had stockpiled enough tasteless sleeping pills to fill a grain elevator.

American GIs painted a fleet of beat-up buses to look like Afghan ones. They were short a few, so they stole some and hid them.

Layla, too, was ready. The widows were at her compound of houses in the South of France. All were delighted to go to Australia. Many were multilingual. As well, each chose her area of work: medical, school, playground, clerical, and the like.

Camp Freedom was ready in Northern Australia. American GIs had set up everything except the playground. Marilyn was ready with a mobile U.S. Passport office there.

"You can't do squat without a passport, and since this is our idea, they'll get U.S. passports. They can always change them."

By chance, on D-Day minus seven, Afghan President Mazoon called Abigail about the Taliban.

"I cannot lead a country in which a major force is totally ignored," he said bluntly.

"You are riding on the back of a tiger, and tigers get hungry. But you must do what you think best, President Mazoon."

"I sense that you are very displeased," he said.

"Has the Taliban built you any sewage treatment plants lately? How many electrical substations have they built?" Abigail asked.

"No, but the Taliban will destroy the ones you build if I don't deal them in."

"Then I do not envy you your job. Goo*d day*."

For the first time in her presidency, she hung up on a world leader.

June 1, Washington

Albright was back at work, relegated forever to driving a desk. He was still in physical therapy and would retire when Abby left office. In the meantime, he used his brain. Let the younger guys use brawn. *Funny, the way Mother Nature doesn't give us both at the same time.*

Abigail summoned the chairman of the Senate Armed Services Committee to the Oval Office that afternoon.

After pleasantries, she said, "You remember owing me a favor?"

"Indeed I do."

"Well, you'd best sit down." Abigail explained what was about to happen. The man was speechless.

"Daring and brilliant," he said, once he recovered his voice. "I'll keep it under my hat until it's all over."

"Oh, and we'll be giving the women a stipend, directly into their bank accounts wherever they go, so no host country can steal their money. I'm calling it a military expense, as it will shorten the war. Five years of minimal support works out to between six and twenty-five days of warfare, depending on where they go. Much of the money is coming from private sources, but not all."

"I've got your back."

"Thanks."

CHAPTER FORTY-THREE

D-DAY

June 6

D-Day dawned cloudy and cool in Sector One. The women came to the market as usual. The pills disappeared in record amounts. "Give everyone staying behind pills in their food. Also into food for any dogs outside." Muslims never had dogs indoors.

"Send your sons eight and over away for the night. If that's not possible, give him a pill. As soon as the men are snoring, leave. Come to the market. Keep quiet. Keep your children quiet. Get on the buses. On the bus, tell us if children are at home. We will not hurt children."

Salazar had things planned down to the number of indelible markers and flashlights each shepherd carried. He also planned water and snacks for all the travelers, especially candy, a rarity for the little ones.

The women left after dark. Most wore all the jewelry they owned. It was their only asset. In the Arab world, women like jewelry as it is an easily portable hard asset.

Once a bus was full of mothers and their children, it left, running with low lights. The shepherds in Afghan clothing passed out indelible markers and flashlights. Each woman who could write was to put her name, address, and date of birth on her arm, as well as the names of her children and their birthdates. For children, the mother would write the child's name, date of birth, and mother's name on either arm.

Translators easily spotted women who could not read or white and helped them without comment. Formal IDs had to wait for Australia.

Most importantly, women gave the name and address of the husband in the Taliban or Al Qaeda.

For women who could not get their boys out or who had elderly relatives at home, U.S. military hunted the Taliban member on foot. Soldiers took all weapons and communications devices. Grandparents and boys eight and over still had a home.

Special ops troops were in two-way communication with the shepherds on the busses. As soon as the busses were safe on a U.S. base, the assaults started.

The buses went to waiting aircraft. Once full, they left for one of the big bases. Or if they were close enough, to a C-5 base itself. Each C-5 had seating, sanitation, and food for over a five hundred people without luggage. Salazar had borrowed some transport aircraft from the Australians, and that made things easier.

Abby was in the Situation Room when the first call came in over a satellite phone that one bus was full to overflowing and another was needed at the site. The military dispatched another.

The destruction of targeted homes was a military operation. They took some out with mortars; others required more expensive drones. That a woman would flee and authorize the death of her husband, and the destruction of her home, spoke to the cruelty in which she lived.

Day one was nerve wracking, and the numbers were staggering. They were exceeding expectations, and Salazar had to scramble to get extra vehicles and airplanes into their hubs. The first load left Afghan airspace a scant three hours after the women arrived at the market place.

"Hey, that's easier than getting on international flight with a first-class ticket," Marilyn said, giving Abby a high five from Australia over their video conference link.

The military destroyed all the houses harboring only Taliban and Al Qaeda by daybreak. Many of the houses contained weapons caches and held vital communication equipment. All that was left was useless debris.

Muslim women greeted the new arrivals in Australia. Many greeters wore headscarves, many did not. They were kind and gentle with their tired sisters. Each woman had an opportunity to bathe, eat, and rest with her children.

Sector two went faster, as personnel knew what to do. Again, a barrage of destruction lit up the middle of the night. Afghan men all over the country knew something was up, but couldn't figure a way to counter it.

Abby slept in snatches, trying to work all day and stay up most of the night. She iced her face three times a day. At least.

In sector three, they hit pay dirt. A woman revealed that Al Zawahiri, as well as six other top Al Qaeda men, were in her home.

"Many are in my house tonight. I put extra pills in the food. They are two stories below ground and will stay until morning," she said through an interpreter. Within moments, her address was relayed, confirmed, and a special forces team attacked, killing all the sleeping Taliban and Al Qaeda members and confiscating an incredible stash of intelligence.

Abigail wanted to teleport herself to Afghanistan and see Al Zawahiri's body herself. She could barely contain herself.

When nothing had come through in terms of identification, she went to the Residence and headed for bed.

As usual, Michael called her at ten for a chat about their respective days.

"So how was your day, my darling Missus?" His voice sounded like warm honey on the phone.

"Oh, you know, another day, another eleven hundred dollars," Abby said nonchalantly. "And you?"

"I had to do a nude scene with Kendra Wallace. The woman smokes like a chimney. Ick," he said. "She didn't even use mouthwash. So I did, twice, after the scene. Plus, I showered."

"I don't know whether to be jealous or not," Abigail said. "The woman's known for her body."

"Of course she is. It's all plastic," Michael said. "Abby, I really, really miss you. A million guys might have wanted to be in my shoes today, but not me. I wanted to be with you."

"Well, I'm out of a job in about eighteen months," Abigail said.

"Well, sleep tight. Call me any time—you're never a bother," he said. She seldom called him anyway, and lately she all but lived in the Situation Room.

It took a week, but at the end of it, nearly a half million people had left Afghanistan, almost all wives and children of the Taliban and Al Qaeda. Of course, many women pretended to be married to the Taliban, but hey, if they wanted out that bad, God bless 'em. As well, many mothers brought very, very tall seven year old sons. Many residences were obliterated, but none with children in them.

Marilyn reported from Australia that many of the women were in horrible shape, but counselors were working with them. Abby had insisted that child life therapists come to help the kids. The kids, according to Marilyn, were having a ball. They liked everything except the dentist and the immunizations. *They're normal.*

On completion of the mission, Abigail spoke to the nation, this time seated at the desk in the Oval Office with vases of Rose Garden roses behind her on the credenza.

"Hello, everyone. I have wonderful news. A very successful secret mission, Operation Women in Flight, has just concluded.

"We undertook this mission to destroy the Taliban and the remaining Al Qaeda cells in Afghanistan. It has succeeded spectacularly. The Taliban and Al Qaeda in Afghanistan are history. We've destroyed their ability to terrorize their own women as well as people abroad. So far, I have heard of no civilian casualties.

"Under cover of darkness on seven nights, the United States, with the assistance of some allies, as well as the International Committee for Afghan Women, allowed wives of Taliban and Al Qaeda members to vote with their feet. The youngest wife is ten, the oldest, eighty-one.

"Nearly a half million women and their children have been safely relocated to an undisclosed location. Those women were so anxious to be free, they risked everything. Once the women were safely out, and with their permission, we destroyed their homes. If elderly family members or older boys were at home, our military left them untouched. We killed only our military enemies.

"Most importantly, Al Qaeda as we know it is gone in Afghanistan. The commander of the Afghan theater has confirmed not only the deaths of Al Zawahiri, but also hundreds of other members and their terrorist plans.

"I can tell you they were planning to destroy another American icon, the Golden Gate Bridge on the Fourth of July. I'm not releasing further details, but we dodged a big bullet.

"Women were allowed to bring out their daughters of any age, but left behind any boy over eight. Children left behind were uninjured. We felt, sadly, that older boys with fundamentalist beliefs would be unwelcome in the rest of the world.

"Under the Department of State, these women and their children will be allowed to immigrate to the country of their choice.

"Each woman will have a stipend for five years, a sort of international alimony from the United States as well a non-profit group, The

Committee for Afghan Women, to help her get her feet on the ground, learn a new language, get a job, and get her kids going in their schools.

"These women will receive their alimony into their own bank account, so they will be net assets to any country smart enough to take them in.

"And before anyone has a heart attack over the cost, the war in Afghanistan costs two hundred million dollars a DAY. We are making money on this deal. Depending on where these women choose to live, their stipend for five years totals between six and twenty-five DAYS of warfare. Shortening the war by under a month lets us break even. Ending it is priceless.

"The stories we are hearing are far, far worse than the stories of any imagination. We have not only saved these women from a life of servitude—we have saved their very lives. Fundamentalist Muslim women are slaves in their own homes. Their husband and in-laws may beat them at will. It is even acceptable to kill your daughter if she refuses to marry the man you've chosen for her, even if she is ten and he is seventy-four. This is an 'honor' killing.

"Many of the women show evidence of multiple fractures, traumatically broken teeth, and some are nearly catatonic from years of abuse. Many men took wives before they reached puberty.

"The children are better than their mothers, as they have youth on their side. We have medical, dental and psychological facilities at their location, and we hope to rehabilitate all as quickly as is humanly possible.

"Lest you think this behavior is just a cultural norm and none of our business, the Afghans are signatories to the United Nations Declaration of Human Rights, which prevents sexual use of children. They have tolerated egregious violations that they'd promised to uphold.

"We took this action primarily for military reasons. With Al Qaeda and the Taliban gone, we have achieved our military objectives in Afghanistan.

"President Mazoon and I spoke last week. I encouraged him to stand against the Taliban. He was not persuaded. Well, President Mazoon, you are on your own.

"We destroyed the Taliban. We destroyed Al Qaeda in Afghanistan and we are leaving.

"As well, I have ordered the destruction of the poppy fields. We will give each farmer the street value of one year's crops. Usually he gets only a pittance—the drug lords get the rest. This should tide them over until they choose other crops, like nutritious food for their own people.

"We hope that the absence of war and drugs will allow a beautiful and ancient country to reflower. Afghanistan is rich in natural resources and the American University will offer degrees in mining so the Afghan people can learn to manage their own resources.

"I've ordered all troops home by Christmas. We will also bring home all our war-making materiel. We will leave behind existing construction supplies to help in the rebuilding.

"Muslim women all over the world have made this possible. They have contributed to the fund for the stipends and are helping with relocation. So next time you see a woman in a headscarf, say thank you.

"We have roughly three hundred thousand Afghan-Americans in this country, and if they wish to sponsor a family, they can contact the Department of State via its website.

"We didn't start this war. Al Qaeda did with the destruction of the World Trade Center in 2001. But we darn sure finished it.

"Listen up, terrorists. Terrorism has no place in the civilized world. Try it against Americans, and I will rain down on you the full force and might of the United States of America in ways you cannot imagine. You might be dedicated, but we are more dedicated and have far superior power.

"Religious wars are medieval. Practice your religion but leave other people alone. Life is too lovely to waste it in hatred. Play with your children, smile at your neighbors, and build strong communities. If you follow the path of peace, you have nothing to fear from the United States. We will welcome you to the global village.

"Thank you and good night."

When Samson told her she was clear, she took out her IFB, took off her mike, and wept tears of joy. She was exhausted, but she felt a sense of accomplishment like she had never felt before.

There was dancing in the streets on military bases. Finally, the end was in sight.

At ten, Michael called.

"So while I'm trying to avoid the horrid charms of Kendra Wallace, you've pulled off the biggest coup of your presidency," Michael said.

"I couldn't tell you, Michael. You know that. But you'd better tell me if Kendra puts moves on you, Mister."

"Well, Missus, we have finished our scenes together," he said. "I might even be able to get home this weekend. Are you free?"

"Let me see. Soul Food is Thursday, Arts night, Saturday, and you might enjoy Sunday brunch. We'd have only moments alone, but…"

"You know that anyone who sees us together will see love radiating off of us," Michael said. Abby blushed. *If I blush over the phone, what would I do in person?*

"We've made a commitment. Do you think the country's ready to see it?" Abby asked.

"No, Missus, I don't. You have a prior commitment the way a mother of quintuplets has a prior commitment. I'd just get in the way right now. The nation wants you to itself right now."

They agreed to keep to their plan of privacy "at least until the end of the year."

Abigail cried herself to sleep on the night of her biggest success.

The stock market leapt two thousand points the next day.

Salazar announced the order in which various units would leave Afghanistan. And since extra planes were in country, he accelerated the timetable. Everyone would be home before Thanksgiving.

CHAPTER FORTY-FOUR

FALLING INTO PLACE

The commission on the events of Abigail's succession concluded that the deaths were freak occurrences. Even the die-hard conspiracy theorists couldn't come up with a vaguely plausible idea. No one could find a grassy knoll.

Abigail created a cabinet level Department of Information Technology and Communications, incorporating the FCC and other entities.

"The information superhighway has to be safe, secure, and easily accessible," she said at the ceremony. "To ensure we get the best talent, I'm appointing an advisory committee of techies from twelve to thirty-five. Computers think the way kids do, and if we leave this to grown-ups, we're all in deep trouble."

Regina's Recipes came out in June and was a best seller. Reege made the rounds of the talk shows. She was her own opinionated self. She even appeared with her male matinee idol, Jeff Washington, on a panel about children. She was some sort of happy that day. The nation was enchanted by her wisdom.

"I don't like anybody who urinates in the subway. I don't care what color they are."

"You don't need anything except soap and water to keep a house clean."

"If you can't afford it, don't buy it. Credit cards are the devil's invention."

"We are all our own worst enemy. When you're down, look up. It's there. Now stop whining and start building yourself a ladder."

"If the first two things on the grocery list are beer and cigarettes, you have your priorities all wrong. That money, over eighteen years, would almost pay for college."

"Anyone who'd buy their kids a pair of two hundred-dollar sneakers is a MO-ron. If all their friends are doing it, then their parents are MO-rons, too. If you have two hundred dollars, take him to the dentist, then go get his teenaged shots free at the city clinic. Put the rest aside for college."

"If you live in a run-down neighborhood, and you don't have a job, get out and clean up your neighborhood. It's YOURS. Get some bags and some gloves and get to it."

"English is our language. Speak it well and people see your brightness. Jive only hides your light under a basket."

"Need a job? Forget a job fair. Iron your church clothes and knock on doors. Sooner or later, someone will hire you."

"If you have cable TV but no books in the house, your kids are headed for the ditch. Get rid of cable. Go to the library, play games, or play catch with your kids and save that money for college."

Naomi wanted her to do her own show, but Regina declined.

"I'm heading for the rocking chair. I've earned it, thank you very much," she said with a firm shake of her head.

On September 1, Poppy and Chaffee got married by an Elvis impersonator in Vegas. Abigail gave them round-trip, first-class tickets to Italy. Michael, for his part, loaned them his villa in Ravello for their honeymoon.

Poppy came back, not only with stars in her eyes, but with a baby due in late June. Abigail was getting baby lust.

Regina and O.T. married quietly in the East Room of the White House in late September. Abigail was thrilled for them. She was glad O.T. and Reege would take care of each other.

"I can't believe I'm a first-time bride at my age," Regina said.

"Hey, you give women everywhere hope," Abby replied.

O.T. took Regina to Paris for their honeymoon. Abby wanted to give them a week at the Ritz, but O.T. would have none of it. "I have a chic boutique hotel all picked out. Mikey's man knew about it." Abby instead gave them a car and driver for the entire time, a luxury by anyone's standards.

Kim's business was blossoming. She was the new Vera Wang. She started in her bedroom and now took over the building next door to Tran's. The downstairs was a showroom, upstairs a workroom. Society brides flocked to her from all over the country.

P.J. O'Neal had a trial date of September 7, but he saved everyone the trouble by dropping dead on the eve of the trial. People were either annoyed or relieved. Abigail was relieved.

The first week in December, she got the six-month report on Women in Flight. Well over half the women and children went to live with distant relatives. The children were bouncing back faster than the mothers were. The American Afghan community was especially supportive, as were those in other first world countries. The Australians had taken a shine to these families, and many of the women were working toward Australian citizenship. These children were attending Australian schools. More than one woman embraced a totally new life.

Arab countries welcomed them slowly. After all, they were widows who had behaved badly by leaving their husbands. After the Arab spring, and the events in Afghanistan, the men began to see things in a less traditional light. Perhaps it would be a good idea to use the talents of everyone in the society, not half.

"If all else fails, we'll take them," Marilyn and Abigail agreed. "After all, it was our idea."

"The most important thing is a correct placement, not a quick one," Layla Farid said. "The women need to feel secure. Freedom is a new thing to them."

Everyone was at the White House on Christmas Eve. After the party was over, Michael and Abby went to Camp David. It snowed in the night, and they awakened to a white Christmas. He serenaded her with the Bing Crosby classic. He was so awful, she ended up in hysterical laughter. How he could persevere in the face of her laughter was amazing.

"Don't give up your day job, Michael. Please." She wept with laughter.

"But Spielberg wants me to do a musical," he said in mock sincerity. "I don't think I could take it."

Later in the day, they played Scrabble. Abigail had yet to win a game and was getting quite competitive about it.

"Missus, I cut my teeth on this game. It's just a game," Michael would say each time she lost.

"I don't like to lose," Abigail would reply.

Finally, she won a game, by three whole points. She was jubilant.

"I did it. I did it. I finally beat you." She reached over and kissed him.

"How about a rematch?"

"Nope. I'm going to savor my victory for a nice long time," she said.

CHAPTER FORTY-FIVE

NEW YEAR'S EVE

New Year's Eve

Abigail and Michael hosted a New Year's Eve Party at the White House to announce their engagement. It was almost redundant, as their inner circle had known they were serious for nearly a year. The non-drinking Poppy came with a proud Chaffee, Duke and Kim attended, as did her parents. Regina and OT held hands much of the evening. She also asked the Salazars, the Lafayettes, Mikey, and Marilyn Chernosky. Albright and his wife Evelyn came. Wicker was there, escorting a smiling Laura Rowe.Michael's mother, Louise Aston, fit right in. She told Abigail she was glad Michael was settling down.

"He was waiting for you, my dear. He said the minute he laid eyes on you, other women never existed for him," Louise Aston said.

"I wondered whether it was me or my job."

"Trust me—it was you. He's the least star-struck man I know."

Abigail laughed. *That was indeed true.*

This soiree was black tie. After all, she'd fallen in love with Michael the first time she laid eyes on him, and he was wearing a tux that night.

She again wore her blue gown, and it was luscious with her ruby and pearl jewelry. Red, white, and blue. Perfect for the President.

For Christmas, Michael had given her matching ruby earrings. Abby gave him a set of gold U.S. coins made into cufflinks, heads on one, tails on the other. Since his birthday fell between Christmas and New Year's, she had Pris's favorite antique jeweler, Past Era in Houston, ship a two-hundred-year-old, eighteen karat gold studs and cufflinks, still in the original case for black tie. *Ah, the things they'd seen.*

Earlier in the day, Michael had formally asked Regina and Duke for permission to marry Abby.

"You may. But if you hurt a hair on her head, young man, you'll have to answer to me," Regina said, wearing her fiery face. She thought about holding a rolling pin for emphasis, but decided that was unnecessary for Michael.

"And, unfortunately, you'll have to answer to me as well," Duke said, looking down on him.

"I'm going to spend the rest of my life making sure no one ever hurts her," Michael said. "I treasure her as much as you do."

At midnight, they drank champagne, kissed and sang "Auld Lang Syne." Then Michael tapped his champagne flute and asked for everyone's attention.

"You might have noticed that Abigail and I are somewhat fond of each other," he said, eliciting raucous laughter.

"With Regina's permission, and with Duke's, I want to announce that Abigail and I are going to be married."

Everyone cheered.

"Some time ago, I asked Abigail to marry me and gave her a ring. It's around here somewhere." He patted down his pockets. Abigail drew it out of the front of her dress.

"Oh, yes, I forgot—she keeps it with the launch codes."

Everyone laughed.

He took the ring and put it on Abigail's ring finger.

"I have finally dragged her, kicking and screaming, to the announcement of our wedding. We will marry as soon as the new President is inaugurated."

Then he kissed her until she blushed. Furiously.

"Get a room," Duke hollered and stomped his feet.

"Plant 'er a good one," Mikey chimed in.

She blushed even more furiously and didn't even care.

The whole group cheered.

Abigail said, "We'll make the announcement January second. I thank all of you for protecting our privacy up to now." She was still bright red from the second best kiss she'd ever gotten. The best ever was the first.

The party broke up about 1 a.m. Regina made sure everyone had black-eyed peas, and then most headed to a bed in the White House. It was big enough for a sleepover for that many, so why not? During FDR's time, the place was like a hotel.

The next morning, Michael made blueberry pancakes for all, Regina did the bacon, and Abigail was allowed to pour the orange juice, with or without champagne, as the guests pleased.

Albright was a bit flustered at having his boss pour his orange juice, but he and Evelyn slept in the Lincoln Bedroom, so they were quite content. The Trans were in the Queen's Bedroom, and they, too, were right at home.

As Abigail looked around the table, she realized her patchwork family had turned into a tapestry of many cultures.

"To all of you, I want you to look around. If America is an idea, you are that idea made real." She raised her glass.

"To America." Everyone raised their glass and drank.

Duke stood up.

"Aunt Abby, I'd like to propose a toast." He smiled at Kim, who dipped her head.

"To Kim, who is going to make me a father in July. If we have a girl, she will be Priscilla Regina."

Abigail and Regina gave way to a flood of tears, while everyone drank to their happiness.

After a lazy morning, everyone went home. Michael and Abby were glad that their days of hiding were over. No one would care if a White House staffer saw him at breakfast.

Their engagement was topic one for the first two weeks in January.

The nation was beside itself that the Sexiest Man Alive was marrying the POTUS. Abigail allotted a total of three full days for publicity, an incredible indulgence. She also announced she would not run for election.

"Two years is enough for an accidental President."

The first White House briefing on the wedding was festive and full of silly questions. Wicker was stumped at some.

"I not only haven't the foggiest idea what the President's bridal colors will be, I don't even know what bridal colors are."

The press drew lots for interviews. Each journalist had thirty minutes, during which Abigail was scrupulous to make sure that Michael got equal billing. That was silly, since most were more interested in Michael anyway. Women all over the country wept that he was off the market.

Not only were Abigail and Michael in demand, so was their inner circle.

Mikey, of course, took full credit as Cupid, and announced he was, of course, going to be the Best Man, even though Michael hadn't asked. Yet.

"You know, the Best Man ends up with his pick of the single ladies that night," he said with his mischievous twinkle.

When she and Michael saw that interview, they convulsed in laughter.

"The man should bottle it and sell it," Abigail said.

Regina was also outspoken, saying Abigail had "met her match," and it was about time someone took care of her. "She's spent her entire adult life taking care of people, whether as a doctor, or caring for her dying sister, or as Senator then President." *Huh? Reege has taken care of me my whole life.*

While the nation burbled with happiness, Abigail went into over-drive on the State of the Union speech. She invited two noted Constitutional scholars to advise her. Andrea Lefkowitz from Georgetown and George Midas from Stanford were pre-eminent in their knowledge of the Constitution. She told them what she wanted, and they got busy drafting not only the amendments, but also the enabling legislation for implementation. The White House Webmaster, Charley Garrett was in on the planning, as the website was a crucial part of the process.

"Congratulations, ma'am," Andrea Lefkowitz said. "These are long overdue."

"Thank you. And thank you for keeping your mouths firmly shut until after the State of the Union Speech. The three of you are invited as my guests."

While they drafted, she drafted a general to lead the charge.

CHAPTER FORTY-SIX

THE GENERAL

Early January

Abigail had been tinkering with her ideas for over a year. Now, she had the political capital to ask for them. She only wanted five things, but they were biggest five things any President had ever asked for.

Thankfully, the country was solidly behind her. The war in Afghanistan was over. Al Qaeda was dust. The economy was turning around, U.S. drug consumption was down, she'd foiled a plot to sell loose nukes, and infants were better off than ever before. The fact she had survived an assassination attempt, killed her attacker, and saved her agent impressed the people enormously.

The nation was optimistic and energetic. Some called her presidency a new Camelot. Abigail hated that phrase. Camelot was fantasy. Abigail wanted nothing less than to Renew the Constitution.

But she had to find the right general to run it. The person must be apolitical, completely credible, and of great stature. He must know politics, but be above it.

Bob McIntosh.

A professional broadcaster, he'd recently retired to fly fish, "all the days God and my wife will let me." He'd covered every major news story of the past forty years, and Americans trusted him.

Abigail invited the McIntoshes to an overnight at the White House the second weekend in January.

His wife, Jeanne, had aged well. Lithe, graying, and elegant, her smile lit up her face. *I want to age like that.*

She put them in the Lincoln Bedroom. Michael was amused that she banished him to the Franklin Towers to sleep. He was invited for dinner, however.

"I do not want your honor besmirched, my darling," he said with great drama. "So I'll watch ESPN, swill beer, and belch at will."

Over drinks, the four chatted about people and places. Jeanne was politely interested in the wedding plans, but Abby had precious little to tell her. "I've got a huge year ahead of me. I'm just glad Michael and I could go public."

"When Bob and I were dating, my mother would sit on the porch under the porch light until Bob brought me home. Then she'd disappear just inside the door while we said good night."

"Yes, we had to marry young, or I wasn't going to get past first base," Bob put in.

"You haven't met Regina," Abby said. "I didn't even have a date till college."

Finally, after dessert, it was time to talk. Michael took Jeanne for an after-hours tour of the White House.

"Bob, I need you to serve your country as no one has since George Washington," Abigail said over coffee in the Yellow Oval Room.

"Oh? Am I that old?" he said good-naturedly.

"No. But I have a sales job similar to the one Washington did with the Constitution. However, I need your word as a gentleman that our conversation doesn't go any further than Jeanne."

"Of course."

I am proposing five Constitutional Amendments in my State of the Union speech. I want you to head the campaign to get them passed as a good government, non-partisan issue."

"You don't want much, do you?" he said with a chuckle.

"I try not to think small."

She gave him a packet, asked him to read it, and said they'd discuss it in the morning.

"Of course," Bob said. Michael reappeared with Jeanne, and then everyone went to bed.

"I'll enjoy my beer-swilling," Michael said as he kissed her good night.

In the morning, Bob, Abby, and Jeanne had breakfast in the family dining area.

"Did you sleep well?" Abigail asked.

"That is one historic room," Bob said. "Makes you realize what an immense man Lincoln was."

"We lost him too soon, but were lucky to have had him at all," Abigail said. "Tell me what you think of the amendments."

"I like them. You're right—you need someone above the fray to sell them."

"But ..." Abby said.

"But it is not a one person job. It is a fifty-person job. If I did this, I'd need a person to push this through in each state. Plus, I'd need some real political clout behind me."

"How about three hundred million Americans who think their government is ineffective at best and corrupt at worst?" Abby replied.

"On another issue, who is going to pay for this?" Bob asked.

"We have a charitable foundation set up. I will be putting in a sizable donation, but most will come from low-dollar, individual donors via the Internet. We need some big dogs on the steering committee. I'd also like the Congressional leadership on it, after the State of the Union."

"These things can drag on for years," Bob said. "I don't want to still be working on this when I'm in a wheelchair."

Abigail laughed.

"I agree. My objective is all five amendments by Election Day."

"WHAT? You do think big," Bob said. Then he paused, "I didn't serve in Vietnam. I had polio as a young child and had a limp. Still do, for that matter. I always felt defective, unable to serve my country. I think this could ease an old man's guilt."

Abby was near tears.

"I promise you I'll give you all my support. I'll make things as easy as possible."

He stuck out his hand, and she shook it, holding back tears.

CHAPTER FORTY-SEVEN

RENEWING THE CONSTITUTION

January 21, Washington, D.C.

"The President of the United States," the sergeant at arms bellowed to clear a path for Abigail. The House chamber was overflowing, and the applause, deafening. As usual, the aisle hogs were the biggest backslappers, going for the most television time. Abigail felt mauled by the time she got down the aisle. *They may not like me so much after the speech.*

She saw her family and Michael in the gallery. Pris was right behind them, looking well, smiling and applauding. And over the roar of the chamber, Abby heard her sister's words clearly.

You are one of the giants now. Square those shoulders. Someone will need to stand on them.

Abigail blinked and Priscilla was gone.

Abigail never wanted this job, but this was her last State of the Union speech. She liked everything except its length. *It is too long.*

She made motions for the chamber to quiet. People settled.

"While the Constitution requires the President to report from time to time on the State of the Union to Congress, I see this speech as a report of a servant to a master. You, the American people are my bosses. I am but your servant, as are all the people who draw a federal paycheck," Abigail said with a sweep of her hand toward the room.

"We have no power; the power resides in each of you. We can only act on your behalf.

"We're definitely better off this year than last. The war in Afghanistan is over; the Taliban and Al Qaeda are dust. They never knew what hit them. All our troops were home by Thanksgiving. We can use the money we were pouring down the rat hole of war on infrastructure repair. We'll put serious money into it, creating good jobs with the money we're saving. And no one will get hurt."

The applause was thunderous and everyone was on his feet.

"Recreational drug use is down 40 percent. Americans now 'get it' that demand, not supply, is the greater problem. We've expanded affordable treatment options and new medications are coming on line to break the ball and chain of addiction.

"We've put over a hundred gun runners at SuperMax in Colorado for a twenty year stay. Federal prisons have no parole. The flood of weapons has slowed to a dribble.

"By dropping our demand for drugs, Mexico is no longer teetering on the brink of anarchy. When illegal drugs become a cultural taboo, these years will be a footnote in history. All it takes is your will.

"Most Presidents come to this speech with a laundry list of laws they want passed. I want something else, something bigger. I want to renew the Constitution, to invigorate it, and bring it into the twenty-first century. We need five Constitutional Amendments. They are a big undertaking, but any nation that put a man on the moon in a decade can agree on a few hundred words in nine months.

"The Founding Fathers knew the Constitution would need to grow and evolve with the nation. It's time to bring it into the twenty-first century. The populace is very upset with Congress's performance. The 2000 presidential election was a debacle. And we are all but broke because we cannot comprehend the simplest of financial laws, the one that says you cannot borrow your way out of debt.

"I am proposing five amendments. All are non-partisan, good government amendments. Their exact wording is on the website that will go up tonight.

The First Constitutional Amendment I propose elects the Presidential ticket by popular vote. Electoral voting is as outdated as powdered wigs. We are one nation and should elect our leaders nationally, not by states.

"If two President/Vice President tickets are on the ballot, the one with the most votes wins. With three or more tickets, the winner must get a majority. If no one does, the two top tickets have a run off in two weeks. In case of a national tie, we will flip a coin. No recounts. No litigation."

Everyone in the chamber gasped.

"I also propose a two day voting period over the first full weekend in November. This lets more people get to the polls, and do so in a more orderly manner. I hope every state will use the National Guard to safeguard the voting places, including computer experts to assure the integrity of the process.

"Voting is a sacred right. Millions have died for it, and I personally look at vote tampering in the same light as treason. It is an assault on the very fabric of our nation. Mess with a single vote and you will go to the federal pen for five years, where there is no parole. Remember?

"The second amendment grants a Single Six Year Term to the President and Vice President. That way, they won't start campaigning for re-election the day after inauguration. Either may run again, but only after being out of office for six years. We have huge problems and the President needs to be working on them ALL THE TIME. If we are to solve our problems, the president can't think short term or look at solutions through the prism of politics."

The gallery was hooting and hollering, but Congress looked perplexed.

"The third amendment is the Line Item Veto. Every President in recent history has wanted this. Legislation giving it has been declared unconstitutional. A Constitutional Amendment is the only way. Oddly enough the Supreme Court may throw out part of a law, but the President can't veto part of one. That's wrong.

"This amendment will cut the pork at least in half. The President can cut out the other party's pork. If she, or he, is smart, all the pork will go."

Abigail paused and looked around the chamber and shook her head.

"The government forgets that we have no money of our own. All of it comes from your pockets. A million dollars for the federal government is barely pocket change. But a million dollars represents the entire after tax income of the average household over a lifetime.

"The people know how much a million dollars is, but the federal government doesn't. No wonder people are clamoring for regime change at home."

Abby thought the gallery was starting to riot, they were so fired up. She calmed them down and pressed ahead.

"The fourth amendment is a Balanced Budget Amendment phased in over six years to minimize economic whiplash. We've been on a debt bender and it has got to stop. The wording is simple: the budget of the United States shall not exceed the revenues for the most recent fiscal year for which revenues are known. Additionally, each year's budget must include money to pay down the principal of the national debt to zero over forty years.

"If you are paying the minimum on your credit cards, you are drowning in debt. That's basically what we are doing. And that's just wrong. We've got to tackle the principal.

Everyone was on his feet applauding.

"In an emergency, such as a war against us, the balanced budget can be overridden with a two-thirds majority of both houses and the consent of the President.

"If we don't have money for a burger and a movie, we'll stay home, eat rice and beans and play cards. But if we have a war or five Katrinas at once, we can borrow money.

"Oh, and everything goes in the budget. We can't hide Medicare or Social security "off budget." That's like saying food you eat standing up has no calories."

At least she got the chuckle she wanted.

"The Balanced Budget Amendment would also ban unfunded mandates. The feds make rules that other governmental entities have to follow, but they don't always pay for them. If the Department of Education says all school busses must be red, white and blue, the school districts must comply, even if they can't afford it. If they don't, they stand to lose more federal funds. That's just wrong. Whoever thinks it up, has to pony up. People are fed up with the federal government as the national nanny."

The Congress applauded, but Abigail knew smaller government entities were thrilled with this.

"The fifth, and last amendment is Campaign Finance Reform."

Abby down-shifted her tone.

"I have wondered long and hard why the presidency fell to me. I am an outsider and that has made all the difference. Every time I thought of something that would be good for 99 percent of the people, I realized the special interest group for the other 1 percent would block it.

"That's just wrong. It's a perversion of what democracy is all about. How does the will of the 1 percent trample the will of the 99 percent? Money.

"Lobbyists run this town, and since this town runs the country, they run the country. And that's just wrong." Abigail was righteously irate.

Congress was fidgeting in their seats, but they were listening.

"We say we have government of the people, by the people and for the people, but we do not. We have government of the fat cats, by the fat cats, and for the fat cats. And that's just wrong."

The gallery was on its feet, whistling and hollering. Congress was ashen.

"I took an oath to preserve, protect and defend the Constitution and the special interests groups threaten it daily. With their money, they negate you, the voter. You are the bosses, not them.

"Lobbyists are not stupid. They give lavishly to both sides, knowing that whoever wins, owes them big time. The definition of a good politician is one who, once bought, stays bought. And that's just wrong.

"Sure, well-meaning lawmakers try to be impartial, but they can't be if they have to hustle for campaign contributions at breakfast, lunch and dinner, 365 days a year. All previous attempts at campaign finance reform have only been gamed. I have an answer.

"I heard this years ago, I don't know where. But its simplicity is great," Abigail said. Men in the chamber were fidgeting in their seats and worrying about their wallets, which were perilously close to their balls. Many could not distinguish between the two.

"All campaign money must come only from individuals and must go only to a candidate for whom the donor can vote. Joe Blow can donate to someone trying to be his U.S. Representative, Senator or the President/Vice Presidential ticket. Congress can set a donation maximum. Let's say they choose a hundred grand as a maximum donation.

"Joe Blow can give up to a hundred grand to one person running in the primaries for his U.S. Representative, Senator and President. That's three hundred thousand dollars. If all of them lose in the primaries, or drop out, he can donate again in the November elections. But if all three win in the primaries, he's blown his budget. He has to put his checkbook away.

"Before you gripe about the fat cats financing the elections, remember, regular folks outnumber the fat cats 99 to 1.

"Now let's look at what you cannot do.

"Joe Blow cannot give money to others to donate. If he does that, they both go to the federal pen for five years. Is there parole there?" Abby cupped her hand to her ear.

"No," the gallery shouted.

"No business, union, PAC, charity or any other entity can give money to a candidate. If they do, the CEO and CFO get a trip to the pen for five years. Is there parole there?"

"No," the gallery shouted.

"No business, union, PAC, charity or any other entity can help or hinder any candidate in any way that involves the expenditure of money. They can stand on the corner and say they are for a candidate, but they can't rent a bullhorn, a soap box to stand on or print flyers to hand out. That involves money. And they sure can't run endless attack ads.

"Also, all donations are monetary, there are no in kind donations. Why? It's hard to account for the value of donuts and confetti. Joe Blow gives money to Sue Smith's campaign, then Sue buys the donuts and confetti. Joe can't loan Sue his jet, but he can give her money to rent one.

"We know Joe Blow is for Sue Smith. But at his company, Blow Software, he cannot punish people who don't donate or reward people who do. Water cooler gossip is speech. Putting it in the company newsletter is a no-no. That newsletter costs money to produce.

"There are strict but easy reporting laws that back this up. Every day, Sue Smith's campaign posts income and outgo into their accounting software. Under the new system, she'd also send it to the Federal Election Commission with the click of a mouse.

"You know, we do something really stupid in this country. Currently we post your name and address on the internet if you give money to a candidate. That's insane.

Your ballot is secret, but we publish your name and address on the internet for any wacko to see? That's nuts. The Election Commission will divulge information only when appropriate.

"This returns financing of elections to the individual citizens, where it rightly belongs. It insures that the elected officials answer only to their constituents, not to special interest groups.

"Sure the special interests groups can still exist, they just can't bring money to the conversation."

Abby let this sink in.

"Let's talk about things people on the federal payroll accept. Under the amendment, anything a federal employee accepts, from a burger to a 'free' trip on a private jet to Idaho, an honorarium for giving a speech, 'free golf' is all income and must be reported as income. The federal employee must pay tax on it.

"And the person who bought the burger or put on the boondoggle? He has to report that to the IRS.

Whoever fails to report boondoggle money, whether donor or recipient, goes to the federal penitentiary for five years.

"I imagine that the wining and dining will go way down. People will be in their offices, sober, in the afternoon, not on the golf course.

"People cannot help but be influenced by their 'friends' who are so 'generous.'

"If you are abroad and see someone pay a cop a bribe to ignore a traffic violation, you call that corruption and look down your noses at that. But when special interests wine and dine federal officials who then act on matters regarding those interests, we call that "the way things are done.

"Corruption on a grand scale is no less corrupt than corruption on a small scale. It's. All. Wrong."

The gallery was going nuts. Members of Congress were either ashen or red-faced with fury. *No one ever thanks you for pointing out they're a crook.*

"People talk a lot about throwing the bums out of Congress, but these people in front of me are not bums. The problem is not the people, the problem is the process. Let me repeat that: the problem is not the people, the problem is the process. Most of the people in D.C. are trying to do their best. But the process corrupts good people and lets bad people have a helluva good time at the taxpayer's expense."

Congress applauded this as least.

"I'm not asking for term limits. That's the job of the voter. Some people are morons in their first term and exemplary in their twentieth. Would you throw a doctor out of practice after ten years? No. You look at performance."

Congress again applauded her.

"These amendments shut big money out of the electoral process. Isn't that the least we owe ourselves?"

"YES," the gallery bellowed.

"These amendments prevent us from borrowing our grandchildren into poverty? Isn't that the least we owe them?"

"YES," the gallery hollered.

"Finally, these amendments acknowledge that the federal government works for you, not the other way around. And that is long, long overdue."

Abby could see weary Congressmen shaking their heads. They were caught and they knew it.

"The nation is demanding a return to sanity, and Constitutional Amendments are the only way. Yes, they are a lot of work. The twenty-seventh amendment languished for two hundred and three years before ratification. These five must pass two-thirds of the votes in the House and Senate, as well as in three-quarters of the states. And I want them before the end of the year so the incoming President and Congress will be bound by them."

The audience gasped.

"The amendments have been drafted by eminent Constitutional scholars Andrea Lefkowitz and George Midas, who have different political affiliations. They agree the amendments are non-partisan. They've also drafted the enabling legislation to support them. Would you two stand, please?" Abigail pointed to the gallery.

The two got a nice round of applause.

"The White House Webmaster, Charley Garrett, has also created a new website www.renewtheconstitution.org. It has sections for Members of Congress, State Legislators, Governors as well as individuals."

"Charley, would you stand please?"

Charley stood and endured the applause. He did not like the spotlight.

"We want financing of this effort to come from everyone who is fed up with the system. As it is a non-profit, you can not only donate, you can deduct your donation. For just ten dollars, you can have a red, white and blue star like the one I am wearing. And you can give as much as you want to give, as often as you like."

"Please log on," Abigail said, "but not everyone at once."

Congress did chuckle at that.

"As President, I have no constitutional role in the actual passage of amendments. So I've drafted a general to lead the Renewal: Bob McIntosh, the most trusted man in America.

Bob stood to roaring applause and saluted the audience

Abby held up her fingers and ticked off the things she'd done.

"I've given you the amendments, a road map to passage, a way to pay for the revolution and a general to lead it. The rest is up to you, my bosses, if we are to bring the Constitution into the twenty-first century. If we fail, our country will follow. We shall not fail. Why? We outnumber the special interests 99 to 1.

"The way will not be easy. The 1 percent will be cut off from their gravy train. They will scream bloody murder. They'll wail that their free speech is being eroded. Baloney. Speech is speech and money is money. You the voters are smart enough to see the truth. You've seen it for years, you just couldn't stop it. Now you can.

"There is no perfect way to passage, but there is a sure way to defeat: dither, quibble, nitpick, bicker and blather. Do those things and we don't stand a snowball's chance in hell of solving the problems in front of us.

"We will go into decline as a nation.

"Health care won't get fixed.

"Climate chaos will worsen.

"In short, your grandchildren won't have a world worth living in or the money to do it with.

"Righting the course of our nation is the least we owe the men and women who have given their lives for this country.

"John F. Kennedy said in his 1960 Inaugural Address, 'Ask not what your country can do for you, ask what you can do for your country.'

"Well, I'm telling you what you can do for your country. Pass. These. Amendments. And do it before Election Day."

Abby waited while the standing ovation that started in the gallery died down.

"Voters, get on your feet and get marching. What should you do?

"Visit the website and donate, donate, donate.

"Get every candidate's pledge in writing to support these amendments.

"Email your Members of Congress and tell them they will not get your vote unless they are for these Amendments."

Abigail paused and changed to a lower gear.

"Veterans, you know that putting your country ahead of yourself is a noble calling. Parents, you know that putting the welfare of your children and grandchildren ahead of your own is a noble calling. These Amendments are a noble calling.

"Millions have died for this country's liberty and we have got to stop selling it to the highest bidder."

Abigail took a sip of water during the applause. Then she started to speak again in the calm voice of a story teller.

"Over the first three days of July, 1863, over fifty-thousand men died in a previously peaceful field in Gettysburg, Pennsylvania. The ground was knee-deep in blood-soaked mud.

"Later that year, on a raw November day, President Lincoln went to dedicate the cemetery of the fallen. His words were simple and enduring.

"We take increased devotion to that cause for which they gave the last full measure of devotion. That we here highly resolve that these dead shall not have died in vain. That this nation, under God, shall have a new birth of freedom and that government of the people, by the people, for the people, shall not perish from the earth."

Abigail paused and looked around the silent chamber.

"Thank you and good night."

The gallery erupted into a standing ovation. Congress reluctantly joined in it. *They're probably cheering that this is the last time I'll speak truth to power in here.*

CHAPTER FORTY-EIGHT

MOVING AHEAD

Late January

Renew the Constitution was Topic One for weeks. One pundit said that lobbyists were "the governmental equivalent of sex offenders." Abby loved that line.

The website had more hits than any website ever. It also went up on all social networking sites. It went beyond viral. Red, white, and blue stars were the hottest accessory in the nation.

Wicker showed her one piece from a local news show where all the dogs in town were sporting the stars in on their collars. Abby laughed and clapped. People were making multiple small donations, seeing who could sport the most stars. *Whatever.*

Bob McIntosh was indeed the most trusted man in America. He, in turn, recruited people from every demographic to spearhead the project in all fifty states as well as in the Congress.

He created a battle plan and stuck to it.

"Madam President," he said on one of their regular morning phone calls, "do you realize this is the biggest change to the Constitution since the Bill of Rights?"

"Yes, I do. That's why I sent you to sell it. It's way out of my pay grade. I just think up this stuff," Abigail said with a laugh.

As predicted, the K Street crowd howled bloody murder. She was proposing things that would put very rich and powerful people on a par with working stiffs. Many of them thought scruples were a shellfish and would be happy to see Abby out of office by any means necessary.

The Secret Service wasn't just worried about the whack jobs or the jihadists; now they had to add half of Washington to the worry list.

The stock market, however, liked the idea of governmental transparency. It went up another thousand points. And it stayed up. Finally, companies wouldn't have to spend billions just to talk to people in D.C.

"I feel like I'm being shaken down every time I go see my U.S. representative," one CEO said. "If I have a problem with the feds that I can't solve, part of his job is to be the point man, but I better pony up, big, first."

Senators and Congressmen had no choice but to agree with the President. What were they going to do? Say they were *for* taking bribes?

Polls showed overwhelming public support for all five amendments. People began calling them the Adams Amendments.

Abigail first heard this term at her desk in the Oval Office. She fished out her sister's copy of the Constitution, and tears welled up. She looked across at Washington's portrait. She could have sworn he had a small smile.

Bob McIntosh's battle plan was simple. First, get the Senate Majority Leader and Speaker of the House as co-sponsors. As it turned out, both were up for re-election.

He softened them up with "airstrikes" before he even went to their offices: commercials ran in their districts, people on his team went on radio talk shows, and polls showed their constituents were overwhelmingly for the amendments.

Finally, for the week before he visited them, he orchestrated an e-mail blitz from donors to the website. They demanded ratification before Election Day.

"History is marching, sir," McIntosh told each. "You can either lead the charge or get trampled by it. Your choice."

They were happy to be on board. That or else they'd both lose their seats.

McIntosh used the same strategy in every governor's office.

General Lafayette officially declared his candidacy for the presidency on February 1. Abigail was thrilled: he had decades in government, while she had a couple of years.

For the candidates who'd frozen their rears off in January primaries, Lafayette's announcement winnowed the field in the majority party fast. It also put the fear of God into the other side. Since he was strongly for the Constitutional amendments, they'd better be also.

He had everything he needed for a successful campaign: name recognition, respect of people from both sides of the aisles, and most importantly, he had nothing to apologize for in an entire career. How many men of accomplishment could say that?

Lynne could not campaign. Abigail spent one day a week on the campaign trail for him. She loved the people she met, but everything else was too much. Too much work, too much noise, too many takeoffs and landings, too much bad food, and way too little exercise.

She talked up the amendments, talked up Lafayette, and deflected questions about her personal life.

"We haven't had time to set a date," she answered. "You might have noticed I'm sorta busy."

Once home at the White House after a campaign day, she dropped into bed like a rock.

Michael again asked her to go to the Oscars®, and this year she accepted. She'd earned a two-day parole. She was truly excited about going to the Oscars®. She not only wanted to go; she wanted to "own" them.

Tom Albright insisted on heading the advance team himself. He'd gotten a little more protective of Abby, if such a thing was possible. He liked Michael's house, as Marine One could land without difficulty. As well, it had high walls on three sides; the fourth was a cliff over the Pacific.

He paid a call on the producer, Roger Webster, who was used to dealing with divas and their entourages.

Albright toured the venue with him, saying very little. He did, however, lock and pocket the key to the elevator to the helipad.

"The President may or may not attend. You won't know until she appears. She will not do any photo ops, inside or outside. She'll require a block of ten seats at stage left, next to the elevator to the helipad, if she attends."

"When will we know if she is coming or not?"

"I'll let you know prior to the event."

"How prior?" the producer asked.

"Prior."

The producer was not happy at having the Secret Service dictate details to him. No one ever really likes working with the Secret Service. They are paranoid, obsessive, abrasive, and totally unapologetic for all of it. But when your mission is "Bring Her Back Alive," nice isn't on the menu.

"What do you do to get ready for the Oscars?®" she asked Michael during a nightly phone call.

"Me? Shower, shave, and wash behind my ears. Oh, and check for nose hair. Just like I'll do when we get married."

Kim made her something as glamorous as possible, considering she'd be wearing a Kevlar vest. She also resumed her workouts with Susan Salazar. Five a.m. lunges were hell. *Oh well, if I'm spending two million dollars of taxpayers' money, the least I can do is suffer a little.*

At last, she'd get to see where Michael lived, where she would live when she left office.

Michael agreed to everything, even to hosting a party, and Abigail looked forward to the first truly frivolous thing she'd ever done as

President. For someone who'd read *People* as well as *The Economist*, it was a real treat. For someone who always watched Academy Awards®, usually alone and in her bathrobe, this trip was the stuff of fantasy.

Kim made her a long, black, silk sheath that was sleeveless with a slight scoop to the neck.

To accommodate the vest, Kim eased out the seams and added a short jacket with princess seams and a stand-up collar. The skirt was long, slim, and slit up the front to just below her left knee, the lining the color of her ruby slippers and the ruby in her necklace. Laura found some lace-encrusted bridal shoes at an off-price bridal store, had them dyed to match the pinky-red lining. No one would have believed the shoes cost under fifty dollars.

"When you have beautiful jewels, you make the dress to fit them," Kim said with her quiet demeanor. "Never put a fancy dress with fancy jewels. Do one or the other."

"And my security pocket?"

"It's inside the scoop of the neck. You can access them even with the Kevlar vest on."

"Thanks."

Kim also made a slinkier dress to wear to the after-party. Turquoise, minimalist, body skimming, sleeveless, it, too, showcased not only her jewels, but her shape. The workouts had paid off.

Michael and she saw less of each other as both were busy. He was involved in the movie business, and she was constantly on the go. Their lives were lived on their BlackBerries and Skype. The Secret Service hated Skype and diplomatically warned her against sexting. *Oh, good grief. That's not our style.*

"Hey, Missus, time's a-flyin. You think we can pick a date?" Michael said one evening during their nightly phone call.

Abby brought up her color-coded schedule that ran until through January 20 of the following year. It was already almost full.

"January 21 is the first I can do," she said.

"Any date is fine with me. I think we've practiced making babies long enough. Let's go for a real one," he said.

She had to smile. He was going to be a great father. Poppy and Kim were both pregnant, due just months apart, and they increased her baby lust big time. Her first view of Michael a year earlier kick-started her back into womanhood.

She and Michael found a rare night together in Washington before the Oscars®. Abby was humbled he would fly six thousand miles for one night together.

"Marilyn has set up a State Visit to China for me this summer. It would be a lot more fun if you went with me," Abigail said.

"I can do that," Michael said. "I don't start my next film until the fall."

"Acting or directing?"

"Both, actually. I get in fewer arguments that way. Of course, when I do, my crew thinks I've gone off my rocker."

"Having you with me on the trip will make it all so much nicer," she said. She got up, walked to his chair, and kissed him on the forehead.

"Could you plant those lips a little lower, please?" he said, reaching up and pulling her down into a kiss that ended dinner. But it began the evening.

Afterwards, she was lying in his arms, and he, as usual, was playing with her hair.

"I love playing with your curly hair," he said. "You've always reminded me of the little redheaded girl."

"Who?" Abigail said sleepily.

"Remember *Peanuts*?"

"Of course," Abigail said. *Doesn't it still run?*

"Charlie Brown always had a crush on the little redheaded girl. He never got her. I'm so glad I got you."

CHAPTER FORTY-NINE

OSCARS®

Abby was working fourteen-hour days and hadn't seen Michael in nearly two weeks. She missed him terribly, both minutes of the day she wasn't working.

She monitored Renew the Constitution as if she was giving birth to it. The country wanted it desperately. It had momentum. She helped keep McIntosh and his army moving forward. The funding was phenomenal, and that eased the burden on Bob.

One backer of the amendments offered his private jet to Bob, "for the duration." He, too, was fed up with the system. "I want my grandchildren to have a decent nation. If we don't change things, they won't."

"Gee, thanks for the jet," Bob said.

"No prob. I have another. But I believe in this so much, I'm giving you the better one," he said.

Abby loved that story.

The Oscars® approached rapidly. The producer of the broadcast needed a blowout preventer for his head; his blood pressure was so out of control dealing with the Secret Service.

Andre gave her detailed instructions on everything from hair to air kissing. "Remember, the more make-up the better for this event.

Laura and Kim helped her pack. Abby was a bit nervous on the flight to L.A., after all, she'd never seen Michael's house. *What if he has pictures painted on black velvet?*

Michael took down the tennis net and poles and Marine One landed in his yard with room to spare. Abigail stepped off Marine One into the bright blue of a perfect L.A. day. It was seventy degrees, low humidity, and bougainvillea grew up the walls, their fuchsia blooms almost too vivid to believe.

At least the outside looks like paradise. Especially compared to D.C.'s slush and muck.

Then she looked up and spotted her very own sniper on the roof. *Sort of like a weird weather vane.* They gave each other a thumbs up.

"Hey, talk about a cheap date," Michael said, kissing her on the cheek after she landed. "I don't even have to come pick you up."

"Yeah, well, your tax money paid my way."

"Then in that case, I don't mind taxes one bit." His smile was wide and welcoming.

"Let me show you around," Michael said.

Michael gave her a brief tour of the house. Originally built in the twenties, the stucco, one-story house had a red tile roof and Saltillo tile floors. Today all the windows were open, and Abigail relished the fresh air. She'd forgotten how cooped up she felt in the White House.

Five bedrooms and four and a half baths did not a palace make, but it was spacious and well-done. And while there was a designer behind the interiors, it was obvious this was a guy house, complete with a weight room and a billiard room. The only tip off that a celebrity lived here were the two Oscars in Michael's bathroom.

"Um, Michael. Why do you keep your Oscars on the back of your toilet?"

"To remind me, that my career can always go in the crapper," he said, agreeably.

"How would you feel about that?" Abigail asked.

"Fine. I like my United Nations work. I could do that full time. And there aren't going to be any wolves at the door, unless, of course, they are looking for you."

"I wouldn't go with one," she said.

He took her outdoors. He had a patio with an outdoor kitchen. A full bath opened onto the patio for anyone who needed a shower after tennis or swimming in the dark-bottomed pool. Abby couldn't decide which was her favorite view: the bougainvillea everywhere or the view of the Pacific far below the west end of the house.

"Paolo is great with the bougainvillea. He says you have to be mean to them," he said. "He whacks them with a stick and tells them they are ugly."

"Are you sure you aren't singing to them?" Abigail teased.

"Maybe that's it," he laughed. "I trust you brought your swimsuit. I heated the pool for you, so feel free to swim whenever."

"Lovely. Too bad we can't skinny dip," she said, gesturing to her sniper on the roof.

She met the couple who worked for Michael, Juanita and Paolo Hernandez.

"We are honored to meet you, Madam President," Paolo said.

"You make Mr. Michael so happy," his wife added. "He deserves a nice lady."

"Thank you. Where do you live?"

"We have an apartment over the garage, and it is just right for us. Mr. Michael, he moved the basketball hoop to the other end, so when he plays with his friends, it doesn't bother us."

The garage, Abby noted, had room for four cars.

When the tour was over, they flopped onto a sofa in the living room. Abby looked around. A picture of them at the State Dinner had pride of place on his living room mantel.

"Gosh, that seems like a long time ago," Abby said, smiling.

"Not to me. Note where my hands are," he said.

"The classic fig-leaf position, so?"

"Not ten seconds earlier, I had put my hand on your waist."

"Yes. I remember your thumb brushed my bare skin. I almost jumped, your touch was so electrifying," Abigail said, smiling at the memory.

"Well, you weren't the only one electrified. When I touched your waist I noticed nothing between my fingers and your skin except the dress and one of those slinky slips. You, young lady, were not wearing any panties. Naughty, naughty."

Abigail blushed, but said nothing. She remembered how aroused she had been.

"Shorty saluted you. I had the biggest boner of my entire life and a camera pointed at me. I put my hands in front of my zipper in record time."

They laughed.

"It was lust at first touch," he said, nuzzling her neck.

"Same for me," Abby said. "Dancing with you later was a life-altering experience."

"Can you believe how far we've come? We committed to spending our lives together before I even saw your house," Abigail continued.

"I haven't seen yours in Houston," Michael said.

"Actually, that's Regina's, I think."

"So where do you live?"

"I'm not real sure," Abby shrugged. "I don't even know exactly where the ranch is."

"The ranch?" Michael knew nothing about a ranch.

"Yes, it's a long story. I inherited a ranch from my sister, who inherited it from her ex-father-in-law."

"You are full of surprises, lady, you know that?"

Juanita left dinner in the oven for them, and when the agents discreetly went invisible, Abby and Michael curled up in front of the fireplace in his bedroom and ate dinner from a tray. It was a cool-ish night, and having the windows open and a small fire made things perfect. She always felt sealed up inside the White House.

"I know why I've never married, but I've wondered about you," Abby said.

"Oh, I fell for a couple of leading ladies, but then I found out it was really the character, not the actress herself I liked." He was easy about it. "You?"

"I've been told I'm intimidating," Abigail shrugged.

"Oh, I was intimidated, all right. Up until I whipped you at Scrabble. Then I figured I might, just might, be able to handle you."

They relished in the sounds and sights of the fire. "I'd rather watch a fire than a movie," Michael said.

"Funny, that was just what I was going to say."

When it had burned down, they turned down the bed and made this house their home. When they had spent their passion, they slept in each other's arms. He even got to sleep on the side of the bed he liked best. That was fine with Abby. Her Blackberry was on the bedside stand, and Hitch or Dabaghi was outside in the living room with the football.

Abby awakened to a view of the Pacific from the bedroom windows. The day dawned clear and gorgeous, and hearing the waves breaking rhythmically was delightful. She looked west to the ocean and watched the ever changing palettes of an ocean at dawn.

Michael ran interference between the Secret Service and the caterers. Everyone entering the property went through full-body scanners and got patted down, even if all they were doing was delivering the flowers. Then the flowers went through the scanner and were searched, as was the food. Juanita prepared Abigail's food with a Secret Service agent hovering over her. He was also in charge of the water Abby traveled with, to avoid tummy upsets or worse.

Abby did her PDB and a few phone calls poolside, even if agents ringed her. They'd never seen her in a bathing suit, and she knew they were checking her out behind their mirrored sunglasses. From her work-outs with Susan Salazar, she was pretty buff, come to think of it. Pale, but buff. The warm L.A. sun felt good on her winter skin.

Michael came in about noon, they had a bite to eat on the patio, and then Michael needed to dress.

"Can you imagine a black-tie affair that starts in the middle of the afternoon?" he said. "They do it so it runs in prime time on the East Coast. I'm In Limo 22. We have a carefully choreographed arrival protocol, and you, little lady, messed it all up." He tapped her on the end of her nose.

She sat cross-legged on the bed and watched him dress. He spent minimal time getting ready. He did, however, make an elaborate show of twirling cotton swabs in his ears.

"Note, my dear, the lengths to which I must go to please my pub-lic," he said, one swab sticking out of each ear. "Remind me to take them out before I leave. No one knows my secret weapon," he said. "I channel my charisma through them."

Abby was in giggles.

Where was Clutter when she needed a photo like this?

He could even tie his own tie, which was good. Abby lacked that skill, for sure. Abby was near hysterics as he finished dressing with swabs sticking out of each ear. She was pleased he wore the antique studs and cufflinks she gave him.

"Oh, I almost forgot," he said. "I got you something. Think of this as a wrist corsage for the prom."

He reached inside a drawer for yet another black box with a pink bow. Inside was a bracelet that matched her necklace, just smaller.

"Something to remember tonight," he said, still with swabs in his ears.

"Thank you, Michael, this is truly beautiful," Abigail said, putting it on. "And you are the most wonderful, wacky man in the world."

"Oh, where's my tiara and sash? I can't leave without those!" He mimed a frantic search for those. Then he kissed her and walked to the limo, tossing the swabs at the last minute. *How did I ever get so lucky?*

After he left, she had time to dress in peace. She showered and did her hair and makeup just like Andre told her. He had given her pearls on fine, copper-wire corkscrews.

"Put these all around your hair when it's up. They'll be smashing with your pearl jewelry. You'll look like a Botticelli."

She got herself into the Kevlar vest, and then the dress and jacket. Thank goodness, it wasn't hot outside; the vest was warm. The last thing she put on was her jewelry. Rubies and pearls adorned her neck, ears, and wrist, and she had a knockout engagement ring on her finger. Pearls peeked out from her hair. She might be President, but she felt like a queen.

The orchestra played Ruffles and Flourishes then Hail to the Chief as she walked from the elevator to her seat. Everyone in the auditorium gave her a standing ovation. She turned and bowed toward them, but then immediately took Michael's outstretched arms. He kissed her cheek. She blushed. Probably a billion people saw it.

Albright was on her right, Michael was on her left, with agents flanking them. The five people behind her were all agents, except for Hitch who was directly behind her. Sally was in a chic white tux and black lace camisole. All were armed to the teeth.

The host made a joke about Michael bringing "a date with an army." Everyone laughed. Then he added, "and a Navy, Air Force, Coast Guard, and Marines."

The evening went without a hiccup. Michael was always at hand. Abby did not let her jaw drop once, even as Hollywood royalty paraded in front of her to get their awards.

Some looked like surgeons had stretched their faces toward the backs of their heads. Many looked like a vacuum cleaner sucked up their lips. Some had the wrinkles of sun and cigarettes, routinely airbrushed out of every photo for public consumption. Many over sixty wore gowns appropriate for twenty-year-olds. *An upside down "V" does not count as cleavage. When they droop, cover them up.* The weirdest ones, though, were the ones with frozen faces.

Plenty of men "had work done." One heartthrob of her childhood barely resembled himself. *I would have loved you craggy and weather beaten.*

Abby was able to go to the VIP ladies' room just off "her" entrance. A scrum of agents, hanging out in "her" entrance went with her. They barred anyone from entering until the ladies' room was empty.

Two women were coming out. "Kendra Wallace tried to get missile lock on Michael Aston," Abigail heard one woman say. She and Sally smiled at each other.

"Then she's dreaming. He's been off the market for a year," the other one said, just as she noticed Abigail.

"Why thank you," Abigail said to the second woman. "I like to think Michael and I have missile lock on each other. But then again, I do have the missiles."

She and the woman laughed. The first woman sniffed and walked off.

She and Michael stayed until he presented the Best Director Award. As soon as he finished, they left. The view of L.A. at night was breathtaking from Marine One. Neither noticed the sky was temporarily empty for Abigail's safety.

Michael's party was lovely, but very, very tame. No one dared act up with the Secret Service everywhere. It was like having a party with a set of uncool parents in every room.

Abigail changed into her other dress, the slinky turquoise one, as no Kevlar was required. It barely concealed the launch codes and thumb drive. It showed off her jewelry to perfection.

She enjoyed meeting many of the celebrities, but was appalled at how many smoked. Michael banished them to the patio. The women were especially heavy smokers. The thinnest ones never ate, just smoked.

James Taylor came to "work," probably because she had mentioned once to Michael that he mellowed her out. He sang off and on for an hour or so, mixing with the guests when he wasn't singing. *How cool is this?*

She and Michael danced until fairly late. They hadn't improved as dancers, but they were happy hugging to the music. She danced, badly, with a few other stars and found them boring compared with Michael. Hollywood had not gotten the memo that one didn't walk out on the President, which was fine with her. She enjoyed pretending to be just a woman at a party.

As the crowd started to thin, Michael took her hand, and she followed him to bed. As she cleaned her face, he came up behind her and nuzzled on her neck. He undid his tie and threw his tux jacket across a chair. He was definitely feeling amorous. So was Abby as he kissed her neck.

"I need to take my hair down," she said.

"May I?" he asked.

One by one he pulled out the pins. He even unscrewed each of the pearls in her hair. Finally, the mass of curls was loose. Then he brushed Abby's hair for what seemed like the longest time. He knew to start at the base of her neck.

"Curly hair requires special attention," he said.

"Ummm. That feels good. Regina used to brush my hair when I was little. I loved it."

"My little sister used to ask me to brush her hair. She had hair like yours, and brushing it took forever. Until the end of course."

"Come here, my love," Abigail said, rising from the dressing table and leading him to the bed.

CHAPTER FIFTY

RENEWAL STRATEGY

Washington, D.C., March

By March, the amendments passed the House by eighty-five percent. "The other fifteen percent are retiring, whether they know it or not," according to Bob McIntosh.

The Senate, however, regards itself as a deliberative body, and it wanted to deliberate until the cows either came home or wandered off the farm. The Senate ran on blather, and it drove Abigail insane. *Hell would be working in the Senate forever.*

McIntosh had a plan for the Senate.

First, he knew that the third of the Senators running for re-election supported the amendments. That gave him thirty-three votes. He needed thirty-four more votes for a two-thirds majority.

He didn't have time to visit thirty-four senators, but he knew the K Street crowd was wooing people mightily. A governmental watchdog group, Pigs at the Trough, monitored every Senator's boondoggles. Bob contacted the group and got their data.

McIntosh scheduled a visit with the Majority Leader, who was cosponsor of the amendments in Congress.

McIntosh showed Schwartz the list of members in his party who needed "persuasion." Then he showed them the boondoggle information on them.

"Bob, I'll get my guys in line, if it is humanly possible." Chuck Schwartz said.

"Well, if it isn't, tell them T.J. would love another Emmy. The nation wants these amendments now."

The Senate Majority Leader realized that for once, the Senate was going to have to get off its ass and actually do something other than yammer. They'd vote before the end of the month.

The Majority Leader got serious: he threatened lost parking spaces, reassignments to lesser committees, and finally, the worst punishment of all, sending them to "Siberia." He could send them to temporary office buildings that were little more than trailers with electronics. In the summer, they were senatorial sweat lodges.

If they weren't on board with one phone call, he threatened them with Bob McIntosh's outing them via Pigs at the Trough and T.J. Most everyone got in line. A few dithered.

Bob did the same with the Minority Leader, who had fewer sticks and carrots. McIntosh would make good on outing the boondogglers. Most just happened to be in the minority party and all were up for re-election. Losing even half their seats would give the other side a super majority, sixty seats, and his party could turn out the lights and go home.

He also told them McIntosh and T.J. would out them, and they caved.

McIntosh had all the votes, except one. Cordelia Laurus.

Lobbyists were her major source of campaign funds, travel, and entertainment. She was the biggest hog at the trough. Truth be told, she depended on them. She seldom bought groceries, since as she ate her meals out with lobbyists paying. (She took home doggie bags for her other meals.) Few lobbyists appeared in her office without a "hostess gift," not unlike the brandy snifter from John Lafferty, which she had sold at a consignment shop for a hundred dollars, tax-free. She told other lobbyists that she "collected" Hermès scarves, and she sold those on eBay. She never paid for a ticket home to Louisiana, as some corporate jet was usually headed that way. Cordelia could not afford to stay in the Senate in the style to which she was accustomed without lobbyists.

Abby could not believe the gall of the woman. The Attorney General had dropped the charges of striking a federal agent and Cordelia wouldn't give Abby one lousy vote?

Abigail thought of inviting her to the White House, but feared she couldn't hold her temper. *Cat fight in the White House. I can see the headline now.* She settled for calling her.

"Cordelia. This is the Abigail Adams. Do you really want to get yourself labeled as the biggest hog at the lobbyists' trough? You do know that's what Bob McIntosh will call you, don't you?"

"He wouldn't be so foolish," she said with disdain.

"Cordelia, your judgment has proven faulty. You stood up for O'Neal, who ended up being a traitor. You brought an assassin to the White House who damned near killed Albright. As a gesture of courtesy, I persuaded the Attorney General not to press charges against you for striking a federal agent."

"The man deserved it," she said.

"What he deserved was a written apology and a case of exceptionally fine whiskey. I'd like your vote for the five amendments. You'll look like a fool if you are the only 'no' vote. I doubt you want to look foolish," Abigail said. She was so mad, she slammed down the phone.

On the day of the vote in mid-April, Cordelia was still undecided. She thought of staying home, but she couldn't. Her biggest supporter was bringing her an enormous check just before the vote.

Her name was in the middle of the alphabet. When everyone up to her had voted yes, she caved. The amendments passed. One hundred to zero.

Cordelia went into her office, locked the door, and began throwing things. When she had smashed everything that belonged to the government, she walked out. She cashed the check and was last seen at the international departures area at Dulles. With what she'd stashed away and her Senate pension for life, she'd be fine.

By May, McIntosh was on to the states. Fifty legislatures needed persuasion, and not all were in session at the same time. He was determined to get them by Election Day.

Abigail was thrilled.

"Ambitious, but if anyone can do it, you can."

"I may need some Presidential arm-twisting in a few states. Their legislatures will have to be called into special session for this."

"No prob. Just give me the governor's name, and I'll take it from there."

CHAPTER FIFTY-ONE

HIGH-FLYING PLANS

June 1, Washington

One year after Operation Women in Flight, everyone had a home country. Some younger women remarried and stayed in Australia where they desperately wanted to fit in.

The women worked on new languages, and their children knuckled down in real schools. They could plan a life without war. Some acquired new work skills, others brushed up on old ones.

In the one-year follow-up, not a single woman regretted her decision to leave. Many missed their older sons, but felt a duty to save as many children as possible. Depression lifted for most, but not all. There is only so much the human soul can take.

Once safely settled, many confessed they'd already been widows when they left. A widow in Afghanistan must send her children out to beg for money. Because of the Taliban, she could not work, even if she had been a brilliant surgeon.

The Infants First group now included all babies. Infant abuse was down 75 percent. More children were hitting their developmental milestones on time, especially in poorer zip codes. This meant their brain hardwiring was proceeding properly. Autism was down, but no one knew exactly why.

milestones on time, especially in poorer zip codes. This meant their brain hardwiring was proceeding properly. Autism was down, but no one knew exactly why.

The economy was much better without two hundred million dollars a day going down the toilet of war. Jobs at home beat wars abroad where the economy is concerned. And no one gets hurt.

The Chinese state visit was rapidly approaching. Abigail hoped to come home with agreements for more Chinese purchases of U.S. goods. As things stood now, the trade was pretty much one sided.

Both Kim and Poppy were too pregnant to travel, so Laura Rowe stepped in.

Just like in junior high school, it was important that she not wear the same thing twice. And Laura could keep her immaculate every moment in China, where she had multiple outfit changes. "I'd love to help, Madam President," Laura said. "Leave your wardrobe to me."

"Great. Just tell me your fee, and I'll write you a check."

"Excuse me, but that is not necessary. I think going to China on Air Force One with the President is compensation enough. Besides, while you are working, I can go sight-seeing."

Abigail relaxed a bit. Laura made sure she had a wardrobe that would have made Jackie Kennedy envious. Kim made her Chinese inspired evening dresses. Laura chose socko items from American designers for daywear, though Chinese workers had sewn them.

As far as jewelry went, Michael found an Asian jewelry specialist in L.A. and the man went on a worldwide quest for antique Chinese jewelry.

Abby was busier than ever. She still had to endure the daily PDB, often with Lafayette on the campaign trail, monitor the various cabinet departments and their problems as well as nudge along the Renewal.

Especially close to her heart were returning veterans. Every vet had an older veteran sponsor to help with peacetime adjustment.

War is hard, but peace can be a soldier's undoing.

The Renewal always needed a phone call here or an arm-twisting there, and she was out of the office one day a week campaigning for Lafayette. All this, and a state visit to China without Poppy who was due to deliver any day.

Briefing books by the dozens appeared on her desk, and Mikey grilled her on the non-classified parts of the books each evening.

"Charm will only get you so far, my dear. In negotiations, you need facts, and you need them by the ton for the Chinese negotiations. So again, what are the three largest components of our Chinese trade deficit?"

Abigail was beginning to remember what life had been like before Michael, and she was quite sure she didn't want to return to it.

Briefing books also went to Michael. As the unofficial "first gentleman," he had to know names, faces, taboo topics, as well as a principal's hobbies and all sorts of other trivia.

On one of their nightly calls he said, "I thought making a movie was complicated, but this is insane."

"I'm overwhelmed, too. I'm so glad you're going with me."

"Oh, I'll go, but I can't see you before we leave," he said.

"Why's that?" Abby said.

"Who has the time? Your books must dwarf mine. I hear from Mikey that you are studying like a fiend."

"Yep."

Abigail read the protocol book from start to finish. Twice. She even had Regina quizzing her when they were together.

"What is the difference between a fish fork and a salad fork?" Regina would ask.

"The fish fork is smaller and apt to have fewer tines. Sometimes it has sushi on it," Abby said. "Reege, are you sure you don't want to go?"

"Not for all the tea in China. And you can cut out the smart aleck answers. Next, what do you do with the finger bowl? Besides, O.T. and I are house hunting."

"Really? When are you planning on moving?" Abigail asked, feeling the tectonic plates of her life shift underneath her feet.

"I think O.T. will retire at the end of your term. He's always wanted a house out in Virginia someplace. So we're looking. This way, I'll still be close to Duke and my grandbaby."

"And what about me?" Abigail asked, feeling rather small.

"When you have your babies, I'll be right with you. You're still my baby, too. But you don't need me like you used to. You're all grown up," Regina said softly.

Abigail went and sat next to her and put her arms around Regina.

"I will always need you, Reege. Always. And I will always be there for you."

Regina patted her in the same rhythm she always did, and Abigail took great comfort from it.

CHAPTER FIFTY-TWO

MILE HIGH CLUB

June 10, Washington

James Chaffee arrived healthy, albeit three weeks early.

Abby visited Poppy in the hospital. With Poppy's permission, she did a full newborn physical on him.

"He's not only perfect, he's handsome," Abigail said, afterward.

"Sweet Baby James" was a good baby, and Regina was a big help to Poppy, who had never even held a baby. With Regina's gentle guidance, Poppy turned into a natural.

"Madam President," Poppy called her from home, "I didn't have a litter. Do you know that?"

"Yes. Why do you ask?"

"Because UPS has been here three times today."

"He's just so cute. And I can shop online."

"I can't nurse with UPS and FedEx always ringing the doorbell. Please leave something for other baby boys with doting aunties."

Thankfully, Kim's baby wasn't due until well after Abby was home.

Abby insisted on seeing Poppy and Sweet Baby James before she left town, and everyone was at the White House when Michael arrived.

He kissed Abby and turned his attentions to the newest arrival. James was indeed a beautiful baby, with his dad's sandy hair and his mother's fair skin. Michael enjoyed playing "pass the baby" with the entire crew. The baby especially took to Mikey, probably because Mikey was still a little boy at heart.

"I remember being three, but what I wouldn't give to remember being this little," Mikey said.

"Who'd want to remember pooping in their pants?" Tran said, to great laughter.

"Well, some other things well worth remembering," Duke said. Regina swatted him on his arm, and Abby once again felt safe and warm in the tapestry of her family. Kim, she noticed, merely ignored his comment, though Abby detected a twitch of a smile. Kim bloomed with her advancing pregnancy.

Michael had never been on Air Force One.

She showed him around the plane before departure, introduced him to the crew, all of whom were terribly star-struck. She also introduced him to the pilot, Colonel Barnett.

"Great to meet you. Now she won't be pestering me to let her fly," Barnett said.

"I've never done that," she protested.

"No, but it's more polite than telling him what a big weenie you were going into and out of Afghanistan," Barnett smiled. The three enjoyed the laugh.

She showed him the back of the plane where the press flew.

"It's easier to take the press with us. Otherwise everything turns into herding cats," Abigail said.

The members of the press were more interested in Michael than in Abby, and that was fine with her. She hated having her every phrase dissected.

They had an early dinner with Laura Rowe, Wicker, Chaffee, and Albright in the conference room. Albright briefed them on details of their arrival into Beijing. Then Abby and Michael retired to the President's Suite. Others had pod seats that converted to flat beds.

"Hey," he whispered in her ear as soon as she closed the door. "Want to join the most exclusive chapter of the Mile High Club?"

"And which chapter would that be?" Abby asked innocently.

"The Air Force One chapter."

"Sure," Abby said. "You're better than any sleeping pill."

"I'm only a drug to you?" He feigned hurt, but continued shedding clothes.

With a plane full of people wondering what Michael and Abby were up to, they were as quiet as mice, until of course, they hit clear air turbulence just when the earth moved. Michael had to put a swift hand over Abigail's mouth, lest the Secret Service knock down the door.

They collapsed in silent giggles, like guilty children.

Michael is way better than the Frenchman on the airplane, especially since we have a real bed.

Deliberately, they flew over Shanghai and up the Yangtze River, now damned to provide hydroelectric power from the Three Gorges Dam.

"For a culture that worships their ancestors, flooding the villages in which their families had lived for thousands of years was an enormous wrench to the Chinese people," Michael told Abby as they flew the path of the Yangtze.

"How come that wasn't in my briefing book?" Abby asked.

"Maybe because it was in *National Geographic?*" Michael replied. "I do have talents other than keeping you quiet at key moments."

Abby slapped him on the arm. *Oh my God, I'm turning into Regina.*

Beijing was enormous and enormously gray. She could see the pall over the city from hundreds of miles away.

A major U.S. city might have two "ring roads," freeways that encircle the city. Beijing has eight. Well-wishers lined the motorcade route, waving American flags and standing, likely, where their government told them. Still the round-faced children were a delight, and Abby made eye contact with as many as she could. Abby loved the elaborate landscaping that was in every square inch of dirt available. *At least the Chinese were trying to make some oxygen.*

The crowds in Beijing were more for Michael than they were for her. His face was on a number of billboards advertising high-end espresso machines. Yes, coffee machines in the land of tea.

"What's up with all this?" Abby asked after she saw the tenth billboard.

"Oh, all American celebrities do it. That actually constitutes a sizeable chunk of my income. Owning that coffee machine is an incredible status symbol. Asia is celebrity crazy and mad for labels. If a shop girl can't afford that machine, she will work an extra job to get one. Go figure."

U.S. Ambassador and Mrs. Thompson greeted Abby and Michael. For large nations, only high-caliber career diplomats get ambassadorships. He'd been a China specialist for many years, and she was Chinese-American and fluent in three dialects.

After introductions, Abigail, Michael, and the Thompsons strolled outdoors.

"Thought you might want to stretch your legs," he said. "Madam President, no building in China is free of rats." He was very matter of fact. "And the Chinese sometimes feed them electronic listening devices. Then they drop off the rats near buildings they want bugged. Although we sweep rooms daily, both for bugs and rodents, you should presume you are overheard."

"Thanks for the heads up. I'll be sure to keep my mouth shut."

"I'm getting pretty good at shutting her up," Michael said with a wink.

She resisted the urge to swat him on the arm.

Before formal negotiations, they had a state dinner in the Forbidden City, the Ming seat of power six hundred years earlier. They drove through the Meridian Gate and parked. They crossed the Golden Water

River. Eventually they were in the Hall of Supreme Harmony where they would dine.

Abigail was agog. Everywhere she looked, she saw only the China of the Ming Dynasty six hundred years ago. The designs were magnificent and all done in wood. Ornate carvings and gilding were the norm, and she was glad she had worn a red dress.

Abigail wore a stunning red silk gown designed specifically to show off an antique jade necklace. An L.A. jeweler not only found it, he gave Michael paperwork in Chinese (and English) to certify it. Hu eyed the necklace frequently during dinner.

"You're sure you bought it outside China?" he said good-naturedly. "I used to be in the Ministry of Antiquities, and that is definitely a Ming Empress's necklace. It should never have left the country. On the back are two pheasants and old characters that say roughly 'may you grow white hair together.'"

Abby turned it over, and saw the pheasants.

"Then allow us to repatriate it," Abigail said, taking it off and handing it to a shocked Hu.

Michael also insisted. *I want to strangle the L.A. jeweler.*

"Thank you very much," Hu said with a catch in his voice. "We revere our ancestors and to have their possessions from seven hundred years ago is a great privilege."

Leung Lu, Hu's wife, was a chic woman, the epitome of a *tai-tai,* a socialite. She only wore designer clothing. This night, she was totally in Chanel and totally into Michael. That was just as well; Abby was well on her way to charming Hu.

Leung Hu's daughter, Lin, and wife Lu, flanked Michael, and the daughter talked his ear off all night. Her English was excellent, and before the evening was over, she had wangled a provisional invitation to visit Los Angeles.

"Only if your parents agree, and only if you are properly chaperoned," Michael said. "You are far too pretty to be let loose on the unsuspecting young men in Hollywood. And we'll have to clear it with the President. By then, she will be my wife."

The girl all but burst into tears.

"There, there. I am far too old for you. I'm almost old enough to be your dad."

She made a sour face but perked up a bit.

At the ritual exchange of gifts, Leung Lu was keen to have a set of Abby's scarves. They had become desired, even in China. She got an entire set.

Leung Lin loved her snow globe set and an autographed, framed picture of Michael. Leung Hu, a great fan of all things "Western," was thrilled with the hand-tooled belt Abby gave him. He immediately took his own off and discarded it. The new one delighted him. It had a "salad plate" buckle, the enormous and intricate silver buckles rodeo riders get as prizes. He looked like a kid with a new toy. His name, in Mandarin characters, was tooled into the back of the belt.

Abigail received a small, exquisitely carved jade box. She prayed it would be under the value limit so she could keep it. Michael received jade cufflinks and shirt studs.

The next day at the trade talks, Abigail started with her line, "How can we be a better neighbor?"

"Please bear with us. We have a billion people still living in the sixteenth century, and we are trying to get them to the twenty-first."

"Is there anything we can do to help?" Abigail was genuinely curious.

"Energy is our stumbling block. We must get off of coal. It is choking us to death, not to mention what it is doing to the environment. I never knew the sky was supposed to be blue until I left China the first time. Then I thought it was only blue in Canada, where I went as a student. For many years, the government told us pollution was what you call 'humidity.'"

Abigail and Hu both raised their eyebrows at the sad irony.

"Funny you should ask about power. I've been kicking around the idea of the U.N. owning and operating nuclear power plants. They're very clean, unless of course they are hit by an enormous earthquake, like Fukishima."

"Why the U.N.?" Hu was intrigued.

"To take the politics out of it. A country would qualify by certain good governance measures. Also, let's face it—a lot of countries are not sophisticated enough technically to deal with a zero-tolerance thing like a nuclear power plant.

"If the country ceded territory to the U.N. and the plant was run entirely with a U.N. force, we might be able to keep the nuclear genie out of the hands of the bad guys."

"Interesting. But what would you do about attacks on it?"

"Well, you'd have a large buffer zone. If it is violated, the U.N. shuts down the reactors. Kind of hard to have a coup succeed in the dark," Abigail said.

Hu laughed.

"It's just an idea," Abby shrugged.

"But an intriguing one. Of course, after Fukishima, it would have to be engineered to higher standards."

"Everything has to be upgraded where Mother Nature is concerned. Her tantrums are getting worse and worse."

Hu was thoughtful. "The French, you know, have cookie cutter plants, all run alike, so the teams could rotate to reduce the possibility of misuse."

"And how can we be a better neighbor?" he asked.

"Well, we'd like more goods in China to say Made in America. I think all the objects on my desk say Made in China."

Leung Hu laughed.

"I am wearing a Ralph Lauren suit and shirt. My country is crazy for your culture. When my daughter heard that Michael Aston was coming, she began shrieking and wailing, wanting to meet him."

"Well, she met him. Do you think we can sell you a few cars?"

"As long as they meet our mileage standards, we would be delighted."

The talks continued the next day. Abigail was shocked to walk away with almost everything on her want list. Finally, the U.S. could get some parity on imports to China. The Chinese were especially interested in micro cars, like the French Smart Cars, but ones that run on compressed natural gas.

"We can do that," Abigail said. "I'll get with Detroit next week."

Repatriating the necklace was the luckiest thing she'd ever done, and none of it would have been possible without Michael.

CHAPTER FIFTY-THREE

THE SLAP HEARD 'ROUND THE NATION

June 20

The stock market rose another five hundred points at the outcome of the Chinese talks. Abby insisted on paying for the necklace she gave away, but Michael would not hear of it. The dealer in L.A. got into serious hot water, but he should have known. Every country had a right to its heritage.

She called the head of the three major U.S. car companies into the Oval Office, announced that the Chinese would buy a micro car that met the certain specs. She also suggested each man spend a little time in China to see what the Chinese people wanted and could afford.

"This is our big chance. Let's not blow it," she said. "The Chinese are label mad, so you might want to partner with American companies and consider licensed cars, the way stores sell tee-shirts of Disney characters. A little market research would go a long way."

The men moaned and whined about years as lead times for new vehicles.

"Buy a micro car. Take it apart. Work round the clock, but get it to them. Please? We're hemorrhaging trillions here and you're quibbling over millions?" Abby pleaded with them.

The men seemed to listen, sort of, but Abigail didn't take it personally. They'd stopped listening to the American people decades ago when the consumer said they'd pay more for better built cars from abroad.

Work had not waited for her while she was gone.

McIntosh needed her ear about an errant governor.

"He says he's not going to call a special session of the legislature for this. Period."

"Fine, I'll call him. He wants hung-up highway funds. When I say the magic word, he'll get in line. It's all a giant con," Abby said. If she'd learned nothing else, she'd learned that things were seldom what they were billed.

The irony was not lost on her that to eliminate pork, she had to deliver it.

Of the fifty states, five had already ratified all five amendments. They needed thirty-seven legislatures to ratify before Election Day, three months away for the next President to have a six year term, be bound by the Balanced Budget Amendment and have the Line Item Veto.

Most importantly, the lobbies would be kneecapped as soon as the new session of Congress started.

Abby worked the phones daily. Governors and their wives dined and danced at the White House regularly. Abby spent a fortune on scarves and snow globes, but they were worth it. She gave them away by the truckload. If she never saw another one, it would be too soon.

McIntosh used the same tactics with state governments as he did with Congress: email blitzes demanding ratification before election day and the threat of outing the biggest hogs at the lobbyists' troughs

July Fourth

Twenty-five states had ratified; none had gone down to defeat. Abby invited the remaining twenty-five governors and their families to the White House Fourth of July Party. Only the South Lawn could hold everyone. Michael matched each guest with a celebrity supporter. It had taken some sleuthing, but if the wife of a governor had a "thing" for one star, he was her dinner partner. Abby thanked her lucky stars for him nightly. The party was a smashing success, and more people moved into the "yes" column.

Kim's baby arrived that evening, so baby Priscilla would go for many years believing the fireworks were for her. Priscilla was a beauty, even in the picture Duke sent over the phone. She was petite like her mother, tipping in at six pounds fifteen ounces and nineteen inches long. Abby couldn't imagine a girl built like Duke. Abby wished she could have been there for the birth, but Kim delivered quickly. Abby visited the next morning, and as she had done with James, she performed a newborn physical on little Priscilla. She, too, was perfect and beautiful.

For his part, Duke thought he had invented fire, or perhaps spun lead into gold, he was so proud of his baby girl and her beautiful mother.

Baby Priscilla focused on Abigail when Abby held her about eighteen inches from her face. Abby saw something of her sister in the baby's eyes. No, nothing genetically possible, but a spark, a curiosity that reminded her of her sister. *How happy Priscilla would have been with her namesake.*

Abby was equally insane with the gifts for Priscilla. Kim, however, did not complain; she merely wrote thank you notes by the dozen to Abby.

September 15

Thirty-five states had ratified. Only two more states were needed for ratification. Virginia and New York had rejected the Amendments, as they were knee deep in lobbyists. Everyone seemed to be sporting the five star pin, not only their lapel, but they were glued onto headbands, belts, even shoes. No one could accuse the effort of being under funded.

Lafayette won his party's nomination. His running mate was the female governor of California. She had turned the state around after its financial woes and was widely regarded as smart and honest. Abby thought they made a good match.

The other party ran a sanctimonious woman governor, Ruth "Tell the Truth" Church of Utah, whom Abby called the Church Lady in private. Abby had to cough up extra highway funds to get her to go along with the amendments.

Her running mate was a Senator from Wisconsin who was a brilliant eccentric. He commuted to the Senate daily on a bicycle, a suicidal move in D.C. traffic. If traffic didn't turn you into road kill, the exhaust would surely give you cancer.

If Abigail thought the Church Lady would play nice because of her generous highway funds, she was terribly mistaken.

On one Sunday morning news show, Governor Church said, "President Adams endorses General Lafayette. Of course she does. When she sneaks off for trysts with her Hollywood boy-toy, Lafayette babysits the White House for her. Her behavior has been scandalous. Here she is an unmarried woman virtually living in sin in the White House. I think she owes the country an apology. She is downright immoral, engaging in sex outside of marriage."

At first, Abby wanted to laugh, and then she wanted to rip the woman's throat open.

A comment like this required a deft, swift and proper response.

Wicker, Lafayette, and Abby met that afternoon in the Oval Office. Michael was on the speakerphone from L.A., livid.

"I supposed I can't punch her in the nose," Michael said.

"No, you can't," Wicker said.

General Lafayette had a different take. "This is a political stab at me. I think I should comment swiftly and briefly."

Then Wicker asked, "Madam President, do you always stay in control of the football when you are out of the building?"

"Yes, of course, why?"

"Just checking, we have to tell the truth."

After some discussion, Michael's publicist released his statement that afternoon.

"Governor Church has seriously insulted my wife-to-be, and I take that as a personal affront. Disparaging Abigail's character this way is totally out of bounds."

General Lafayette's statement was also released immediately in Washington.

"I am proud to be the Vice President for Abigail Adams. I have taken over for her only once, after someone tried to assassinate her. Even so, she saved the life of the Secret Service agent who nearly died trying to protect her. She took an evening off to recover. As to her personal life, Michael Aston is a great guy and a very lucky one. My wife and I wish them every happiness."

Abby decided to present her statement personally to the press. Wicker argued against it, but Abigail would not budge. And she would not show him her text.

"I stand up to my own bullies."

Wicker shook his head. No telling what she'd say, but she'd always been spot on, so he left her alone.

She walked into the Monday one-thirty briefing without introduction. She strode in, wearing her highest heels, a scarlet red suit, and her prettiest pearls. *If I'm a scarlet woman, so be it.* She spoke without notes.

"Please sit, everyone. As President, I take my responsibilities very seriously. I took an oath to serve my country, and I do that duty willingly and, I hope, with honor, day in and day out. I have taken exactly one day 'off' during my presidency. I thought it prudent to give General Lafayette acting Presidential powers for under twenty-four hours after a bloody assassination attempt.

"The nuclear football is always with me, even when I was at the Oscars®. The launch codes were inside my Kevlar vest.

"Anyone who is mature enough to carry the launch codes is mature enough to have a private, committed romantic relationship with another single adult. I am *not* some hormonal teenager unprepared for the consequences of her behavior. Sex is for grown-ups, and the last time I checked, anyone who carries the launch codes had better be a grown-up.

"Michael and I would have been married sooner but for the demands of my job. He has asked many times, and my response has always been that I have a prior commitment. Patient man that he is, we are waiting until I leave office to marry.

"Governor Church is entitled to her opinion. I can understand that my choices are not everyone's. However, I have nothing to apologize for, to her or to anyone, about the conduct of my personal life. Nor do I take lightly nasty comments about my fiancé. He is a serious, thoughtful, delightful man and the love of my life.

"Governor Church, with all due respect, I believe you are out of line. I do hope, for our country's sake, that you do not become President. Your mind is simply too small for the job."

Abigail turned on her heel and left.

CHAPTER FIFTY-FOUR

VICTORY

Governor Church had done more than shoot herself in the foot; she'd blown off both legs. Her poll numbers went into free fall. She went from having a chance of being President to the dustbin of history. Abby was the first female President, albeit an accidental one. Church was an inept politician who had exceeded her sell-by date.

Lafayette considered cancelling the debates, but Abigail encouraged him to speak in his own words to the electorate. They wanted to know about their next President. Church, having lost her nerve, just sloganeered to the annoyance of voters.

The lobbyists knew that if they were slammed out of the federal governments, the state governments would be next. They'd have to get real jobs.

A handful of states could put the initiative over the top before the election, but their prices were high. Abby felt like she was playing political Monopoly, but with more zeroes on real money.

Abby decided to turn the tables on them. She called each of the remaining governors and said she had infrastructure money ready to release. She could allot it anywhere. Then she dropped the bombshell; it was for road repairs. Potholes. Yep, potholes.

Mikey taught her that all politics is local. Bad roads annoy voters, and they equate them with bad government. Smooth roads win votes.

The governors queued up at attention. The two running for re-election were the biggest money sluts.

"Ma'am, I'll be happy to pass those Amendments pronto, if you'll release that money," one said. The second said the same thing.

"Pass them. Then I'll release the funds." Abby knew better than to pay in advance.

Both states passed the bills within the week. Abby had the checks cut. She'd be the last president to reform government with pork, or so she hoped.

Abigail declared the following Sunday Constitution Day. The committee already had party plans ready to go across the nation. People turned out for a smorgasbord of patriotic music, fireworks, and all manner of folderol. McIntosh's Army came through with Uncle Sams on stilts, Betsy Rosses on stilts, even images of all previous Presidents on stilts. They marched up and down the Mall, throwing red, white, and blue beads to the well-wishers. The White House sported red, white, and blue spotlights, as did the Capitol, the Washington Monument, and the Lincoln Memorial. Military bands played at several locations, and the city celebrated. People even painted fireplugs red, white, and blue.

All across the country, communities had their own celebrations. Jet formations of three flew low over cities, with red, white, and blue contrails; schools planned activities for that afternoon. People brought picnics and painted their kids' faces red, white, and blue.

Finally, the government was back in the hands of the people.

Abby invited Michael to come for the weekend, but he couldn't leave production on the movie he was both starring in and directing. Abby would celebrate with a small hole in her heart.

Abigail would miss having a front-row seat to history when she left office, but she would not miss the enormous responsibilities.

Even Halloween was patriotic this year. Abigail Adams and Michael Aston were the most demanded costumes, and Abby's came with a red, white, and blue curly wig.

Election Day dawned, and as always, Abby was emotional about voting. She and Regina flew to Texas to vote at the fire station near the house. She hated the expense, but it was important for people to see her voting. She sent ahead red, white, and blue snow globes for everyone at the fire station where she voted. Lots of people brought the firefighters goodies on voting day. She liked that. She stood in line to vote, like anyone else. Regina did, too. Many of their neighbors said hello, and Abby was glad to be in Houston, even if it was for just a few hours.

As soon as they voted, they returned to the White House.

They arrived about seven, when the polls on the East Coast had closed. Each network brought in the numbers for the states in the Eastern Time Zone. Lafayette was a sure winner, but the networks didn't call it until the polls on the West Coast closed.

Church could not even take her home state, Utah, but did manage to get Kentucky and for some reason, West Virginia, a very unlucky thirteen electoral votes. She won 18 percent of the popular vote, which sounded little better.

Lafayette was at the Hay-Adams, the historic hotel that overlooked the White House from the other side of Lafayette Square. Neither the name of the hotel nor that of the square eluded the broadcasters.

Church called Lafayette to concede at about ten-fifteen. She then made a rambling cliché-ridden speech which Abby muted and got ready for bed. She waited up to see the Lafayettes in their well-deserved spotlight.

The entire Lafayette family entered the ballroom a few minutes after Church finally shut up. Lynne looked rested and well. She should; she'd spent the whole day in bed, resting up. Then she would go back to bed and stay for several days. Their two children, daughter-in-law, and two grandchildren were with them.

Lafayette's remarks were brief, humble, and personal. Just after his remarks, Abby's BlackBerry rang. It was Michael.

He was on location in Vancouver and had finished for the day.

"So, now, Missus, you got the whole ball of wax. Lafayette's in, Church is toast, the amendments have passed. When do you become my bride?"

"January 21. Anything before that, and I'm superstitious."

"I get that. Where?"

"The penthouse?"

"Who'll do the ceremony?" Michael asked.

"Hmmm. How about the Chief Justice?"

"Can't get more official than that."

"Michael, do you want a wedding ring?"

"Yes, I do. It would mean a great deal to me."

"I'm thinking of getting one with a female detector in it. Whenever a woman other than me gets too close to you, the ring says sternly, 'Step away from my husband.'"

"Hey, you might be onto something. You could make those and sell them. Bring in a little cash after we're married. Add a GPS so they'd know where hubby was, and you'd make some serious money."

"Do you want to help me pick out your ring?" Abby asked.

"Missus, I can get home for two nights max at Christmas. We'd have to do it then."

"I'm sure some jeweler would be happy to pay a call to the White House," Abby said.

"Yeah, that'd work. I'll call Past Era in Houston. Regina turned me onto them. That's where I got your pearls. What kind of ring do you want?"

"Something that looks good with my engagement ring and good alone. I may not want to wear the engagement ring everywhere. It is rather large, you know."

"I just wanted to mark you as taken," he chuckled.

"How is the shoot going?"

"It's raining, the director's a real prick, the male lead's a jerk, and the female lead has permanent PMS."

"I can't believe all that," Abby laughed, as Michael was directing himself in the lead role.

"No, but I'll be working eighteen hours a day until our wedding day. Can you put up with that?"

"Sure. But I'll still miss you more than words can say."

"But we are going on one helluva honeymoon," Michael said.

"Really, where?"

"It's a secret." He sounded happy.

"But the Secret Service and Air Force One have to know, so I'll need to tell them," she said.

"They already know."

"But I need to know what kind of clothes to take," Abby said.

"Honey, you're going to be naked most of the time."

"Michael, I want to ask you something serious. You don't have to answer now. Do we need a pre-nup?" Abby asked. "You have assets and I have assets."

"How about you show me yours, and I'll show you mine?" She could hear the leer in his voice. Then he turned serious. "Besides, I'm in this till death do us part, for all the days of our lives, until time ceases to exist, and then beyond."

"I love you. Get some rest, Mister."

"You too, Missus."

CHAPTER FIFTY-FIVE

END RUN

November 15

Jerome and Lynne Lafayette took a well-deserved vacation. He returned to the White House a week later, looking refreshed.

"Ah, Mr. President-Elect, you look well rested," Abby said, giving him a hug.

"It's still not real to me." Jerome said.

"It will be on January 21. You'll wake up and go, 'Oh, holy crap, what have I gotten myself into?'" Abby said with great good cheer.

Lafayette wanted to keep on most of Abby's staff. Poppy, however, wanted to "consult." That was Poppy-speak for staying home with the baby unless the proverbial excrement hit the fan.

"I'm thinking of calling my consulting company ShitStorm. What do you think?" Poppy said.

"Well, it does have a certain cachet," Abigail said.

The first American-made micro-cars hit Beijing in late November. They were an instant hit. The cars were cheap, colorful and met mileage standards. U.S. companies and Chinese consumers both paid dearly to advertise their favorite products. The one with the red Coke® bottle was the hottest seller, but a close second was one painted with a huge Mousketeer® hat.

Finally, we could sell something in China. More importantly, China had agreed not to rip off the patents and build their own. And Leung Hu was taking the idea of U.N. owned and operated nuclear plants to the United Nations.

Michael, as predicted, would be working over Thanksgiving. He shot only part of the movie in a studio, where taking a day off is possible. But on location, meters keep running, so people keep working.

Thanksgiving Day saw everyone except Michael at the White House together. Abigail invited the Lafayettes and their daughter and was delighted when they accepted. She knew their son would be at the home of his wife's family this year. Lynne deserved a rest. Mikey brought Marilyn, Wicker brought Laura Rowe, the Salazars came, as did Duke and Kim, Poppy and Chaffee, and the Trans. Sweet Baby James and Baby Pris made the table even more fun.

Abby remembered her first Thanksgiving in the White House. She ate in the Mess and was scared to death. If memory served, she threw up every morning and cried herself to sleep for what seemed like weeks.

This year, Abby sent the Navy stewards home for the holiday. Everyone brought a dish, and food was abundant. As usual, Regina presided over the turkey and dressing.

Abby would set the table and do the dishes. She actually enjoyed putting on the rubber gloves and working off the billion calories she'd just eaten.

The meal itself was scrumptious, and Abby was thrilled to have two babies at the table, both old enough to be delighted with the social aspect of eating. With their mothers' permission, Abby fed each small bites of mashed potatoes, and they clamored for more.

Regina and O.T. announced they had found a house.

"It's a real Colonial, circa 1750," O.T. said, "We're going to live over the garage while I restore it properly. It will be historically correct."

"But we'll have indoor plumbing and a gas stove," Regina said. "And he's got six months. I'm not sure about that garage apartment. I may stay at the penthouse."

"Nonsense. It'll be good exercise for us," O.T. said.

"And don't expect me to put on a do-rag and help paint. I only paint my fingernails," Regina retorted. *Happiness is a life-long bicker partner.*

Duke announced that when his clerkship with the Chief Justice was up, he was hoping to become an assistant U.S. attorney.

"I'll remember not to tear off any mattress tags," Abby said.

"That's almost as nice as when you told me, in front of my teen-aged friends, that I was the gentlest creature God ever put on earth. You might as well have told them I was a girl."

"I did not say that," Abby retorted.

"Did too."

"Not."

"Too."

"Don't make me go get my switch," Regina interfered on cue. Everyone laughed at the routine.

The afternoon passed in a blur of family stories. Mikey told steal-ing candy when he was five. Realizing he had no place to store it, he ate it all.

"I ate so much, I threw up on mother's freshly mopped floor. See-ing the evidence of my crime, she spanked me. Saved me from a life of crime, she did. I was headed in the wrong direction, even at an early age," he said with a smile.

"And you've gotten me into a lot of mischief," Abby said. "The Middle East trip, setting me up with Michael."

"Ah, but what a wonderful thing that was. You two have made me very happy," Mikey smiled indulgently.

"Oh, but I was so scared of him that first night. He was such a hunk. I was petrified and so rude to him."

"Yes. He told me you barely spoke to him all evening and then refused every entreaty of his to see you again. Perfect strategy to land him," Mikey said.

"It wasn't a strategy," Abby protested.

Everyone at the table guffawed.

"Uh-huh, sure," Duke said. "Reege, go get the switch."

"It may not have been," Marilyn said with characteristic diplomacy, "but it worked brilliantly."

Everyone drank to Michael.

Poppy wanted to know about the wedding plans.

"As soon as possible after the inauguration is as far as we've gotten."

"I have a great idea," Lynne said. "Let's have it in the East Room of the White House that afternoon. I'd love to give you a wedding. You've been a great friend to me," Lynne said.

Everyone liked the idea. Especially O.T., on whose shoulders the work would fall. After all, he was moving out one President and moving in another the same day.

"What a wonderful idea. Just a small wedding, though, a few more people than are here now," Abby said.

"Like the groom?" Duke asked.

Abby asked Poppy to stand up with her, and Poppy accepted.

"Actually, I'd take out anyone who got in my way," she said. "I've had your back for a couple of years, and this is the least I owe you."

"There is one hitch, though," Abby said.

Poppy's eyes narrowed to slits.

"I'm giving you the dress to wear. It will be red," Abigail said.

"Okay, I can live with that." Poppy was thrilled.

"Besides, Kim gives me a major discount," Abby said.

"You are so lying. You pay full freight. I see the bills, remember?" Poppy said.

"Well, we won't discuss it further," Abby said, sticking her nose in the air. "So say thank you and shut up."

"Thank you and shut up," Poppy replied.

Later that night, Michael called.

Abby was all but overflowing with wedding details. The women had everything planned, but she wanted Michael to know that his wishes counted.

"So it's okay to do the wedding here after Jerome's inauguration?"

"Of course." He was thrilled with the idea, actually. This topped any celebrity wedding. Period.

"What do you think of lobster mousse in the tea sandwiches?" she asked.

"I want you, naked in a bed. Everything else you can plan."

"What about the wedding cake? I like a chocolate cake with raspberry filling. How about you?"

"Can I smear it on your naked body later?"

"Has anyone told you that you'll make a perfect husband?" Abby said.

"No, but remember that the first time I tick you off. I'll leave nose hairs in the sink or something," he said.

"If we can get through our courtship, Mister, we can get through the rest of our lives just fine," Abigail said.

The White House mailed the invitations six weeks before the wedding, and they were spectacular in themselves. The Presidential seal in gold topped the ivory card stock. They had a thick gold border and navy engraving. The protocol people wanted more flowery language, but Abby nixed it.

President-Elect and Mrs. Jerome Lafayette
Request the pleasure of your company
At the wedding
of
President Abigail Adams to Mr. Michael Aston
January twentieth at three o'clock in the afternoon
East Room of the White House
Reception to follow
RSVP

Abigail all but wept when she saw them. It was really going to happen. *In the White House but without the launch codes. Hallelujah.*

Michael was in Washington for two days only at Christmas. He was working flat out to finish the movie before the wedding. The jeweler of the black boxes with the pink bows made a house call.

A Brit by birth, Marion Glober from Past Era in Houston was a world-class expert in antique jewelry. Luckily, she had no part in the Empress's necklace debacle. She was tall and slim, very chic, and wore her own jewelry well. Her plummy accent made everything sound better. As well as wedding rings for the two of them, she brought a selection of gifts for Abigail to give Poppy, Regina, Kim, and Michael's mom, Louise.

She arrived at the White House at noon on Christmas Eve. Michael, thoughtful man that he was, had arranged for her and her precious cargo to come by private jet.

"Thank you so much for coming. I'm sure it interrupted your holiday plans," Abigail said.

"It got me out of a neighbor's Christmas Eve drinks party. She hasn't changed the menu in thirty years. I can assure you I'll be eternally grateful. Besides, this is quite an honor," she said warmly.

"Well, we appreciate it," Michael said.

Marion opened a black velvet ring case, full of diamond bands in Abby's size.

"The stones in your ring sit up nicely, so the bands won't 'fight' with it," Marion said.

"Ooh," Abby said, rubbing a finger across the jewels. Michael and Marion exchanged glances and grinned. Abby looked like a little girl contemplating which cookie to eat first.

She tried on rings for about a half hour, and then they took a break for coffee. Marion set aside the ones Abby liked best.

"Let's look at rings for Michael now. I want something big to ward off the women," Abigail said.

"Wise move, with a man this charming," Marion said, smiling. "I have one I think you will like especially. Oddly enough, it is engraved with your initials and dated two hundred years exactly before your wedding."

The band fit Michael perfectly, and while Abby would have preferred a wider band, the idea that AA and MA married two hundred years ago meant a lot to each of them.

"I like it. Michael?" Abby said, trying not to sound too eager.

"I just hope they were as happy as we are," he said, kissing Abby on the tip of her nose.

Marion had gotten the ring on a hunch. It had paid off.

Abby and Michael settled quickly on an Edwardian diamond band in platinum for Abigail. It looked lovely with and without the engagement ring.

For Poppy, Abby chose a diamond and ruby brooch. Abby got a bow pin for Regina, not unlike one the Queen wore at Walter Harrington's funeral. After all, Regina was the queen of the family. Kim was harder, but she settled on an emerald and diamond brooch. As well, she chose an amethyst and diamond brooch for Michael's mother Louise.

Marion gave them boxes and ribbons for their purchases, and as no sizing was required, she left the rings with Michael. Marion left the invoices with each of them. Abby and Michael both paid the invoices online.

That night, as they were getting ready for bed, Michael was in his robe and rummaging around for something in the bathroom.

"What on earth are you looking for?" Abigail asked.

"Your birth control pills."

"They're here on my nightstand, so I won't forget to take one every day."

Michael picked up the package, noted several pills were gone and walked out of the bedroom again. Abigail grabbed a robe and followed him. She waved at the Secret Service, so they wouldn't jump at anything.

He strode through the Yellow Oval Room and opened the door onto the frigid Truman Balcony, the Secret Service still observing from a discreet distance. Abigail watched in helpless delight as he threw her birth control pills like a Frisbee as far as he could into the black night.

"I've been wanting to do that for a year or more," he said. "Come back to bed, woman. I want to get you well and properly knocked up."

Christmas Day was about the babies. They were wide-eyed and eager to eat bows and paper.

The family had a small dinner at noon, and Michael left the next morning. Before he left, they took their rings for another trial run in the bed. Making love wearing only their wedding rings was wonderful for them both.

"I'll be back three days before the wedding. We have a seventy-two hour cooling-off period, after getting the marriage license," Michael said. "Let's hope I don't have to go back and work those next couple of days. I'd rather stay and practice for the honeymoon."

It was just as well that Michael was gone until three days before the wedding. Abby was frantically busy, tying up loose ends. She had plenty to do.

Every President has a portrait done for the White House, and Abigail wanted hers done by John Singer Sargent. Unfortunately, she was over a century too late. She chose the artist from one of the people at an arts night, Boone Franklin, a Maine artist whose style reminded her of Winslow Homer, another favorite.

He came, and they talked about the portrait. She confessed her love of Sargent and saw his eyes light up.

She put on her long blue dress and her pearl and ruby jewelry. Boone took a number of photographs in a variety of poses and from a number of angles. It took a half hour to dress and an hour to shoot, and then she had to redress for a yet another reception.

Abigail put the meeting out of her mind as soon as it was over. The painting would be ready in July or something.

She had cleared as much of her schedule as possible to begin the moving process. All her personal archives were to go to the National Archives. She couldn't see the need for a Presidential Library for half a President. Besides, who would donate? She'd ticked off every high-dollar donor in the world.

She went through all the pardons and denied the requests of all white-collar criminals. Those people were well enough educated to know better. She approved one of an elderly golfer playing as a guest on a military golf course. He took a leak in the woods and was arrested as a sex offender when a female colonel saw him and reported him. His only "crime" was having the plumbing of an old guy and being too far from the rest rooms. *Good grief. I should bust the colonel for stupidity, but I just want out of here.*

Abby did a photo session with each member of the White House staff, a tradition for outgoing Presidents. When the photos were ready to sign, she added a personal note to each.

But giving each just a photo seemed lame, even vain.

Abigail called Marston Mills and established a scholarship for children of permanent White House employees who showed academic promise. She named it the O.T. Wagner Scholarship. She endowed it with a sizeable donation and hoped that Presidents following her would add to the endowment. She called the two former Presidents, and gentlemen that they were, they matched her gift.

"I'm just mad I didn't think of this," President Wells said.

She had O.T. set up a staff meeting in the East Room and announced the scholarship to thunderous applause for O.T. He teared up and hugged her. The scholarship passed his lifelong love of learning forward.

She would really miss the staff. They were all gracious and kind. Mabel, the head phone operator on the night shift, knew things that the tabloids, if not the CIA, would want to know. The groundskeepers loved the White House lawns and it showed. When an ice storm took out a famous old tree, they all but had a funeral for it. People took pride in their jobs.

The move from the White House was sad. She and Regina would no longer be living under the same roof. She could not remember a time when Regina was not right there for her. Whether Abby needed a shoulder to cry on or a piece of wisdom dispensed, Regina was her constant, her North Star.

Abby could picture life with Michael, but she couldn't yet picture one without Regina nearby.

Abby went around with colored stickers and put them on her own things. Yellow ones went back to the penthouse. Red ones went to Michael's home in California. Regina had her own set of stickers, yellow for the penthouse and green for Houston.

Realizing she had no clothes for the honeymoon, she called Laura.

"Michael says we'll spend one week someplace tropical and the other has weather like Houston in winter. Sooner or later, I'll have to learn to dress myself. But I'm not sure. I haven't gotten very far with cooking," Abby said.

Laura laughed, "Leave it to me."

"And I have nothing to wear in California," Abby said.

"Let me see to it, Madam President," Laura said.

"And Laura, please put in some really snazzy lingerie. I am after all, marrying the Sexiest Man Alive."

≡≡≡

Michael had arrived, as promised, on January 17. The D.C. clerk brought a marriage license for them to sign. Michael gave the man five hundred dollars and told him to take his wife away for a night without the kids.

"Thanks. We could use a little R&R." His face lit up.

"I need a shave, a shower, and some sleep," he said, when the man left.

"Did you finish your shoot?"

"Yep. Sometimes finished is better than perfect."

"I'll drink to that," Abby said, downing a glass of water.

They showered together and fell into bed, exhausted. Michael slept most of the next day. Abby asked Regina to feed and water him from time to time.

"Think of him as a potted plant, not a house guest," Abby said

On the eighteenth, Abigail got a half day of maintenance: haircut, condition, threading, mani-pedi. Maybe she'd get to indulge in a massage on their honeymoon. She'd never had one. At first she'd been too frugal, putting herself through med school, and then she'd been too busy.

Laura brought a new, non-Presidential wardrobe for Abby to try on. Of the things Abby liked, some went into the honeymoon pile. The rest they tagged to go to California.

"The clothes for California came from the Los Angeles Neiman's," Laura said. She gave Abby the card of the personal shopper there. *Great, she can dress me because I sure can't.*

"Michael won't even give me a clue as to where we are going," Abby said.

"Colonel Barnett must know, as Air Force One is taking you," Laura said.

Abby called him.

"Sorry, ma'am. Air Force One destinations are secret," he said.

"Barnett, have you forgotten what Commander-in-Chief means?" Abby asked.

"No, ma'am. However, Michael is a great guy, and he asked me to keep your destination secret. I am retiring after this flight, anyway. But you'll like where you're going, I promise."

Abby laughed. "You win."

Next, she tried Albright.

"Ma'am, it's called the Secret Service for a reason. Your destination is a secret," then he laughed his growly laugh. Abby gave up.

As Laura packed up her things to go, Abby teared up.

"I won't see you until the wedding," Abby said. "Laura, you have been so very, very kind to me. From the first packet of handkerchiefs…"

Both women were weepy.

"I'll try not to cry too loud at the wedding," Laura said.

Abby and Michael had just sat down to a quick lunch on the nineteenth when O.T. came in.

"Boone Franklin is in the building and has something for you in the East Room," O.T. said.

It took Abby a moment to place Boone Franklin.

"Oh, yes, the artist," Abby said. "I guess it's a preliminary sketch for the portrait. Want to see?" she asked Michael.

"Sure," Michael said, shrugging his shoulders.

The three went into the East Room. Abby thought it an odd place for a quick peek at preliminary sketches.

It was no sketch. It was the portrait.

Abigail burst into tears, and Michael held her.

Franklin had painted her exactly as John Singer Sargent would have.

Abigail was life-sized, in three-quarter profile in her midnight blue gown, her left hand on a Bible and Constitution on a table, complete with engagement ring. She wore her ruby and pearl jewelry, and even her silver shoes.

"Finished it early for a wedding present," he said, with laconic Maine humor. "Figured you'd cry, being an art lover. Couldn't have that at the unveiling."

O.T. beamed.

"Thank you, thank you. Every time I walked past Teddy Roosevelt, I was jealous."

"Well, I know you're busy, so I'll take my leave. O.T. will put this away until the unveiling."

Michael left a weepy-smiley Abby after lunch.

"Just think, the next time I see you, you'll be walking down the aisle."

He kissed Abby good-bye, went to pick up his mom at the airport, and then headed to Camp David. Lynne put his friends with him. The tabloids were ticked off that they couldn't fly over either Camp David or the White House. Putting the celebrities out of sight was brilliant.

Michael left two large suitcases with Abby's baggage at the White House. Abby was tempted to open them, but didn't. Wherever they went would be fine with her. Their passports were atop the bags.

Hitch, who had spent the last two years carrying the football around for her, volunteered to make sure everything was loaded onto Air Force One.

"What a dear you are, Hitch," Abby said, putting her hand on his cheek. "I will miss you very much."

Kim made sure Abigail's wedding dress, veil, and cape were perfect and waiting. She added special hangers and covers for them to the pile of luggage.

Kim hung a shopping bag with her shoes, the frilly white bustier and panties over the hanger of the dress. She put Michael's ring over a strap that snapped in one pocket, a handkerchief and lip gloss in the other. She forgot the tampon, but unbeknownst to all, none would be needed for the next nine months.

CHAPTER FIFTY-SIX

DAY OF DAYS

January 20
Inauguration Day/Wedding Day

Andre appeared to do her hair and makeup for the first time that day at 8 a.m.

She loved the icy towels for her face.

"I am so happy my invitation to the wedding included a guest. I'm bringing Don, my investment banker. He's finally coming out of the closet, and what a classy way to do it. He'll send his mother and father a picture of us at your wedding."

"Just don't embarrass me, Andre," Abby said. "Not today."

"No, way, Baby President, I love you," he said. "I'll be the soul of decorum. Remember, I knew you when you were the 'before' picture and said things like 'huh'?"

Abby would miss Andre's outrageous humor.

Andre would stay at the White House, watch everything on television, and then do her makeup and hair one last time before the wedding.

Soon Abby was dressed for the inauguration, the launch codes and thumb drive in the pocket of her favorite red suit for the last time. She tossed handkerchiefs, lip gloss and extra pantyhose into her purse. *For the last friggin' time.*

She and Jerome attended the PDB together, and she was grateful she'd never hear this filth again. Jerome could handle it far better than she.

After that, the day became ceremonial.

The Lafayettes came to the White House for coffee with Regina, Abby, and O.T., as well as the former Presidents and their wives. Everyone was relaxed except Jerome. Abby had never seen him tap his foot.

O.T. was the center of attention on his last day on the job. Both former Presidents had a story of how O.T. saved some day or other. Jerome relaxed. A little.

Michael was still at Camp David with his friends. She would not see him until the ceremony.

"Do you know why I wanted Jerome to take this job?" Lynne asked.

"Not really. But I'm awfully glad you did," Abby said sincerely.

"We read the same chick novels," Lynne said. "I felt I could trust you."

"What a lovely thing to say," Abigail said. *I wish I could tell you in detail how much better Michael is than the Frenchman on the airplane, but I can't.*

Soon it was time to go. Presidents filed into their limos one by one. Abby rode with Regina, Duke, and Kim. O.T. stayed behind to do what he did better than anyone did: move Presidents and put on a wedding for the history books. He was unflustered, as always.

The Chief Justice swore in the President and Vice President, and Abby felt like jumping for joy.

Hallelujah, I am free.

Lafayette's speech was brief and optimistic. He was very kind to Abby.

"As an outsider, she knew our process was broken and she helped us fix it. Thank you, Abigail Adams, for your vision."

Abigail got a standing ovation.

Then she stood and bowed to her people, as servants have bowed to their masters for millennia.

Lynne nixed the idea of walking to the White House. It was too much for her, so both Abby and she had extra time for a nap. Abby slept through the parade, literally. Lynne napped down the hall. At two, Regina knocked on Abby's door. O.T. would pack her room after the wedding. The Lafayettes' boxes waited on the floor above.

"Sweet Pea? Time to get up," Regina said.

"Okay, I'm awake," she said. She jumped in the shower and was ready for Andre at two fifteen. She spritzed herself with the Bulgari Green Tea, making sure none would touch her beloved pearls. She had a bite to eat. It would be a long time till supper.

Then Regina went down the hall and woke up Lynne, who was napping in the Queen's Bedroom.

"This may have to be my official nap station," Lynne said. "Very restful room."

Unknown to Abigail, Michael and his friends were already in the White House. O.T. had put them in the Diplomatic Reception Room with refreshments.

Michael checked repeatedly that Abigail's wedding ring was in one pocket and that the marriage license was in his jacket. His uncle Mikey arrived, attired in his tux, and held his hand out for the ring.

"I believe I am supposed to be in charge of this," Mikey said, holding out his hand.

Michael's hand shook a bit.

"That's a good sign, Michael. You should be a little nervous. You've waited a long time to find the right woman," Mikey said.

Michael's mom, Louise, sat in a comfortable chair and watched Michael, nervous for the first time in his very public life. *Good. About time. And about time for real happiness for him.*

She wore a lavender suit, edged in sheer lavender silk ribbon. Her bouquet of lavender and white sweet peas gave her something to do with her hands. The amethyst and diamond brooch from Abby was stunning and such a lovely surprise.

Then it struck her. *Emma would have been about Abigail's age. With Abby's curly, strawberry-blonde hair, I can almost pretend that this is Emma's wedding day. In a way, I am getting a daughter. Again.*

At two-fifteen, Andre entered Abby's dressing room. Abby was ready for him to take her from President to bride. She could blush on her own. Hair and makeup took thirty-five minutes. He put her hair up in a loose knot.

Poppy was lovely in her red dress, adorned by her diamond and ruby pin. Her bouquet was red roses in full bloom, set off with white rose buds. Regina and O.T. drifted down from upstairs, both looking regal in their finery. O.T. like all male members of the wedding party, wore a red rosebud boutonnière. Regina, too, had chosen to wear a red dress, and of course, a red hat. She also wore what she called her "Queen pin." For her bouquet, she too carried red roses with bits of lily of the valley tucked in it.

Andre disappeared while Kim, wearing a lovely emerald brooch, helped Abby into her dress.

Abby could finally go barelegged. No more panty hose. Ever.

It took almost forever to button up each of the tiny covered buttons that ran down the back of the dress to below the waist.

The off-white duchesse satin dress stood out at the hemline to about shoulder width, its silk crinolines rustling softly. The circular neckline to the edge of her shoulders was edged in the same fabric, but cut on the bias and embroidered with lace. The same trim adorned the hem and the bottom of the long sleeves. In the front, the hemline was just at the top of Abigail's foot. At the back, it skimmed the floor. Abigail adored her white lace bustier and frilly panties, and luxuriated in going bare-legged.

"I don't have the launch codes. Hallelujah." She did a fist pump and all but crowed.

"Please, let me put on your pearls," Kim said softly. This settled Abby.

The choker glowed against the satin dress. Abby put in her earrings. No panic button was required.

"Please, hold still, so I can put on your veil properly," Kim said softly.

Abigail looked stunning. The tulle veil, edged with the lace on her gown, grazed the neckline of the dress.

Abby picked up her bouquet of creamy white roses sprigged with tiny red rose buds. Just like the roses Michael had first brought her, these white roses were also fragrant.

She felt light and free of any responsibility except to Michael, for the first time since they had met. At the stroke of three, Abigail appeared downstairs on Duke's arm. She had not yet turned onto the red carpet into the East Room. At the far end, Michael was standing, waiting for her. Mikey stood next to him, beaming. George Washington stood above them, looking down on them all, as music from his era filled the room.

Everyone sat while a string quartet played Beethoven's "Ode to Joy," and Poppy walked down the aisle. Everyone oohed at Poppy's outfit, a short, and chic, red silk version of Abigail's dress.

The quartet segued into Bach's "Jesu, Joy of Man's Desiring." Abby and Duke turned the corner onto the red carpeting. Everyone in the room stood, and all eyes were on them. Abigail saw George Washington first. *I hope I did you a good job, sir.*

Then she saw Michael. The room was full of people she loved, but she saw only one: Michael. He was beaming. *He is my dream come true.*

Abigail Adams walked down the aisle and took her rightful place at the side of Michael Aston. She turned to Poppy, who lifted her veil and held her bouquet.

The Chief Justice performed his second big job of the day. In ancient and simple words, Abigail and Michael told the world they would spend the rest of their lives together.

Abigail cried when Michael put the ring on her finger.

Michael beamed when she put the ring on his finger.

When told he could kiss the bride, he did. She blushed furiously at the passion that was obvious to all.

CHAPTER FIFTY-SEVEN

LEAVING HISTORY

The reception was easy and fun, with good food, champagne, many pictures, and delicious cake. For once, Abby ate as she pleased, unworried about spills. As luck would have it, she spilled nothing at all. They didn't have time for dancing, which was fine with Abigail and Michael. They wanted and needed to be alone.

Everyone had something to say.

"Man, you are one brave dude to take on Aunt Abby," Duke said. "Call if you need backup."

"If she gets stubborn, give her a pecan ball. It works every time," Regina told Michael.

Michael's mom said, "If he gets too big for his britches, remind him he sucked his thumb until he was seven."

"Mom, I did not," Michael protested.

"Oh, well, maybe he just wet the bed until then. I can't remember back that far."

Abigail and Michael lingered at the reception longer than they had planned. Abigail enjoyed meeting his friends and relatives. She liked them all, even the famous ones.

When it was time to leave, she tossed her bouquet into the group. Laura Rowe happened to catch it. Wicker looked delighted.

Hitch got everything into Marine One, as promised, and he'd wrangle the entire pile onto Air Force One.

Dusk settled in quickly in January, so Abby and Michael said their fond good-byes to their friends and loved ones. It was time to leave. Abby could easily believe she was leaving the White House. She'd entered that building out of duty.

Duty. Honor. Country.

The words still gave her goose bumps.

But it was unfathomable to her that she was leaving Regina and Duke, but then she realized that not only had she gained Michael, but she'd also gained Mikey, O.T., Kim, the Trans, baby Priscilla, Poppy and Chaffee, Sweet Baby James, the outrageous Andre, Laura Rowe, Wicker, Marilyn Chernosky, the Salazars, Peggy Mellon, Albright, Hitch, and so many more.

Then, as she was preparing to leave, she saw her sister in the crowd.

Well done, thou good and faithful sister. In my death, you found your true life.

Abigail blinked and she was gone.

Abigail needed the off-white velvet cape that Kim had made. It had turned colder and clouded up. Fat snowflakes were falling around them as they walked to Marine One on a red carpet. The barrage of flashes helped light their way in the gathering evening's snow.

Once up the stairs, they turned and waved at everyone, lit by the barrage of photographers' flashes. Abigail and Michael disappeared into the cabin, the pilot started the rotors, and they headed for Andrews Air Force Base.

Abigail watched as the White House, once so huge, became smaller and smaller. It finally disappeared in the snow. Just like in the winter snow globe.

At Andrews, Michael helped Abigail negotiate the steps up to Air Force One in her bridal gown and cape, again lit by a barrage of flashes. Again, they turned and waved with big smiles for everyone.

They only looked alone. Hitch had gone in through another entrance, wrestling suitcases and other paraphernalia to the appointed spot. Then he left.

On board were two flight crews, one to spell the other, as well as the full Secret Service contingent that would shadow Abigail. Between them and Michael, she felt safe.

"Colonel Barnett, will you now tell me where we are going?" Abigail asked of the pilot.

"No, ma'am. You'll find out soon enough," he said with a grin.

Michael and she retreated to the Presidential Suite.

They looked around. All their bags were stowed along with their passports. Regina made a box of reception goodies for them to nibble and Hitch put them in the little kitchenette. In its fridge, someone put a bottle of chilled champagne. Kim put in hangers and covers for her wedding gown, veil, and cape in the closet.

A real football sat on the table, inscribed by a permanent marker.

"For Abigail Adams. You don't throw like a girl. Hitch"

Abigail laughed, as did Michael. Abigail took off her cape and hung it up in its garment bag.

"Do you want anything to eat now?" Abby asked.

"Later, Mrs. Aston," Michael said. "First, we'll need to work up an appetite."

They buckled in for takeoff. They held their rings up and admired them. Michael's looked wonderful on him.

The plane began to accelerate. With such a light load, it was airborne quickly. Abigail always got a rush when they went wheels up. Flight was physics made magic, except, of course, in Afghanistan.

Finally, Barnett turned off the seat-belt sign.

"My darling husband, would you help me get out of this dress, please?" she asked, taking off the veil and packing it away.

Abby turned her back to Michael.

"How many itty-bitty buttons does this thing have anyway?" Michael grumbled good-naturedly.

"Enough to constitute foreplay?" Abigail asked.

"No, my dear," he whispered into her ear. "This is foreplay."

Each button took a while to undo. After each one, Michael paused to kiss where the button had been and to say, "I love you."

She had goose bumps at his whispers and every kiss sent the butterflies rioting deep below her belly button.

Michael will always give me goose bumps and butterflies.

TO BE CONTINUED

THE ACCIDENTAL PRESIDENT RETURNS

January 24
A private island in the Caribbean

Michael bounded up the stairs to their thatched pavilion, hot and sweaty from a morning of fishing. He caught dinner for the two of them and got just enough sun to invigorate him. He might, just might, shave today as a treat for his new bride.

He noticed Abigail had not moved in hours. Heaven knew she needed the rest. She was still asleep; her strawberry blonde curls in disarray, a small smile on her face and her long legs sprawled in the bed. *She even sleeps pretty.*

Abigail stirred and looked up at her stinky husband who sat down beside her on the bed. *Stinky or not, "husband" is the sweetest word on earth to a woman who never thought she would marry.*

"Honey, I went out and caught dinner," he said with exaggerated pride. "I left it with the chef. I thought it was a bit early to start you on cleaning fish."

"You thought right, Mister," she said, rubbing his scruffy beard. She didn't have the heart to tell him he looked more like a refugee with a skin disease than the Sexiest Man Alive right now.

"Hey, let's cancel the rest of our lives and live here. Go native. I won't shave, and you can grow hairy armpits," he teased.

"Mmm. Can't wait," she said, rolling her eyes. "Are you planning on shaving any time soon?"

"No, I thought the Tarzan look would turn you on." He started making chimp noises and scratching at his sides. Abby giggled.

"Think again, Tarzan," she sat up and pecked him on the cheek. "Only one problem. Your face would leave rug burns anyplace it touched. No shave, no shower, no sex."

She stood and stretched. He reveled in the sight of her naked. While he was tan, she had the milky skin of a Botticelli. Paint her standing on half a giant clam shell and she'd be right at home in a museum.

"Join me in the shower?" she asked, slinging a towel over her shoulder and giving him a sultry backward glance.

"You don't have to ask twice," he said, taking off his sweaty fishing clothes and leaving them in a pile by the open air shower.

19885634R00212